the House *on* Malcolm Street

Books by Leisha Kelly

Julia's Hope
Emma's Gift
Katie's Dream
Till Morning Is Nigh

Country Road Chronicles
Rorey's Secret
Rachel's Prayer
Sarah's Promise

the House *on* Malcolm Street

A NOVEL

LEISHA KELLY

Revell
a division of Baker Publishing Group
Grand Rapids, Michigan

Published by Revell
a division of Baker Publishing Group
P.O. Box 6287, Grand Rapids, MI 49516-6287
www.revellbooks.com

Printed in the United States of America

Library of Congress Cataloging-in-Publication Data

Kelly, Leisha.
The house on Malcolm Street : a novel / Leisha Kelly.
p. cm.
ISBN 978-0-8007-3328-5 (pbk.)
1. Widows—Fiction. 2. Boardinghouses—Fiction. I. Title.
PS3611.E45H68 2010
813′.6—dc22 2010021068

10 11 12 13 14 15 16 7 6 5 4 3 2 1

To my wonderful family
with love always

1

Leah Wiskirk Breckenridge

September 1920

I plopped Mother's old carpetbag next to the railing and grabbed for Eliza's thin glove. "Don't step too close, please. The train is almost here."

"I won't, Mommy," little Eliza promised, her rounded cheeks flushed pink with excitement. "I just want to see."

Our other bag, still slung over my shoulder, was weighting me terribly, and I tried to shift it. Here we were on the wide oak platform, though I would have preferred to run the other way and never come near this or any other train station. My feet hurt, I'd grown hot despite the coolness of the day, and though I'd tried to fix my hair as best I could out-of-doors this morning, such a long walk in the breeze surely had it looking disheveled again. I would have liked to be almost anywhere else, at least to have some other option. But despite all my fretful efforts, I could think of none.

Six-year-old Eliza, whom I sometimes called Ellie, was just as eager in this new experience as I was wary. Her rag doll dangled limply in her free hand as she strained forward in an effort to see the approaching locomotive through the press of the crowd gathering around us.

"How big is it, Mommy? Is it really, really big?"

"Yes. Terribly. You'll see soon enough."

The train whistle blared, painful and shrill, piercing right through me. Clouds of steam and dust rolled toward the platform, and my heart fluttered violently in my throat. As the locomotive roared to a stop, I tightened my grip on my daughter's hand but then clutched as well at the iron rail to squelch the urge to snatch her up and flee. Little Eliza would not have been so thrilled with the prospect of a train ride, nor even with the sight of the awful thing, if she knew everything that I knew about trains.

"Mommy, Mommy! Can't we go closer?"

"No! We must wait till it is stopped completely!"

The huge black locomotive slid nearer, churning out plumes of smoke, steam, and choking dust. For a moment it seemed to be coming straight for me, and I could scarcely breathe. The whine of the great wheels grinding to a halt jarred me to the core of my being. It was utter foolishness to come to this train station, even for the hope of a fresh start. How could I go through with it?

"When can we get on?" Eliza persisted.

I froze, trying to regain composure. My grip on the rail was painful now but my knees were so weak and my head so unsteady I was afraid to loosen it.

How had John felt when he'd stood here on this platform? I could hardly think of him without tears filling my eyes, but in this place it was even harder. *Why did it have to happen? We'd had so little time together!*

"Mommy, don't squeeze me so tight." Eliza squirmed uncomfortably.

"I'm sorry." I relaxed my grip, took a deep breath. *John would always do what he had to do. No matter how hard it was. He would never let fear stand in his way. Especially foolish, irrational fear like mine.*

Eliza stared up at me. "Are we really going to ride?"

I nodded, mustering all the courage I could. "Yes. We are going to Aunt Marigold's in Illinois."

"Marigold is a lovely name," she mused.

I sighed. My dear daughter had always been quick with bright and cheerful observations. I could only hope Marigold McSweeney's disposition matched Ellie's enthusiasm.

All the women in my husband's family had been named for flowers, including his long-deceased mother, Azalea. There was a Daisy. Petunia. Violet. Even Zinnia. That John and I had given our little girl "Rose" for a middle name might not be good enough among such folk. Marigold had written a letter recommending the name "Peony" before Eliza was even born.

I had no idea what to expect at Marigold's, but we couldn't stay here in St. Louis. After John's death I'd tried to find work, but it was next to impossible with no one to care for my children. And then the influenza that had killed so many in 1918 and 1919 took another dreadful sweep through our neighborhood. I became gravely ill, and late in January little Johnny James had died. If I'd not had Eliza, I would have wanted to die too.

The landlord had been patient for a while, but we lost our home when a businessman offered him more for it than he was willing to turn down. I'd already been selling our furniture and household items for the money to live on. We barely had anything left. Not enough to find another home on our own, not even for the first thirty days. Aunt Marigold did not know all of that. And yet she'd invited us months ago to the large home where she took in boarders. She'd offered to let us stay until we could get a fresh start. It had seemed like such a strange proposition when I first got the letter last winter. I'd never met Marigold face-to-face, had never been any farther into Illinois than Alton. But now, what option did we have? I couldn't move in with my father. I absolutely could not put Ellie or myself through that, ever.

The station platform grew more crowded now that the train had stopped. Where had all these people come from? I knelt beside Ellie and drew her close, just to be sure of her in the press. City crowds still made me nervous, despite my years in St. Louis. If there was one thing positive about having to start over in Illinois, it was that I'd be in a small town again, no bigger than the one nearest the farm where I grew up.

"Are all of these people going to ride the train with us?" Eliza asked.

"No. Some are surely here to greet people just arriving, or to say good-bye to their loved ones going away."

She looked around uncertainly. "Did anyone come to tell us good-bye?"

"No." There was nothing else to tell her. Who would come? We'd already said good-bye to Anna Butler, our former neighbor, days ago. Father didn't know we were leaving, and we had no other family.

We watched and waited as people began to exit the train. I had already been told that this train would not linger long. Soon there was a general press toward it and then a shouted announcement for passengers traveling east.

I picked up the carpetbag that along with my heavy shoulder bag held what little remained of our belongings.

We're destitute. Relying on the mercies of John's relative. Where is God in all of this? Where was he when we needed him so badly?

Maybe a couple of deep breaths would help calm my nerves. It would be wrong to cry in front of these strangers, and especially in front of my daughter right now. Somehow I needed to find a way to be strong and not look afraid. "Come on," I told Eliza as cheerfully as I could. "They're beginning to board."

It was not easy to step so near what I'd always thought of as a horrid, belching, man-eating monster. I'd heard people speak of their admiration and even gratitude for trains. But to me, from my earliest days, they'd been quite literally the stuff of nightmares, to be avoided as much as possible.

My hands shook ever so slightly, and I fought with all the strength I could muster against the threat of tears as I led Eliza through a swirl of leaves to the line where a conductor had begun calling passengers to board. I could not let myself be stopped. If we did not leave St. Louis for Marigold's boardinghouse, if we did not get on this train, where would we spend another night? In the park again, among the birds and beasts, and who knew what else, wandering the city after dark? I could not do that to my daughter. Nights would be so much colder soon. I had to find a way for her, even if it was with a strange woman in an unfamiliar town.

Eliza bounced up and down as though we were in line for a carnival ride. She was a boisterous little girl, despite our sorrows less than a year ago. I couldn't help thinking of her father and his death on a day not unlike this one, clear and beautiful with a flurry of dancing leaves. It had been a freakish accident, the result of his short train ride to Florissant to investigate a job opportunity. And as soon as I knew something had happened, I'd prayed. I'd begged God for John to come home to us safe and sound as always. But my prayers had been useless. John had died needlessly, because trains and train tracks were horrid, unpredictable places where metal and steam rule like tyrants over human life.

My heart thundered as this train blew its whistle again, as if taunting me. I tried to lay such thoughts aside when it came our turn to board. But I still found myself shaking as we climbed the metal step and moved to find a seat in the narrow railcar.

"Mommy," Ellie begged. "I want to be by the window so I can look out the whole way!"

"Just sit down wherever you find a place and hold on," I whispered. She looked at me and dropped to a passenger chair in an empty row but then slid over until she could look out easily.

We didn't start moving. Not yet. I sat beside her, stiff and uncomfortable, wishing the ride would start so it could just be over. A ghastly scene flashed into my mind of blood, a mangled leg. Trains were killers, pure and simple. How could I possibly endure riding miles in the belly of one with such memories assaulting me?

It's just too soon. That's the problem. Ten months is not enough time to feel normal again after losing my precious husband. And then our only son.

I sniffed, at the same time arranging our bags near my feet and hoping Eliza did not notice the trouble I was having. I could not imagine being happy about a train ride when I was six. At that age, giant locomotives had pursued me in my dreams, and even in my waking hours the sound of their whistle had given me chills.

But I was grown now. Despite the circumstances of John's death, it was time to block such things out of my mind. I opened one of our bags and pulled out a comb to fix my hair and Eliza's. Hopefully, we wouldn't arrive at Aunt Marigold's looking like vagabonds.

We certainly didn't have much baggage to speak of. The conductor had offered to place it in a baggage car for me, but I wanted to keep everything by my side. We had so little left in this world. Clothes. A few pictures and personal items, nothing more. I'd had to sell what little else we'd had in order to purchase the train tickets.

Hopefully the two nights we'd spent without shelter would be our only ones in such condition. We had no money for a return trip, but what was there to come back to? A park bench? Our first night on one of those had been horrid. I'd felt so empty and hopeless. I'd hardly slept, struggling to make up my mind what to do. The second night was just as unnerving because of a man I'd seen watching us from a distance. But he went away and I found some peace in my decision to leave Missouri and show up on Aunt Marigold's doorstep. She'd offered. And I'd have to be brave and humble enough to accept the offer. If I'd only known to arrive at the station for the early train in the wee hours of morning, we could have been there by now.

Eliza was more aware than I wanted her to be of my quiet thoughtfulness. And despite her excitement to be taking this trip, she was probably nervous as well. She leaned into my shoulder and gently stroked my hand. "Are you sad today, Mommy?"

"A little." I sighed. I really hated to admit such a thing, but there was no point denying it when she seemed to read me so easily.

"You wish Daddy and baby Johnny were here?"

Sometimes my daughter's directness was more than a little unnerving. She seemed terribly grown-up in moments like this, and I knew she wanted me to be honest. So I nodded and tried to sound as positive as I could. "I'm sure it'll be wonderful for us in Illinois. But in a way I feel that we're leaving them behind."

"Anna told me they're always with us," she said softly and turned her eyes to the window where we could easily see over the heads of the people remaining on the platform outside.

I sat in silence. How could I possibly respond? Despite Anna's words, John and the baby were *not* with us and would never be with us again. Nothing would ever be the same, or feel right again.

I leaned back and closed my eyes, holding Eliza in my arms as the train began its slow crawl forward. Maybe if we sat very still and were both very quiet as the train began its acceleration, I wouldn't get too anxious, nauseous, or upset. Soon we'd be rushing out of the city and into the countryside, leaving St. Louis and its memories forever behind us.

"Will we sleep on the train tonight?" Ellie whispered.

"Not all night," I answered, hoping my little girl would be satisfied with the vague reply. I simply couldn't discuss things more. Not yet. I had to regain my equilibrium, my composure, first. We were riding in a ten-ton monster. Maybe even the very one that had killed John. There was no way to know for sure.

Ellie continued her words at a whisper. "I think it will be lovely to sleep on the train, even if it's just for a little while." She squeezed my hand. "But I wasn't scared to sleep in the park. Not one bit. That was a good adventure too."

Adventure. Of course that was the way a six-year-old would

see the state our lives were in right now. Lovely. I smoothed her brown muslin skirt and glanced at the heads of the couple in the seat in front of us, hoping that no one had heard her speak of sleeping in a park. Before we reached Andersonville, I must tell her not to mention a word of such things to Aunt Marigold. That we were destitute and coming so suddenly to share her roof was shameful enough.

I'd thought that Eliza would be tired and ready for a nap once the train got going. She'd been up far too early this morning and couldn't possibly have slept well overnight on the wrought-iron bench I'd chosen to keep her up off the ground. It had been a tiring day too, walking all the way to the mission church where I knew breakfast would be served, past the memorial garden where John and the baby were buried, and then across the city to the train station.

But she was far too interested in the view out the window to consider closing her eyes for even a moment. Did she remember being anywhere other than the city? Maybe not. She'd only been two the last time we'd ridden out to Sugar Creek, where I grew up.

It seemed like only yesterday. A beautiful April morning. John had driven the shiny Ford coupe he'd gotten from his best friend, trying not to be edgy about taking us out to see my parents for only the second time in our marriage. And I'd been far more nervous than he. Of course I'd longed to see Mother, but I'd never had a good relationship with Father. Walter Wiskirk had despised my choice of a husband from the beginning, and he made no effort to hide it. He'd scoffed when we chose to name our girl Eliza, after my mother, but he'd been even more spiteful when we'd named our second child John James. He scarcely knew how to be civil to anyone.

Life and death were so cruel. I needed my mother. I would have loved to have her at my side right now. And Ellie would have loved it too. Why would God take her away, two years ago this very month? Why would he not have taken my father instead, who never bothered with a kind word, never tried to be a decent father or grandfather? He had always been red-faced and yelling from my earliest memories of him. It was good to be putting distance between us.

"Mommy, look!" Eliza cried suddenly, pointing to the wide expanse of river the train was about to cross. The mighty Mississippi. I took a quick glance and then averted my eyes so I'd catch no real glimpse of the narrow bridge that would be supporting the train's weight over the rushing current.

I need to be strong. I must be strong. I must not let fear stand in my way.

John had understood the fears that troubled me, though they'd never been as bad when he was around. He'd been patient, gentle, in praying for me and helping with so many things. But trains were absolutely the worst. They'd always been the worst.

Eliza pulled my sleeve and pointed out a small herd of cows grazing placidly within a fenced pasture. So quickly we were across the river and into the colorful leaves and drying cornfields of Illinois farmland on the other side. I did my best to smile and nod pleasantly for my daughter's sake, though the train's steady speed was unnerving. Thirty miles an hour? I couldn't be sure. It might have been even more. What would happen should one of those cows escape its fence and wander onto the track? I shuddered to think about it.

Ellie looked into my face for a moment, as though she sensed the unrest inside me. But she broke into a tender smile. "This is fun," she said softly. "Ill'noy's gonna be lovely."

There was that word again. So many things were "lovely" to Eliza lately. But that was better than "blessed," her favorite word just a few short weeks ago. Hearing "blessed" so often had been a trial for me, a dismal struggle with my faltering faith because it constantly reminded me of God and what he could do, or should do. Or should have done.

John and I had wanted a big family. I'd always wanted a big family. And despite our hopes and prayers, that dream had been brutally stolen away. Now Eliza and I had nothing but lack. How long would it be before she grew hungry, if she wasn't already? Hopefully, her excitement with the trip and the sights would keep her from noticing. It was long past lunchtime. But we hadn't eaten since breakfast, and I'd had no money to provide food to bring along, nor even a penny to purchase any once the train was stopped. We'd be leaning on Aunt Marigold's mercies indeed.

Eliza should have been able to enjoy a day at school like other children and then come home to a warm house and generous supper. But I couldn't give her any of that yet. She would've started school in St. Louis if we hadn't become homeless. But the beginning of first grade could be such a crucial time. I just couldn't send her off for such a new thing when I didn't know from one day to the next where we'd be. Hopefully, she could begin in Aunt Marigold's town. And hopefully, missing the first few days would not be a problem and she wouldn't be set back a year.

Taking Eliza's hand to hold, I closed my eyes and leaned my head back again. I really should pray. The way Mother had taught me and John had always encouraged me. The compulsion was strong, but I still resisted. I'd been able to believe in prayer once. But I was afraid now. If I dared try again only to find disappointment, I wasn't sure how I could take it. I hadn't been able to pray aloud since John died for fear that Ellie would be hurt if the prayer weren't answered. That was bad enough. But I hadn't prayed at all since losing the baby. And silence toward heaven grew increasingly painful. Why should I pray? What had it gained us? And yet my guilt only grew stronger over not doing so. It wasn't fair.

Eliza was quiet, looking out the window, leaving me to my thoughts. But eventually, the weariness of the day won out as she turned and snuggled with her head on my lap. I stroked her generous curls, wondering if she already knew that asking about dinner would gain her nothing. She seemed so content, so at peace. How was it possible? She was an amazing child, to be without her daddy and yet to remain so cheerful, so appreciative of everything around her.

If I could just be more like her! Maybe I could get past our losses and find real hope in making a new life.

I combed through her pretty hair with my fingers, at the same time watching her face. So peaceful, so trusting. She did not seem to have the slightest doubt that Marigold would welcome us and everything would work out beautifully for us there. *She's not like me. She's like her father. Fearless and confident. Unshaken even in hard times.*

I could see out of the corner of my eye that someone had approached in the narrow aisle, but I did not look up.

"Excuse me."

The unexpected voice was jarring, and I found myself resenting the interruption. Who would disturb my solitude with my daughter or have reason to seek my attention on the train? Reluctantly, I looked up into the face of an elderly woman from a seat a few rows in front of us.

"Excuse me," she said again, passing a large orange between her hands. "We get off at the next stop, and we just won't be needing this." She extended the orange in my direction. "My husband and I thought your little girl might like to have it."

I could barely respond. I'd have liked nothing more than to claim the orange before the woman changed her mind. I'd wanted desperately to be able to offer Eliza something to eat. But a gift from strangers?

"Are you sure?" I asked the woman quickly. "Wouldn't you use it later if you took it with you?"

"No. If we eat it now, it'll spoil dinner with my niece. And if we take it along to that household, it'll cause a ruckus over how to split it among her seven children. Better to share it with someone who might need and appreciate it now. Does your little girl like oranges?"

Eliza had opened her eyes and was looking up at the woman with a smile, but she didn't respond.

"Y-yes," I answered, receiving the gift with a shaking hand. "Thank you."

"You're very welcome. Have a wonderful trip."

The train was beginning to slow, and the old woman and her husband made their way to the end of the car. I watched them, still holding the orange. How could they have known our need? Did we look so poor? Could complete strangers read our situation that well?

Eliza sat up, her eyes shining and her face aglow with excitement. "Mommy! God is good to us! I prayed! I asked him for something to eat, and he sent us this orange right away! Can we open it up? Right now?"

I stared at her, barely able to keep back tears. God had answered her prayer so readily? Sure, it was a good thing. The dear child needed a decent meal, and this would at least keep her from going completely hungry. But I felt anger stirring in me, deep and bitter. *You think this is enough, do you, God? One orange? In the face of all our need? I begged you! I cried and prayed that you wouldn't take first her grandmother, then her father, then her baby brother! And now you decide to send us one orange?*

"Mommy?" Ellie repeated. "Can we open it?"

She looked so happy, so hopeful, her joy tempered only slightly with concern for the look that must have been on my face. I was practically shaking inside, afraid of my own feelings, yet unable and unwilling to change them. But I must not let her know. I must not pass along to Ellie the worry of my resentment and ingratitude when she was feeling so . . . blessed.

"Of course," I told her, careful to smile. "I will peel it for you right away."

"For *us*, Mommy," she corrected. "I prayed for us *both* to get something to eat."

I could not stop the tears from filling my eyes now as I tore into the orange rind with my fingernails. My precious, saintly daughter intended to give me half. And for fear that the tears would take charge, I could not tell her that I couldn't eat what she alone had gained by her prayer of faith. I had no right.

"Isn't God good?" she went on. "I never, ever seen a prayer answered so fast before."

Neither have I, my restless, embittered mind answered, fortunately not aloud. Ellie was watching my face, keenly aware of my tears.

"Have you got real hungry since this morning?" she asked.

I shook my head, miserable with the understanding that she'd probably been suffering in silence. I *was* hungry. But I couldn't admit it to her now. Setting the bits of rind aside, I pulled segments of the orange apart and gave her the first one. It looked so juicy and sweet. I expected her to eat the first bite quickly, but she paused, her face lit again with a smile. "Thank you, Jesus, for sending an orange when we needed one."

Now she was ready to eat. But not quickly as I'd expected. She took small bites, savoring, making it last.

"You have some, Mommy."

I shook my head again and kept passing her the orange segments, one by one. "I'm not really hungry, dear." It was a lie, but she'd have no way of knowing that. I was glad for her to eat it. I wanted her to eat it all, though some fire of indignation still burned hotly within me that God would do this—send just this little gift now, as though that could make up for all the pain, all the negligence, of the last months.

Today you hear? my mind raged on. *Where were you in November when John was killed? Where were you in the winter when the baby and I became so sick? You brought John through the war only to come home and die the way he did! And you brought little Johnny James through a difficult childbirth only to die such a few short months later! You left Ellie and me alone, not knowing how to go on! And now—now you hear?*

My own depth of anger frightened me. I didn't know the Scriptures very well, but there must surely be a warning there about railing and complaining against God. I knew it wasn't right. It scared me to be in such a place, yet I couldn't let it go. *It's not fair, God!* You're *not fair!*

How dare I be this way? Mother would be horrified at me. John too. They would think that I should cheerfully accept everything that had happened and keep on thanking God.

Eliza was down to the last orange piece. She had tried to offer me several others, but I turned them down. "Please, Mommy," she suddenly begged. "Please eat this one. I want you to know how sweet it is."

Her bold words seemed almost like the voice of God telling me to open my heart and listen. I was missing something, something he wanted me to know. I swallowed hard.

"Please, Mommy."

How could I continue to refuse? She looked very near tears. *Because of me.* Finally, I nodded. She'd prayed for food for *both* of us. She did not want me to deny her answered prayer and make it only half complete. "All right," I acquiesced. "It would be nice to have a taste."

I ate the orange slice slowly as Eliza watched my every move. "Wonderful," I said when I was done. "Imagine such a sweet orange in the middle of the country in September. I wonder where they got it?"

She laughed. "It doesn't matter, Mommy. *We* got it from God. Isn't he good?"

She was waiting for my answer. I nodded, knowing it was the best I could do to respond. I would not be able to argue the point with her. In a way, I still wanted to believe it myself. But my pain had built a formidable wall that grew broader and higher with each passing day. I wasn't sure I'd ever feel the presence of heaven unhindered again.

2

Leah

It would have been nicer had we been able to arrive in Andersonville in the daylight. But fortunately it was such a small town that I'd surely be able to find the proper address without much trouble even at night. Ellie had dozed on the train and was dreadfully sleepy when it came time to step off. That bothered me considerably. How could I manage a drowsy girl and two large bags? What if one of us tripped on the step or caught our skirt on something? What if the train was in too much of a hurry to notice and started moving before we could step away?

I needn't have worried. One of the railway workers apparently had a home in this town. He was getting off the train at this stop and offered to carry my bags to the station platform when he saw me struggling with my arms so full. "Thank you so much," I told him.

Eliza stared up at the stranger but didn't say a word. I was glad to have my hands free. She was so groggy she nearly stumbled as we left the railcar. I took her in both hands and guided her safely down.

This station was nothing like the one in St. Louis. It was much smaller, and no crowd stood waiting. No one at all. I'd expected that, of course. Though I'd written Aunt Marigold weeks ago to say that we might come, I'd had no idea whether it would be practical for her to meet us, so I hadn't asked. I hadn't even told her the day of our arrival, because when I'd written her, I wasn't sure about the whole thing. If there'd been any way for us in St. Louis, I might have taken it.

I couldn't see much of the little town beyond the depot, but the moon shone almost full, and it was such a beautiful evening that I told myself this would prove to be a pleasant place. A very large windmill stood not far away. A row of businesses lined the narrow street in the opposite direction.

The stranger had just set my bags down, and I was wondering where Malcolm Street might be when he looked around a bit and shook his head. "Someone coming to meet you? Doesn't look to be anyone here yet."

I wasn't sure at first how to respond. But he could see for himself that nobody was hurrying to greet us. And I did not want to appear the least bit troubled by that. "No, sir. We're not expecting anyone. But we'll be fine from here alone. Thank you very much for your kind help."

Still holding one of Ellie's hands, I leaned and picked up a bag.

"Um . . ." He reached to lift the second bag again before I could get to it. "You mean to walk to wherever you're going?"

I did not like his persistence, nor his bold reluctance to turn loose of my luggage.

"We've made it this far, sir. I'm sure it won't be difficult for us to walk the rest of the way."

He tilted his head sideways a bit. "What street you headed for?"

What if he followed us? What if he refused to give up my bag? The train was already beginning to move away, and there was no sign of anyone on these sleepy streets. How could I get this man to leave us alone? "I am not in the habit of telling strangers my personal affairs," I told him coolly.

He smiled. "Maybe not. But I daresay you could use some

help out here with so much to tote. I don't mind packing the baggage if you're not going far. Too many blocks, though, and I'd bang on Melvin's door right across the street there and ask him to take you in his truck. Save you both some walking."

"No, thank you, sir," I said as firmly as I could. "There's no need to disturb a complete stranger. And we'll be quite all right without your help, though I do appreciate the offer. I wouldn't want to keep you from your family. Good night." I tried to take my bag from his hand, but he wouldn't turn loose of it.

"Don't have much family to speak of. Just an elderly aunt. And I'm trying to save you some trouble, ma'am. Your little girl there looks awfully tired."

I was well aware of Eliza's exhaustion as well as my own. And I knew we would be far more exhausted by the time we reached Aunt Marigold's door. It wouldn't be difficult once we found the right street, but that could take a while in the dark. Oh, why hadn't the train schedule brought us here in daylight? I had considered trying to rest the night right here at the depot and locating the boardinghouse in the morning, but I couldn't admit such a thing to this forward fellow.

"We'll be fine, I assure you," I insisted again. "It was very kind of you to help us off the train, but you've no reason to concern yourself further."

He was quiet for a moment, but he still didn't let go of my bag. What now? I had not expected such a predicament as this. Could I trust him to help us? How could I be sure he didn't have something less chivalrous in mind?

"Look, ma'am," he finally answered. "Maybe you're perfectly comfortable, and maybe I ought to leave you and the youngster to find your own way. But I'm walking home from here myself. Forgive me for saying—it wouldn't seem right to leave you and your little girl out after dark without any help. So just point the way or start walking. Your bags aren't heavy, and it's a small town. I'll pack them for you. Won't take long for me to see you to whatever door's waiting and go home from there. Or if you won't let me do that, I'll just have to follow to make sure you make it where you're going all right."

His response may have been sincere, but it rankled me nonetheless. "I told you. We'll be fine. I am not in the habit of—"

"Taking help from strangers. Obviously."

I stared. Eliza pulled at my wrist, but when I turned to her, she didn't say anything. I leaned to take her into my arms for a moment, and before I could speak, the man was saying something more.

"Maybe you're scared of me. I understand. But if you're really frightened of a stranger out here at night, all the more reason not to be walking alone. That might not make sense to you, but it does to me." He set my bag down, but then he sat on it. "Look. I'm willing to help you. But if you won't have it, I'll knock on Mel's door. Maybe you'd let him *and* his wife take you home. Maybe you'd be more comfortable then. It's your choice."

I could tell he was stubborn and I was stuck. He was going to have his way, one way or the other. But for some reason, that made me less apprehensive than I was before. "Well, if you must insist, we are going to Malcolm Street. To a boardinghouse there."

"Really?" He cocked his head again in the moonlight. "That's easy. No sense bothering Mel and Dotty for that. They'd think I'd lost my mind." He stood up and lifted my bag, then took the other from me and threw it over his shoulder. "Can you and the little girl keep up all right? It's only four blocks."

I pretended I'd known that all along. "Of course."

He started off toward the row of businesses with long strides, and Eliza and I indeed had a struggle to not be left behind. For a moment I worried that he might purposely abscond with my bags and lose us, but he soon glanced behind him and slowed a bit.

"So what brings you to Andersonville?" he quizzed. "Can't say we get travelers here every day just to stop over at our illustrious boardinghouse. How'd you even hear of the place?"

"The proprietor invited us," I told him, feeling generous to share even that much information.

"Really?" he asked again. "What did you say your name was?"

"I didn't say."

He walked on a few steps and then laughed. "All right, then. What's your name?"

"I am unconvinced that you need to know any more of my business."

He smiled. "Pleased to make your acquaintance, Miss Unconvinced. My name is Josiah Walsh."

I suppose he thought he was being pleasantly funny. I might have told him otherwise, but he spoke again before I had the chance. "So tell me, the proprietor you were talking about—is she expecting you *tonight*?"

"I can't imagine why you'd need to know."

"Maybe I don't." He shrugged. "But it does pay to be considerate to your pack mule. A little conversation on the way to a destination never hurt anyone."

Something about his tone rubbed me the wrong way, and I wished I could yank my bags out of his hands and make him disappear. "I did not ask you to carry my things, Mr. Walsh! I would never call anyone a pack mule. And I see no reason for personal conversation with a stranger, as I have already told you."

"Whatever you say. Can't make a lady converse, I guess. Won't hurt to try, though. Pleasant train trip?"

I ignored his question. The sooner we got to the boardinghouse and were rid of him, the better. I hoped he didn't ask payment for carrying our things. I had nothing to give him.

Eliza stumbled on a rock, and I reached quickly to keep her from falling. "Do you want me to carry you, sweetie?"

"No, Mommy, I can make it just fine." She held my hand and looked all around us, taking in what she could as Mr. Walsh glanced back at us again and turned a corner.

"The stars are pretty," she observed. "Aren't you glad it isn't raining?"

"Yes. Very glad."

Four blocks, he'd said. Surely we were almost there. Eliza was thoroughly awake now, kicking at the occasional rock in front of her toe. Then as I tried to hurry her along, she began skipping.

"Do you think Aunt Marigold's gone to bed already?" she suddenly asked. "I hope not. It's a lovely night and I want to meet her."

Mr. Walsh stopped in his tracks and turned to look at us.

"We're right behind you, sir." I tried to sound pleasant. "I can carry the bags the rest of the way if you'd like to go on to your home. Thank you again—"

"I'll be finishing what I started, if you please, ma'am." He took a few steps and then stopped again. "Marigold McSweeney is your aunt?"

"Yes, sir."

He shook his head. "I didn't think there could be more than one Marigold in a town this size. Least not without me hearing about it."

I wondered if he thought everyone's business was his own. Why would it matter who my relatives were? But he wasn't done with the questions.

"Is she kin on your father's side or your mother's?" he asked on.

"My husband's," I said tersely, hoping he'd decide to drop the subject.

He looked Eliza and me both over a little more thoroughly. "All right," he said almost absently. And then he took such a big breath that I could see his shoulders rise. "Any notion how long you may choose to stay in our fair village?"

Once again, his prying fed my ire. "Mr. Walsh, I have no intention—"

"Of telling your business to strangers. Right." He turned and started walking again, faster. If we'd had a long way to go, he surely would have left us far behind this time, even with Ellie's determined skipping. But in the next block of houses, he suddenly stopped.

"There she is." He pointed to an old two-story home, large but not particularly extraordinary. "Marigold McSweeney's boardinghouse."

I expected him to set my bags on the walkway, but he didn't. What would I tell him if he expected payment? I couldn't ask Aunt Marigold for money first thing. It was enough to expect her to provide us a bed.

Eliza had stopped just to stare at the house, but I hurried her along, glad to be done with our walk.

"Thank you very much," I told Mr. Walsh. "I'll gladly take my bags so you may go—"

He didn't seem to hear me, just marched right on toward the house with my luggage still in hand. We had to hurry to keep up until finally he stopped at the front door.

"Thank you so much," I said again. "You may set my things here on the porch, sir, and be on your way—"

Once again, he ignored me, stunning me this time with seemingly overwhelming audacity. With one of my bags in hand and the other slung over his shoulder, he turned the knob, flung the door wide, and tromped right into the house.

Eliza moved to follow, but I held her back and stood on the porch, uncertain. Mr. Walsh dropped my bags recklessly at the base of a curved stairway and turned to motion us in. "Don't worry," he said in answer to my silence. "I live here. Aunt Mari!" he called toward the back of the house. "You've got guests!"

Aunt Mari? I was struck speechless. Did he mean Marigold? Was this—this—gentleman a relative of my husband? My John had never mentioned his name. I was absolutely certain.

"You might as well come in," he said. "Aunt Mari'll probably be a minute. She doesn't move very fast right now."

I stood still, not quite able to do as he said or find the words to explain why not. Eliza looked at me, expecting some kind of response. When I gave none, she broke the silence.

"Mommy? Do we live here now?"

"We're just visiting for a while," I answered, afraid to voice more than that in front of this man. It should have occurred to me that Marigold might have boarders, even several boarders, including male ones. But I hadn't given it much thought, and I'd never considered the possibility that she might have other relatives staying with her. She hadn't mentioned it. And I wasn't sure how it might affect the situation for us here. I looked past Mr. Walsh into the house, hoping to see Aunt Marigold approaching us, but there was no sign of anyone.

He seemed amused by my discomfort. "I suppose you think I should've told you we were going to the same place."

I could readily agree with that. "Someone so quick to inquire of other people's business should certainly be willing to disclose their own."

He smiled. "You didn't ask. But I gave you my name anyway. And yours is . . . ?"

"Breckenridge," I told him, feeling a pinch of nerves in the pit of my stomach. "Leah and Eliza."

He nodded. "John's wife." It wasn't a question, just a statement of what must have been obvious. I almost asked if he were a cousin to my husband, but a shuffling sound drew my attention and then the door behind him swung open. A short, white-haired lady in a fluffy apron ambled in, limping in such a manner that I could not determine which leg she might be favoring.

"My—you must be here off the train—so late at night with a young'un." She stepped closer and eyed me carefully.

"It's Leah Breckenridge," Mr. Walsh told her solemnly.

"Leah? Oh my stars! I might have guessed."

"Where do you want me to put their bags?" he asked just as soberly, the attempts at levity in his previous conversation somehow gone. Now he seemed pensive, anxious to be away from us. I wasn't sure if it might be because of his aunt's presence or because he knew for certain now who we were.

Aunt Marigold gave me a hug I didn't expect and then

squeezed Eliza just as much. "Oh, my dears! Did you have a good trip? Are you hungry? I wish I'd known you'd be here tonight. I'd have had some scones all baked and ready."

Scones? I'd never in my life even seen any.

"Take their things to the master room, Josiah," she quickly directed. "Best place to put the two of them together."

I wasn't sure what the "master room" was, but it didn't seem quite right for us to be placed there. "Oh, I don't want to put anyone out," I ventured. "Any room will do, and I am so grateful that you'll have us."

"Not to worry, dear," Aunt Marigold told me. "Used to be my room, but I haven't slept upstairs in months. Can't take all those steps the way I used to."

Josiah went straight up the stairs with my luggage, but she called to him quickly. "Come on down and join us for a bite to eat once you get their things up there."

He shook his head. "I believe I'll just go on to bed."

"Nonsense. You're always hungry when you get home. Don't be playin' shy now. I know better."

He disappeared, and she shook her head. "Never mind him," she whispered conspiratorially. "He can be quite the character sometimes, but God love him, he's a real good boy."

Josiah Walsh must have been nearly thirty years old. To hear her call him a boy was a bit unusual. But she looked ancient. I wasn't really sure how old. John had never told me.

She took my arm and started back in the direction she'd come from. Eliza stayed at my side, watching her every move.

"Now, tell me, dearie," Marigold asked as we went through the doorway and into a generous dining room. "How have you been? God love you, what a rough go of it! How'd it come about for you to be gracing me today? I got your letter and I wasn't sure when to expect you, but I'm sure glad you've come."

She talked a mile a minute, but her steps were so slow and careful I thought surely her hand on my arm was more to steady herself than to lead me anywhere. I decided to make what I hoped would be considered a polite inquiry. "Have you been well?"

"Oh yes. No complaint 'cept the rheumatiz that just gets worse and worse. You know how that is." She stopped and smiled. "No, I suppose you probably don't, young as you are. And you're a beauty too. John never told me he'd married up with someone so pretty."

I'd never thought of myself as pretty. As far as I was concerned, my nose was too big, my hair too unmanageably curly, and my figure more like a stick than anything to be noted with admiration. No one but John had ever countered my opinion, and I'd concluded that that was just John. Outspoken and generous with his praise, sometimes to a fault.

"You know," Marigold talked on, "I wanted to come over for your wedding, but dear Petunia was ailing so poorly with the dysentery that I didn't want to leave her. Expecting her eighth child too. A miracle we didn't lose them both."

"I remember that. John's aunt Daisy was beside herself with worry for both of you."

She shook her head. "I told and told that Daisy. I was far too stubborn to take the dysentery or anything else off of Petunia! She needn't have worried on my account." She turned her eyes quickly to me. "But tell me, dear, how have you been making it? God love you, I cried over your last letter. All you've been through! Are you fully recovered? Are you and your little Rose both well?"

I wasn't sure what to think of her calling Eliza by her middle name. Or her talkativeness when I was little more than a stranger, relative or not. "We're well," I answered simply. "I'm so sorry to surprise you like this. I would have written again and told you for certain when we'd be arriving, but . . . but our departure was so sudden that there wouldn't have been time for the letter to get here."

Barely seeming to hear me, she ushered us through the dining room and into a small kitchen with bright yellow walls and fringed curtains. "Do you have plans? Have you just come to visit? Or can you stay a spell? Have you worked out what's next? Poor dear, you've hardly had time to get your feet under you again."

I don't know what I expected from her. She had every right to ask. But I was tired from the trip and my two nearly sleepless nights. I didn't want to talk. Not yet.

Eliza was not so minded. "We come to see you 'cause you was nice enough to invite," she announced. "We don't know yet where we're gonna live after this."

"Dear child," Marigold said with a sigh. "You're welcome to stay as long as you need to. I'm pleased to have you."

I felt I needed to tell her something our letters hadn't addressed. "I—I'm afraid I can't pay. Not yet, at least."

Marigold waved her hand and dismissed the notion. "I'll not be asking for pay. Just a hand with things now and again. Josiah, though, that's different. He's got a good job with the railroad. A man can afford to pay a mite for his board. It's only right."

I almost protested that if one relative were paying, it wouldn't be proper for me not to. But I decided instead to take a more realistic approach. "I don't want to just lend a hand now and again, Aunt Marigold. As long as I'm here I want to work daily at whatever it is you need done. I can see that you need the help."

"That's not the reason I asked you," she said, her eyes filling with tears. "I know how hard it can be after—after you lose a husband, to make ends meet on your own. I wanted to help."

I wished she hadn't gotten teary. Now there was no way I could hold back. I didn't want to cry in front of her, but it was just no use.

She hugged me again. She didn't say anything at all this time, only led me to a chair and held her arm around me the whole time. When I saw her reach her other hand to Ellie, I knew I'd made the right decision to come here, at least for a little while. For a safe and accepting shelter where I could take the time to think things through and decide what to do next. "Thank you," I managed to tell her again.

"Don't even think of it. I'm glad I've got the room. Though I'd have squeezed you in sideways if need be."

"I still mean to help you all I can."

"I'll let you, I suppose. Eventually," she agreed. "Especially upstairs. I haven't gotten up there to clean in an unspeakably long time. Ashamed to have you see it."

I heard a sound behind us and turned just enough to know that Mr. Walsh had come in. I looked away quickly, toward the window above Aunt Marigold's sink, hoping to clear my eyes and regain my composure.

"Josiah says he's been helping me," Marigold said with a wink in her nephew's direction, "but I haven't been able to get up there to inspect. Who really knows the shape those rooms are in by now? It's no wonder my other boarders moved out."

"They both took jobs away from here," he answered her quickly. "Don't blame me."

Marigold left my side and hobbled over to start water heating in the large teapot on the stove. "Don't just stand there," she admonished her nephew. "Grab the teacups and the sugar for me. Would everyone like a slice of soda bread with some ground-cherry preserves? I've got chicken and dumplings too, if you want something more substantial."

"Oh," Ellie said quickly. "Lovely!"

She'd been so patient. Aunt Marigold had no idea. Eliza looked at me with her eyes aglow. "Oh, Mommy, doesn't that sound really good?"

My face grew hot and I hoped they wouldn't realize that my poor child was half-starved for want of a decent supper. "Yes. It sounds delicious."

If Marigold realized, she didn't let on. "Well, I do love guests with hearty appetites. Help me, Josiah. Bring the pot from the icebox and cut the bread for me."

I watched as they worked together, the short squat old lady, and the tall, well-muscled man. I tried to discern some family resemblance, but neither of them looked a thing like my John at all. I knew Marigold was John's mother's much-older sister. But

I had no idea where Josiah fit into the picture. Another sister's son, most likely, but I couldn't bring myself to ask.

His presence was my only uncertainty about staying here. I knew I'd not be comfortable with a man about. Even bearing no resemblance, he would still be a reminder of John, and it was difficult to watch him working beside his aunt already. But besides that, his manner toward me on the way here was a concern. I'd always been wary of men. It had taken John a long time to win my confidence. How could I be sure this man could be trusted, a relative or not? He was bold to do a kindness, admittedly. But bold nonetheless.

Aunt Marigold served the best chicken and dumplings I'd ever eaten. With homemade bread, preserves, and a cup of tea on the side. Eliza ate hungrily, and I admonished her to be careful of her manners.

Aunt Marigold didn't think I needed to worry about it. "It's just a late snack after traveling," she said with a smile for Ellie. "There'll be time for being ladylike another day."

Josiah ate a remarkable amount amazingly quickly despite his earlier hesitation. But then he tried to excuse himself.

"Wait just a minute," Marigold told him. "You know I can't show these ladies to their rooms the way my knees have been lately. You'll have to do it for me, as soon as they're ready. And please make sure there's plenty of water, clean soap, and fresh towels at the washstand too. Be extra nice and I'll have a pie made before you're home for supper tomorrow."

She smiled and turned to me, not giving him a chance to respond. "Wasn't it just the blessing of God to put you all at the depot at the same time? Most days Josiah's on a different train and you'd have missed him altogether. The good Lord must have seen fit for you to have an escort right to our door. I don't believe in any such thing as luck. Nor coincidence. Must all have been divinely arranged, no doubt about it."

Her words stirred a bitter response in my heart. Divinely arranged? Why should God care if I met anyone to carry my baggage? He hadn't cared about my far greater needs. John should be here enjoying dumplings with his aunt. And I should have a babe in my arms.

Mr. Walsh didn't seem to appreciate her comment any more than I did. He stood with a frown and began clearing the table though Eliza wasn't finished yet. I couldn't eat anymore. What appetite I'd had disappeared quickly as Ellie excitedly related the story of the orange and her prayer on the train. What I'd wanted to remain hidden was now fully in the open. I sat like a stone as Aunt Marigold exclaimed with joy over Ellie's tale of provision. Only once did my eyes stray unintentionally to meet Mr. Walsh's, and he looked away. No doubt he thought us little more than beggars who'd come to cadge what we could off his aged, rheumatic aunt. No wonder he looked so solemn.

Soon enough, Aunt Mari hugged and kissed Eliza and we followed Mr. Walsh up the stairs to our room. He said nothing at all, nor did I, but Ellie was humming all the way. We'd been given a large room, a most generous room, with lace curtains and a full brass bed. I was too tired to care that there was dust on the dressing table and the crystal lamp. I only wanted to sleep and put the day behind me.

Apparently in this house, running water extended only to the lower floor. Josiah filled a bowl at the washstand with the pitcher he'd carried from downstairs. He opened a drawer and pulled out a cake of soap. I thanked him, but he simply set the pitcher down and walked away as if he didn't hear me. Eliza was still humming as he stepped out into the hallway and shut the door behind him.

He might prove difficult to have around, though he'd graciously done what Aunt Marigold had asked of him. Except set out the towels. But that was a small thing and not something he should have to think about anyway. I'd be taking care of my own needs and Eliza's soon enough without his help. I'd have the entire upper story of this house spotless as soon as I could manage it. And do what I could to help Marigold with the downstairs too.

For a moment I considered her words, that our timing tonight had been divinely arranged. She seemed to be talking only about our meeting Josiah at the depot, but perhaps she'd meant the possibility of having my help too. Obviously, her nephew was a benefit to her, but he was gone through the day. She needed me here for a time, that seemed clear, the way she struggled just getting from one room to the next.

I wasn't much in a temper to give God credit for anything, but maybe good could be at work here. At least I wouldn't have to feel like a useless burden, and that would be a decent start.

3

Leah

Bedtime was bittersweet and much the same as it had been in our own home and even in the St. Louis city park. Eliza used to love the tender good-night ritual her daddy had developed when he came home to us after the war. The first few nights after he died she'd cried for hours, inconsolable to be without him. But eventually she'd created a ritual of her own that seemed to enable her to shut out the world and close herself into a secret place alone. Though I had my small part, her daddy's memory was the focus of her new nightly ritual, and I made no attempt to draw her attention away from it because she seemed to have found peace.

When she was all washed and changed, she came to me for hugs and kisses. And then she lay down and curled into a ball. Now the humming that had already started would be almost constant until sleep carried her away. Through the little drawing motions she made in the air, and the hair twirling, and the rolling side to side as though her bed were on rockers, she would continue humming the tune her daddy had sung to her night after night. This night I stretched beside her, and though she snuggled near me, she kept up the motion and the song and I lay with tears in my eyes, wishing I could hear John's voice one more time. A bird I didn't recognize called outside our window, and somewhere nearby I could hear low footsteps and the creak of furniture. Mr. Walsh, presumably, preparing for bed.

Why had Eliza and I come to this? A borrowed bed. Charity from a relative. We should have been a complete family, in the happy life I'd dreamed of since I was a child. We'd had plans to purchase a home of our own. It wouldn't have been hard, even on the paycheck John had already brought in. But he'd wanted to provide more and kept looking at other jobs, hoping for a higher salary.

If he'd been satisfied, maybe he'd be alive today. But there was no telling such a matter as that, no point entertaining it in my thoughts. John had done the best he knew, and had he survived, we'd have moved to a home all our own this past spring. That had been his plan. We'd looked at several houses together. But now, such dreams were worthless as the dust.

The bed was comfortable, but I found it difficult to relax. Even when Eliza finally lay still and her humming had ceased, I had a hard time shutting off my thoughts and closing my eyes to really rest. Somewhere I could hear the tick of a clock. Except for Eliza's gentle breathing, and my own, everything else was still. In the dark of night the same prompting that I'd felt on the train came to me.

Pray. This is the perfect time.

But I didn't know what I could possibly say. If my anger jumped to the fore the way it had the last time I'd had such a thought, it would be better to stop before I even started. How might God respond to my ungrateful feelings? It was frightening to consider, and I didn't want to make things worse.

But prayer brings peace. Without it, you've no foundation.

I rolled to my side, doing my best to shut off such uninvited thinking. Sleep. That was the most peaceful thing I could consider right now. My most immediate need. Eliza bumped her arm against my shoulder, and I let it rest where it landed.

Morning would come soon enough, and a new day—a new beginning—for our lives with it.

Every sound and every worry faded into the night as eventually I managed to sleep. But the peace I'd longed for proved evasive. Black metal death was bearing down on me at breakneck speed. Huge. Spitting steam. I cried out soundlessly, every noise I made swallowed by the piercing devil scream of a train whistle. There was no way to flee in time. Unforgiving track stretched endlessly ahead and oddly to both sides, and I could not make my bloodied knees and trembling legs lift me from the rough-hewn ties where I'd fallen.

"Mommy!" I screamed, my tiny arms flailing in search of help.

But Mother was nowhere in sight, and my voice could not penetrate the train's roar. Nothing could. It was a hungry monster with its hardened mouth wide open. It owned me already, and there was no escape.

I rolled, I jerked. My leg caught in a jumble of fabric, and I fell headlong to the braided rug at the side of the bed. My heart thundered so viciously that it hurt, and I lay still, trying to recover myself from the paralyzing effects of the dream.

A train. Again. My worst fears, my worst memories, encompassed trains. When I was a child younger than Eliza, I would panic at the sound of one, freeze at the sight of one, without knowing why. Even then I must have had such dreams. The memory of them had been vague, almost invisible, yet it had plagued me nonetheless.

"Could a train cut people in pieces?" I'd asked my mother one day, barely able to speak at all. I was trembling so badly after being frightened at the sight of one in the town near where we lived.

Never would I forget her doleful answer. "It could, Leah-love. It's happened."

Mother's sorrow filled my mind so much that it took me a moment to realize that I lay on the hardwood floor in Aunt Marigold's master bedroom. Mother had been terribly sad so often. Partly because of Father's unkindness, I'd always thought. But partly for the sake of my older brother, who'd died when I was a toddler. If she were here now, if she were alive to be at my side, she would understand what I was going through with the loss of Johnny James. She would understand the bitterness, the pain and doubts because she'd probably gone through much the same herself.

Thank God my awful dream hadn't wakened Eliza. I sat up, stiff and tense, suddenly annoyed at myself for the almost-prayer. What did God have to do with it? My daughter was a sound sleeper, which was a mercy often but especially at times like this.

Was it morning? Someone was awake somewhere close by, almost surely Marigold's nephew again. His movements were quiet, and I hoped the tumble I'd taken was not the reason for him stirring. The darkness in the room made it seem like the full of night, but as I looked, I began to realize the first hint of dawn light at the big bay windows and I felt out of place. I'd never before lived in a house with bay windows, nor in a bedroom as spacious as this one.

I should pray about this new start, I considered again. But I was too stubbornly out of sorts over the day's unpleasant beginning to heed my own admonition.

I'll not do it. I'll not pray. Why should I talk to God until he shows me why he continues to torment me this way? All my life I've been haunted by trains, and by the deaths of those who shouldn't have died. The least he can do is tell me why!

I heard a door click somewhere beyond our door. Having John's unfamiliar cousin in such proximity was more than a little unnerving, but to my relief the next sound I heard was footfalls on the steps. He was leaving. Perhaps he'd already be gone to work by the time Eliza and I went down the stairs for the day.

I'd have my work cut out for me. Aunt Marigold might not want to see it that way, but I felt obligated to start helping immediately. I could cook breakfast if it weren't already done.

And I could begin cleaning every nook and cranny that she couldn't reach.

I dressed quickly and folded my bedclothes and the traveling clothes I'd worn yesterday. We had so few garments left, but they'd have to do until I could earn money for the fabric to make more. Perhaps it might be possible to find some employment in this small town, though I would need to make sure Aunt Marigold's needs here were taken care of first.

I had no idea how many bedrooms she had available to let out, but with only one paying boarder now, she might be struggling. We must not become a burden. With a job, I could pay her what was due and continue to contribute in other ways as long as we stayed here. That would be ideal.

I washed my face in the washbasin and checked the cupboard and drawers beneath it. Good. There were several other washcloths. Surely Aunt Marigold would approve of me using one for a dust cloth so I could use my time wisely while Eliza still slept. I didn't want to go downstairs without her. Certainly not on our first day here. She had seemed far more cheery and adaptable than one might expect in our circumstance, but I didn't want to risk her being alarmed at the unfamiliar surroundings upon wakening.

As the light from the window began to grow, I looked around carefully at the space provided for us. Obviously, this room had been furnished by a woman for a woman. The bedspread was ruffly, with a delightful quilted pattern of flowers. Aunt Marigold might be very handy with her sewing. Perhaps I could learn a thing or two to improve my own skills.

But the morning did not brighten quickly enough to suit me, and I lit the crystal lamp, knowing Eliza would sleep on despite it. What might I learn about Marigold, just from the room around me? The bedclothes were predominantly a soft pink, and indeed, most carefully hand sewn. The pale cream-striped walls were adorned with only two pictures: an inviting painting of hummingbirds flitting about a backyard bush and a tintype photograph of someone bearing a slight resemblance to my daughter. Her grandmother perhaps? John's mother? I studied the picture but had to turn my eyes away in tears.

Perhaps being here was not such a good idea. I would be constantly reminded, constantly bombarded with the injustice of John's absence. Because of that, I should not make plans to linger in this town any longer than necessary. I should see our visit only as Aunt Marigold had suggested, as a time to rest and prepare until I could get on my feet again. Elsewhere.

I lifted the lamp gently to dust beneath and around it and then wiped its crystal surface carefully. I would have to remember to remind Eliza to be extra careful not to touch this. I'd never seen one like it anywhere. Perhaps it had been quite expensive.

When the entire dresser top was clean, I opened a drawer, expecting to find it empty and in need of airing. Instead, I found folded garments, neatly tucked away with a sachet of cedar chips to prevent the infestation of moths. Marigold had probably not anticipated sharing this room with us. Maybe she hoped to be well enough to climb the stairs and use it herself again soon. It made me feel that we were intruding.

4

Leah

Eliza rolled a little on the bed and then sat up and looked around. I pulled the lacy window curtains wide and let the outside world rush in to greet her.

"Mommy—everything looks different in the daylight!"

Indeed it did. By the dim light last night, the room had seemed angular, shadowy. Now it had a comfortable air. I moved to the center window and looked out over Aunt Marigold's side yard and the town beyond it. Everything appeared more alive and promising than it had last night. I saw an automobile and a milk wagon, a neighbor's garden shed, several swaying trees, and standing tall above everything else, the big old windmill slowly turning in the distance.

Ellie leaped up to stand at my side. "Wow. What's the name of this town again?"

"Andersonville."

"It's lovely."

There was that word again. I nodded and tied the curtain in place with the sash I found dangling from a gold tie hook at the window's edge.

"Can we take a daytime walk?" she asked excitedly.

I hadn't expected that. Going out for a stroll was the last thing on my mind. But perhaps it was a reasonable idea. I would need to become acquainted with the town and its businesses if I hoped to find a position and pay for our board here. "We'll not go walking this morning," I said, giving her a quick hug. "We need to have breakfast with Aunt Marigold and help her with some cleaning chores first. But perhaps this afternoon, if she hasn't any other plan for us—"

"Maybe she would want to come walking too!"

"Oh, Ellie, I doubt she's able. She's having a lot of trouble right now with the rheumatism in her legs."

"But I prayed for her last night to be all better."

Her words stabbed at me. Not because my beautiful little daughter maintained a faith and commitment I now lacked but because I was afraid for her, afraid of the hurt she'd feel if Aunt Marigold did *not* get better. "Such things take time," I said simply. "Let's not ask her on a walk so quickly."

"Maybe that Mr. Walsh will come then," Ellie persisted.

"He has to go to work today," I admonished. "But even if he didn't, it would not be appropriate for young ladies to ask him out walking."

Ellie continued looking out the window. "I'm glad he carried our things last night. I'm glad we met him so he could show us the way."

I almost expected her to say she'd prayed for someone to guide us here from the train depot. I wouldn't have been the slightest bit surprised. But instead she bounced back toward the bed and told me she was hungry.

"Already? You ate like a horse last night."

"It was yummy. An' I promise to eat like a young lady today."

I smiled. "Of course you will." I pulled her blue cotton dress from one of our bags, wishing I'd had opportunity to iron it. But it wasn't too badly wrinkled. I'd folded and rolled it carefully.

"I like Aunt Marigold," Ellie said. "She sure was nice to us last night. This room is lovely. Don't you think? An' I know she'll be nice today too an' prob'ly even after that. You think we'll live in this town always?"

Quite a mouthful, but for Eliza Rose, not at all unusual. "I don't know the answer to that, honey. And I'm not sure when I'll know."

She shrugged her shoulders. "That's okay. I think livin' at Aunt Marigold's is gonna be perfect fine, an' if we ever do move, I hope it's right down the street at one of them other pretty houses."

"Let's keep such discussions between ourselves, shall we?" I told her uncomfortably. "I'm not sure how long Aunt Marigold would like us to be here, nor am I ready to ask."

I had her wash her face and get dressed while I continued to dust all around the room. I'd been too tired last night to think about it, but now I wondered how long it'd been since the bedclothes had been laundered, considering that Marigold hadn't been able to climb the stairs. It wouldn't be appropriate to ask first thing this morning, of course, but maybe later I could offer to do the washing, including all the bedding in the house. The windows could use a good wiping too, the floors dust-mopped, and the rugs shaken out—eventually. There might not be time for it all the first day. And I certainly didn't want Aunt Marigold thinking that I disapproved of her housekeeping. I just wanted to pitch in with things that must be especially difficult for her.

I could smell something baking as soon as we reached the bottom of the stairs, and then I felt guilty that I hadn't been down earlier. If Aunt Marigold prepared breakfast this early then I should be up helping in the kitchen. I would have to tell her that I did not want to be treated like a special guest. I wanted to work for our board starting immediately.

But it was quickly apparent that Marigold had different ideas.

"My goodness!" she exclaimed as soon as she saw us. "You're up so early! Did my clattering about wake you? I wouldn't have called you down this morning at all. You need your rest after the trip."

I knew what had wakened me, but I didn't want to say a word about that. "We've become accustomed to rising with the sun," I said simply, neglecting to add that the habit was a by-product of my own restlessness.

Her nephew seemed to be nowhere about. Perhaps he'd already left for work. If that were the case, we'd only need to concern ourselves with encountering him directly in the evenings, which would be far easier for me. Marigold seemed matronly in an immensely likeable way. And to all appearances she even needed us, as we needed her. Without Josiah Walsh's presence throwing an unpredictable cog in the works, we could have a happy arrangement here.

Marigold was rolling out biscuit dough and Eliza was immediately fascinated. "Can I help?"

"Why, sure, child. You're just the right age for this kind of thing." Marigold reached to the wide pickle crock that held her kitchen utensils and grabbed out a much smaller rolling pin, just the size for Ellie. The handles were painted bright red with little yellow knobs on the ends. The little roller had probably been carved from a very lightweight wood, but it rolled just as easily as the big one.

Eliza was eager to do her part rolling out the biscuits, and Aunt Marigold was just as eager to teach. They made quite a pair, just as I'd expected. Ellie was beaming ear to ear as she bore down with her rolling pin over the smooth dough. I busied my hands with the little bit of dishes in the sink, and Marigold left Ellie alone for a minute to check the oven and pull out what I'd been smelling—the first pan of biscuits. She had the biggest cookie sheet I'd ever seen brimming full, and there'd be at least that many more. I'd never known anyone to fix such a big batch who didn't have eight or nine children standing ready to eat them.

"I'm slow anymore," she told me. "'Fore I get the second tray of dough ready, the first ones are comin' out."

"Do you always make so many? Goodness, we couldn't begin to eat that much."

She smiled. "Won't have to. Twice a week I send a bundleful on the train."

On the train? Biscuits? I didn't have time to ask what she was talking about. The back door creaked behind me and I turned in time to see Mr. Walsh step into the kitchen with a wire basket filled with eggs.

"My, oh my, that's a generous many," Aunt Mari proclaimed. "Did Mr. Abraham insist on sharing again?"

"That he did," Josiah answered. "Of course he knows it's Tuesday, but he also said he saw the light in your room upstairs and knew it wouldn't be you up there. So he figured you'd rented it out and had another mouth to feed."

"Nosy old coot," Aunt Marigold said with a mysterious smile. "It's no business of his what we're doing over here."

"Maybe he's hankering for a fresh-baked pie again."

"Maybe. But it'll have to wait. It's biscuit day and when we're done with these, I'm going to let the oven rest at least until this afternoon."

Josiah set the egg basket on the counter, glancing in my direction for the first time. He looked so tall, far taller than he had last night. Fair-haired like John but broader of shoulder. I hoped he'd be in a great hurry to leave for his work.

"Sleep well?" he asked.

I nodded, not wanting to elaborate in any manner.

"Somebody have a bumpy start this morning?"

Had he heard my precipitous tumble from the bed? Or worse, had I cried out? I couldn't remember, but it was certainly a possibility. John had wakened me from the nightmare more than once after hearing me yell.

I stared at him, wondering what I could answer without having to explain myself. He didn't walk away and busy himself at something, which would have been the gracious thing to do. He just stood watching me and waiting.

"I assure you that we're both fine," I told him, a bit more curtly than I'd intended.

He narrowed his eyes a bit, as if questioning me, and then turned abruptly away. "Good. Has anyone carried the milk in?"

"Haven't got to that yet," Marigold answered immediately.

"I didn't mean you," Josiah told her. "I'll get it."

Why hadn't I thought when I saw the milk wagon down the street that there might be milk on the front step? I could've saved someone some steps. Mr. Walsh obviously believed I should've. I'd have to be on my toes around here or he'd quickly draw the conclusion that I wasn't doing enough. Maybe Marigold had told him she was letting me stay without paying. I could understand that the apparent double standard could be upsetting, but there was nothing I could do to remedy that yet.

He brought the milk in silence and then without waiting for anyone else, plopped jam onto a warm biscuit and began gobbling it down.

"Want eggs?" Aunt Marigold asked him without a shred of criticism.

"Sure."

She turned to me. "How do you ladies like your eggs? I'll be making some for everybody, but Josiah first. He'll be out the door before we know it. I've got to get the rest of these biscuits in the oven. Don't want to make anybody late."

"Train won't leave without me on biscuit day," Josiah added, and I still had no idea what they were talking about but didn't think it was my place to ask.

"We'll eat eggs any way you fix them," I answered Marigold. "But I'd be happy to cook them if you wish."

"That'd be wonderful, dear," she said quickly. "It'll give me a chance to help the little baker here finish cutting the last few biscuits. Josiah likes three hard fried when he can get them and I'll take one scrambled." She turned happily to Ellie. "You're doing a great job, sweetie."

Eliza smiled as Marigold helped her fill a second tray of biscuits for the oven. But I noticed Josiah's frown and got the sinking feeling that he was very unhappy with our presence.

"I can cook my own eggs," he said.

"Nonsense," Marigold told him. "I want you to read to me, same as usual."

I wasn't sure what to think as he moved to the table in silence and picked up a leather-bound book from a small shelf in the corner that I hadn't even noticed before. Obviously, he respected his aunt enough to do what she asked even when he didn't like it.

"Chapter 139," Marigold prompted.

I didn't know what to expect as he turned pages and began to read, but it was a psalm, from the Bible. I recognized it immediately, though I couldn't remember when or where I'd heard it before.

"O Lord, thou hast searched me, and known me. Thou knowest my downsitting and mine uprising, thou understandest my thought afar off."

Did Mr. Walsh appreciate the Scripture as much as his aunt did, or was he simply being nice? It was impossible to tell, but I wished he would refuse her request, or at least stop after the first verse or two. Marigold had set a skillet and grease beside the stove for the eggs, but it was frightfully hard to concentrate with the Word of God going on in the background.

"Thou compasseth my path and my lying down, and art acquainted with all my ways."

I tried to busy myself and pay no attention. He wasn't reading to me, and the words had no bearing on my situation. Why bother with them?

"There is not a word in my tongue, but, lo, O Lord, thou knowest it altogether. Thou hast beset me behind and before, and laid thine hand upon me."

Marigold's wonderful gas stove lit with ease. Noisily, I fumbled in a drawer for the utensils I needed and melted a dab of grease in the pan. Mr. Walsh wanted three eggs, hard fried. Just what John had always requested. Must be a family thing. I reached for the egg basket as he read on.

"Such knowledge is too wonderful for me; it is high, I cannot attain unto it. Whither shall I go from thy spirit? Or whither shall I flee from thy presence?"

The words stopped me cold. An egg slipped from my hand, I don't know how. But before I could catch it, the thing cracked against the corner of the stove and slid to the floor with a squishy plop.

Josiah stopped reading and looked up at me. Wonderful. I certainly was not making a very good impression. Staring down at the egg on Marigold's hard wood floor, my eyes filled with tears. This was so stupid. It was absolutely the worst moment to draw attention to myself. I hadn't been trying to flee God's presence. I'd only wanted a roof over our heads. And now—now here we were in this strange house in Illinois with perfect strangers. And I was acting like an absolute ninny in front of them, to be so clumsy and so . . . so emotional.

Marigold hurried toward me with a cleaning rag. "Don't you worry about it, now, dearie," she admonished quickly. "One egg is no big thing. Nobody here's starvin'."

Glancing over at my daughter, I could see the hint of anxiety in her eyes. Had she wondered if Aunt Marigold might get mad at my carelessness? Or even ask us to leave? Such an outcome would be devastating.

"I'm sorry," I managed to say, maybe as much to Eliza as to anyone else.

"Like I said, it's no big thing," Marigold repeated. "We've got plenty more this morning."

True enough. But that started me wondering. Did they have other mornings when they did without? Josiah had said a neighbor sent the eggs at least partly because he thought Marigold had extra boarders. Did she have any chickens of her own? Had she been struggling for enough food to put on the table? We would be a terrible burden if that were the case.

"Go right on readin'," Marigold told her nephew, and I wished she'd let it go. I couldn't remember the number of the psalm she'd chosen, but it had started out unnerving and hadn't gotten any better.

"If I ascend up into heaven, thou art there: if I make my bed in hell, behold, thou art there. If I take the wings of the morning, and dwell in the uttermost parts of the sea; even there shall thy hand lead me, and thy right hand shall hold me . . ."

Suddenly I remembered where I'd heard those words before. John had read them late one night as I walked and prayed, trying to coax our baby to sleep. Poor little Johnny James had been so ill several times in the few short months of his life. And John had been so confident in his recovery. All for naught.

Marigold motioned at me to keep cooking. She insisted on cleaning up the mess herself. I tried to concentrate, to show her and her nephew that I could be a decent cook, a decent help to them. But I broke an egg against the side of the pan and another got a little overdone as I tried to scrape up the splatter. They'd not be very pretty eggs, but hopefully they'd taste all right.

Marigold had the last of the biscuits in the oven in two shakes and then sat down across the table from her nephew, bringing him more biscuits and jam. Eliza sat beside her and accepted a biscuit immediately. But Josiah just kept reading.

"Thou hast possessed my reins; thou hast covered me from my mother's womb. I will praise thee; for I am fearfully and wonderfully made: marvelous are thy works; and that my soul knoweth right well."

I took him a plate of eggs. He stopped and looked down at it but didn't say a word.

"Go ahead and eat," Marigold told him. "You'll have to be out the door pretty quick."

He set the Bible aside, glanced at me, and then bowed his head for a moment before lifting his fork. I wished I knew if prayer was his regular habit or only a precaution under the circumstances. But I tried to act as if I hadn't noticed and set to work scrambling a batch of eggs for the rest of us.

"What does 'possessed my reins' mean?" Eliza suddenly asked.

I drew a breath. It was hard enough to answer some of her questions privately, but in front of Aunt Mari and Mr. Walsh? I was about to reluctantly admit that I wasn't sure when Marigold answered confidently.

"That means God had control of the making of you before you were even born," she explained. "He knew all about you and worked out every detail to make you the special person you are."

"Before I was born?" Ellie questioned. "Did I have curly hair even back then?"

"In God's eyes you did."

I hoped they would stop before the conversation progressed any further. But my Eliza was too much of a thinker and too full of questions for that.

"Did he know all about my baby brother too?"

Marigold put her arm around my daughter's shoulders. "He knows everything there is to know about every one of us, child. No matter how old or young. He made us who we are."

"Then did he make my brother sick?"

I would not have been prepared for such an abrupt question, nor would I have handled it very well. But the words were not spoken with any kind of bitterness, and Marigold didn't seem troubled by them in the least. Her words were steady and strong, as though she'd had plenty of time to think them through.

"Whether God formed him weak of body or whether the enemy in this world caused that for trouble, I can't say. But I know that child was purposed of God and loved by him just as much as anyone that's ever been born."

I suddenly realized that Josiah was watching me as he ate, probably waiting for some kind of reaction. Did he know about my baby? Surely he did. How could a relative staying here with Marigold not know? So what did he want to see? More tears?

I turned off the burner beneath the eggs and excused myself to find the washroom. I wouldn't give him a reaction. None at all. Let him call me a poor cook or anything else he liked. I'd not give him occasion to think me any more of an emotional weakling than he might already.

5

Leah

Josiah was finished eating when I rejoined them in the kitchen, and Marigold was taking the last of the biscuits out of the oven. I didn't realize until that moment how hungry I was, but I said nothing and did not venture to the table. The eggs were still on the stove where I'd left them. Marigold separated a plate of biscuits and piled the rest in a heap in the middle of a large double cloth.

"This'll keep 'em fairly warm. They'll be nice and soft too," she explained.

Josiah was lacing his work boots as she pulled two corners of the cloth over her biscuits to the center and tied them. Then she did the same with the remaining corners and, using the knot as a handle, lifted the bundle and swung it around a bit.

"Nothing's gonna fall outta there."

Eliza was fascinated. "Is that Mr. Josiah's lunch? It's the biggest lunch I ever seen. Must be four whole plates heaped full, maybe five."

Marigold laughed. "He can snitch him a biscuit or two for his lunch, same as the brakeman always does. But the rest of 'em's going to the Kurchers."

"Where is that?" I asked, genuinely curious about this "biscuit day" idea.

"The Kurchers live close to Maple Falls, east by the train track. Lovely family. He passed on a couple of years ago, but she keeps things together the best she can. Most amazing thing you ever saw, with twenty-one children—"

"Twenty-one?"

She smiled. "I suppose they're down a few by now, with her oldest girls grown and married. They had fourteen of their own, then took in five when her younger brother and his wife both died in the influenza epidemic." Her voice grew quieter. "Someone they didn't even know left the other two. Just abandoned them on the front porch. A baby and a little thing smaller than your girl. Can you imagine? Hilda didn't have to, but she kept them. A lot of love, that woman. I send her biscuits every Tuesday and Friday, just to help a little. Eggs too, when we can. What do you think, Josiah? Can you carry eggs today without any getting broken?"

He nodded. "Pad the layers with a towel."

I stood and stared at them. My parents had never been givers. John and I had seldom had the means. Was it just routine for them here? Had I been mistaken earlier? Was Aunt Marigold well-to-do? Or saintly despite her own need? Either way, I surely did not belong here, and I felt terrible that I had broken an egg earlier that might have fed one of the Kurcher children. For a moment I forgot that we had not yet eaten, but Marigold quickly reminded me.

"We'll sit down and breakfast leisurely as soon as Josiah's gone," she said. "Can you help me pack the eggs?"

Marigold only kept back two besides the ones I'd cooked. We layered the others carefully in a basket between folds of dishtowel, and Josiah was ready to leave as soon as we were done.

"Don't forget you promised me a pie," he told Aunt Marigold right before he left, his rugged features softened slightly by a youthful smile.

I didn't know what to think of either of them, but Marigold gave me little time to wonder. As soon as he was gone, she set my pan of cooked eggs on the table beside the biscuits and jam that were already there and motioned to me to sit down.

"Sorry we didn't have a chance to finish our psalm today. That happens sometimes, but we can finish up tomorrow. I'd have you read me the rest, but I think it's good for Josiah to be a-listenin'."

I wasn't sure why she thought it might be important to me. I would have been more comfortable for her not to bring up the subject of Scriptures again at all. But as usual, Eliza was overflowing with boundless curiosity.

"Can't you read it by yourself?" she wanted to know.

"Oh, I used to. Every single morning. But my eyes is dim for that sort of thing now. The print's too small. Been a godsend for me to have Josiah here reading for me. I started him on it the very first day he came. Been good for both of us."

Now *my* curiosity was piqued. "How long has he been here?"

"A little more than a year. But enough about him. Tell me more about yourself. What sorts of things you like to do, that sort of thing."

"I—I'm afraid I don't have many real preferences. And I wouldn't want you to cater to them if I had. I'd like to help you while we're here. Starting today. If there's any housework—"

She smiled. "Actually, it's supposed to be a beautiful day. I'd much rather spend some time getting a few things done out-of-doors if it's all right with you." She looked at the food on the table and then at Eliza, who was breaking open a biscuit. "Has anyone asked the blessing?"

"Mr. Josiah did," Eliza answered cheerfully, and I hoped Marigold wouldn't think her cheeky.

Apparently she didn't. "Well enough, then." She passed me the eggs. "Do help yourself. It's delightful to have your company. I'm so used to being left alone anymore."

I took a spoon or two of scrambled eggs and gave Eliza a

scoop of them because she wouldn't eat them if I didn't set them on her plate. The girl loved biscuits more than anything else, and I'm sure the fun of helping roll them herself just made the appeal that much greater.

Soon I could discern the sound of a train in the distance, and my stomach knotted. I'd heard it in the city sometimes, not quite so close at hand. It helped to know that the tracks were four blocks away at the closest point. The whistle wasn't terribly jarring, at least not in the house with the windows shut. I was sure it was something I could manage to get used to. I decided to try to make conversation to take my mind off it.

"Aunt Marigold—I appreciate so much you welcoming us here."

"You told me that last night. And believe me, it's a pleasure to have you. But I do want you to tell me more about yourself. Do you sew or crochet? Do you like to bake? Or embroider, perhaps?"

"I'm acquainted with all of those. But not terribly good at any of them, I'm afraid."

"You mentioned that you might seek work in town. Did you learn marketable skills before you married?"

Gracious, she was straight to the point! Maybe she did need a rent payment from me as soon as possible. "I'm afraid the only thing I did before marriage was help with the chores and orchard work."

"Orchard? Really? Did you grow up on one?"

"Yes, you could say that, but a very small orchard. Father only had two acres of trees not far from town."

"A person could put a lot of trees on two acres if he was of a mind to. At least I could. Apples?"

"Mostly. A few pear and peach."

"Wonderful. You are exactly who I need today."

She took a bite of egg and buttered a biscuit, leaving me wondering what she was talking about. But when she was ready to resume the conversation, she changed the subject entirely. "I realize it might seem a little strange to have Josiah about.

But he's a good fellow. He may be standoffish part of the time, but I know he understands me asking you here. So don't think nothing of it if he's not always as friendly as last night."

I wasn't sure "friendly" was the term I would use. And there were so many things I wanted to ask, about both of them, but this was probably not the time. "I appreciate you telling me."

"Now, about this little one." Marigold abruptly switched subjects again. "Your darling Eliza Rose. Did she already start school in St. Louis?"

"No." I almost felt as though I needed to apologize. "She's ready for first grade, but I—I didn't want to begin the year there just to uproot her. I thought it would be better to wait until I knew we were settled somewhere."

"There's a good school here," Marigold said between bites of a biscuit. "And only three blocks, when you feel you're ready."

I didn't. I was far from certain we were "settled" in the long term. And though I expected Eliza to be excited with the idea of school, she seemed wary and glad I didn't push the issue immediately. "Maybe when things aren't so completely new," I said. "We're barely off the train."

"I realize that," Marigold admonished. "But the sooner a routine is established, the better."

"I'll visit the school," I decided. "And talk to them. Soon. Just—just not today."

"Good enough. A child this bright ought to have an outlet for all that brilliance."

Eliza didn't smile or say a word. I don't think she knew how to respond, so she just sat watching me and buttered another biscuit.

"Um—Aunt Marigold. About my orchard work—you said—"

"Oh, I didn't mean I was going to farm you out or anything like that," she chuckled. "I only meant I need your help if you will. Looks like we're gonna have fruit to beat the band, and it's more than I can handle by myself."

"What kind?"

"Apple and pear. One tree of each. And if I don't get some picked, the squirrels are going to wreak havoc. Already they're knocking down aplenty, in addition to what's been dropping off the tree on its own. But I'd just as soon have some fruit not so bruised and pecked upon. I hate to ask Josiah, as late as he's been getting in. And I just can't do it myself."

"We're gonna pick apples?" Eliza brightened. "And pears? Can we really? Can I climb right up in the tree?"

"I couldn't say about that," Marigold warned. "It'll have to be your mother's decision whether she wants you clamberin' through limbs and branches up off the ground. But I can find a job for you one way or another."

Eliza was so excited she could scarcely finish her biscuit. And I thought of my father, how I'd loved climbing in his trees, and how he'd scolded me for it time and again. Not because he was afraid I'd fall; he was more bothered that I might knock down his fruit, even when I was carefully picking.

"So did he sell the fruit commercially?" Marigold asked me.

I looked up, only half sure of what she'd said. "What?"

"Did your father sell the fruit himself?"

"Oh. He sold some to the local market and a peddler he knew. But he also traded a good bit of it for other goods." I didn't tell her what goods. I didn't want her asking more questions, requiring me to talk about him.

"Was that near St. Louis?"

"About forty miles south."

"Are your parents still living?"

My breath caught in my throat. If I told her the truth, would she question why I'd come here instead of to my father's farm? Yet how could I be deliberately untruthful? It wouldn't be right, even for my comfort's sake. "Mother died a couple of years ago," I said with a sigh. "But Father is still living."

"Is he well?"

"Yes, the last I knew."

She looked at me rather oddly and I knew she had more

questions, but she didn't ask them then. "Would you like a cup of coffee?"

"Yes, ma'am. But I can get it." I jumped to my feet so she wouldn't have to. "Would you like me to pour you one as well?"

"Yes, please. And you may as well pour a glass of milk for your little Rose."

There it was again, her using Eliza's middle instead of her first name. I wasn't quite sure what to think. Maybe she thought the flower name should have come first. But I didn't say anything. Just poured her coffee and then proceeded to get Eliza's drink and my own.

Marigold and Eliza were both nearly done eating. I didn't have much appetite, but I hurried to finish the rest of what was on my plate, not wishing any of it to be wasted.

"Does your father still have his orchard?" Marigold persisted.

"Yes, ma'am."

"Well, then, I suppose it must be nearly harvest time there."

"I suppose so."

Of course it might occur to her that for me to go there and help with the harvest would seem like an ideal arrangement for my father and me both. But she said no more about it, perhaps realizing that I wasn't going to open up very much on the subject. When she started to clean up a bit, I hurried to help and soon had breakfast dishes washed and the whole kitchen looking neat and tidy. Eliza was itching to get outside, and Marigold seemed to be too, though I wondered how she'd manage it. She seemed to be having trouble with her legs again this morning.

"Would you like me to carry a chair out for you?" I asked when she was ready.

She frowned. "How am I going to pick apples from a chair?"

"You can just sit and tell us what to do and we'll do it. Or, if you like, we can carry the drops to you and you can sort or even start cutting some while we pick."

"I certainly need to be cutting a few if I'm going to get pies made. Josiah knows it's high time we had an apple pie, and I'm sure Mr. Abraham's had his eye on them too."

With my help, she gathered baskets, buckets, and boxes to hold the fruit we picked. Eliza thought we had an impossible number of containers, but I knew from experience that if Marigold had healthy trees, it might not be enough.

While carrying everything out to the backyard, it was impossible not to think of Father and his trees again. Marigold might think it shameful that I knew so little about his health or his harvest this year. She might think I should have gone to him after John died. She might even get around to suggesting it if things did not work out well here. But I couldn't. There was no way. The last time I'd tried to talk to him, the only time I'd been to the farm since Mother's death, he was so hateful, so horribly painful, that I'd left, never wanting to go back.

"Can we make applesauce and pie? An' even cimmanum apple tarts?" Eliza asked, evidently remembering the fun we'd had when our good friend Anna had given us a bushel basket full of cooking apples last year.

"Cinnamon apple tarts, hmm?" Marigold asked. "That's something I've never done. You'll have to show me how."

We set down the baskets and buckets beneath an old tree, rather small and misshapen but loaded with apples nonetheless. There would be plenty for tarts or anything else that Marigold wanted to make. The pear tree across the generous backyard, though taller, was not nearly so laden. But there would be plenty of those too.

"Do you want to just pick what's hanging down in reach?" Marigold asked me. "Or are you comfortable enough with a ladder to get some of the high ones too?"

"I'll pick whatever you want picked. A ladder won't bother me a bit," I promised. "As long as we give it level footing."

"I should've had Josiah set it up for you. Do you think you can manage it? It's in the shed over there."

"Not a problem at all."

Marigold smiled. "You're a go-getter, aren't you? I used to climb the ladder myself and do all of that. Might try it today, but—"

"I can easily do it," I stopped her. "There's no need at all for you to."

She nodded. "Then I suppose I might take the chair you offered. In a bit. I mean to take a load of weight off some of these low-hanging branches first."

I wished I could caution her even about that. I was a little worried about her limp and the stability of her footing in the yard. If she were to fall, would I be able to get her up again? What if she broke something? Such fears were probably completely unfounded, and though I couldn't quite shake them, I kept my mouth shut. Marigold struck me as an independent sort who wouldn't appreciate me thinking like that, at least not out loud.

"May I climb in the tree, Mommy, please?" Eliza looked up with her shiny eyes twinkling in the sun.

Before I could answer, my father's red face and roaring voice came to mind again. "You knock another apple down outta that tree, an' I'll be knockin' you out of it!" he'd yell. "My customers won't buy bruised apples!"

"Would you mind if her climbing shook a few more from the tree?" I asked Marigold, just to be sure.

"Lord, no. I want most of 'em picked so they'll keep a while, but drops'll cook up good as the rest. Besides, I've got you here to help me cut them now."

Eliza was itching to get into that tree, and I wouldn't have let her if there'd been any boys about. But there was not so much need to be ladylike on a job like this with only Marigold and me with her. I let her try, knowing how much I'd loved tree climbing when I was little, despite my mother's cautions and my father's scolding. I used to think I was trying to be like the son my father had lost, but that couldn't be Eliza's reason. Her baby brother had been far too little for climbing, and we'd lost him before we'd even had time to speak with her about the sorts of things a bigger boy might do.

She didn't try to go very high. Content to sit on the lowest branch, she leaned to pluck the apples within reach. I gave her a little basket with a handle she could hook over her arm.

"I'm helping, Mommy," she said with a smile.

"And a fine helper you are," I replied.

It was a happy moment, but I found it suddenly invaded by my bitter thoughts. If everything were truly right in this world, Father would be a kindly sort who'd love having a six-year-old join him in his orchard. We could stay at his farm, helping with the peak of harvest, and perhaps even enjoy our time as a family. But Father had never wanted my help, as a child or as an adult. And if he cared at all for Eliza, he'd scarcely shown it. That was nothing but a dead and empty dream.

I fetched the ladder. We were here now, so there was no point thinking of anywhere else. Eliza was smiling, Marigold truly did need us, and we would do the best we could.

Marigold picked busily at the low branches while I reached as high as I possibly could on the ladder. I carried my own baskets down, so she wouldn't have to reach up for them and then hand me empty ones.

I had just stepped from the ladder when another train went through town. I jumped at the sound and Marigold smiled.

"There's no more than six or seven a day," she told me. "You get used to it."

I took a deep breath. Hopefully I could. But this one didn't bother me much. Perhaps I was already getting used to it. *Four blocks*, I told myself. *I'll not be able to see it, and it could not reach us even if it jumped the tracks.*

Maybe something about working with Marigold made my train anxiety fade into the background a little. It really wasn't hard at all to turn it from my mind and focus with renewed energy on the work at hand.

We filled five baskets in practically no time, and I thought Marigold must surely be getting tired. So I went to the house for a chair and a paring knife so she could do sit-down work. But she wouldn't use them till we'd filled most of the baskets and started in on the buckets and boxes. By that time, she admitted she'd have to sit. Her legs just couldn't keep on.

So Marigold sat and peeled and cored the bruised apples that I brought to her. Eliza shifted several times in the tree in order to reach just a few more apples, but most of the fruit was hanging way outside of her reach. I let her stay in the tree anyway. It had occurred to me that she could fall, but she stayed low and seemed far more cautious than I'd ever been, so I had little to worry about. I just kept picking, bucket after bucket, at the same time looking around the yard a bit. A garden stood in one back corner, nearly spent and covered with weeds, a sure sign that Marigold had been unable to tend it regularly and that her nephew was not enough of a gardener to have taken it in hand.

"Is that turnips you've got growing?" I asked from the ladder, trying to identify the healthiest deep green row of leaves among the jumble.

"Such as they are," Marigold confirmed. "Good year for apples, but not much of a year for root crops. Hardly anything below ground on any I've pulled, and they should've been fist-sized long before this."

"Looks like a splendid batch of greens, though," I suggested.

"Indeed you're right," she said with a smile. "And I almost forgot they were there. What a waste if I don't make us up a mess. Would your little girl eat that for lunch?"

"Oh, certainly. At least a little. I'll not allow her to be too choosy."

She asked me to cut some so we could have fried apples and greens at noon. That sounded good to me, and whether or not it was anywhere near that time, I was already hungry and figured Eliza might be too, though she was good enough not to say so. I climbed down from the ladder and gladly fetched a bowl and knife from the kitchen. From the ground, the row looked longer than I'd realized. I knelt at one end of it and started cutting the leaves an inch or two above the ground. If I left the roots, they might get bigger. At the very least, they'd set on new leaves for another batch of greens, or even two, before winter. Grand! Renting in the city I'd missed having a garden and the extra security of knowing there was at least some small thing growing outside that we could pick and eat when we needed to.

"Cut half the row today, and we'll get the other half in a day or two," Marigold told me.

Eliza eased herself out of the tree to join me. "Doesn't look like turrips," she observed.

"The part you're used to seeing is still under the ground," I explained. "We're going to eat the leaves today. The last time we had that, you were a little bitty thing. Too young to remember, I guess."

She reached and touched a leaf and quickly pulled her hand back. "They're prickly."

"Not too bad. Not nearly so prickly as some wild leaves get. And they cook up limp and soft. You won't find anything prickly to them at all when we eat them."

Her little nose was all scrunched, and I knew she mistrusted the whole idea. "Are they yummy?"

"They're perfectly good. Not like cake or anything like that, but a decent enough vegetable. You'll see."

She knew not to question me further. She'd accept them, like it or not. There was no use otherwise. She turned her attention to the weedy garden around us, turning in a circle to look at the green growing things. "Will we eat other leaves too?"

"Oh, probably. The smartest thing to do this time of year is harvest all that can be harvested to eat or store for winter."

"That makes food without even any money," she declared, catching the gist of what I was saying immediately. "Purty smart. But isn't there any pickin' food in the city?"

"Not as much, unfortunately."

"Oh. That's why we was so hungry."

Too late I realized that Marigold was listening to every word.

I hadn't wanted her to know how our last few weeks had been, struggling with so little and then nothing at all. But she didn't look our way or comment.

"Is there more things to pick right now?" Eliza asked eagerly.

"I think those are cherry tomatoes there in the corner. Why don't you see if there are any truly red ones on the vines? I'm sure Aunt Marigold wouldn't mind if you were to find a few ripe tomatoes."

"Goodness, if you find anything at all worth pickin' out there, you're welcome to it," Marigold called to us. "I thought the tomato vines had died and most everything had given up, the weeds are so bad. Sorriest garden I ever had in my life."

Eliza only found three ripe tomatoes, but there were more stubbornly coming on through bristle grass as high as my knees.

"Mr. Walsh doesn't garden much?" I asked, though such an inquiry was really pointless.

"Goodness, girl," Marigold half scolded. "You may as well call him Josiah. Or just plain Joe. He'll wonder at you calling him Mister much longer after you've been proper introduced. But he doesn't take to gardening natural, and he hasn't got the time anyway. You'd be surprised how much I've put him to fixin' on this old house of mine, besides his railroad job. He does enough already that I wouldn't want to ask him for more."

I would've asked, I thought instantly. Just a few hours a week in a garden never hurt anyone and did a world of good. But it was none of my business to say anything about it. I finished cutting the tops of half the turnip row, and Marigold was happy that it filled my big bowl to brimming. I lifted her cane from the grass and steadied it for her while she got to her feet. Then we all went in the house with the greens, the little tomatoes, and Marigold's bowl of cut apples.

It was a dandy lunch, plain as it was, and almost seemed festive, with a scoop of turnip greens next to a big serving of fried apples and a plump cherry tomato for color. A biscuit left from breakfast was all we needed to round the whole thing out. Though it was an odd lunch to Eliza, she ate everything, even the turnip greens. "I sure do love fried apples," she said happily. "And I love it here where there's plenty of dinner."

Not again. I would have to speak to her later about such talk. Aunt Marigold would get the idea that she'd been without a decent meal her whole life. Or at least since John died. It was too late to give the impression that I'd been able to manage very well, but to keep bringing up our lack only made things painfully worse. At least for me. But maybe it helped Eliza somehow, as if voicing our struggle helped her to drive the reality of it forever into the past.

To my surprise, Marigold began singing as we cleaned up. I recognized the hymn immediately as one I had sung often enough in church with John. Eliza joined in happily. I didn't feel like singing, especially not such a song as that, but I didn't want to seem like a wet hen among such happy larks, so I did my best to sing along at least a little.

It made me feel like a miserable hypocrite. The words were all light and praise, not at all the way I'd been thinking toward the Almighty. Maybe I should've felt deeply grateful, for Marigold's hospitality and Eliza's cheery good health. Perhaps I did, at least a little. But in a good moment when I might have felt warm and comforted, the darkness still filled my eyes and I feared I'd never see the sun.

6

Leah

The afternoon was filled with apples. First we sat on the back porch and cut and peeled a bucket's worth. And then Marigold and Eliza went in the house to make pies while I got back to picking. Alone with my thoughts and a fruit tree, my mind jumped to Father again. He'd grown potatoes and sweet corn in addition to his orchard fruits, and people loved his produce but not his demeanor. I'd overheard more than one customer cautioning another about the half-drunk, stony-faced farmer you had to be careful not to rub the wrong way. I'd also heard a few whispers about his awkward tomboy daughter. I'd been glad to marry, to move away and start a new life away from the wagging heads of that community.

I picked until I could see apples with my eyes shut. Marigold had said I could stop whenever I wanted to, but she'd also said she'd like to get them all picked and put in away from the squirrels, so I did all I could. There was no way I could get the top branches, even with the ladder, and the tree branches were too thin there to hold me. There were scads remaining, but we'd have to wait till they dropped and use what we could for applesauce or something. Maybe the highest apples were the squirrel's due anyway.

There weren't as many pears and they were still mostly green. That harvest could wait, but probably not for long if we wanted to get them while they were good and firm. "Pears like to ripen wrapped in newspaper or paper sacks," Mother used to tell me. And they'd certainly ripened well that way for us every harvest. I wondered if Aunt Marigold had ever made pear honey, or apple pandowdy, or any of the other wonderful out-of-the-ordinary things my mother had done. John had loved apple pandowdy. The memory nearly brought back tears.

I didn't see much sign of the squirrels bothering the pears, probably because of the abundant apple supply nearby. But with that diminished, the pears would be in danger too. Despite that, I started moving the apple baskets and buckets to the porch instead of setting up the ladder again. We had enough to deal with for now. Many of these apples would store, but equally as many, maybe more, would have to be cut and cooked, or canned, as soon as possible.

Aunt Marigold had no root cellar, but there appeared to be a generous basement under her house. I'd seen more than one window practically level with the ground. I was about to go inside and ask if she wanted me to carry some of the buckets down there when I saw movement from the corner of my eye. An old man coming from the yard next door. Just like Mari, he walked with a limp, and though his face was blotchy and practically shriveled with wrinkles, I saw the hint of good humor in his eyes as I looked his way.

"Well, does Marigold McSweeney have new hired help? Or a new boarder today?"

"A new boarder," I answered, sure Marigold wouldn't mind me speaking to him if this was the neighbor she'd mentioned before.

"Making off with all my apples, eh? Did Marigold tell you I planted that tree myself, years ago? I came right over, dug the hole, and stuck it in the ground 'fore anybody come out of the house to tell me not to."

"I certainly hope you put it where she wanted it," I ventured.

He cocked his head a bit. "I put it in the very best place for it, and she knew it too. Didn't move it an inch. I put the pear tree in too, but she caught me at that one."

No wonder Marigold wanted to make him a pie. I almost said it aloud but thought she might want to surprise him. "Shall I tell her you've come to call?"

"Oh no. I haven't done any such thing. I came to borrow the hedge trimmers from her shed. Got a lilac bough bent over and hanging at nose height over the garden path. Figured I better cut it 'fore I forget it's there and whap myself in the head."

He was certainly a friendly enough sort. Far more willing to talk to me than I would've been to him. "Shall I go and ask her for you?"

"Can if you wish," he said with a tiny grin. "But I'll probably be whacking with them 'fore you get back. She won't care. We share things back and forth all the time."

"Just the same, I believe I'll tell her, just in case she were to look for them."

He nodded. "Name's Saul Abraham. What's yours?"

"Leah Breckenridge. Glad to make your acquaintance."

He nodded again. "Nice name. Aristocratic. You from around here?"

"No. Sugar Creek, Missouri. Near St. Louis."

He nodded, as if he knew exactly where I meant. "Have a nice day, young lady."

"Yes, sir," I told him. "You too, sir."

I went inside and found Marigold and Eliza busy with the rolling pins again, merrily making pie crust. So quickly my daughter seemed to belong here. Maybe I would eventually feel more comfortable too.

"You have a very nice neighbor," I told Aunt Marigold. "Mr. Abraham. He's borrowing your hedge trimmers from the shed."

"Lordy sakes, those are his. That ladder you were standing on is his too, and he very well knows it. I never remember to return anything. It's in my shed near year-round."

"If Mr. Abraham would appreciate the ladder being brought back to him, I could take it over there. But we'd need to borrow it again to pick the pears in a day or two."

"He hasn't got the room in his shed for it. Don't worry. He's not mindin' it being over here, and he'll come after it if he needs it for anything."

Aunt Marigold seemed to have quite a remarkable and unusual relationship with her neighbor. But maybe such things were normal around here. I had shared pleasant conversation with Anna, my old neighbor in St. Louis, but not much else except the extra apples fallen off her tree. And I didn't remember any particularly good relations with any neighbors back home, but that was because of Father's gruffness.

I asked her if she wanted me to carry any of the apples to the basement where they'd keep longer, but she said she'd rather sort them for spots first in case any had been bird pecked or affected by insects. "Separate a basket of the plumpest, nicest looking," she instructed, "to take over to Mr. Abraham. That's probably why he decided to trim the hedge on apple-picking day, to make sure we'd notice and remember to give him some."

The thought of Aunt Marigold and old Mr. Abraham purposely doing for each other made me smile. They must have been neighbors a long time for the trees Mr. Abraham had planted to be so big now.

I separated out about a peck of wonderful-looking apples, just like she'd told me, and then set to work on the back porch sorting more. Quite a few had spots as she'd thought, but most were in good shape. There'd be far too many, though, to keep through the winter for eating raw. We'd have to can applesauce, apple butter, or pie filling to deal with the excess. Quite a marvelous problem to have. I wondered about the Kurcher family, if they had an apple tree. If only I'd been here in time to pick some yesterday, we might have sent a bucket or two with

Josiah along with the biscuits and eggs. Aunt Marigold sure had plenty for sharing.

My mother had always been delighted with harvest bounty. Father forbade her to give away fresh apples because he wanted the people we knew to buy from him. But she had found the occasional opportunity to share pints of apple butter, and even turnovers once or twice. Now the pleasant memory saddened me, and suddenly it seemed that sitting to sort was not nearly the job I needed. So I set aside a box of apples to be cut and another for storage in the basement and headed for the weedy garden to see what I could do for it this late in the season.

Physical work in the sunshine seemed to be just what I needed to keep my mind occupied away from troublous thoughts right now. Of course I needed time to think and make decisions about the future. That was at least part of why I was here. But I didn't want to think yet when everything here was so new, lest I overwhelm myself with worry.

I walked over every inch of Marigold's garden, row by row, foxtails, chickweed, and all, certain I'd find something besides turnip greens and the few specks of red tomato in the weeds. Some of the rows were empty of anything useful, already harvested if they'd been planted at all. But in others I began to find hidden surprises: first scraggly carrot tops indicating an undug supply below, and then two abandoned pattypan squashes, covered with squash bugs and half buried in sedge grass.

"Shoo, shoo," I fussed at the beetles as I tried to brush them off. Big and grayish or little and white, they shared the same tenacity, but I was claiming these squash whether they liked it or not. Their vines were shriveled, but they didn't appear too tough. There was no reason at all that Aunt Marigold shouldn't get some good use out of them.

I set the squash aside on the stone path that ran from the back door to the garden and threw myself into weeding with a will, uncovering more treasures as I went. Two gangly pepper plants and an eggplant were nearly choked but still surviving. Perhaps there'd yet be time for them to bear fruit before the frost if I cleared a little breathing room for them. A row of abandoned bean plants were brittle-dry and ready to be pulled. They'd been harvested green no doubt, but a few plump pods still clung here and there to the lifeless plants with beans now dry as stones inside. No reason I couldn't collect them for Aunt Marigold to use for seed or add to a soup pot one of these days.

I also discovered rhubarb and a patch of winter onions along one edge of the garden, and best of all, in what appeared to be an empty row, I began to discover tiny new growth: baby lettuce coming up volunteer from plants gone to seed earlier in the season. My mother used to love when that happened. She'd leave lettuce to go to seed on purpose, hoping for the fall surprise. Unless we had a serious early freeze, there'd be time for it to grow large enough for a salad or two.

I pulled weeds around the lettuce and peppers until my back and arms grew tired, then I rested by sitting to sort apples again. That would be an ongoing job because even the best apples stored in the basement should still be checked every few days for the bad spots that could develop.

We had filled four boxes, three bushel baskets, and buckets and smaller baskets besides, all from the one generous tree. With this many apples, Aunt Marigold could probably be cutting and cooking some every couple of days right into winter, even if we canned oodles this week and left many for eating raw besides. Even if she gave several baskets away. What a blessing.

I stopped for a moment, staring down at the crimson fruit in my hands. A blessing? A gift from on high, like my mother used to say? Perhaps so. And perhaps that was just a wee inkling of gratitude I was finding in myself. For the plenty, at least of apples, that we were here to share. For Aunt Marigold's kindness and hospitality. For an abundance of chores waiting, so I wouldn't have to feel like a useless beggar.

Maybe things were going to work out all right, and this new start would grow eventually to happiness. I should have voiced the spark of gratitude and hope that had risen in me, no matter how small. Maybe it could have been the beginning of a rekindling of matters of faith in my heart. But I was still afraid. It felt good to have something to apply my hands to, and to know for certain that my daughter would have plenty to eat tonight. But there was so much more to consider. So much more uncertainty about where we would go from here.

I'd been sitting too long. Sorting apples all alone allowed my thoughts free rein, and I still wasn't ready for that. Not yet. So I jumped up and pulled the row of bean plants, collecting the few dangling pods and stuffing them in my skirt pocket. The gangly dry vines I piled in a heap, along with the weeds I'd pulled, on a bare patch of blackened ground that looked like it'd been used before to burn off brush.

A bushy-tailed squirrel scampered from the neighbor's bushes into Marigold's yard, and I watched for a moment to see what he'd do. The creature noticed me, but apparently unconcerned, skirted the garden and headed straight for the pear tree. Well. Maybe that harvest had better not wait. I ran at the tree to scare the pest away and then stopped to take a good look at the fruit. Obviously not ripe, just as I'd thought before, but if a fruit grower waits for his pears to soften on the tree, they'll be full of bruises and half bad before he can get them to market, even if his market is a corner stand across the yard. "That's just pears," my father used to say. "Pick them three days before they're ready."

As if I could tell exactly when that would be. But these pears were as good as I'd seen anywhere. They should ripen just fine.

I wondered if I should go in and ask Aunt Marigold about picking them. But she'd already said she wanted it done. The problem was, we'd filled all our containers with apples. Present need or not, we might have to cut and can a while just to empty something to pick the pears into. With a sigh I turned back to the porch.

We might lose a few of the pears, but to pick them all now would just overwhelm Aunt Marigold. We already had fruit lined up everywhere, waiting to be dealt with. Sit-down job or not, that was really what she needed me to help with first. So I carried in the pattypan squash and my pocket full of dried beans and got a pan and a knife from the kitchen to start cutting bruised apples for a batch of applesauce.

Eliza was thrilled that I'd stepped inside again. "We've got three pies in the oven, Mommy! Three!"

"You're quite a baker today," I told her with a smile.

"And you're a bit of a wonder-worker," Marigold said. "Finding any squash in that weed patch. I thought it was long since dead and gone. Haven't even seen any vines left in that corner."

"The vines are done, true enough. There won't be any more squash, but these should still be good."

"Bless you, child. You've supplied the vegetables for lunch, and now supper too."

"It's your garden. All I had to do was walk out there and pick."

"Oh, I expect it's a bit more of an adventure than that."

"We'll have to pick the pears soon. A neighborhood squirrel is interested in the tree. But I thought I'd better cut apples first, to empty at least a basket or two."

"Squirrels are in the pears already?"

"At least one. I shooed him out, but of course he'll be back if he's not already."

That quickly, Marigold was incensed. "Get the washtub. Can you do that for me? We can fill it and have at least that many out of their reach. I had one year that I got nary a pear that wasn't squirrel bit or bird pecked. Nary a one. But it's not happening again. Not when I've got such good help."

Eliza was looking at me with a big smile, immensely enjoying such a fruit-picking day.

"Squirrels are maddening as all get out," Marigold talked on. "The way they won't eat the whole fruit but just nibble a bite or two and then move on to the next one. The washtub's below the shelf to the left of the door out in the shed. Bring me some more apples to cut. I'll stay in and watch the pies and you girls can go and pick if you've a mind to."

She picked up a bucket of drops we'd carried in earlier to cut up, dumped what was left in the sink, and handed the bucket back to me. "You're a godsend," she told me. "An absolute godsend. I'd have never saved even half my crop working alone. And just think what we can do with all that fruit."

I wasn't sure how to answer her. It was a little overwhelming to find her grateful for me, considering my circumstance. She was the one providing.

Eliza jumped to join me. She was joyous, enough to worry me just a little. Quick and spontaneous like soap bubbles, such delight could be so easily broken. What if we suddenly had to move again? Or something happened to drastically dampen Marigold's enthusiasm at having us here?

"Did you set aside a basket of the best apples for Mr. Abraham?" Marigold suddenly asked me.

"Yes."

"Good." She looked at me with a lively twinkle in her eye. "When these pies come out of the oven, I'd thank you to take the basket over to him. And invite him right over for tea."

Suddenly it occurred to me that Marigold might consider Saul Abraham more than just a pleasant neighbor. And if that were so, I had no doubt that the feeling would be mutual. What if the two should decide to marry? Marigold might not be running a boardinghouse at all anymore then.

Feeling tight in my stomach, I stepped out to the porch and collected the bruised apples I'd already sorted. Eliza helped me carry them in to Marigold, and then we went together out to the shed for the washtub.

"Daddy's auntie sure is nice," she told me on the way.

"Yes. But remember, this is her house. And not ours. We'll eventually have to find a place of our own."

She nodded, though she seemed less than convinced. "I guess so. But I think she's going to need us here a really long time. She told me we made her happy just by coming, before we even started helping her any. And then we was working too, and she thought it must be like heaven on earth."

"She said that?"

"Yeah. That people working and being happy together is like heaven."

I moved a rake to one side and started dragging the washtub from its place. "Aunt Marigold seems to be very religious."

Eliza wasn't fazed by my comment. "I like her."

We headed for the pear tree, and I could see right away that the squirrel was back. I thought that running at it again, especially with the washtub in my hands, would scare it away. But this was a stubborn squirrel, and it only retreated to a higher branch in the pear tree and hunkered down, chattering at us.

"I'm sure we'll have to leave you a few," I told it as I scanned the top limbs. "Just like in the apple tree. I'll never be able to reach up there. So you can have those."

Eliza laughed at me talking to a squirrel. She shinnied right up to the lowest branches without my help this time. I hung the bucket from a branch near her where she could reach it, and she stretched her arms to pick what she could find.

I got out the ladder again and picked into the bowl I'd brought along. When that was full, I'd climb down and transfer the pears into the washtub. Slow going, but it'd get the job done.

We'd been at it a while and Eliza had changed position twice when she suddenly sat stark still and stared across the yard. I turned my head to see Mr. Abraham, still a complete stranger to Eliza, coming toward us with a bucket in each hand.

"Thought you could use these," he said, bringing them close. "Will Marigold be making apple butter and pear jelly?"

"I expect," I said simply, watching his face for any sign of what I thought I'd seen in Marigold.

"Well, it's nice she's got good help this year."

"We made pies!" Eliza announced, suddenly not shy anymore.

But I wasn't sure Marigold wanted to disclose that information. Perhaps she wanted to surprise the gentleman with pie if he accepted her invitation to tea later. So I said no more about that. "We enjoy helping," I told him. "And it's only right while we stay here."

"Are you kin?"

"Yes, sir," I answered, wondering briefly why I found it so much easier to answer his questions than Josiah Walsh's last night. Because he was so much older, surely. And therefore in some fashion not as much of a threat.

"Might you be John's family?" Mr. Abraham asked on, and I was surprised that he could know enough about us to understand that so quickly. Marigold, or Josiah, must have already mentioned us to him.

"Yes, sir," I said again, hoping he wouldn't ask anything about our losses or our present circumstances.

He didn't. He only set down the buckets, gave Eliza a friendly nod, and then looked up at me briefly. "Shalom."

Was that Hebrew? I wasn't sure what to say. And he turned without another word and began walking slowly back to his own yard. "Thank you," I called, though I wasn't completely sure what he'd meant. *Shalom* was a blessing, wasn't it? Or a greeting? I didn't think it meant good-bye. "We very much appreciate the extra buckets. I'll be over in a while with a few apples for you, and maybe some pears as well. Have a good day."

He turned with a little smile. "Thank you."

Eliza and I worked on in silence for a moment or two before she finally spoke up again. "Maybe *everybody* here is nice. At least everybody we've met so far. You think so, Mommy?"

I wasn't going to say one way or another about Marigold's nephew. He was probably a good man, but he hadn't been at all pleased when he realized who we were. Now I wondered why. It hadn't bothered him to be taking strangers to the boardinghouse. In fact, he'd rather seemed to enjoy himself with that. It was only when he knew we were John's family that he cooled toward me. Maybe he'd just wanted idle banter with a stranger. Or maybe he was genuinely concerned that I was here to use his aunt's good graces to my own ends.

We picked till the washtub was full. Then we had to stop. I simply couldn't reach anymore. But it was plenty, and Marigold was pleased.

"Now those squirrels can eat and I won't begrudge 'em," she said. "We got us enough to speak of, if we don't get even another one. Praise the Lord that it's a good year for fruit, 'cause I've not been able to work the garden worth my salt, and it's sure a blessing to have something else to can."

Again I wondered if Aunt Marigold struggled to make ends meet. I expected that soon enough I'd be seeing what, if anything, she had already stored on her pantry shelves.

But she wasn't ready to think of canning yet. "Go take Mr. Abraham his apples," she told me. "Put 'em in one of his buckets and fill the other with pears. Ask him over and don't take no for an answer. It's time for a break, and he's entitled to join us."

So I walked boldly to the neighbor's house and knocked soundly at the back door. His yard was kept up a bit better than Aunt Marigold's. Everything was nice and trim and orderly, even the lilacs. The chicken house was painted a crisp cream color and the trim was even painted to match the house, which appeared to be in immaculate condition. I imagined Mr. Abraham must be retired but a hard worker nonetheless. How old might he and Marigold be? Sixty? Sixty-five? It was impossible for me to tell. In a moment I saw him through the screen, walking slowly to the back door and looking far more somber than he had earlier out-of-doors.

"Aunt Marigold sent you apples. And pears," I said quickly, though I knew he'd already expect that to be why I'd come.

He opened the door and took the buckets from my hands, barely looking at me. "She's a dear heart to think of me so often. Thank you."

He might have turned away again, but I continued before he had the chance. "If you planted the trees, sir, I don't know how she could help but think of you. Anyway, she wanted me to ask you to tea. Right away. And not take no for an answer. Can you come?"

I could still see the touch of solemnity in his eyes, but he smiled. "I would be glad to. Right away, eh? I suppose that would be all right."

He set the buckets down, then stepped out the door and followed me across his smooth lawn and into Marigold's, which was not quite so neatly clipped.

"Will you be able to stay long?" he suddenly asked.

"I . . . uh . . . I don't really know yet."

"That's all right," he answered, his voice suddenly as soothing as the breeze blowing gently against my face. "The Lord has good thoughts for you, and not evil, to give you paths of peace and a satisfying future."

I stopped. I turned. There was something strange, something different, about those words. Why would he say them to me?

"Are you familiar with Jeremiah the son of Hilkiah? He recorded that. In his book among the prophets, of course."

The prophets? He must be speaking of the Bible, though I'd never heard anyone identify a book of the Bible in quite such a manner.

"How old is your little girl?" he asked.

"She's six."

"Yes." He nodded. "Old enough to remember but too young to understand the things that have happened. May I have my Shabbat group pray for you both?"

I had no idea what "Shabbat" meant, but dumbly I nodded, unable to respond in any other way. Maybe Mr. Abraham was a recent immigrant from the old country and things were done differently and referred to differently over there. But no. He could not be a recent immigrant. Not if he had planted that thick-limbed apple tree capable of bearing such an amazing bounty.

We reached Marigold's back door and I was glad to go inside. Not that it bothered me to be with Mr. Abraham. There was something very peaceful about him, but at the same time now strangely intense.

Marigold had places set very cheerily with cups and plates

and a teapot ready and on the table. Eliza sat prim and still as if taking tea were an everyday occurrence for her. Mr. Abraham seated himself, and Marigold happily served generous slices of her pie as I filled each cup with the fragrant blend that somehow reminded me of flowers.

"What have you put in the tea this time?" Mr. Abraham inquired gently. "It doesn't smell quite normal."

"Rosehips. And they're perfectly kosher, so don't question me. I checked."

"Just curious," he replied. "I trust you, good neighbor. Don't doubt."

I took a sip of my tea and watched them, fascinated.

"It's a very good-looking pie," Mr. Abraham continued. "The same as the last time?"

Marigold smiled, almost mischievously. "Of course not. The last one was cherry. Your memory fails you."

"You know that's not what I mean." He lifted his fork.

"Of course it's the same," Marigold acquiesced. "I learned the kosher pastry from Mrs. Liebwitz just as you suggested. I haven't even any lard in the house anymore. At least not today, so you needn't worry."

"Just curious, as I said before." He took a generous bite, winking at Eliza at the same time. "Did I hear someone say memory fails you? Did you remember the sugar?"

"Yes!" Eliza was quick in answer. "Yes, we put in sugar. And cimmanum too."

"You make a worthy pie, ladies. Many thanks."

Eliza drank milk from a teacup and enjoyed a bigger piece of pie than I'd ever given her, but after all the work today she'd definitely earned it. I'd never had rosehip tea before, not even with Mother on the farm, though she'd grown roses aplenty. It was tasty, and the apple pie was even better. But the lightness of the conversation between Marigold and Mr. Abraham soon faded.

He looked at the floor for a moment and seemed to need to draw in a deep breath. "You should know that my father will return to my house early next week, or perhaps sooner. He's not been well, and he should be where I can care for him."

How old might Mr. Abraham's father be? He must be ancient!

"Is he willing?" Marigold asked. "I mean, are things well between you again?" She suddenly glanced my way, then Eliza's. "Oh, my. I'm sorry to have completely left you out of the conversation, dears. We shouldn't be so rude."

"Oh no. You've been talking to us plenty in the midst of everything," I assured her. "But it's your first opportunity to sit down and speak with Mr. Abraham all day. Go right ahead. We'd rather eat pie than talk right now, anyway. Right, Ellie?"

Eliza nodded and shoveled a big bite into her mouth. Mr. Abraham took another sip of tea and got around to answering Marigold's question.

"Papa knows my heart, good neighbor. And he trusts the promise I gave him."

Marigold stared down at her plate. "Then I suppose I'll not see you for tea in a good long while."

"Maybe not. He's been very ill. When he is in my house, I should not leave his side for long."

"Then we'll have to bring the next pie right to your door. And apple butter, when I've got it made." Aunt Mari smiled. "And jelly. Does your father like pear jelly?"

"He does." Mr. Abraham returned the smile warmly. "Even if it is made by a Christian lady friend, though maybe it would be wise this time not to tell him so."

By the time our tea was finished, I was sure that Mr. Abraham must be Jewish and that he and Marigold had more than purely neighborly feelings toward one another, though I was not quite sure how to define the sort of relationship they had. I had plenty of questions, but their business was not mine, so I made myself keep quiet.

I realized it was already evening when Mr. Abraham returned to his house, carrying the rest of the pie we'd shared. We must have been pouring tea at the time most people begin preparing for their evening meal. And I soon realized that Aunt Mari had planned it that way, to hold us over so we could sit down and eat a late dinner with Josiah when he came home.

Marigold already had a pot on the stove of cut apples cooking down for sauce, and we worked together to fill a second pot. I wished I could ask Marigold about herself and Mr. Abraham, but it was far too soon for me to be prying.

"I suppose I'd better leave a couple of burners open to get supper going after a while," she said. "How would you like corned beef without any cabbage?"

"That would be fine," I told her. "We're not picky. And I'd like to help if I could."

She said she had home-canned corned beef in the basement if I wouldn't mind fetching a couple of jars. And we'd have apples and creamed squash and pie.

"I'll need an order from the grocer before long," she told me. "To add a little variety around here."

"You have quite a bit of variety already," I said. "Do you have a digging spade? There are carrots in the garden to be dug whenever you'd like to get them out of the ground."

"Oh, did they make anything at all? They were choked by weeds last I saw them."

"They may not have grown large, but there are definitely carrots out there."

"Now see what a blessing you are," she told me. "I'd have left them to the gophers and never known the difference. We'll dig them tomorrow, Lord willing. We've got enough to do tonight getting some of this fruit canned and put away."

She told me exactly where to find the corned beef in her "fruit room" in the basement, and I made my way carefully down the dimly lit stairway. She must have been sending Josiah down here for things lately or only using what was within reach in the kitchen. These stairs were far more difficult to maneuver than those going up to our bedroom. Darker, steeper, with two turns and a crack in one step wide enough to catch the heel of a shoe. I wouldn't want Aunt Marigold to even try going down them.

Her basement had two generous rooms, the second of which was lined with shelves. Jars and jars filled over half of the available space, unfortunately most of them empty. It wasn't hard to find the corned beef. There weren't very many canned meats left. I was a bit surprised that she had home-canned meat at all, since she lived in town and had no livestock. But maybe she'd gotten extra from a local farmer.

I looked through the other jars, still wondering if we would be a burden to John's aunt just by being here to eat her food. There was not near so much as I would like to see. Several pints of pickles and a few quarts of green beans. Six or eight jars of beets, and a few other things, but not much to speak of. Especially for the fall of the year with the summer garden nearly done. No wonder it had been important to her to save the pears from the squirrels. But maybe there was no real cause for concern. Maybe Marigold had an abundance of store-bought canned goods upstairs. Or plenty of money for the grocer when the time came.

I grabbed two jars of corned beef like she'd told me, though I really doubted we'd need more than one, even with Josiah likely coming in with a hearty appetite. I didn't think I'd need very much after already eating pie, and I wasn't sure my start at work today had been enough yet to earn my keep.

Marigold was cutting the squash when I came back up, and Eliza was enjoying the freedom we'd given her to try to cut an apple on her own.

"Thank you so much," Marigold told me when I set the jars on the table. "You go right ahead with the apples if you don't mind while I set these other things on to simmer."

We'd cut most of the fruit in the kitchen, so I went to the enclosed back porch for another bucket. Marigold hadn't let me carry any of the apples down to the basement yet. And she'd had me cover the washtub of pears with an old blanket and not carry it in from the yard yet, either. It was all far too heavy for someone as small as me to maneuver on the stairs, she'd insisted. Josiah would have to help.

We cut, cooked, and mashed apples in Marigold's soup pot. I lifted the boiling-water-bath canner down from a high shelf and carried armloads of empty jars up from the basement to be washed. Aware of the hour, I knew that Josiah was later than Marigold had expected him, and though she didn't say anything, I could tell the slightest difference in her demeanor. She thought highly of him, that much was clear, and worried when he was late.

We were filling the first of the jars to go into the canner when we heard the train whistle again faintly in the distance. I'd thought it hadn't taken us long to walk from the depot last night, but much more time went by than I'd expected before we finally heard the front door. Josiah strode in looking far less perky than he had last night. He was a sight, his clothes, face, and hair all a filthy mess. He set Aunt Marigold's empty egg basket and dishtowels on the table and sunk into the nearest chair.

"What happened?" Marigold asked him.

He seemed reluctant to talk. "Train hit a car. Outside of town."

Breath caught in my throat, and I had to steady myself suddenly against the side of the sink. An image leaped into my mind of the ashen-faced man who'd arrived at our door last November with the horrible news. *Train accident*. I couldn't keep my heart from racing.

Marigold set down her canning tongs and limped to Josiah's side. "Was there anything to be done?"

He shook his head. "We stopped when we could. Wreckage went over the slope by Bud Peterson's place down into the slough. I went . . . hoping . . ."

He glanced at Eliza and stopped. From the look of him, he'd fought the mud and muck with some determination, searching for any survivor. But the outcome was evidently too grim to speak of in front of a child. Though I couldn't possibly know whoever the victim or victims had been, still I felt sick to my stomach and utterly broken.

Josiah pulled himself up from the chair and staggered to his feet. “I better go clean up.”

Aunt Marigold, her eyes filled with tears, took him in her arms and held him. He stood, straight and still, his neck quivering just slightly, until he broke from her and walked away.

“Dear Lord,” Marigold said almost under her breath. I couldn’t clearly hear the words that followed, but I could well imagine them to be a prayer for Josiah, for the family of the deceased, or both.

Eliza was staring at me, looking frightened. “Is Mr. Walsh all right?”

“Yes, dear,” I told her somberly. “He will be.”

My heart continued to thunder even as I made an effort at outward calm for my daughter’s sake. *Train wreck*. On only our second night here. It was like the devil’s mockery. And to have to see it happen? Marigold hurried back to her business, but I knew her thoughts were surely centered on her nephew and what he’d been forced to witness. What must be going through his mind? It was just too horrible to think about.

7

Josiah Walsh

It wasn't easy to push away the image. Bloodied skirt. Crushed body. We'd known immediately that there was no life in the man whose remains had become so entangled with that of his automobile, but I'd held out hope for the woman. To no avail.

Now every step took extra effort, and I ached inside, as though what I'd witnessed had produced some physical injury in me. The encrusted mud seemed to weigh a ton, and though I wanted to be rid of it, I could scarcely coax the movement from my hurting body to cleanse it away. Only gradually did I realize that the heavy pain with each breath, the horrible soreness down my entire left side, was an echo of the days after the accident that had taken Rosemary, when life had seemed nothing but a bitter, monstrous fog.

How quickly it must have ended for the couple in the gray topless coupe at the rail crossing. Perhaps they did not even see the approaching train. Perhaps their last thoughts, their last words, were ones of love and joy. If so, their end might be thought a mercy. At least they'd died together. At least one of them had not been left behind to grieve and struggle with the endless appraisal of what he should have done differently.

Aunt Mari's washroom was down the hall from the kitchen, with running water and a large tub. But I did not want to wash so near everyone, with their words and their worries. Instead I filled a bucket, which smelled strongly of apples, and carried it up with me to the wash basin beside my bed, where the plumbing did not go.

For the moment I was glad Aunt Mari was too feeble for the stairs, and Leah Breckenridge surely kept herself too aloof to notice my struggle. I did not want them to offer help, nor follow, nor speak to me at all again until I could push away the cloud that had surrounded me.

The woman had been nothing like Rosemary. She was larger. And older. But I could not seem to separate the two in my mind anyway. Rosemary's pale fingers and strawberry blonde curls filled my eyes even when I closed them. The bulge of new life beneath her dress still pressed at my heart. They were gone. Together and in an instant. But like a lone tree after a cyclone's devastation, I'd been left behind.

I set down the pail of water at the doorway to my room, ripped the soiled shirt over my head, and threw it against the wall. I heard the *pip* of at least one button hitting the hardwood floor, but I didn't care. I never wanted to wear that shirt again because it was tainted. I'd dug through the bog in it, I'd held death. And I'd cried.

Why, God? Why did it have to happen? Why does it have to affect me so?

I poured what was left of the tepid water from the pitcher into the wash bowl and buried my hands in it. I didn't even have to scrub to darken the water, I'd carried so much of the slough home with me. When that water had done all it could, I drained it into the slop pail beneath the washstand and poured fresh water to clean my face and hair.

Little by little, I washed every part of me, leaving my encrusted denim trousers in a heap on the floor. When I was finally ready to dress, I felt too stiff, and almost buried myself in the covers of the bed instead. But if I did not manage to take myself downstairs again, Aunt Mari would send John's wife up looking for me. She'd be that concerned, I knew without doubt, and I did not want our sudden visitor to be put in such a position. I did not want her inquiring after me at all.

Better if Leah Breckenridge were not here. What good could it possibly serve? But there could be no argument that I was as much a subject of Aunt Mari's benevolence as anyone. So if I could not stomach the presence of another "wounded spirit," it might be time for me to move on.

I tried to dress more quickly than I'd managed to wash, hoping Aunt Mari was patient enough to give me the space I needed. But as I started buttoning yet another of the shirts given to me by Mari's neighbor, I heard the faint sound of footfalls on the steps. Too strong to be my aunt, with her worsening arthritic limp. Too light to be Mr. Abraham, though Mari'd sent him up my way more than once when I'd first arrived here.

In moments came a timid rapping at my door, and when I did not answer promptly, a far more timid voice.

"Mr. Walsh . . . your—your aunt sent me to see if—if you might need anything. Dinner is ready. When you please. She said I could carry it up to you if you wish."

I almost accepted the offer, but I knew it would send Mari to her knees in prayer for me, and I didn't want her to worry. "No. I'll be down."

Silence from the other side of the door. I'd have thought she was gone, except there'd been no more footsteps.

Finally, her voice ventured once again through the wood of the door. "Are you all right?"

"Yes." Somehow I could say no more.

"You could become friends," Aunt Mari had said when first she'd told me about inviting Leah and her daughter to stay here. "The things you've both been through, you could understand each other so well."

I didn't want understanding. I didn't want Mari's well-meaning attempts to draw me from what she imagined to be some sort of hidden quarter within myself. It was not hard to be friendly, to be a kindly nephew to my generous "aunt," to joke and banter with the men I worked with and idle acquaintances here and there. But John's wife? Looking past her frosty demeanor into the pain that must rest inside would be almost like ripping open pages of my own hurt to air in the public view. I couldn't do it.

Softly, slowly, her footsteps moved from my door and down the oak stairs. I took a deep breath, willing myself to somehow find the appetite Mari would expect. After a long day's work, I should be ravenous. But my mouth felt like cotton, my stomach like lead. I couldn't imagine enjoying anything placed before me tonight.

For some reason my mind traveled back to the burnt roast beef Rosemary and I had enjoyed together on our first full day as man and wife. She'd been so excited to prove to me her abilities, only to have almost everything go wrong. But I didn't care. That roast beef had been the best I'd ever eaten, or could ever imagine eating, because her hands had prepared it and offered it with hope and love shining from her soft green eyes.

No gourmet meal could hold a candle to that.

I left my work boots upstairs and padded down in my stocking feet, hoping to be able to grab a few bites and be done with the obligation without having to say more than a few words at most. I could smell now what I probably should have noticed before. Apples. Fragrant and abundant. Leah Breckenridge must have picked from the tree today. Good for her. At least she wasn't too stymied by her grief to lift a helping hand.

I don't know why I didn't smell the corned beef sooner. Or the pie. Aunt Mari had chosen a couple of my favorites, as if she'd tried to bless me especially. I could take or leave the pattypan squash, but for Mari's sake I accepted a generous share. She said the prayer, and I wondered if she knew that I didn't have the strength tonight.

John's wife and daughter sat and ate in silence, surely feeling as awkward as I in this new arrangement. Only when I noticed the tiny glint of a tear in Leah's eye did I remember what Mari had told me of John's death. A train accident. God Almighty.

I'd been too consumed by the cloud over my own thinking to consider what such a subject would call to mind in this woman and her daughter. No wonder they both picked at their food, grave-faced and still. But there was nothing I could do now. The hurt had been driven home without remedy. And Aunt Mari had been right all those months ago when she'd said I'd be able to relate to the pain they were enduring.

"We've filled the back porch with fruit," Aunt Mari said lightly. "With the old washtub full of pears in the backyard to boot. Mostly Leah's doings. She's been such a help today. I was going to ask you to carry some of the baskets down to the basement for keeping, but it can wait till morning when you're rested."

"I can do it tonight," I told her, pushing my fork into the corned beef on my plate and careful not to look up.

"I think it might be better for everyone to turn in early," she protested. "None of that fruit'll be going anywhere."

I nodded, and Aunt Mari kept right on talking. "Leah's discovered the garden. That's where this squash came from. And she tells me there's carrots to be found, and the chance of more tomatoes and peppers."

How could I respond? My only experience with gardens had been brief here with Aunt Mari. And the loving labor at Rosemary's side as she toiled to create a vegetable patch out of rough sod in the home we'd shared. Now the planted rows made me think of her and filled me with an empty longing. I didn't ever want to garden again.

"You can't go on grieving," Mari had told me once. "At least not to the exclusion of everything else life has to offer. Rosemary would want you to live on and be happy again."

Perhaps the words were true, but they rang with emptiness for me nonetheless. Rosemary would never have chosen to die in a ditch alongside a narrow street, and to take our unborn child with her. She'd had more hope for the future than that.

I finished my meal and did what Aunt Mari said in returning to my room and retiring early. The clatter of dishes behind me said that Mari and Leah would clean up before doing the same. I was sure I'd been woefully unpleasant company this evening, but there was precious little to be done about that. It would have been worse had I tried to talk. Bad enough to have to face Leah Breckenridge here at all. For her to see me shaken, bowed by the gruesome events of the day, was just a cruel jab at us both.

8

Leah

"Don't let it worry you," Marigold told me after Mr. Walsh had finished his meal and retired. "He's exhausted. And shaken by what's happened."

"I know." Somehow it was hard for me to hold my equilibrium together, as though the very mention of another train wreck had pulled the footing away from me. Eliza was watching me, had been watching all of us through our quiet meal, her eyes wide and wondering, perhaps not completely understanding the reason for our solemnity. Of course she knew that a train wreck was a serious matter, but I'd never told her the manner of her father's death. I hadn't wanted her to be plagued by dreams and fears the way I had been for as long as I could remember.

"Are you finished with your squash, honey?" I asked her.

She nodded, looking up at me with her bright eyes full of question. "Did Mr. Walsh know the people that got hurt?"

Again, my breath stuck in my throat. Somehow she had failed to realize there'd been no survivors left in the wreckage. "No," I said softly. "Most likely not. But it's difficult to come upon such a scene nonetheless."

"Daddy told me about a wreck once."

My heart thundered. I had no idea what she could be referring to. I could not remember John ever discussing such things with me.

"He was a little sad because a girl my size got her leg broked up. He hugged me and said it made him think of me when she was crying and he hoped I never got hurt like that."

"I hope not too." It was all I could say. I could feel the threat of tears and did my best to push them away. Eliza did not need to see me crying. We were here for a new beginning, for hope. Not to let the tragedy of strangers drag us down.

"Your father loved you very much," I told her. "He was a wonderful man." Quickly, I gathered the dishes and hurried them to the sink. Putting my hands to work in the dishwater was like a safety, keeping me from dwelling more than necessary on the pain that had presented itself so abruptly.

Marigold worked beside me, lifting her voice in a tender hymn. And though I could not quite bring myself to sing along, it seemed a most appropriate way to draw what had become a difficult evening to its close.

9

Josiah

Leah Breckenridge would think me weak. And Aunt Mari in her worry would surely explain to her all about my loss and my struggle. I should have pretended nothing at all had happened. I should have told them I'd fallen in a puddle and let them laugh at my foolish ineptitude. It would have been far easier to take.

I don't want my pain rubbed raw in the view of others, Lord God! I directed bitter thoughts toward the ceiling.

I don't want the things inside of me to be shared! Maybe I don't want to die anymore, but I still think you were unfair not to take me along with my family. You know I didn't want to come here. I didn't want to do anything after Rosemary's death but fade away to dust. Don't open me up before a stranger. Don't hang my weaknesses in view like so much tattered laundry.

My filthy trousers lay in a heap inside the door, and I kicked them across the room to join the spoiled shirt. Maybe in the morning I would pick them up and dispose of them. Or maybe I would let Mari talk me into allowing them to be washed and used again for thrift's sake. It didn't really matter. What I needed now more than anything was sleep.

I plopped onto the bed, glad I'd already taken off my work boots so I wouldn't have to loosen the laces now. The pounding at the back of my head was worse than usual tonight. But maybe the rest I needed would come easily.

Lord, I know you work all things for good and according to your will, but why does life have to be so hard?

I didn't want to pray anymore tonight because thinking would go along with it and I didn't want to think. Better to be dead to the world and every struggle that's a part of it. I lay down for a moment, shutting my eyes and wishing for instant sleep. But thoughts of Rosemary intruded on my efforts, and eventually I heard footsteps again on the front stairs. Leah and Eliza coming up to bed.

Why did Aunt Mari have to give them the master room? Right next to mine? Sure, it was the biggest, so it would suit a woman and her child. But I could already hear the little girl's humming, just like last night. I could hear the whisper of voices, even without being able to discern a single word.

Leah had more than I did. She had a piece of her John beside her, to cherish and hold. I had nothing but this empty room. The voices of a woman and child just one thin wall away were like mockery.

Why didn't she just tell her daughter to be still and go to sleep? Even after their talking was done, the humming continued, incessant, overwhelming, as if the sound were something alive, reaching on and on into the night for something impossible to grasp.

Maybe there was peace in it for that little girl. But to me it shouted only of her lack. Rosemary had been prone to humming. But her hum had been the sound of contentment, of quiet pleasure that needed no words. Eliza's was different, which was obvious to me even at a distance. It was noise to fill up the silence, to cover over an empty spot that would never go away.

I tried to push it all out of my mind, but then Rosemary's image returned to me, sitting in the cherrywood rocker in front of the fire, her knitting in her lap and a soft melody teasing forth from her closed lips.

In a fit of grief and rage, I'd smashed that rocker into a hundred pieces. And then I'd burned every sliver, so I wouldn't have to look at its emptiness and remember the dreams I'd lost. But memories aren't disposed of that easily.

I rolled slowly from the lumpy mattress and knelt by the side of the bed, knowing that the way my mind was plagued, sleep would not come unless I prayed. But tonight it might be difficult to form the words. Perhaps I could pray in my thoughts alone for Aunt Marigold. That would be easy enough. She'd been a blessing to me and it was not hard to ask a blessing for her in return, as well as help in her continuing struggle with the rheumatism that tried to cripple her.

It was also not as hard as I'd thought to pray for the relatives of the man and woman who had died together today. But that was as far as I got. Leah Breckenridge and her daughter surely needed prayer too. But I couldn't bring myself into their pain right now without being slammed down again by more of my own.

Aunt Marigold will pray for them, and that will be enough, I managed. *You know, Lord. You know their need.*

I rose and climbed between the covers of the bed. The humming continued for what seemed like an hour before finally tapering off. Silence. At last. But sleep proved evasive nonetheless.

This bed, any bed, was just too big. I grabbed at the extra pillow and scrunched it against my chest. Same as always, the pillowcase smelled like Aunt Mari's lavender-scented detergent. Too delicate. Too feminine. I hurled the pillow across the room, rolled onto my stomach, and jerked the bedsheet over my head.

10

Leah

The next day, Mr. Walsh seemed to be trying to make up for the somber mood of the previous night by a hefty dose of levity as he hauled the finest looking of yesterday's apples and pears into the basement for storage. Even after Marigold called him for breakfast he persisted at singing some sort of "jazzy" music I'd never heard before.

Last night, he'd seemed touched by the tragedy, and I'd been deeply surprised and moved at the depth of the feeling I thought I'd seen. But maybe he was just tired, like Marigold had said. This morning, he'd put it all behind him and seemed to have nary a thought that somewhere in this town or a town nearby there was at least one family in mourning, and preparations of the most solemn kind being made. Almost I wished to ask if he had any idea where the memorial services would be held and whether or not the railroad company would send any representative. But I did not dare to voice the words, uncertain of his reaction.

He ate heartily of Marigold's oatmeal, avoiding looking at either Eliza or me as he relayed to his aunt the Kurcher family's thanks for the biscuits and eggs she'd sent yesterday. "Dodie Elmira is getting married," he said. "Only sixteen, I think. Her beau is the son of a neighboring farmer. They'll be building a Sears Roebuck house practically a stone's throw from both in-laws."

"Well, that'll be keeping the family together," Marigold made conversation in return. "Is he farming like his father?"

"Helping, I think. But she said he wants to inquire about a railroad job too."

Eliza picked at her oatmeal, and I gave her a sprinkle of sugar across the top as enticement to finish what she could. She smiled.

"The whole family's well?" Marigold asked on about the Kurchers.

"Well enough, I guess. Dodie didn't say anything different."

"I would love to visit them again. Dearly I would."

Josiah let his aunt's words go, and I was very glad. The thought of her hopping a train with him to ride off to an unknown town was quite unsettling.

I was hoping he would leave after breakfast with the jazzy music still on his lips and no more thought of the Scripture he'd left off in the middle of reading yesterday. But Marigold reminded him, scurrying dishes out of the way when he was finished with them to make room for her big, leather-bound book.

He read all the rest of that chapter and the next, and I tried not to listen as I washed up the dishes yet again. But one verse stuck with me, and I couldn't quite get it out of my mind.

"How precious also are thy thoughts unto me, O God! How great is the sum of them!"

Did that mean that God's thoughts about me were precious, or that I was supposed to consider his thoughts precious, whatever they might be? I couldn't quite decide, and either way it seemed unfair and unjust. How could I be expected to think his thoughts precious if they allowed for agony and pain? Or could he truly be thinking good things for me? If so, why was I now being forced to live as a widow and provide without means for a fatherless child?

Josiah Walsh shut the book when he finished the chapters and rose to his feet. "Got to be going, Aunt Mari. I'll see you a little earlier tonight, Lord willing."

The words seemed harsh, like a slap at last night's pain. He turned away and would have gone, but Marigold stopped him to give him the last pie she and Eliza had made yesterday.

"Lunch," she told him. "Eat it all if you want to. There's plenty more where that came from."

With a brief nod to her and not a word in my direction, he was out the door and gone. And just like yesterday, it was a relief.

Now we could get to the business of the day. More canning, of course. We'd barely gotten started with that. And there were the carrots to dig. And the laundry and such things to be done about the house. But Marigold had other things in mind, at least at first.

She pulled a picture album from a cupboard and took us to the sitting room where we could join her on the settee. Eliza was excited, I could easily tell. But I trembled inside at the very idea of viewing pictures of John's family and talking about them.

"Thought you might appreciate the chance to see these," she said. "No sense in slaving away the whole time you're here."

She showed us John's parents, her own parents, and an immense assortment of siblings, cousins, nieces, and nephews.

"Some of them don't live too awfully far away," she said. "Maybe we could have a little get-together."

I hoped not. I'd met many of them, but John had not made keeping in touch with them a priority, so I didn't feel I had any real relationship with these people. And even if I had, to be put on display in front of them now would be awkward at best.

I wondered if Marigold would say anything about Josiah or his parents. She didn't mention them, but she spoke more about her sisters, and John's mother in particular, than anyone else. I would have liked to know their relationship, to know if John had been close to Josiah as a boy, but I couldn't quite bring myself to ask.

On one of the last few pages, Eliza found a tiny photograph of an infant draped with a lacy coverlet and staring intently at a wooden pony someone held overhead.

"Pretty baby," she remarked.

"That, dear one, is your father," Marigold stated warmly.

"Really?" Eliza exclaimed with a deep intake of breath, as though she'd found a sublime treasure. She moved her fingers to the very edge of the picture but didn't touch the face of it. "It looks a little bit like my baby brother."

My eyes filled with tears, and through them the photograph looked far more like Johnny James than I could ever have expected. I could almost see his tiny, frail fingers clutching for the pony, his plaintive wail letting me know that all was not right with his world.

Aunt Marigold suddenly took my hand in hers and squeezed it, then she closed the book and set it aside on the lamp table.

"I'm glad baby Johnny and Daddy are together," Eliza said. "If only one was in heaven alone, they might be lonely. It's better that I gots Mommy and Johnny gots Daddy so nobody gots to be alone."

I couldn't answer, but Marigold gave Ellie a little hug and nodded her head. "That's a very good way to look at it, and I'm sure that they're glad to be together just like you said. But nobody is ever alone in heaven or here on earth, because the good Lord is always with us."

There was nothing I could say, and I didn't want to sit and listen to any more. "The sun's shining," I said, standing to my feet. "Looks like perfect weather for digging those carrots. Are there digging tools in the shed?"

Marigold looked up at me for a moment. "You know it's all right to slow down enough sometimes to remember and reflect."

"Maybe so," I agreed. "But it doesn't seem as practical as bringing in a harvest that's in the ground and waiting."

She smiled. "You're quite the go-getter. But we all cope in our own ways."

I found her reference to my grief irritating. I didn't want it mentioned. I wanted only to move on into the work that needed to be done where I could maintain my composure and feel like I was accomplishing something. I was about to go on outside when she mentioned something I'd already thought of but felt too uncertain to mention on my own.

"You seem to take natural to the garden and such, but I was hoping you wouldn't mind helping me with another chore first." She took Eliza's hand in her own and continued. "I hate to ask you to help with the washing, but it's become awfully difficult for me anymore and we've got such aplenty waiting. I meant to ask Josiah to bring down anything that might be in his room yet, but I forgot. If you could check for me and then help me get everything started, I can wash and you can rinse and put on the line."

"That would be fine," I told her. "Would it be all right if I add a few things of ours?"

"Of course."

"You needn't wash if you want to continue working apples," I told her. "Just show me what you use and I can take care of the washing. We could get two jobs done at once that way."

Despite my preference for working alone this morning, Marigold was not about to let me have my way. "The work goes quicker when it's shared," she said. "I won't be able to dig the carrots later, but I can still get my hands in my own laundry, and I won't have it any other way. Not just yet, at least."

So she started drawing water from the sink, and I went upstairs to gather any dirty clothes I could find. Walking into Mr. Walsh's room was a little strange, even with him gone to work. There was nothing about it even remotely similar to the room Eliza and I had been given. This was a man's room, through and through. There were no flowery curtains or pretty pictures on the walls. Even the bedspread was a plain brown, trimmed in blue.

The room was not tidy, with clothes and even part of the bedding strewn about the floor. I felt like stripping all of the bedding and carrying it down with me along with the clothes, but I wasn't sure if we'd have time or room on the clothesline for all of that today.

I gathered up the filthy clothes, wondering briefly about the man who occupied this room, who'd at first been altogether too friendly, and now rather like a closed door. There was nothing at all in here to give me any indication of the sort of person he might be, no personal effects except one small picture, laid flat on the dresser. A woman, quite young and rather attractive. She wore a button hat and a tiny, almost mischievous smile. It would have been nice to know a little something about her.

I carried my load down carefully, glad to be here to help Marigold with such a chore. We filled the barrel of her wringer washer and then a couple of tubs for rinse water and worked side by side. It was difficult to keep Eliza back, she loved the wringer so much, but I didn't want her hand getting pinched. We'd never had one of these, and she'd never even seen one before.

"Fancy," she called it, and I had to agree, compared to washing by hand, which I'd been used to doing.

"Does make things faster," Marigold agreed. "That's important when you get to be my age. But I expect it'd help a young wife with a big family get to the other needs of her day a lot quicker too."

"How old are you?" Eliza asked before I could stop her.

"Sixty-two," Marigold answered without hesitation. "But sometimes I feel older. I'm not as spry as my mother was at this age."

I knew that Marigold's mother had had fourteen children. Marigold was the second oldest. And Azalea, John's mother, had been thirteenth. There'd been six girls and eight boys in a span of twenty-two years. John's grandmother must have been an amazing woman.

I put clothes through the ringer from the first rinse into the second, and then again from the second rinse into a laundry basket to take and hang the clothes outside. Marigold handled rubbing any special stains, putting everything to churning in the wash and then ringer-pressing it into the first rinse tub. Josiah's work clothes were the absolute worst, and she threw those back into the washing tub three times.

I asked about the bedding, but she decided on another day for that simply because, just as I'd thought, there wouldn't be room enough on the line for it all with the other clothes. The water in the washtub was too dirty after the work clothes to do a good job at anything else thrown in now anyway. So we went ahead and drained it.

With that chore behind us, we moved with a will into the canning and the digging. I was disappointed to find no more than two pecks or so of fresh carrots, but Marigold was pleased as she could be, and so was Eliza. We cleaned carrots on the spot and each had one for a snack. Marigold thought they'd all keep all right and we wouldn't need to can any of these. She separated a mess of carrots to cook, and a bundle for the icebox, and sent the rest downstairs with me to a bin in the basement.

Meanwhile, Marigold kept the canner boiling with our second batch of applesauce, and, not sure what else to do, I kept sorting through the apples and cutting more. We started apple butter and made a canner load of pie filling, and then I showed Marigold how my mother had made cinnamon apple tarts. I felt good about the whole day.

The following day was almost like it. We canned more apples, kept up with what little the garden held, and got a start at cleaning the house. I gathered more turnip greens and even wild greens enough to can a mess. Occasional interruptions by a train whistle had become predictable and not too terribly difficult to put from my mind. And despite Eliza's initial enthusiasm to explore the town, I kept myself busy with everything around me, hesitant to venture into the wider unknown.

But after Friday's biscuit making, the flour supply was low, and though we'd been making do with what was around, the time had come when groceries would have to be ordered. Josiah had given Marigold grocery money from his paycheck before he left with the biscuit bundle and a bucket of apples for the Kurchers, but he wouldn't be able to pick up the groceries himself because he wouldn't be back before the grocer closed. Marigold said she could use the neighbor's phone and have her items delivered, but she preferred if I would take the order to the store myself.

"You'll have to go right by the school on your way," she said. "And you can register Eliza Rose for classes starting next week. The time has come. I'm sure you'll agree."

Of course she was right. I couldn't continue to ignore that detail, as much as I might like to. Eliza had scarcely left my sight since we'd lost Johnny James, and part of me preferred to keep it that way. But she was a big girl and ought to be in school. I was confident there would not be a problem with her starting late.

She walked with me that overcast day, excited to be finally exploring but a little apprehensive just the same.

"I wish you were a teacher, Mommy. Then you could go to school too."

"Oh, they prefer unmarried women to be their teachers," I said without thinking, and we both fell silent.

We'd brought along Marigold's wheelbarrow to manage the groceries on the way home and parked it carefully beside a pair of bicycles in the schoolyard when we went in.

The teacher I spoke with was very polite and offered to take Eliza immediately to her class, but I told her we felt it best to wait until Monday. She showed Eliza around the building anyway and let her peek at her classroom from the doorway so she would know a little of what to expect. The children were all reciting their alphabet letters, which Eliza already knew, so she felt at least a little at ease. The teacher stepped out for a moment to introduce herself, shaking Eliza's hand kindly. She also offered to let Eliza stay for the rest of the day. But Eliza shook her head determinedly, and since I'd already told her differently, I didn't make her stay.

I'd been glad to find the school such a short walk from the boardinghouse. It would be easy to take her there in the morning and meet her again in the afternoon. And the grocery store was not much farther. I let Eliza sit in the wheelbarrow on the way there. The clouds were passing for the most part, and I was enjoying the breaking sun. The store where Marigold sent us was a big cheery place with rows and rows of most any food I could imagine. I couldn't quite remember the last time I'd shopped at a grocer for any real order of supplies. For our last few weeks in St. Louis, we'd been unable to afford more than an item or two at a time, if anything at all.

Marigold had a generous list, and it made me feel rich to relate it all to the helpful man behind the counter. Flour, oil, bacon, and potatoes. Corn meal, sugar, sweet peas, tea, and much more. She'd even said I should get us each an orange as a special treat, which of course made me think of the orange on the train.

"God has taken very good care of us," Eliza suddenly said, as if she'd shared the same thought. "He's given us Aunt Marigold, and Mr. Josiah, and plenty of food to eat. I never see'd so many apples in all my life, plus the other stuff. It's blessings just like I prayed for."

I nodded to her, willing to share in her gratitude if only from a distance.

"Mommy, did you ever think we'd be so blessed?"

"I—I hoped for the best."

"Ill'nois is happy for us, just like you said."

Things *had* been going rather smoothly, with Marigold at least. But Josiah seemed to be doing his best to ignore or avoid us. Obviously he was not pleased to have us around, and I wondered how much longer the friction of those feelings could continue without coming to some sort of a head.

The grocer offered to walk our wheelbarrow home for us, but

I told him I'd manage just fine. Eliza would have liked to sit in it again. She seemed to be getting a little tired, but there was no room for her now. I almost forgot that Marigold said I should check the mail while I was out. Hers was always delivered to the post office, and she usually had Josiah go and check it once a week, but since I was out and about anyway, I might as well find the post office for myself and even give them my name, in case any mail ever came for me.

As it turned out, they hadn't gotten my name quite soon enough but had graciously held on to a letter anyway. From my old friend and neighbor Anna in St. Louis. She'd placed only my name, the word "Boardinghouse," and the name of the town on the envelope, but it had gotten here just the same.

I had no idea what to expect from her letter because I really hadn't thought she'd ever write. And maybe she wouldn't have on her own. Her words were short and to the point:

Dear Leah,

Your father called looking for you. He is ill and wishes to speak to you. I wasn't sure from the way you talked whether you'd want me to tell him where you are. So please let me know because I told him I might be able to find your new address and he said he would call me again. If you have access to a telephone, could you call and give the information yourself? I would prefer that. I hope that everything is going well for you in your new home.

Sincerely,
Anna

I could not remember my father ever looking for me before. I thought of Mother's sudden illness, and my heart pounded, yet at the same time a bitter resolve tried to raise its ugly head. He'd never cared to have much to do with me before. Why now?

Of course I couldn't call, because even if I used the telephone of a neighbor or businessman here, I had no idea what number to use. The last I'd known, Father had no telephone at home. But why should I try to reestablish communication? I didn't need his thunderous assaults jabbing at my ears, pounding on my heart. So many times I'd left his presence emotionally in pain. I wasn't sure I ever wanted to hear his voice again.

And yet he was my father. And I was the only child he had left in this world. If he was really ill, if this might really be serious, maybe he only wanted me to know, or maybe he had something else that he wanted to say.

My eyes filled with tears, hoping he'd choose to do more than relay, by word or impression as he'd done so many times before, just how grievous a disappointment I was to him. I'd known almost for as long as I could remember that it had been my older brother James that Father had really loved and had hopes for. Despite all my tomboy efforts, I could never be more than a poor replacement.

"Did you get a sad letter?" Eliza asked, waiting quietly beside the wheelbarrow on the post office walk.

"No, honey," I tried to assure us both. "Not terribly sad. Your grandfather is not feeling well, but there's nothing to indicate that it's serious."

"We should pray for him," she said immediately. "And tell Aunt Marigold to. She'll pray. I know she will."

The suggestion jarred me, and I was tempted to tell her to keep the letter a secret. Of course Marigold would pray. But she might also think that I should go to my father's side, and I did not want that, not for me or for my daughter. Eliza would not really understand. She'd seldom been with her grandfather, and then only when sheltered by her father's special watch care as well as my own. She had no idea how ugly he could be.

Still I could not refuse the prayers. If it came up, I would simply have to tell Marigold that my father did not want my presence and I did not want his. Strange as that might seem, it had been the truth for most of my lifetime, and I could not really picture it changing now.

I expected Eliza to ask Marigold to pray for her grandfather immediately, but she didn't. While we put away groceries and ate a quick lunch, the subject of the letter never came up. But I knew I could not just ignore it. I would have to at least reply to Anna, and like it or not, writing to my father directly would probably be the right thing to do.

I borrowed paper and sat down. First I wrote to Anna, telling her that things were going well for us and that I appreciated her letter and would contact my father myself. Then I began the far more difficult letter. Simple as it should have been, nothing seemed to suit me, and I ended up restarting the letter three times. Finally I decided that if I couldn't find any words I could feel secure sending my father right now, then maybe I didn't really need to say much of anything at all. So I wrote only that we had moved and supplied the new address. Marigold had no telephone number, so I told him that too. That was enough. I could not even express my endearment at the end but instead signed it only, "Your daughter, Leah."

He hadn't come when John died, nor Johnny James. He had barely tolerated my presence at my own mother's funeral. I did not know why he would be seeking me now, and I wasn't sure I wanted to know. But at least I'd done what might be considered a daughter's duty, and let him know where to find us.

It was pouring down rain by the time the letters were written, and I was very glad to have finished our errands in the morning. Mailing the letters could wait till tomorrow. There were more pears and apples to cut and can, and that was the perfect job for a rainy afternoon.

"Grandpa doesn't feel good," Eliza finally told Marigold as we were filling jars once again.

I hadn't disclosed the content of my letter and she hadn't asked, but now she looked at me with considerable concern. "Oh, I hope it's nothing serious."

"I don't expect so," I said solemnly.

"But we're gonna pray for him anyway," Eliza quickly added. "Will you pray too?"

"Of course I will."

It pricked my heart for a moment to realize that Eliza had given the impression that both of us were praying individuals. Hypocritical or not, I just couldn't manage to tell Marigold otherwise. And I know she would probably have appreciated me volunteering a bit more information, but I didn't want to talk about my father. John had told me about his family, how they could be distant, too caught up in their own lives to take much time in each other's. But that wasn't the same as giving each other any real reason for avoidance.

"Mr. Abraham's father moved in today," she told me. "I saw them this morning while you were gone."

I'd wanted to ask questions before. Now I finally felt bold enough. "Why were you concerned about not seeing much of Mr. Abraham while his father is here?"

She lifted jars carefully into the rack of the boiling-water canner. "To tell you the truth, child, the man feels that we think too highly of each other. Mr. Abraham's father and son are both rabbis, and they are both terribly concerned about him becoming too close to a woman who is not Jewish."

"That seems a little unfair."

She shrugged. "Oh, I don't know. If I had a son, I would want him to marry a Christian, so my grandchildren would be taught about what the Son of God has done for us. Even if they had no children, I would still think it right for them to be able to share and support each other in their faith. So I suppose I understand their position readily enough."

"But you and Mr. Abraham haven't spoken of marriage. Have you?"

"No. At least not directly. But I'm quite sure it's crossed his mind, the same as it has mine."

It was unsettling for my earlier thoughts about them to be confirmed, but I tried not to let on that I found anything unusual about it. "It shouldn't be any of his family's business to keep you apart," I told her, hoping to sound supportive.

"But it's right to show the proper respect. To the elderly Rabbi Abraham, of course. Saul will not directly dishonor his wishes, and I support him in that." She gave me a sly grin. "But that being said, let's make them a pie in time for dinner."

It was startling to find in Marigold the sort of attitude I might expect in a strong-willed twenty-year-old. Behind her gray hair and wrinkles, she seemed to have a steel determination.

"Is Mr. Abraham your beau, then?" I asked her.

"A dear friend. And it is perfectly sufficient to leave it at that."

But I couldn't quite stop with the questions now that I'd started. "Can you share and be encouraging in your faith, even though it's different?"

She nodded. "We've spoken of it often. He has shared the basis of his beliefs just as I have mine. And we agree that there's really only one difference. I say his religion is incomplete without the Messiah who waits for them to receive him. And he says my religion is based solely on the teaching of an uneducated carpenter's son."

I sat down, and Eliza climbed into my lap. "How in the world can you reconcile that?"

"Oh, we're much nearer than you might think."

"I don't understand how you could be."

She smiled. "One afternoon over tea he asked me why, apart from the traditions of my family, I could accept Jesus's claims to be the Messiah. And I asked him why, apart from the traditions of *his* family, he could not. That turned out to be a very fruitful discussion."

My curiosity would not stop. "Did Mr. Abraham come to believe in Jesus?"

"Not outwardly. Not openly. But passages like Isaiah 53 and Psalm 22 are doing their work in his heart to this day, and I completely believe that."

I should have known better than to delve so completely into a religious discussion. At this juncture, I wasn't quite sure of my own beliefs anymore, so I was certainly in no position to speak of others'. But oddly, I just couldn't keep my mouth shut. "I'm afraid I don't remember those passages," I told her, hoping I really had heard them somewhere so I could consider my own words more than just a bold lie.

"Oh, my. Psalm 22 is a prophetic picture of Christ on the cross. Really remarkable. And Isaiah 53 is an amazing statement of the real reason why the Messiah would come, far too often overlooked. It's very clear about his substitutionary sacrifice."

"You seem to know the Scriptures very well, Aunt Marigold."

"That's what Mr. Abraham thought. He was rather impressed, actually. So I told him how important it was to my preaching grandfather that girls learned the Word as well as the boys, because it's so often the women that teach the children what they need to know."

"*I* don't know," Eliza suddenly spoke up. "Not about any of all that, I don't think."

"Oh, goodness, you're young," Marigold immediately told her. "And even if you weren't, that is easily remedied."

I'd really started something. Marigold was all fired up and determined. As soon as we had the canner going, we worked quick as we could to get pies in the oven, and then, when they were finally baking, she got back to my non-thought-out questions.

"Fetch the Bible. Over in the corner."

I didn't want to read. I didn't want to ponder the words or risk the flame of bitterness they so often sparked in me. But I couldn't tell her no. Eliza seemed eager to learn. Who was I to stand in the way?

So at Marigold's direction, I read both Psalm 22 and Isaiah 53 and then listened while she explained to my daughter how both were fulfilled in Jesus. I didn't remember ever hearing a better teacher. If Mr. Abraham's heart had been pricked, it was no wonder.

But I didn't question the Son of God's deity or his station as Savior of men. That was not my problem. The thing I questioned was the goodness of God the Father. How could a being of complete and ultimate good allow such dreadful sorrows to take place in this world?

Checking the pies in the oven was a convenient excuse for distancing myself from the discussion. And it was easy enough to keep myself busy after that. Every jar in the last canner batch had properly sealed, but we had more fruit yet to cut, so I began again. Somewhere Marigold had recorded just how many pint and quart jars I'd taken to the basement filled with fruit, but I'd lost track, happy in the abundance. We'd even gladly shared fruit with other neighbors, and the minister of Aunt Marigold's church, in addition to the Kurchers, yet still had plenty more.

I wondered briefly how I'd manage church on Sunday. I hadn't been to a regular service since before my son's funeral, and I wasn't sure I could sit through it without anger or tears. Perhaps I could convince her that I didn't feel well enough to go. But how long could I continue to be dishonest? By now Marigold surely thought me to be quite strong in the faith. Primarily because of the words of my daughter, which I never refuted. What would she think of me if I dared tell her of my struggle?

Josiah came home surly and peevish. He wouldn't even talk to Marigold when she asked him what was wrong. I couldn't help thinking that surely it must be me that was troubling him. Here I was, eating Marigold's food, sitting across from him at the table, and not yet paying a single dime into the household, when he, as far as I could tell, was the one who supplied every bit of the groceries the yard did not produce, and probably considerably more besides. In the time I'd been here I'd seen nothing at all to indicate that Marigold had even a smattering of income other than what came from her one paying boarder.

"Maybe you need some thinking time before you sit down to supper," Marigold told him. "That'll give me time to get the rest of these canning jars out of the way. The rain is done. Could you take Mr. Abraham one of the pies, and while you're about, walk over to the post office and put Leah's letters in the box for her?"

I could imagine that such a request might not sit well with him, so I offered to mail the letters myself. I preferred it that way. But the words from me only served to raise Mr. Walsh's ire all the more.

"I'll take them. I won't make *you* set after it when Aunt Mari wishes otherwise."

He was so abrupt, and his tone so harsh, that I let him leave without another word. Eliza was quiet, wide-eyed.

"Don't worry," Marigold told her. "He's surely had a bad day with his work. Or some other difficult matters churning about in his mind. It happens now and again. Don't let it bother you."

We had the table cheerily ready before Josiah returned. Still I was uneasy and quite sure, despite Marigold's words, that his ill temper was somehow because of me.

"Should Eliza and I eat before he gets back?" I asked timidly. "Or, take our meal to our room so he can eat with you alone? I'll bring the dishes—"

"Nonsense," she interrupted me. "He doesn't bite, and you've as much right to be at my table as he has."

"But—"

"If everyone ate alone every time anyone was out of sorts, families would scarcely know each other," she maintained. "The world would have no use for tables any bigger than a nightstand."

Eliza smiled, just a little. "That would be funny. We could line them all up, or put them in a really big circle on the days when nobody was out of sorts."

"Far better to be civil and hospitable, whether we feel like it or not."

Her words, though seeming to be about her nephew, put doubt within my heart about her own feelings toward us. Of course she would be genial and welcoming, because she believed that was the right thing to do. It didn't mean she really wanted us here after all.

Dinner that night was a trial for me, though the potato soup was the best I'd ever eaten and the corn muffins were so much like my mother's that they'd have been a treat in any other circumstance.

We didn't belong, regardless of how much we might like to. Marigold had her heart set on winning the heart and soul of her neighbor. Though we'd helped her with her harvest, she wouldn't continue to need our help, and then we'd just be in the way. And Mr. Walsh had scarcely any patience left for us at all. I had to consider. Where could we go from here?

That night the difficult dreams returned. But instead of calling out for my mother as I'd done so many times before, I found myself crying for my father as the belching, bellowing metal monster bore down in my direction. Father turned away. I could barely see him through the smoke and the haze. He seemed frantic, distressed, desperately searching for something alongside the endless tracks. But he was not searching for me.

The locomotive rushed on, rushed over me, and I could not breathe. Finally, in the midst of the screams and the blood, my mother was there, clutching me to her breast and crying.

Oh, why? Why did I have such dreams? This one was not quite the same, but they all were so similar, filled with the terror of that devil train. I clutched the blanket to my breast after being shaken awake like so many times before in the middle of the night.

At least I hadn't waked screaming again, or fallen from the bed with a thud loud enough to be heard by Mr. Walsh no more than a room away. When I was a wee child, my screams had wakened both my parents, night after night. Mother would kiss me and hold me in her arms until the tears faded. Father would holler from his bedroom that I wasn't hurt and shouldn't be "coddled" at the expense of everyone else's sleep.

Mother had prayed for the dreams to go away. I remembered that now and wondered why she'd never gotten upset that the prayers were not answered. The dreams still shook me. Not as often. Sometimes they were weeks apart. Months, when I'd been with John. But they always returned, like a plague that had attached itself to my spirit and would not let go.

We used to live beside a train track, that much I knew. But the wail of the monster at night had been far too much for me to bear. Father moved us to the farm he still occupied, five miles from the nearest rail crossing. But the dreams did not cease, and he lost patience with them, sometimes disappearing outside and slamming the door behind him when I cried out at night.

Eliza rolled beside me, her dark curls flopped haphazardly across her face and pillow. Thank God I hadn't wakened her. Thank God she wasn't plagued by dreams like mine.

I took a deep breath, realizing that those almost-prayers had risen from me without a moment's thought, automatically, as though spirit-breathed. Many times in the last few months, I'd squelched my own inklings in that direction, or ridiculed myself because of them. But I realized now that I really couldn't change who I was, and some part of me, despite everything, still believed in God's sovereign hand.

God was real. To Marigold and Mr. Abraham. Definitely to my dear faithful daughter and in some measure to my own heart. I couldn't truly deny him. But I had yet to reconcile my feelings. Though it would be fruitless to pretend someone did not exist, that didn't mean you could pretend you weren't angry with them. I still felt betrayed, forsaken, and I didn't know how that could ever change.

I hadn't ventured to my knees in such a long while, and I came close to stumbling from the bed and making some attempt that night. It might have been a new beginning for me. But before I could completely coax myself, my eyes filled with tears and my head stopped my heart.

I couldn't pray. I didn't know how anymore. With my misgivings and hard feelings, any attempt I made would be pitiful and futile anyhow. What was the use?

I felt drained, utterly spent the way it used to be when I finally caught my breath after a long cry. Why did I dream such things? Why did I have such turmoil in my heart? Why could I not just sleep and forget all the questions, all the pain?

Eliza rolled against me, her cheeks oddly damp as though she'd been silently crying. For a moment I thought she might have awakened, but my dear daughter slept on, touched by the sadness of some nameless dream.

"Why, God?" I suddenly found myself pleading. "Please, please give her peace."

11

Josiah

Dawn light woke me to the new day, but it didn't take long for thoughts of yesterday's funeral to cloud my mind. I wouldn't have gone except that my boss had said some of us should, and he'd chosen me to go with him. It should have been easy just to sit in the back of a room full of strangers and wait out the time until it was done. But my mind had refused to stay so separate.

Even now I thought of the nearly grown children of the couple that had died in Tuesday's train wreck. What would they be doing this morning? How long would it be before anything began to feel real or ordinary again?

It didn't help me to be thinking such things. But maybe if I took the time to pray for that family again, there could be at least that much good in it.

Seeing the grieving mourners had taken my mind back to rushing and straining to pull that woman from the mud, only to find her already gone. It was too much like the horrible day when I'd lifted Rosemary from the ditch after our awful accident.

Mr. Abraham's rooster jarred me with its belated crowing,

and I shoved away Aunt Mari's bedspread and pulled myself up. As much as I'd like to lie in bed all day, I'd have to present myself downstairs before long or Mari would send Leah Breckenridge my way, thinking I might be late for work. I hadn't told them I wouldn't be working today. I usually knew several days in advance when I would be free on a Saturday, but this time Mr. Behrens had simply said to stay home, take some time. Of course it was because of the way the funeral had affected me. I wished he had decided to attend alone.

I would rather have worked, to take me away from here until evening. I tried to think of errands, but there weren't any. I wouldn't be able to just close myself in my room or aimlessly wander about town when there were chores Aunt Mari needed done. But how would I find solitude with Leah and her daughter around? I didn't want them to witness the struggle I was having. That would make everything worse because it wasn't just the train wreck this week that was giving me trouble, hard as that had been. John's family was a large share of the problem. Their loss kept staring me in the face, reminding me of everything I wanted to bury away inside me.

It didn't help matters that Mari expected me to be able to minister to Leah in her loss. She hadn't told me in exactly those words, but I knew what she meant when she first shared her intention to invite them: "You can understand better than other people what they're going through. They'll need that sort of friend."

It was too much for me. Because I *didn't* understand. I tried. But I couldn't understand why tragedies happen, why we can never know from one day to the next whether our loved ones will remain healthy, safe, and whole. I'd prayed when I was a youngster for God to give me a complete family. Yet here I was alone in this world, except for Mari.

A lot of things about God I just didn't understand. I couldn't doubt his power, considering the world and everything he'd made. And I didn't doubt his love after being saved in Aunt Mari's living room and realizing the forgiveness he'd sent his

Son to gain for me. It was his reasoning that had me puzzled sometimes. The choices God made. Like accepting me, with no particular reason to. But also giving life within Rosemary's womb and then allowing that life to be cut short before it ever had a chance to blossom.

I pulled on trousers and sat back down on the edge of the bed. In some ways, the loss of our child had been harder on my mind than the loss of Rosemary. At least Rosemary had lived long enough to bless me and others with a little of her sunshine. But that baby—what could be the purpose of a few short months in the womb, never even being held by its mother? At least John and Leah's baby had lived long enough to be rocked and cuddled and to offer a loving look or contented smile in return.

Lord, you know Mari wants me to be a comfort to John's wife. But she'll be sadly disappointed. I'd make a miserable comforter. I don't know how to begin.

I took a deep breath, wondering if Leah Breckenridge had the same sort of questions I did. I hadn't been praying for her. I hadn't thought I could manage it. But I should at least try.

Give her peace. Help her realize your love for her, just as you showed me. Help her to know that you are good, even when we don't understand.

With my head in my hands, I thought of the John I'd known, so sprightly and full of life. I'd only seen him briefly once or twice since the summer we turned eleven together and got in enough trouble to remember for a lifetime. It was difficult to imagine such a boisterous boy grown up, let alone dead and gone already. If Leah had trouble accepting that, it was no wonder. With a sigh, I tried to continue my prayer, but my thoughts seemed muddled now, my mind almost numb. It was suddenly hard to string one word after another, but I did the best I could.

Lord, I know there's tribulation in this fallen world. I know there's an enemy who wants to destroy our lives and our faith if he can. I don't understand why you seem to let him have his way sometimes. But I know you're not at fault for all the wrong that happens. You're the one who's been reaching out with answers since time began. Help Leah understand that somehow. Help her to know your comfort and love.

For some reason the prayer exhausted me, and I felt like climbing right back into bed. But I heard a distant *clank* and knew that Aunt Mari was up already, just like always, working in the kitchen despite the arthritic pain that now accompanied almost every movement she made. *Bless her too,* I added briefly. *Bless her deeply. You know where I'd probably be without Mari. Thank you so much for her.*

I pulled on a shirt that had hung from a hook on the wall. Maybe it would be nice to have a day to work at home. Mari's home. It was still strange how deeply my heart had accepted her love and God's love along with the shelter here. So of course it wasn't right that I should resent her opening her home to John's family in the same way.

But it did lead to questions: What was this place anyway? A boardinghouse? Or a halfway house for the disconsolate? Mari would never turn a profit by giving space to the struggling, as she so often did. But she didn't care about the money anyway. She'd make do and trust the Lord, content with the ministry he'd given her. She'd probably never stop opening her doors to the needy, even if she succeeded in wooing and winning Saul Abraham to Christ and gaining him for a husband. She'd just add him in to the work at hand, which in many ways she already had.

Through the wall I heard little Eliza stirring, whispering to her mother, and then apparently jumping rather emphatically out of the bed. I wondered that I hadn't heard even the slightest noise sooner. Usually I heard small sounds first thing in the morning. Leah's delicate movements, I'd decided, as she started her morning being careful not to disturb anyone else.

Before I knew it, Leah and Eliza were on the stairs together, their quiet footsteps barely out of rhythm with each other. This was the first morning I hadn't gone down ahead of them.

Aunt Mari would be wondering about me by now. I crossed the room for a pair of socks, but my mind was suddenly stuck on Leah.

I'd wondered that first night what sort of a time we'd have with her. She'd seemed snobbish and curt. After that immediate impression, I'd expected a whining, aristocratic sort who only wanted to be waited on while she sniveled over her misfortunes. But instead, she'd proven herself a hard worker. She'd helped Aunt Mari accomplish things that we'd thought might not get done at all, and Mari loved her for it.

We might be in for more than a visit. Mari was liable to invite Leah to stay just as long as she liked, even after she got "on her feet" again. And that would mean Mari's expectations of me in the situation would not go away. Instead, they'd only increase. And I wasn't sure I could handle that.

I pulled on the socks and finished buttoning my shirt. Aunt Mari might be putting breakfast on the table by now. I didn't take the time to lace my work boots but carried them down with me instead. I could lace them in the kitchen and at the same time appear to be at least somewhat sociable.

Suddenly I thought of a job I could do that would leave me entirely to myself. There was a hole under one side of the attic roof just big enough for a squirrel to squeeze through. I'd have to seal it before winter, or regret not doing it, almost certainly. And that meant time at the top of Mr. Abraham's ladder, two stories above Leah Breckenridge and her troubles. It made me feel better just to have that in mind as I went down.

12

Josiah

"Sleep well?" Aunt Mari asked me as I got to the kitchen and sat down to put my boots on.

I nodded, very aware that little Eliza was watching me while her mother, across the room, was very careful not to.

"Train leave at the regular time today?" Mari continued.

"Far as I know. But I won't be on it. Mr. Behrens told me I needn't work today."

Aunt Mari flipped a pancake and turned and looked in my direction. "Is everything all right?"

"Yeah. Fine."

She could read me like a book. I knew she could. So of course she knew I was lying, or at least covering the truth as much as I was able. But she didn't say anything. And before she could ask me for help with a job that would have me in the middle of things with her and Leah, I spoke up quickly with my own plans for the day.

"Looks like good weather. I'd better take the long ladder and fix that squirrel hole under the attic overhang. We don't want nestlings running around up there all winter wreaking havoc."

"Indeed we don't," Mari readily agreed. "Thank you for thinking of that. I completely forgot."

"Will you see squirrels in the squirrel hole?" Eliza suddenly asked.

"Possible, I guess. But not likely. If there're any about, they'll probably hear me coming and be long gone."

"They won't go far," Leah added. "They're still enjoying the apples and pears I couldn't reach."

She'd been avoiding words in my presence, so for her to speak so conversationally was startling. Especially since I'd been so abrupt with everyone last night. I'd thought she might be even more cautious now.

She was gathering dishes to set the table. I watched her a moment, content that she was turned just enough not to notice my gaze. What in the world made her tick? Was she an aristocratic snob or not? A cheerful laborer? A saint?

Whatever she might have inside her, she was certainly a closed book to me. Even her words this morning seemed to be designed to offer just a moment's friendliness, her contribution to a smooth-flowing superficial day, rather than revealing anything consequential about herself or her thoughts. But maybe she was finally trying to break the ice and be congenial. As Mari had once told me, just because I so often hid myself behind an outward face didn't mean everyone else did the same.

We barely talked at breakfast. Eliza quietly watched me pack away six of Aunt Mari's pancakes before she ventured a word.

"Jeepers."

"What is it, dear?" Leah asked.

"Mr. Josiah eats a lot."

Leah's face reddened just a little at her daughter's bold comment, but Aunt Mari spoke before she had the chance.

"Working men need to eat aplenty to keep their strength up."

"Oh."

Eliza watched me down my coffee and two more pancakes. Then I thought I'd better quit before she thought me a glutton.

I rose from the table and set my chair back in its place. "Think I'll go drag out the ladder and get started."

"Josiah," Aunt Mari said in a soothing sort of voice. "You haven't read this morning. Would you mind doing that while we're all here handy?"

Eliza was looking at me with such expectation and once again Leah wasn't looking at me at all. I should have agreed. There was no real reason not to. But for some reason, I couldn't manage it this morning. Not yet.

"I'll be here all day. Can I read to you later? I feel like I need to push myself right into the job first thing."

"All right," Mari told me. "But mind you, I won't forget, even if you do."

"Okay."

I walked off, glad to leave them in the kitchen and get myself up under the eaves where they were sure not to follow. I couldn't cope today with that little girl's bright eyes and quiet curiosity. Nor her mother's cool civility. So I dragged Mr. Abraham's tallest ladder from our shed and set it up against the east side of the house. Maybe I would encounter squirrels, despite what I'd told little Eliza. I could see what looked like shredded leaves and weed stalks poking out from under the eaves. Something had been preparing a nest.

I was halfway up the ladder with a stick in my hand when a voice suddenly called behind me.

"Is that really a squirrel hole?"

Eliza. Down at the base of the ladder.

"Sure looks that way."

"How does a squirrel get to it?"

I took a deep breath. "You've seen squirrels hop from one tree to the next, haven't you?"

"Yep. That looks scary."

"Not for squirrels. God made them that way. They hop from tree to tree, and from a branch to the roof of the house. Then they just have to walk over and chew a spot till they get a hole big enough to crawl through."

"Is there a squirrel in the hole right now?"

"Hope not. I wouldn't enjoy having to pull him out."

Maybe with her questions answered, she'd run back in and join her mother and Mari at whatever they were doing. But the questions weren't finished.

"Why can't the squirrel stay in our house if he made himself a spot? Will it hurt the house?"

I stuck the stick into the hole and started raking out the debris. Fortunately there was no sign of an occupant. "If we let squirrels do as they please, they'd make an awful mess and damage more of the wood chewing more holes. Rain can come in the holes and do a lot of water damage to the walls inside."

"Oh."

Why did this girl linger? Me cleaning out a hole could not possibly be fascinating viewing. And I wanted to be alone with my thoughts. I wasn't the grouch I'd been last night, but I wasn't ready to be completely civil yet either.

"If they can hurt people's houses," Eliza asked on, "why did God make them able to get inside like that?"

I let go of the ladder for a moment and scratched my head. "Does your mother know you're out here?"

"Yes. She said I could follow you if I don't get in the way. So did Aunt Marigold. And Aunt Marigold even said I might learn something."

That figured. Leave it to Mari to be an instigator and make me uncomfortable. All for a good cause, of course.

"So how come God made squirrels like that?" she persisted.

I was some kind of expert now? Unbelievable. But I couldn't just refuse to answer. "God made them to have homes in trees. That's what they're supposed to do. But sometimes they get out of order, like some other critters, and invade our space. They aren't supposed to. They just do, and we try to drive them out."

"If God don't like it, then why do they do it?"

I glanced down at her. This was more than a little odd, to be having a discussion bordering on the theological with someone so small. "I can't say that critters know God didn't make them to get in people's houses," I answered with a sigh. "They're just looking for the easiest possible way to get shelter and food. That's really all they want. Easy survival."

"Isn't it easy for squirrels to make homes in trees?" she persisted.

"I don't know why it wouldn't be," I told her offhandedly, at the same time yanking down a big chunk of nesting material. "It looks like all they have to do is cram a bunch of leaves into a fork or knothole in the branches."

"So why do they like people's houses?"

"Maybe storm protection."

"Did you ever *make* a squirrel house?" she asked on. "Like people make birdhouses?"

"No. Never even thought of such a thing."

"Maybe they'd like it. Maybe they'd not make holes in people's houses anymore."

"This is the most I've heard you talk since you've been here," I told her.

She smiled. "It's the most I've heard you talk too."

"Yeah."

She watched me in silence but only for a moment or two. I had the hole cleaned out as well as I could, still with no sign of an inhabitant. Now I'd have to fetch a board and nails to cover it over.

She looked around the yard as I was climbing down. "Is all that stuff you pulled out a squirrel's bed?"

"Probably."

"Will the squirrel get mad?"

"Won't be able to do much about it if he does. I'm going to board up the hole."

I moved past her and she followed me to the shed.

"Is there more squirrel holes in this house?"

"I guess I should check. This is the only one I've noticed." I selected a piece of scrap board from a heap in the shed's corner. It was a little long, but it would do. I grabbed the hammer from its hook and handed her the can of nails from a shelf. "Fish out four about an inch and a half long." I figured that if I had to put up with her sticking around, I might as well give her a job to do.

She shook the nail can and then felt around in it for a while. I wondered if I should have asked her. She was pretty little, and a girl besides. "Do you know how long I mean?"

"Yep. Mommy showed me once how big a inch is."

"How old are you?" If Aunt Mari had told me once, I couldn't remember now.

"Six," she said, barely looking up.

"Isn't that old enough for school before long?"

"Yep. Mommy says I have to go on Monday."

Monday? I hadn't expected that answer, though there was no reason for it to be a surprise. Of course she'd have to be enrolled in school. It was just that for her to be enrolled *here* gave Leah incentive to stay. And I'd never felt as positive about that as Aunt Mari had.

I'd been under the impression that Leah had nowhere else to go, and if that were true then I couldn't fault her being here. But then I remembered the letters I'd delivered for her last night. Obviously, she had loved ones elsewhere. People important enough to her that she'd felt the need to write when she'd been here less than a week. Other than Rosemary and perhaps Marigold, I'd never had such a relationship, and it made me a little hot inside. She wasn't truly destitute. So why was she here?

"I wish I didn't have to go to school so soon." Eliza kept right on talking. "I'd rather be here and bake some more with Aunt Marigold. We've made pie and cimmanum tarts and all kinds of stuff."

"I know," I muttered.

"Did you like them all?"

"Yes. I guess I did."

She smiled, a happy, generous smile showing one missing front tooth. "I found a good nail for you. Maybe two. I'll find some more."

"That's a good start." I walked back in the direction of the ladder and she followed me again, bringing the nail can with her.

When I'd first moved to Marigold's boardinghouse, the son of her sister Petunia had stopped to tell me that if I'd come to get anything from his aunt except a room at a fair price, then I'd have to answer to the whole family. Now I wondered if Petunia and the others knew that Leah was here. Would they distrust her too? Maybe not, because she was John's widow. But what kind of person was she? Would it matter to her what Marigold had said back then, that there was no use anyone squabbling over her material things because it was all promised to her church when she was gone?

Leah didn't seem like someone who would strive to get into someone's good graces for the hope of material gain, but she had endeared herself rather quickly. Made herself indispensable, more like. What was I to think? She didn't carry herself like the frail, distraught, helpless creature that Aunt Mari had initially described. On the contrary, she seemed quite capable. So much that I wasn't sure why she'd needed to come.

Now here was her daughter, with bright eyes and childish innocence, searching through the nail can again. What was I to do?

"Here you go," she said cheerily, handing me three nails to get started with. "I'm trying to find another one the same size."

"Let me." I set down the board and hammer and dumped the little can into my open hand. In moments I found what I was looking for, fished it out, and then plunked all the rest back in the can again.

"Jeepers," Eliza exclaimed. "You have really big hands."

"Compared to yours, I guess." How could I get her to leave me alone? "Thanks," I muttered to her. "You've been good help. But maybe your mother has something for you to do in the kitchen now."

"She said it was fine for me to be outside on a nice day. She's coming outside in a while too, to work in the garden."

What could Leah hope to accomplish in that sadly neglected corner of the yard? "You ought to go help her," I said, hoping to sound dismissive. "You could learn something there too, and it's your mother you ought to be learning from, not some odd fella up a ladder."

"But I *like* watching you. I never seen nobody fix a squirrel hole before."

Somehow I couldn't argue with her and ended up mumbling under my breath. "Exciting, I guess. In a town this small."

I went back up the ladder with the nails in my mouth and the board and hammer in hand. "Can I come up and hold stuff for you?" she suddenly asked.

I grabbed the nails. "Absolutely not! Wouldn't want your mother to come outside and find you two stories off the ground."

"I could go ask if it's okay."

"No," I said quickly. "Forget it. She might get the idea that the notion came from my head."

I pounded in the first nail.

"Aunt Marigold says you'll be friendlier when you've knowed us longer."

"Really?" I looked down at the girl. "She told you that? I guess she thinks I'm being unfriendly."

"I don't think you're unfriendly," she assured me. "Just busy on the inside same as on the outside."

"Where'd you hear that sort of thing?"

"From my daddy, I think. He said when grown-ups get that way, they don't have time for the things kids want to do. Then they need prayers, for God to hush them up and give them rest."

I smiled. "Your father was a wise man."

"I know. He's a angel now, helping my baby brother grow up in heaven."

Her words expressed an absolute certainty, without a shred of doubt tainting her assertion. Faith like a child indeed. This girl could probably picture the two of them together, doing all the normal father and son things, just like earthly life, only so very much better.

I also believed that my family was in heaven. I could imagine Rosemary with her beloved grandmother, both of them joyful and satisfied. But I still wondered whether our unborn child, such a tiny person, could ever really have the sense of purpose, the feeling of fulfillment, of someone who had lived to grow up and experience life.

I pounded in the second nail, remembering some of the verses of the psalm I'd read earlier in the week:

"Thou hast covered me from my mother's womb . . . Thine eyes did see my substance, yet being unperfect; and in thy book all my members were written, which in continuance were fashioned, when yet there was none of them. How precious are thy thoughts unto me, O God."

The words had not sunk into me as I'd read them that morning. Were they really saying that God had each of us in his mind and heart before we were born? My eyes misted wondering the sort of precious thoughts God had held for my dear little unborn son or daughter.

I dropped a nail and nearly lost the other one sputtering a frustrated complaint at myself. Incredibly quickly, Eliza found the nail in the grass for me and called with real excitement. "Can I bring it up to you?"

"No! Stay there!" I nailed the third corner and then started down the ladder to retrieve the last nail. Eliza was looking at me far too seriously, and I was glad she didn't ask for my thoughts the way Marigold sometimes did.

Just in time, I heard the back door. That would surely be Leah coming out. Good. It gave me the perfect excuse to send this child away. "Go see if your mother needs help," I commanded. "Hurry, so she doesn't have to come looking for you."

She still didn't want to go. I could see that plainly. But she obeyed. Glad to be alone, I returned to the top of the ladder, very quickly absorbed again.

You're a fool to get emotional in front of a six-year-old, I thought to myself. *She's liable to tell her mother, who'll think I'm an imbecile.*

But then I scolded myself further for caring a hoot what Leah Breckenridge thought anyway. She'd been maddening since her first night here, when she'd refused to give me even the courtesy of an introduction. I'd only been trying to help, and she'd treated me as though I were a supreme nuisance.

I pounded the last nail and gave the board a tug, satisfied that it wouldn't budge for the most hardheaded squirrel. But then I noticed that a trim board along an upper-story window had pulled loose an inch or two. Might as well fix that while I was out here. I only had to move the ladder a foot or so to the left, and it didn't take long to have the piece hammered back into place. But then I wondered if rain might be able to seep around those window cracks where it had come loose. Maybe I ought to have some sort of sealing putty to smear around it just in case.

I didn't want to ask Aunt Marigold what she thought because she would tell me to do whatever I thought best. That was her usual response to most of the repair efforts around here, and maybe that was the best she could do. Mr. Abraham, on the other hand, was very knowledgeable about all sorts of home repair. He'd know the kind of putty I needed and where to get it. So I left the ladder and walked over to his yard, hoping he'd already be outside.

He wasn't, and I realized that I'd completely forgotten Marigold sending me over to his house with a pie last night. His father was visiting, an incredibly old man. Hopefully, it would not be a terrible time to disturb them. Hesitantly, I knocked at the back door.

"Ah, Josiah," Mr. Abraham greeted me quickly. "Good morning. What can I do for you?"

I apologized for disturbing him, explained the problem with the window, and asked for his advice. "Does Schuller's Hardware have what I need? I wasn't completely sure what to ask for."

"They'd have it, but no need going across town," he said. "I've told you before. My tools are yours, any time you need them. I've got what you need for decent window putty right here. The box of whiting powder is in the drawer of my worktable. Mix some of that with a squirt of linseed oil from the can on the top shelf to the left. All you need is a stiff paste. But not too stiff, so it doesn't dry before you're finished working with it."

"But you don't have to supply—"

"I've got the stuff. Why not?"

"Can I pay for your ingredients then?"

"Oh no." He smiled. "Ask your aunt to make me another pie someday. What a blessing. That's all I want right now."

He was the blessing. Most definitely. Mr. Abraham had been the best neighbor a person could ever ask for. It made me glad to know that even when I was away at work, he was here if Aunt Marigold needed anything. She had a big old farm bell she could ring in case of emergency. I'd made her test it and we could easily hear it at Mr. Abraham's house even with the doors and windows closed. But even without the bell, I knew he would check on her.

Sometimes I wondered why he was so kind. But when it came right down to it, there was really no mystery at all. Saul Abraham loved Marigold McSweeney, it was as simple as that, and was always willing to help when it came to Mari or her property. I wasn't sure how long he'd loved her, but it was plain that he did. I could tell it in the way he looked at her and spoke of her.

I wasn't sure if either of them had done much thinking about their feelings for each other. And I'd wondered if they'd ever be open enough about their feelings to marry each other. It would make the newspaper in this town if it ever happened. And it'd be time for me to move on.

I went to Mr. Abraham's shed, found the whiting powder and linseed oil, and mixed them like he told me in an old tin can. Then I walked back to the ladder in Mari's yard, still considering the notion of her marrying again, so long after losing her husband who'd brought her here. I'd never seen a gray-haired bride, but it was a dandy thought in some ways. I liked the sparkle in her eye when she spoke of her neighbor. I liked the idea that love could be found in the later years, and that, whether they ever married or not, friendship meant the widowed didn't have to grow old alone.

Leah and Eliza were in the garden. I couldn't tell what they were doing and told myself that I didn't care. With the can of putty and the mixing stick, I was back up the ladder in a jiffy, smearing the whitish gunk into the biggest cracks around the window.

The sun was growing warm on my back as though it had forgotten that fall was supposed to bring chillier days. From my vantage point on the ladder I could still see Leah with her back bent in the weeds. Her chestnut locks waved slightly in the wind, just like Rosemary's had on the cool spring day when she'd planted the garden that was supposed to be our "winter larder." Eliza bent beside her, plucking something off the ground. Her hair nearly matched her mother's, and I breathed a little heavier. With their faces hidden from me I could almost imagine it to be Rosemary there with a perky child just as she'd always planned. She would raise gardeners, she'd told me more than once, to work at her side and grow far more than their share of flowers, fresh fruits, and vegetables. Enough to bless the world.

I dropped the putty stick and decided I'd put enough into these cracks anyway. Maybe there were other windows that would need putty before winter. I should check them all, since this was an old house and it'd probably been years since anyone had thought about this sort of thing.

On my way down the ladder, my eyes wandered toward the garden again. Leah was pulling weeds in one corner as if she had hope that there might still be something growing there. A quick burst of breeze tugged at her skirt, and she caught it with one hand and kept right on working. Then Eliza was on all fours; something tiny on the ground must have suddenly caught her attention. And I noticed that I'd simply stopped, halfway down, purposeless, watching them.

What a numskull I was becoming. I'd get far more done if I could just keep my mind on the task at hand. It made no sense for me to be reminded of Rosemary. Leah was nothing like her. Her hair was longer, and darker. She might be a little smaller. She was certainly more abrupt and far less amiable. There were women and little girls all over this world. I might encounter them anywhere. There was no reason for these two to arrest my attention on a fine work day like this.

But they had my attention, like it or not. I couldn't seem to shake them from my mind. Leah, aloof and untrusting, yet a capable worker indoors and out. And little Eliza with her shining, inquisitive eyes and nightly incessant humming. Maybe there was a reason Leah hadn't found work and stayed in St. Louis. Maybe circumstances prevented her being able to stay with the loved ones she wrote letters to. But even if she'd had a hundred job offers and a thousand other places to stay, them being here was still just between Leah and Marigold. It was really none of my business.

It was time for me to move on soon. Maybe already past due. My lingering here wasn't so much about Aunt Mari needing me, though it was easy to tell myself that. It was really more about not trusting myself to start over somewhere else.

But I didn't belong here with a child in the house. She might get used to me. She might decide she liked me. And I would look in her eyes and wish to God she was mine, that my own baby had lived, that I had some family to my name.

Father, why did you bring them here? I know Mari wanted them to come, but do you have to listen to her so well? It's better for me to be alone, puttering about fixing on an old woman's place. It's easier to think only of her and the Kurchers and her other old friends, and feel like I'm accomplishing at least a little piece of good in this world. But Leah being here—she makes me think of my lack too much.

I could feel the tension rise in me just seeing the mother and daughter talking to one another in the weedy garden. And then Leah turned her head and caught me looking at her. I turned away quickly, moving the ladder to reach the next set of windows and acting as though my glance had been nothing more than incidental.

Father, help me. It's just too hard. Her loss. And mine. We've too much in common. Whether she even knows that, I never want to discuss it. I don't want to talk to her at all because my mind won't be able to push it all aside. And yet how can I be here and not talk to them? Aunt Mari will think I've become an even worse lout than I ever was before.

Suddenly I had a nearly overwhelming desire to drop the putty can, leave the ladder where it leaned, and hurry downtown to see if Miller's Eatery was open. The place had been a tavern before the prohibition, and I knew Jake Miller had found ways to keep it stocked for those willing to pay under the table. A couple of drinks—that would drive Leah and her daughter from my mind, and though liquor had never been able to banish Rosemary from my thinking, at least it had seemed to temporarily dull the pain along with any other sensation the day might bring.

I didn't have to work today. I wouldn't have to work tomorrow. And it wasn't even ten in the morning. This would be the perfect time to get slammed-down drunk and stay that way for nearly two days. If I hadn't changed. If I hadn't promised the Lord, and Mari, and Rosemary's memory, that I wouldn't do that anymore.

I picked up the putty stick from the grass and threw it against the house. It had been months, seven to be exact, since I'd had a drink or wanted one. What was wrong with me now?

Taking the putty and a fresh stick with me, I went to the next set of windows and checked them for any loose cracks around the molding. These were in pretty good shape so I moved to the next ones. Two of the windows outside the master bedroom were in need of a little putty, as well as the one that looked out from my bed to the side yard. No wonder I'd been able to hear it rattle in a stiff wind at night.

I kept my hands busy and my eyes to the house so they'd wander neither to the garden nor out across town looking for traffic in front of Miller's. *Help me, Father. Something's wrong with me or I would not be so weak!*

"Did you find more squirrel holes?"

The tender voice broke into my desperate prayer, and I didn't have to look down to know that little Eliza stood at the base of my ladder again, ready with more questions.

"No," I said simply, hoping that was all she'd bother me with.

"What're ya doin' then?" she persisted.

"Fillin' cracks." I knew my voice was cold, hard. So I cut short my answer, hoping she'd go away before I upset her.

"What is that stuff?"

"Sealing putty."

"Does it seal the glass in?"

"Yes." I gritted my teeth and plunked the stick into the can.

"And the squirrels out?"

"Squirrels don't come through windows. Even loose ones."

I climbed down the ladder, turned my back on her, and started back to Mr. Abraham's shed. I could hear her following, but I had no patience for it. "Stay with your mother."

"Are you busy thinking?" she asked.

That sounded like a thought her mother or Mari might have planted in her head, and I didn't want to give it credence. "Just busy. Stay with your mother."

Silence behind me. Finally. And though I'd been rude, I was glad she was leaving me alone. I was ready for a break. Maybe it wouldn't hurt to walk downtown. For one drink. Just a soda pop, of course. Nothing alcoholic. Just a change of scene, a short walk . . .

I knew the reasoning. I well recognized the convoluted logic being laid down in my brain. I'd told myself the very same thing so many times before. *I'll just take a walk. Go pick up a soda pop.* And then of course, my intentions got all twisted and I'd end up stumbling home drunk.

I was closer to falling away from a sound path than I'd been in seven months, and I didn't even know why. At least I could recognize myself being on the verge. But would it be so bad? If Josiah Walsh, professing Christian and Marigold McSweeney's special project, were to go and get a stiff drink just one more time?

13

Josiah

In Mr. Abraham's shed, I leaned against the wall, glad for the shadowy dimness behind the door. *Lord, what is wrong with me? I can't do this.*

I closed a lid on the putty can and just stood for a moment, trying to put my head together. Why was I so off track? What was the problem? Why would I want to run and hide myself in the darkness that had buried and almost killed me before?

Was it Leah? John's wife in front of me every day, reminding me that life was unfair? Truly I didn't need a reminder. Dreams of Rosemary and the life we could have had were not faded and probably never would be.

But putting the two together was just too much to face. Mari's boarders had all been strangers before, and I liked it that way. Other men, either drifters or struggling gents trying to find a way to settle down, and either way they were no problem to me. Easy to work with or ignore completely as it suited me, and it hadn't seemed to make any difference.

But this situation was different. And very dear to Mari's heart. I needed to leave here and not stand in her way.

Eliza was with her mother in the garden again as I strode

across the yard on my way back to the house. They were probably looking at me. I got that kind of feeling but wouldn't turn my head to find out for sure. Mari was in the kitchen working on pies again, the room already smelling like a little slice of the heaven I'd known here so often.

"I need to read now," I told her, heading for the Bible on the shelf behind the table.

Marigold barely lifted her eyes. "Oh, well, that's fine, dear. Why don't you call Leah and 'Liza Rose so they can listen in?"

"No. Just us this time, Mari. I don't want them here."

She looked long at me, and I plopped in one chair with my back to the wall and stuck my feet up on another.

"What's wrong?"

I ignored the question, spreading the Bible open in front of me. "Where were we? Psalm 142?"

She dropped what she was doing, wiped her hands, and limped to the table. "Josiah Mark. Tell me what it is troubling you."

"I think we did leave off at 142," I talked on. "I cried unto the Lord with my voice; with my voice unto the Lord did I make my supplication . . ."

"Josiah, if there's a greater need for talk—"

"I poured out my complaint before him; I shewed before him my trouble . . ."

The words seemed to swim on the page in front of me and inside of me. Why did they have to speak to the sort of thing I was feeling?

"Josiah—"

"When my spirit was overwhelmed . . ."

I had to stop, and just stared down at the page.

"What's wrong?" Mari sat beside me and reached her hand to my arm.

I could barely get the words out. "I want a drink."

"You've been working outside," she said quietly. "I can get you some water or make a cold lemonade."

"That's not what I mean." I knew she already understood that, even as I said the words. And I knew she wouldn't condemn me, but I felt condemned anyway.

"It's the grieving this week," she said softly. "Seeing that awful wreck. Such a thing can't help but trouble your mind. But you can't get a drink around here anymore, can you?"

"Oh, Mari. I know right where to go if I wanted it badly enough."

"Did you drink? Last night?"

It plagued me considerably that she would think so. I was here, in front of her, confessing my temptation. If I'd already given in to it, there wouldn't be much point. "I turned Harvey down last night. That's easy enough. I don't want to drink in company. I just want a quiet corner and a bottle all to myself . . ."

"Have you been struggling with this for very long?"

"No! Today!" I knew my tone took her aback, and I tried to temper the fire I couldn't quite understand. "I can't do this. I can't be your godly assistant reaching out to save all the needy and fatherless! I don't mind taking food to the Kurchers. It makes me feel good inside, seeing 'em smile and knowing they'll eat a little better because I could carry your love and concern in their direction. It don't touch me any deeper than that. But right here. With John's wife—I come home and find her in the kitchen with you. I go to bed hearing that child humming late into the night. I wake up seeing them and I think of Rosemary. I don't know why it bothers me, but . . ."

She gave my hand a pat, and I stopped.

"Why did you come inside, Josiah?"

It took me a moment to answer. "I was afraid . . . that I'd head on over to Jake's and I wouldn't be able to stop myself. I thought maybe, if I came in and read . . ."

"The good Lord would help you?"

I nodded. "Or you would." I stared at the ceiling, hating the weakness in myself that had me leaning on an old woman. "Aunt Mari, I shouldn't be here."

"Why not?"

"You've done enough straightening me out. It's not right putting more on you. If Leah Breckenridge is needy like you said, then you oughta be able to concentrate on her."

"You don't think I've got room for both of you?"

"Yeah. Maybe. But you wanted my help and I can't give it."

"Who says you can't?"

"I do! This crazy hunger for a drink again says it! I remember running around the yard and up and down those stairs with John when I was a kid, and I can't help but think that you and Leah and her child are carrying an awful burden, an awful emptiness without him. But I'm no help. I just think of Rosemary and my own pitiful loss. I don't even want to see it, Mari, but it's in front of my face whether I like it or not. The world stinks! Sometimes God doesn't even seem fair, and I'm supposed to be strong and reasonable anyway. But I can't."

She sighed. "So what will you do?"

I couldn't answer for a minute, and my eyes were drawn back to the psalm in front of me. "Just complain, I guess."

"I cried unto Thee, Oh Lord . . . thou art my refuge and my portion in the land of the living . . ." The words on the page drew my soul and somehow quieted me. "I don't know what to do, Aunt Mari. I haven't thought of drinking for months. I don't want it anymore. But I know how weak I am. And I don't want to cause you trouble."

She suddenly leaned and hugged me. "You won't cause me trouble. And you're stronger than you think you are or you wouldn't be sitting here."

"I probably upset that little girl."

"How?"

"I was pretty short with her. Flat-out rude, I guess. But it's too hard, talking to her."

"Why?"

"I don't know. I guess 'cause she's a kid. Without a dad. And I'm—" I looked at Mari. She was waiting, and I turned my eyes to the floor. "I'm not a father. I just wanted to be."

"You don't think you could be good for each other?"

I shook my head, trying to picture what Aunt Mari could be alluding to. Some kind of substitute relationship. "It's not even healthy to think about. I'm not her father. And she's not . . . not mine. And there's Leah to think about, who has no reason to want anything to do with me."

Mari smiled. "She might like to hear sometime about you and John playing together."

"I can't imagine how that would help anything."

"And I think you should tell her about Rosemary."

I shut the Bible. "I know that wouldn't help matters."

"How do you know? Talking about her again would help *you*, Josiah."

I stood to my feet. "Thought this was about helping Leah and her 'Liza Rose."

"It is. I think it would be good for them to feel that we're making them a part of our lives."

"Well, I guess we have, sharing a house with them."

"Yes. But Leah's still apprehensive, I can tell. She's still not sure she can fit in here, or what to do with herself. And you know from experience, Josiah, how difficult it is to start over when the life you knew is taken away."

"So do you. Longer ago. Why don't you tell her about Uncle William?"

"Oh, I don't know. So many years have passed since then that it's scarcely real even to me anymore."

"I remember."

"Do you? When you were only five years old?"

"At least I remember that you had a husband when you first moved in. And then he was gone and you took in boarders. It was fun to meet the new people. As long as they were strangers. I never liked it when they stayed too long."

"Oh, Josiah."

"Now I think maybe I've stayed too long."

"Nonsense." She rose and glanced over at her half-rolled pie crust. "What sounds good for dinner today?"

"Anything. If I can eat it alone."

"Josiah Mark, you needn't keep such fears about you."

I drew a heavy breath. "What fears?"

"You know what I mean. To connect again—"

"I'm going for a walk."

Her eyes flashed concern.

"Don't worry. I'm not going after a bottle."

"I wasn't concerned about that, son. I trust you in the hands of the Lord."

I wasn't sure right then if *I* did, but I didn't want to tell her that. My problems with drink weren't the Lord's fault, after all. They were of my own doing, but he'd definitely helped me turn away. I felt I really could stay in the opposite direction of Miller's now. And I needed to pray.

"I'll have dinner in about an hour," she told me. "Maybe sooner."

"Need anything from the grocer?"

"No. Leah picked things up for me yesterday."

No surprise. Leah had become Mari's right hand. And feet. I smiled a little. Maybe it was fitting.

I went out the front door, mainly to avoid seeing Leah and Eliza again. The wind had picked up, and a few leaves blew across the porch floor in front of me. I could remember years ago sitting out here on a fall day like this one, feeling depressed because summer was over and John's mother had come to take him back home so he could start school again in Alton. And I'd be the whole school year without him. More, because he couldn't come the following summer.

But at least I'd still had his Aunt Mari. Her cookies. And her listening ear. Thank God I'd remembered her when the police officer told me as I sat in jail, "You're in a heap of trouble, son. Don't you have nobody to call?" If it weren't for her, I might be there still.

14

Leah

I'd expected to eat the noon meal with Josiah and was relieved that he didn't come back from wherever he'd gone. But Marigold was quieter than usual, and I wondered if they'd had words before he left. It made me a little angry that Josiah may have been short with his aunt just as he'd been with my daughter, but she didn't say anything about it. As I helped her clean up, she saved back the leftovers on a plate for Josiah. And then we started the afternoon's work with a will.

I could tell, by the time we'd mopped and scrubbed and were ready for a break for tea, that she was watchful, wondering, expecting Josiah back. But he didn't come and she didn't give me any inkling of where he might have gone. I wanted to ask, but it wasn't my place. I almost hoped that Eliza would ask, because at her age less restraint would be expected and then we'd get an answer to the question. But she didn't ask, and I knew it would be improper to prompt her.

By late afternoon, I'd almost decided that Josiah Walsh was a thoughtless cad even if he did pay for rent and groceries here. Marigold seemed terribly uncomfortable, and I figured it was somehow his fault. Nonetheless, she still wasn't talking about it, and I still couldn't bring myself to ask. With our housework done, Eliza started sorting another basket of apples for Marigold on the back porch, and I went back to the garden again where my thoughts strayed to the letters I'd sent. It was far too soon to expect that the letters had arrived, let alone been answered, but I still wondered about the sort of reaction I'd get. Especially from my father. Would he write back? Surely he'd never consider actually coming here.

I'd told Marigold I would fill a bowl of greens for supper, but there were not enough of the turnip tops to go halfway. My mother used to forage for the edible yard weeds in the spring before the garden came into its own or in the fall like this when she thought the winter might be fierce and she wanted to preserve as much food as she could. I was walking about Marigold's yard gathering what I could find of the wild greens to make enough for a mess, when Mr. Abraham stepped outside to carry something to his shed. When he saw me he waved and then motioned for me to come closer.

"Marigold is well?" he asked.

"Yes. I believe she's all right."

He looked into my bowl. "She would not like me asking this, but is there food enough for her table?"

I could see the honest concern in his eyes, and I knew I should reassure him quickly. "Oh yes. It's all right. I offered to gather greens. It's something I can do, and like to do this time of year. My mother used to say that the more of God's bounty is harvested the less is wasted, and he put it under our noses for a reason."

He smiled. "Your mother had a great deal of wisdom. You may harvest all you like in my yard too if you see anything you can use."

"Thank you. That's very kind of you."

He nodded. "Marigold might think I set you to pickin' weeds so I wouldn't have to trim them."

"She might joke, but of course she'll understand."

His smile broadened a bit. "Greet her for me. Tell her my father is well and has greatly enjoyed her pie."

"She'll be glad to hear that."

He began to turn back toward the house. "Take her some of my rhubarb, will you, please? All you want."

"Thank you, Mr. Abraham."

I continued my gathering as he went back inside. He was a pleasantly odd character, careful to check on Marigold and find something to share. Maybe I should have told him that she seemed a little preoccupied today because of Josiah. But she probably wouldn't like that, and Josiah wouldn't either.

I didn't expect to see any more of him, but he came back out with a knife and cut an incredibly generous supply of rhubarb stalks for me as I finished filling my bowl.

"Thank you so much," I told him again.

"My pleasure."

Marigold was whistling when I went back in the house with the bowl of greens and Mr. Abraham's bundle of rhubarb. When I first heard the sound, I thought Josiah was surely back and it was him doing the whistling. But Josiah was nowhere in sight, and she was beside the table with her back to me, cutting rolled dough and laying wedges of it on a baking pan.

I set the bowl in the sink, and Marigold suddenly jumped as though she hadn't noticed me coming in.

"So sorry. I didn't mean to startle you."

"Oh, it's all right," she answered quickly. "Not your fault if my mind was several blocks away and about some other business."

I wasn't sure what she was referring to. I just set the rhubarb beside the sink and started washing the greens so they'd be ready to fix for supper. Marigold started whistling again absently. It seemed so strangely out of character. I couldn't recall hearing any grown woman whistle before. Marigold certainly hadn't done it any other time since we'd been here.

"That's a catchy tune," I told her.

She shook her head and looked rather dismayed. "Oh, you caught me at it, didn't you? Used to aggravate my sisters something fierce. I only whistle when I worry. And then only if I don't catch myself soon enough. Must have let my mind get in the way of what I know to be so."

Her words made little sense to me, so I asked her what she meant. Maybe she was inviting questions by being so open.

"I shouldn't worry and that's all there is to it," she answered. "The good Lord is still in control." She stepped a little closer. "All that rhubarb! Did you find that much in my yard?"

She surely knew I wouldn't cut all hers without asking, and it wouldn't have made quite this much anyway. "Mr. Abraham sent it to you."

"Oh, bless him. I need to make him preserves again, like I did last year."

"He said his father is well and enjoyed your pie."

She smiled. "Wonderful news. Thank you so much."

How could anyone not like Marigold's pie? That part was no news at all, so surely she'd meant the good report about the old man's health.

"There's always a bright spot," she said. "In the middle of every day."

Before I could say anything in reply, her face changed, revealing again the concern I thought I'd been seeing most of the afternoon. "Josiah's needing prayers. I guess you've noticed he was a bit out of sorts last night, and left today before lunch."

"Yes," I agreed, not sure if I should say more.

"I don't know why he's been so long. But I know he's being tested."

"Eliza thought she might have upset him," I admitted. "He seemed rather unhappy to have us around this morning."

"That's not the trouble."

She didn't look convincing. And I decided I might as well be honest. "I don't think he's favored having us here since the moment he found out who we are."

Aunt Marigold sat in the nearest chair and looked up at me sadly. "Truth be told, dearie, that's probably right."

"But why?"

She sighed. "Maybe it's not really so much who you are as who you aren't."

Eliza came in from the porch where she'd been selecting the "shiningest" apples to set in a bowl on the table.

"Was he expecting someone else to visit?" I asked Marigold, hoping for some further explanation. I didn't like having the confirmation that her nephew and only other boarder did not appreciate our presence here.

"No." Marigold gave Eliza a welcoming little smile. "He's having a difficult time finding peace. Considering those who have gone on before us. I'm sure you understand."

I thought I did. "Was he very close with John? I don't remember ever hearing his name."

"It's been a lot of years." She sighed again. "The boys weren't but ten or so the summer John stayed with us. And they were quickly inseparable, day or night."

This subject stirred my curiosity. "Did Josiah live here back then?"

"No. Not really. But I guess you could say he was here pretty much the whole summer too."

"Then they must have become great friends in addition to cousins."

She looked at me a little strangely, and I had to wait a moment before she answered. "I guess you could say that. Josiah would certainly have liked every summer to be like that one. He thought the world of John . . ." Her voice trailed off and I got the feeling there was more she wanted to tell me.

"Is everything all right?"

"I pray so, dear. I'd say aplenty more, but I don't think he'd want me to."

Whatever could this be about? Had there been trouble at some point between John and Josiah? If not, then why would Aunt Marigold hesitate at me calling them friends in addition to cousins? What might Josiah not want me to know?

Such uncertainty made me more than a little uncomfortable, as well as her admission that Josiah needed prayers. She was asking the wrong person for that. I'd made a couple of feeble attempts at prayer for my daughter's sake but felt like that had accomplished nothing other than making me feel foolish and inadequate. I wasn't sure it would ever do me any good to try again. Why would God care to listen? He wouldn't hear anything the least bit worthy from me anyway.

I wanted to know more of what Josiah's problem could be and what was troubling Marigold. But she'd been pretty clear that she didn't think she could say. Still I wished I could press her for details. I didn't like not knowing any better than this what was going on around me.

Marigold turned back to her dough and began a hymn instead of whistling again. But she stopped almost as soon as she'd gotten started. "You know the Scriptures very plainly say that God answers our prayers," she said. "I've got no cause to worry. The Lord's got everything in his very capable hands."

I continued rinsing the greens at Marigold's sink. Eliza rocked back and forth on her heels beside the table, arranging and rearranging the apples in the wooden bowl Marigold had given her.

"The love of God is the most wondrous thing in all creation," Marigold talked on. "I just wish I could get Josiah to see it more completely. Do you know what I mean? I think he struggles so much with it, without even realizing."

Her words shocked me. Didn't she and her nephew share a common faith?

"I wish he'd learn to rest in the Almighty and not try to reason so much in his own strength. Every one of us is weak. We have to learn to trust in the strength and compassion of God." She glanced in my direction. "Perhaps your presence can be a little difficult for him in that way. People say there's no loss so difficult as that of your own child. And second to that, a spouse. But in spite of all that, you seem to be managing so well, resting in faith, as though you've already allowed the healing balm of the Almighty to heal your heart and enable your hands."

The bowl of greens slipped from my grasp and hit the bottom of Marigold's sink basin with a clatter.

"Maybe I'm saying too much," she continued as though she hadn't even noticed my racket. "Lord love him, Josiah hasn't learned to handle grieving, and any reminder makes things worse. I thought the train wreck this week might weigh at him terribly. And apparently it has, even more than I realized. I wish to goodness I'd known about yesterday's funeral ahead of time so I could have prayed a special strength for him."

I picked up the scattered leaves, re-rinsed them, and plopped them back with the others in the large bowl. She honestly thought I was doing well? Resting in faith?

"I'll pray for Mr. Josiah," Eliza suddenly spoke up. "I didn't know he was sad today, or I'd a' already prayed."

"That's very sweet of you, child," Marigold told her. "But he'll be all right, I'm just sure of that, 'cause I'm trusting him in the Almighty's hands."

"You'll pray for him too, won't you, Mama?" Eliza asked innocently.

But my hands shook. The question stabbed my heart, my conscience, and brought tears to my eyes before I could stop them. How could I tell her no? She so much wanted our faith to be one and the same. But I couldn't find it in my heart to trust God when my prayers had failed so miserably before. I didn't think I could pray for "Mr. Josiah." It would be a farce coming from my bitter heart. And I couldn't lie to my child and tell her that I would. So how could I possibly answer?

"Of course she will," Aunt Marigold answered to fill the silence. I could see a sudden change in her expression as she turned to me. "Let me finish with the greens, dear. You've found so many. Sit and read a passage from Scripture for me. We missed that this morning."

Still trembling, I wasn't sure I'd be able to read, but I dried my hands and walked obediently to the chair beside the shelf. I opened the Bible slowly, turning to the marker in Psalms where our reading had left off. But she directed me instead to the book of John. I fumbled with the pages, uncertain which way to look, but stumbled on the right book completely by accident.

"Chapter 14, verse 27," she said as she skillfully cut the last of her dough and laid it on the pan. She wasn't looking at me, but I got the feeling she was watching me just the same.

"Peace I leave with you," I began, barely able to make my voice cooperate. "My peace I give unto you: not as the world giveth, give I unto you . . ."

"That's Jesus talking," Marigold said softly.

I stared down at the page but from the corner of my eye saw her motion for me to go on. "Let not your heart be troubled," I tried. "Neither let it be afraid . . ."

I couldn't continue. My eyes were too cloudy. I didn't even see Eliza approach me, but she was suddenly at my side, wrapping me in her tender little arms.

"I'm so sorry, Leah," Marigold said. "Please forgive me. You've been so strong, I just didn't think. I shouldn't have brought up that train wreck again. What an awful thing to put your mind to, considering your John."

"No," I managed to tell her as I pulled a hanky from my pocket and wiped my eyes. "I'm all right, and it's not your fault at all."

"Dear Lord in heaven," she went on as if she hadn't heard me. "You'd think I'd learn to contain my tongue. Right in front of your little girl too."

"I—I don't fault you for anything said," I told her again.

So much had been going through my mind that, surprisingly, I really hadn't dwelt on that train wreck. But now that she'd persisted to bring it up again, I could feel my heart patter. No wonder Josiah had come home out of sorts yesterday if he'd just been to that funeral. What might it have been like to see what he'd seen, and stand helpless at the site of a train's awful destruction?

A horrid picture of a bloodied leg leapt into my mind, as it had so many times before. As far as I knew it was just something from a dream, but it always seemed so real. I felt choked, suddenly thinking of my John on the railroad track, helping some poor old man . . .

Eliza hugged me tighter, and I worried that my tears must have frightened or saddened her. I kissed her forehead, trying to put the awful pictures out of my mind.

"Don't worry 'bout Mr. Josiah, Mama," she whispered. "Don't be sad."

I hugged her tight, feeling miserable that she thought my tears were for someone else's sake and Marigold thought I was only shaken by her mention of the train wreck again. There was so much more to my inadequacy than that. I was living a lie in front of them, and I truly should confess the truth of my struggle with the Almighty, but my chest and throat felt too tight to choke out a word. I took a deep breath, trying to muster the courage to try, but then a train whistle sounded from across town like a taunt from the devil himself, and my heart raced inside me as badly as it did in the midst of my awful dreams.

The train whistles in Andersonville had not been bothering me greatly. I could usually shove them to the back of my mind. So this time was just an attack. Satan's effort to keep me agitated and make Marigold think I was a broken-up mess after all. I closed my eyes, willing away the tears, and then heard the front door slowly open and close. Josiah must have come back.

Eliza didn't seem to notice. I wanted to pretend I hadn't either and lower my head into her hair so he wouldn't see my face when he stepped in. But despite my own intentions to the contrary, I lifted my eyes to meet him as he came into the kitchen from the front of the house.

"Aunt Mari, I—"

He stopped in mid-sentence, looking at Ellie and me, and just stood in silence for a minute.

"Oh, Josiah, I'm so glad—" Marigold began to speak, but he didn't let her finish.

"I—uh—stopped to see Mel a while. Thought I'd better get back." He finished quickly and turned and walked away. I could hear his footfalls in the hallway and then on the stairs. What might he have said if he hadn't found us here all teary-eyed like we ourselves had visited a funeral?

"Thank the good Lord he's back already," Marigold whispered to me. "But I wish he hadn't gone upstairs. I would have liked to talk to him a minute."

I should've immediately offered to hurry and ask him to come back. But he'd already gone and I was afraid to follow and knock again on his bedroom door. He'd always seemed too forward, too standoffish, or too strangely intense for me to want to be anywhere near him. So I kept still, hoping she wouldn't ask me to go.

"At least he's in the house," she consoled herself. "Still himself too, as far as I can tell. We can call him down for supper in a little while. Thank the Lord for the victory."

She started to whistle again, just a quiet note or two, but quickly caught herself and began to sing the same hymn she'd sung before. She had her pan in the oven in two shakes and was pulling a cook pot from a cupboard beside the stove.

"Please let me help you," I told her.

Reluctantly she agreed, giving me a hug and telling me she was sorry again, though I told her she had no reason to be. I still thought I should try to explain my sudden burst of tears, but the effort now would probably only serve to bring on a fresh cascade. So I busied my hands, knowing that was the quickest way to convince Marigold and perhaps even myself that I was on an even keel again.

We fried ham and made mashed potatoes to go with the yard greens, and Marigold told me she'd finally gotten around to making us the scones she'd mentioned the first night we arrived here. I dearly hoped Mr. Josiah would smell the fixings and venture down on his own, but when we were nearly finished and he hadn't shown himself, Marigold asked me to go and call him down.

I went to the stairs with a nervous tremble, though there was no reason to be afraid. He wasn't any sort of vile man. He simply made me uncomfortable in an indefinable way. I wouldn't have to enter his room. How nice it would be if I didn't even have to go up the stairs, but it would be unseemly for me to stand at the bottom and yell. My voice might not carry that far anyway.

Slowly I climbed, thinking again of the account of the train wreck he'd told us. Did it play itself over and over in his head the way my strange dreams did in mine?

Maybe just seeing me here reminded Josiah constantly of train wrecks because of the way John had died. How horrible that would be when he had to go and work on a train nearly every day! I couldn't imagine how he'd been able to return to his job the day after the wreck he'd seen. I couldn't have done it. Not for a moment. Why hadn't I wondered about this before? I must have been woefully self-centered not to consider what an awful week this must have been for him. It was no wonder he'd been testy and out of sorts. And no wonder Marigold had expressed her concerns when he was gone.

"Mr. Walsh?" My voice seemed to echo in the large, nearly bare upper hallway. I hoped he would hear me already and open his door, but there was no recognition at all.

"Mr. Walsh?" I said again as I reached his oak door and gently rapped.

After a moment I thought I heard the creak of his bed. His voice reached through the door, sounding groggy and strangely tense. "What?"

"Your—your aunt wishes you to come down for supper."

I nearly turned and headed back down the stairs, confident that my message had been delivered. But the door suddenly opened and Josiah stood in front of me in his bare chest and feet, looking somehow forlorn. What had Marigold meant when she'd said he wasn't troubled so much by who we were as by who we weren't? I thought of the picture I'd seen on his dresser and wondered even more than before who the woman could be.

"I can eat later if you'd rather go ahead without me," he said, much to my surprise. He was looking at me far too intently, studying me, for anything at all he might find.

"It doesn't matter what I'd rather," I answered, perhaps a little too abruptly. "Your aunt would like you to come down."

"I'm sorry if I upset your little girl this morning," he said then with a strange mix of emotion in his eyes.

"You—you didn't," I stammered. "She just wasn't sure why you suddenly seemed upset with her."

"I wasn't. Not really."

I started to turn to the stairs, but before I got a chance he reached and touched my arm and then pulled his hand away again. "Wait. Just a minute."

Something in my stomach pulled tight, and the tension spread to my toes.

He sounded as though he felt the tension too. "Is everything all right?"

"Yes. We're fine." Why would he ask? But then I remembered the tears he'd seen when he came back in. Was he genuinely concerned?

"You'd tell me you were fine regardless of whether it was true, wouldn't you?"

There it was again. Josiah Walsh and his probing questions. Despite the sadness in his eyes, his forwardness irritated me. "I have no reason to lie."

"But you hide yourself. And apparently you don't consider that to be the same thing."

I stared for a moment and then whirled around to the stairs.

"I'm sorry," he said as I walked away. "I didn't mean that the way it must have sounded. I'm very sorry. Really."

For some reason my eyes welled up again, making me suddenly very angry. How dare he do this? How dare he stop me and question me and make me teary all over again?

I quickened my pace.

"Leah?" he called behind me. "I just worried—that you and your daughter—that your tears at the table might be my fault."

"No, Mr. Walsh," I said quickly. "They were not." The softness of his tone confused me. It was on the tip of my tongue, spiteful and bitter, to tell him that my world did not revolve around him, but I kept back the words because of the emotion in him and the worry Marigold had held earlier. I must remember, I must, that this troublesome man was in the midst of a trying time. For a moment I thought I heard another train whistle across town and almost shuddered.

"Would you rather I let you and Eliza eat first before I come down?" he offered again.

Maybe he wasn't quite himself as Marigold had thought. But he hadn't been drinking, if that was what she'd wondered. I'd smelled enough of my father's liquor that I was sure I would know. I stopped at the top of the stairs and tried to make my voice sound patient and kind.

"I told you before. It doesn't matter what I'd rather. Your aunt asked for you. She would've liked you to stay downstairs to begin with. She was quite worried while you were gone."

"Thank you," he answered. "For talking to me."

I turned just a little, wondering if there might be a hint of sarcasm to his words, but I didn't see it if there were any. He went back to his room instead of following, saying that he would get his shirt and shoes and be right down.

I went on down the stairs, wondering all the more about him and the things Marigold had said. Why had it worried her so much for him to be gone in the middle of the day? He'd only visited a friend. And if he was so unhappy with my presence here, who might he be longing for instead? The woman in the picture? Or some other woman, any woman not related to him, so he could pursue the pert sort of conversation he'd been attempting the night we'd met?

We were all quiet at dinner, though I knew Marigold still wanted to talk to Josiah. Because of that, I hurried through the meal and cleanup so they could be alone.

"Are we really going to church with Aunt Marigold tomorrow?" Eliza asked me as I helped her with her bath later.

"Yes. We really should," I acknowledged. "It's the right thing to do, since she's been so nice to us."

"And God too," she affirmed. "He's been nice to us 'cause he gave us this good place to live."

"You're right," I had to admit. "We should be grateful."

But I didn't want to think about church until I was faced with it. Fortunately, she changed the subject.

"Do I have to go to school on Monday? I like to stay here and cook and wash with you and Aunt Marigold."

"I understand that. But you'll learn so much at school. You'll like it. And it won't take all day anyway. You can help us when you get home."

"What if I get lost?" she asked with real concern. "I only been there once."

"Oh, honey, I'll walk you there in the mornings and be there when school lets out in the afternoon to walk home with you."

"Okay," she said rather timidly. "But I don't remember which classroom I belong to."

"I'll take you right there, and if you need any help after I'm gone, just ask one of the teachers."

"Will there be lots of kids?"

"I don't know how many, but it'll be more than you're used to, and that can be a lot of fun."

I rinsed the soap from her wavy locks and helped her dry off and climb into her bedclothes.

"I love you, Mommy," she said softly as I gently brushed her hair.

"I love you too."

She was already humming on the way to our bed. I worried a little about leaving her alone in our room. "Honey, when you're settled, Mommy needs to go and bathe before tomorrow."

"I know."

"Will it bother you for me not to be right here close?"

"No. 'Cause you won't take long and you're getting ready for Jesus."

She went back to humming, leaving me to wrestle with the strangeness of her words. I knew she was referring to me being in church in the morning, but I certainly didn't feel "ready for Jesus," nor did I have any confidence that I could get that way in one night. The Almighty and I were at a standstill. Neither of us had done any repenting over the bitterness I'd felt since John's death. And neither of us were likely to.

The incongruity of where that left me had me uncomfortable indeed as I gathered my hairbrush and bedclothes. *What's wrong with me? Why can't I trust the way my mother did? She struggled. She endured things. She even lost a son once, when I was too young to remember. But she continued to worship God and find strength in him. Why can't I be more like that?*

Shamefully, I knew the answer almost as soon as I'd posed the question in my mind. I wasn't praying, I wasn't worshipping nor honoring God in my every circumstance because in my heart, in some wicked little seat of being that I so often hid even from myself, I didn't want to. Standing in the way for me was one big question with a million tiny parts: why? Why did John have to die? And my baby? And my mother? Why does anybody have to die before they're old and gray? Why does there have to be so much pain in this world?

I wanted the answers. And I wanted to hold out until I got them before I bowed my knee again. In my foolish stubbornness, I wanted to insist that God be the first to move in our impasse. Let him explain himself. Then I'd respond with the worship and prayer he wanted.

Oh wretched man that I am! Somewhere I'd heard those words, I couldn't remember where. But whoever had said them could not possibly have been more wretched than I. After all, their words had seemed to be a cry to God, just the sort of thing my stubborn heart kept refusing. My precious daughter was right. We had much to be thankful for here. We could still have been homeless and alone on filthy city streets, but instead we were comfortable, welcomed, and even mentored in faith by John's dear aunt.

All our most immediate needs had been provided. But that didn't erase the hurt of the past or the uncertainty for the future. Marigold might up and marry or suddenly die, and then we'd be left homeless like before.

I want answers, I thought in my heart again. *But not just the why of what has happened. I also want to see my way clear to the future. I want to know where to go from here, and have some assurance that everything will be all right for my little girl. Why should that be too much to ask of a God who knows everything?*

I went to the bedside and leaned to kiss Eliza. She was already rolling side to side and just like always when she was in the middle of that part of her humming routine, she barely acknowledged me. She'd have to stop first, curl up, and snuggle the blanket to her cheek before she'd open her eyes and return my kiss.

Smoothing her still-damp hair away from her face, I waited, tears coming to my eyes. She did this because her daddy wasn't here. I knew that as well as I could know anything. Despite her smiles, her sunny disposition, and even her words of strength and faith by day, she missed her daddy so much at night that she'd invented her own bizarre sort of substitute ritual, as if anything could take the place of his gentle arms.

I kissed her again, thinking of my own mother's soothing kiss and wishing she were here beside me. *Oh, Mother! If you were with us, you would pray for my dear little Ellie and help her find peace. You could comfort her so much better than I can.*

The tears spilled to my cheeks, and I knew how selfish I was being. My hardness toward God did not affect me alone. It kept me from being the mother Eliza wanted and knew that she needed. In so many ways, she was much wiser than I.

Oh, God, help me. If I can't love you for you, *then please help me to find worship again for my daughter's sake, because she needs me to be strong in faith.*

I knew such a prayer was wrong somehow, that I was still off-kilter in my approach to the Lord, but it felt like a small beginning anyway. A little step on my part instead of more bullheaded insistence on my own demands. *Help me,* I repeated in my mind. *Help me. Because we need you.*

Eliza's rocking motion stilled and her breathing evened out. The humming subsided, and I thought for a moment she was already asleep. I petted her hair and forehead again gently and was about to kiss her and go on to my bath when she opened her eyes and smiled at me.

"I think God is happy that we're going to church tomorrow," she whispered. "It's been a real long time."

It hadn't been long at all since we'd set foot inside a church building. Just the morning that we left St. Louis, we'd taken advantage of a church's advertised fellowship breakfast in order to get a free meal. But we hadn't attended an actual worship service in a much longer time.

Eliza kissed me good night, snuggled with her blanket, and closed her eyes again. I hurried with my bath and back to our generous bedroom, but in that short amount of time, Eliza was already asleep.

15

Leah

In the night's stillness, I sat at the dressing table and carefully combed my hair, wishing I had hairpins and rollers to put it up the way I used to. Fortunately I'd let it grow long enough that I could pull it all back if need be, to look presentable for church in the morning.

I wasn't tired, but I didn't want to putter around and wake Eliza or even make any noises that would let Josiah know I was still awake when he came upstairs. Better to have the light off and the room perfectly still.

I wondered now if Josiah went to church with Aunt Marigold. I'd assumed all week that he surely did, and not heard anything to indicate otherwise, but Marigold's words made me wonder. He hadn't seemed to have any trouble with praying aloud or reading the Scriptures. Did he have his own struggle with faith?

I suddenly wished I knew more about him. Marigold had never said which of her many sisters might be his mother, and I couldn't remember him being in any of the pictures she'd talked about in that album she'd showed us.

Where had he grown up? Had he and John been able to get

together very often, besides the one summer here? Probably not, from what Marigold had said. And John had told me once too that his family's gatherings were rather few and far between. At least he'd had some, I'd thought at the time. My mother had few relatives, and most of my father's family wanted nothing to do with us. I'd only ever met one actual cousin of mine, a man much older than I who was only passively interested that there was any kinship between us.

I was still combing my hair, slowly and carefully, when I heard Josiah's footsteps on the stairs. If only I'd been a little quicker, I might have had the lamp off before he reached the upstairs hallway, but there was no use in hurrying now. I expected him to go on past our doorway just like every night, to his own room. But the footsteps ended before he'd had time to get past my door.

He'd stopped. I knew it even with the door closed. Whatever for? Surely he'd go on quickly enough, but instead, there came a rap at my door and I jumped.

Would he go if I didn't answer? Maybe not since the light was still on. He would know I wasn't in bed yet or I would've turned it off. What could he want? I didn't want him waking Eliza by rapping again, so I moved to the door as quickly and quietly as I could and slowly opened it.

He must have stepped back a foot or two into the dim hallway. He couldn't have reached the door from where he stood. It was a little hard to discern the look on his face.

"Yes?" I asked him, my heart suddenly pounding. I knew that he noticed my nightgown and robe.

"I hope I didn't disturb you."

"I was still awake," I answered simply as I stood with most of the door between us.

"Is your daughter asleep?"

"Yes."

"Aunt Mari told me we should talk. I didn't agree until a little while ago. And then I told myself that if you'd already gone to bed, I'd forget the whole thing."

"I'd have been in bed if you'd waited just another minute or two," I answered apprehensively. "Or if I'd combed my hair a little more quickly—"

"Then you wouldn't be bothered?" He looked somehow younger, and far less sure of himself than usual.

"No, that's not what I meant. What seems like a chance thing can have a purpose to it."

"Then you're willing to talk to me?"

"I suppose." My stomach was a nervous jitter, but I wasn't sure I had any good reason to refuse. It wasn't late, not by any means, and I ought to trust Marigold's opinion on this after she'd been so good to us. "Is she waiting for us?"

He ducked his head for a moment. "Um. No. She's still awake downstairs and will be for quite a while if either of us wants to speak to her again. She said she'd be praying. But she'd rather I talk to you alone. Don't worry. I promise I'm a gentleman."

I didn't know what to say. I opened the door a little wider but couldn't quite bring myself to go out.

"Would you like to step downstairs?" he asked. "If you don't mind that, I thought we might be more comfortable there."

More comfortable? Most definitely. Nearer to Marigold, for one thing.

He turned slightly, toward the stairway, and I made sure my robe was secured around me before I stepped into the hall. "I understand you and John were wonderful playmates."

He smiled. "We had some times, all right. I would have liked every summer to be like that. But his mother wouldn't leave him here again. At least not for so long."

"Why not?"

"He must have told her a little too much about some of the things we did. John's mama thought I was definitely a bad influence."

I could imagine family strife over that sort of opinion. "Didn't her sister object to that?" I asked, thinking that Josiah's mother and John's must surely have been sisters.

But I didn't get the response I expected. "Oh, Marigold

thought they ought to give me more of a chance, true enough. But I probably would have led John into more trouble. His mother was probably right."

He started down the stairs, and I stood for a moment, puzzled. Had he ignored my question or misunderstood it? Slowly I followed him, trying to turn things around in my mind. Finally I decided on an inquiry that might not seem too obtrusive yet would answer at least some things for me. "Which one was your mother? I mean, what was her name?"

"Maxine," he said without looking at me. "Littleton Walsh."

Maxine? Not a flower name? I was stunned. If that were true, he might not be related to Marigold after all. At least not in a very immediate way.

At the bottom of the stairs, he turned and waited for me. "Where would you like to sit?"

His hair was a bit disheveled as though he might have run his fingers through it haphazardly and left it standing on edge. His shirt was not buttoned to the collar, and he was looking at me far too intently again. Why had Marigold wondered if he were himself tonight? What might he be if he wasn't?

I felt a little weak-kneed as I tried to remember if I'd ever heard Marigold call Josiah her nephew. I'd been thinking of him that way all along, but now I couldn't recall her ever referring to him except by name. Yet he'd called her "Aunt Mari" right from the start.

There was a lovely little woven chair beside a table in the lower hall, set against the hollow curve of the stairwell. Josiah didn't make any move to go to any other room, so I sank into that chair, not sure what else to do.

"Well, if you're comfortable here . . ." He seated himself on the bottom steps just to my right and leaned back against the lowest of the oak banister columns. "Probably strange for you, I know, being interrupted so near to bedtime. But I figured this might be the time, while my courage is up. Tomorrow or the day after, who knows? I might not be able to get a word out."

I looked at him, wondering what he could possibly be getting at. Maybe it would be appropriate to ask a few questions, especially since Marigold had thought we should talk. "Who exactly are you?" I said a little too abruptly, my mouth getting ahead of the tact I'd hoped to utilize.

He laughed. "When you decide to talk, you get straight to the point."

I waited warily. Would he even answer my question? He did, and in more detail than I needed.

"Who am I? Well . . . Josiah Walsh. You know that much. So I suppose you'd like me to tell you that I'm just the poor hooligan who lived down the street and I'm only related to Marigold McSweeney through her late husband. And that's at least thrice removed on my mother's side. And I only started calling Marigold 'aunt' because John did and it stuck and we liked the habit. I'm not really John's cousin, except by our druthers back then, I guess, and I'm not even blood kin to Mari, though she says she wishes I were her son and I wish it too."

I stared down at the hardwood floor, completely uncertain how to respond.

"Got more questions?"

I shook my head. "Not yet."

"Like I said. Tonight I've got my courage up. Tomorrow, who could tell? I might not speak a word all day."

"I can't quite picture that."

"Well, nothing of any significance anyway. Light talk's the easiest kind."

I continued to stare down at the floor, not wanting to meet his eyes, not sure exactly what any of this was about.

"You don't make it easy, do you?" he asked.

"What do you mean?"

"Talking. Ditch gets dug faster with two shovels going at it."

"I beg your pardon?"

"Never mind." He shifted his weight and leaned back again on the banister post. "Aunt Mari thinks I should tell you about

Rosemary. You—um—you don't object to me calling her Aunt Mari do you?"

"Not if she doesn't."

"Thanks. Some people would. Petunia's family sure does."

"It wouldn't be my place to say," I assured him. "Or anyone else's either. Marigold has every right to claim whomever she wishes to claim."

He smiled again. "And she likes to claim the needy or alone whenever she can. She calls it her ministry to the world. You've benefited by that a bit yourself."

"Yes," I acknowledged, my cheeks feeling suddenly warm, though I knew I shouldn't be embarrassed to admit the obvious.

"She told me she first began doing things for Mr. Abraham when he moved in years ago because he was a widower living alone and she just wanted to show him the love of Jesus. But he started doing things for her right back, and now there's only one way they could ever be closer. You know what I mean?"

"Yes."

"She sends me with food to the Kurchers' every week. Whether or not she's got plenty here. She gives more than anybody I know through the church's aid society too. And that's just the beginning. Tramps passing through know where to stop for a meal, that's for sure. And I couldn't tell you how many people she's put up in the boardinghouse here without getting so much as a nickel."

"Like me?"

He looked at me sideways. "Couldn't say yet. Remains to be seen whether you'll pay her eventually. You might."

I couldn't tell if his words were a judgment on my situation or not. "Why did she want us to talk?" I decided to ask him directly.

He took a deep breath. "I was hoping to ease around the corner to it a little," he said. "But there's really no use to that. Something that's hard to say will still be hard to say whether it's five minutes into the conversation or thirty."

I couldn't imagine him having trouble talking about anything. He liked to talk. Very plainly so. But it occurred to me that his skirting the real point for a while was rather like his chatter walking over here the night we got off the train. Maybe covering over the silence between us was more important to him than the words themselves.

But I wanted to find out whatever it was that Marigold thought I should know and then be done with this whole conversation.

"What did you need to tell me?" I prompted, hoping I wasn't asking for trouble. "Who is Rosemary? The woman in the picture in your room?"

He looked like I'd struck him. "When . . . ? Why were you looking at my things?"

"I didn't touch anything," I explained quickly. "I wasn't really looking. Marigold sent me up to fetch your laundry, remember? And I happened to see it." His visible angst made me very nervous. "I didn't mean to offend you in any way," I added quickly, my stomach feeling like a leaden lump and my cheeks now burning.

"It's all right," he said with a sigh that made his tone just a little sour. "I suppose you couldn't help it, and if I'd remembered to carry my own laundry down, it wouldn't have happened anyway."

He looked over at me squarely, and I wished I could avoid his eyes. But it probably wouldn't be right to hide from them completely.

"No harm done," he said. "I just didn't feel comfortable thinking of someone else in my room. I don't suppose you'd like it if you found out I'd been in yours."

"No," I emphatically agreed. "I wouldn't."

"Don't worry. I haven't been."

We were both silent for a moment. I heard a sound from the direction of the kitchen and wished Marigold would come in here, or that I'd chosen to walk back there before sitting down.

"That was Rosemary you saw." He finally answered my question. "A great picture, don't you think? I wish I had a hundred more."

"She's very pretty," I agreed.

"She was," he said sadly. "I don't know if folks are still considered pretty up in heaven, do you?"

The question seemed more like something my daughter would ask than a grown man. "I don't know why not," I tried to answer him. "I'm sure in the perfection of that place, no one could possibly look less attractive than they did here on this earth."

The words were somehow painful to both of us, and I wished I hadn't said them. But he persisted at the idea. "It just doesn't seem right though, you know. Like if some people are all that pretty, there must be others that aren't, even in heaven. And that's a pretty odd idea."

I didn't feel qualified to comment on heaven at all, but I wasn't sure I could get out of it now that I'd started. So I tried to say what I supposed I should. "The only thing ugly to God is sin. And there isn't any of that in heaven. So everything and everyone there must be beautiful, I'm sure."

"Are you really sure?" he asked. It was almost like a dare.

"No," I said, looking down at the floor again.

"You surprise me," he said then. "I can tell when someone's just spouting the right words. But I didn't expect you to be honest about it."

As insightful as his observation may have been, it felt like a personal attack. "Who was Rosemary?" I asked him bluntly, hoping once again to get this conversation over with.

"My wife. My love. She was killed in an automobile wreck almost three years ago."

I hadn't expected that. Not at all. "I'm sorry."

"Thank you. But there's no need for you to say anything. I know you understand grief. And yours is even more recent."

I nodded, realizing that I'd misunderstood at least some of what Aunt Marigold had told me earlier. It wasn't John that the grief of yesterday's funeral had Josiah thinking about. Rosemary was the one he mourned, vehemently. Still.

"Marigold wanted me to tell you about my loss because she thinks we should be friends. She thinks we can help each other."

Somehow the words frightened me, and I did not react well. "I—I don't think . . ."

He rose to his feet. "That's fine. Her ideas don't obligate you any."

"I—I only meant that I don't think I'd be very good at helping anyone."

"My thoughts exactly. About myself, I mean." He smiled, much to my surprise. "If we cordially agree to not be friends and to not even try at the helping part, she can't argue with that, can she?"

I didn't know what to say. Did he feel as inadequate as I did? Or was he simply telling me he wanted nothing more to do with me now that he'd fulfilled Marigold's request? "I don't know what she'd think."

"I know what you mean," he said immediately. "She doesn't always see that other people just aren't like her. I'm not. I've got nothing—"

He suddenly stopped, as if the words caught in his throat. He stared at the wall beyond me for a moment, collecting his thoughts. "There's no reason to think that just because we've both lost a spouse and child that we could help each other make peace with it all."

"And child?" I asked, my curiosity now prompting me past the pain I could see in him.

"She was with child," he explained. "Less than a month from her due date."

My eyes filled with tears, and I could see that his did too. Despite the length of time it had been, the wound was still raw in his heart. Would I be that way in two more years? Or even worse? It was hurt I could see in him, but only hurt. Not the bitterness and anger all too often alive in me.

"I'm so sorry for your loss," I told him softly.

"I'm sorry for yours," he echoed. "John should have lived to be an old man. And any son of his should be sliding down drainpipes and playing Catch the Can with the best of them."

He turned his eyes to the wall again, and I knew it was in an effort to keep me from seeing all that was in them. I was glad, because he wouldn't be able to see what surely would show itself in me.

"Do you ever get angry at God about it?" I ventured without thinking. Maybe I was hoping he'd say that he did, just so I wouldn't feel that I alone entertained such faithlessness.

"At God?" He turned his back on me. "You think I'm gonna blame him for the utter stupidity in this world? For my own evil choices or that of the next guy?" He seemed to choke up. He brought his hands to his face, though his back was still to me. I couldn't respond. I was afraid, though I wasn't sure why, to make a sound.

It took him a while to speak again.

"I don't know how you look at what happened to John. It'd be pretty tough to reconcile a God of order with such a senseless accident. I understand that. But I can't question him when it comes to Rosemary. I could never think it was his fault. I'm the one who took that drink. Even though she asked me not to. I'm the one who thought I was such a man that there was no way a little liquor could ever affect my reflexes. We hit a truck, and she was thrown to the ditch. Broke her neck on impact."

He turned around. "There you have it. Josiah Walsh killed his own family. The truth's out about Mari's other charity case. Most of it, anyway. I went half loony for a while. Did a lot of damage getting drunk and trying to forget what I'd done. Marigold took me straight from the jailhouse to board, and there were a lot of people who thought she was making a big mistake. So you see, I'm not really good friend material for you anyway."

Speechless, I just watched him run his hand through his hair and turn his eyes toward the hall leading to the kitchen.

"So do we have an agreement?" he asked.

"What?"

"An agreement. We've talked. I already knew about your family. Now you know about mine. Nothing more to be said. No use being friends or pushing the subject with each other any further. You can't help me anyway. And there's no way I can help you or anybody else. I'm not called the way Mari is, despite what she wants to think. I just can't. And there's no sense in pushing you."

I knew he wanted me to voice my immediate agreement. And though I had no plans to bring up this subject again, or attempt to engage him in conversation about anything, I couldn't do what he asked. I'm not sure why not.

"Well?" he prompted. "Do we have an agreement?"

I took a deep breath, trembling inside. Marigold had been afraid for him today. I understood now that she was afraid he might go to drink again, that there might be something unpredictable, possibly even destructive, in him still. "Please forgive me," I answered, feeling suddenly tiny and vulnerable. "But I don't think I can agree with you."

He shook his head. "You're not asking to be my friend. And you know it's ridiculous that either of us could help the other. So why not agree with me? Do you just have to be contrary?"

"It—it's not that."

"Then what?"

I almost couldn't speak. I really didn't think I was in danger from him, but I could scarcely form the words anyway. What was I saying really, and why was it so important to me when it would be so much easier just to tell this man what he wanted to hear?

"M-maybe it's because I appreciate Marigold and what she tries to do for us," I stammered. "Maybe it's wrong for us to decide even the smallest piece of our own future like this, to close a door that might otherwise be open just a little. How do we know that something we do or say might not be some small help to one another, without us even realizing it?"

He didn't answer me. He just turned his back again. I thought he would go upstairs, but instead he crossed the entry hall and without a word went out the front door and closed it behind him.

16

Leah

"Oh, Aunt Marigold, I'm afraid I upset him. I don't know where he might have gone and I feel terrible."

She sat in her robe and slippers at the kitchen table, rubbing warmed camphor oil into her knees. "Put on the tea water, dear. We may as well have a cup. Hopefully he'll be back in a moment to join us."

I knew he wouldn't. Or at least he wouldn't be joining *me* for a cup of tea any time soon. "I don't know how to be his friend," I confided in her as I rose to fill the pot and put it on to heat. "Especially since he has no desire for me to be that. But it just seemed wrong to pledge not to become a friend to anyone."

"Of course it's wrong," she agreed. "It would be like telling someone you're not ever going to extend the love of God to them, regardless of what the Lord might choose to do with your heart."

"I didn't expect anything like this."

"Of course not." She wiped her hands on a dishtowel. "But I'm afraid it's more my fault than it is his."

"Why?"

"I shouldn't have been pushing him past where he's comfortable. But I did. I tried to get him to see that he's more than he thinks he is and the Lord will use him to comfort hearts and accomplish great things if he'll let him."

I could understand why all that would make anyone uncomfortable. "But you mean well," I told her.

"Still, if he can't turn off *my* expectations, I suppose the next best thing would be to get you to close the door."

"What does he have against me that it would be so important?"

"Oh, dear, nothing. It's not you he's trying to shut out but the very idea that he could minister so directly to anyone else's hurts. It's all my fault, like I said. Because he thinks he has to live up to something he's not ready for. Join me praying for him. I don't think he'll succumb to the temptation of drink again. I know his experience with Christ was real and he truly was set free. But he needs strength."

I wasn't sure what she meant by "his experience with Christ." And I probably should have been honest enough to admit to her that I wasn't comfortable praying, but I was too ashamed. So she prayed, and I bowed my head and nodded agreement as though I was as spiritual as she. Why had it been easier to admit my doubts to Josiah than to this trusting soul? Why was I so intimidated?

I'm not sure where Josiah went, nor how late it might be before he got back. Marigold and I had our tea and talked a while longer, then I went up to bed, mulling over his plight.

I could think of only one thing worse than losing a loved one, and that would be carrying the guilt of the death being your fault. No wonder he was still struggling with it. For a moment I wished I were so solid in faith that I could pray for him with real hope of benefit. That was what Marigold wanted and expected from me. Apparently she wanted it from both of us for the other.

Her logic seemed a bit skewed to think that two souls caught in grief could be of much use to one another. It was almost like expecting a pair of travelers mired together in quicksand to pull each other out. Still, she meant well, just like I'd told her, and it certainly wouldn't hurt anything to be considerate of each other's circumstances. I would certainly be a bit more patient with Josiah's less-than-friendly moods. And a bit more cautious too, since despite Marigold's confidence in him, he seemed more than a little unpredictable.

He didn't come home before I snuggled into bed beside Eliza, and I dropped off to sleep with our strange conversation still in my mind.

I don't know how much time passed. Off in the distance I heard a train whistle again, first low and slow and then gradually nearer. Before long it grew so deafeningly loud that it sounded like the track must be right behind the house. Strangely, instead of being horrified I was somehow fascinated. Spring was in the air. Mother's daffodils and hyacinths were poking their heads above the ground. It was a grand day to be outdoors, and I wanted to travel as fast as my toddling little legs could carry me.

New lilies poked their heads above the uneven ground near the tracks. Just beyond them I saw the rocks. Lots of delightful little round stones of varied colors. Just the sort of thing to catch my attention despite the ominous rumbling again now in the distance. I picked up handful after handful just to let them fall through my fingers again. It was a wonderful game that led me farther and farther up the gentle slope among the seemingly endless pebble array. It didn't bother me to have to step over metal and wood at the top. That was just another part of the adventure. But my shoe caught on the track and I fell. And not until then did I realize the menace of the growing sound that had seemed so benign.

The metal monster was huge, capable of devouring me in a single gulp, along with all the rocks, lilies, and shrubbery anywhere near its path. I was suddenly paralyzed, fear rushing at me with an all-consuming insistence. I screamed. But though

I wanted to run as fast as I could and hide, I could not seem to move. The devil locomotive barreled down on me with an unearthly metal grin. I could do nothing at all. Until John, young and beautiful John, emerged from the haze around the tracks with urgency and determination written all over his face. I reached my arms to him, trying to forget the menace beyond him. If he could only reach me, if I could only be folded safely in the comfort of his arms . . .

He grabbed at me so suddenly that one of my shoes fell to the tracks. I felt a trembling but couldn't tell if it was me or the dreadful shaking of the ground as that metal monster came rushing at us. John had been running and he ran still, pushing me ahead of him with such force that I couldn't hope to maintain my balance. I fell headlong into the stubbly ditch. He was right behind me. He should be tumbling head over heels any second into the lilies and clumps of bristle grass, and then we would be safe in each other's arms.

But I heard a scream and a horrid mechanical screech. John was not beside me as he should have been. Instead he'd been thrown, and all I could see was one leg that should have cleared the tracks in time. One broken and bloody leg.

Panicked, fighting to breathe, I woke to a sob that must have been my own. I was cold and hot at the same time, sweaty and shaking so badly I could scarcely believe Eliza was yet asleep beside me. I gulped, twice, three times, trying to catch my breath and quiet my racing heart. And then I sobbed, unable to stop myself, because I'd seen John again. I'd seen his death as though it were my fault, as though I were the old man he'd lost his life to save.

The dawning sun had begun to lighten the sky outside my window. This was Sunday, the day we were to accompany Marigold to the church that was so dear to her heart. How would I be able to steady my legs beneath me? How could I stop myself from shaking? It'd all been too vivid, too horrid, and I felt that I'd never be able to push the ghastly image from my mind.

I pulled the blanket as close as I could around me and curled tight into a ball as I used to do when I was a child. How comforting it would have been to have my mother's tender hand caressing my cheek, banishing the moment's terror with her soothing touch. So many mornings I'd cried in her arms until I hadn't the energy left even to lift my head.

"Shhh," she'd always whispered. "It's over now and you are safe."

Mother's words had been good. Kind and true. But it was not enough anymore that I was safe. The monster had accomplished its horrible deed. It had devoured, had stolen life and then moved on to steal and kill again.

It was absolutely foolish, to lie in that bed and sob like a child. But I couldn't help myself, even when Eliza began to roll and stir. I wiped at my tears, tried to swallow down the despair I was feeling, but to no avail.

"Mommy, what's wrong?"

"I—I had a terrible dream, honey. But it's—it's over now. I'll be all right."

She laid her head on my shoulder and her hand on my cheek. She said nothing for a moment and I wished I could be stronger for her. So often she was the one being strong for me.

When she finally spoke with uncharacteristic solemnity, I felt completely unprepared.

"I had a dream too. About Daddy and Johnny. I dreamed we was in our house in St. Louis and they was still there."

New tears came to my eyes and I hugged her. "I'm so sorry, honey," I managed to say. "I'm so sorry he's not here for you."

She was quiet again for a moment, motionless in my arms. But then she asked the question I'd dreaded for months even though I'd known it would eventually come. "Daddy wasn't sick like my baby brother, was he, Mommy? I know he was supposed to go away so he'd be ready for Johnny James, but doesn't something always got to happen when somebody goes to heaven? What happened to make Daddy die?"

Why now? After all this time, why did I have to face her inquiries when my insides felt like they'd been wrenched sideways and I could barely hold my thoughts together? I'd told her only the bare minimum when her father died, just as I'd been advised by John's minister, hoping she wouldn't ask for details of his death until she was much older. Now how could I answer with such awful pictures still vivid in my mind?

She waited in silence, clinging to me, petting my cheek with her hand almost the way my mother used to do. And I knew I had to answer her. My daughter was mature beyond her years sometimes, certainly mature enough to have honest questions addressed. I took a deep breath, determined to forge ahead.

"Honey, do you remember that Pastor Woolner said Daddy'd been in an accident?"

"Yes." She looked sober, pensive. "But what kind of accident? Once he got his finger pinched in a door."

"Yes. I remember that. But this—this was far worse. He—he was a hero, honey. I probably should have told you."

I steeled myself to go on in the face of her intense gaze. Should she really hear this story? If I still had difficulty handling the reality of what had happened, how could she? Yet she wanted to know. How could I deny her the truth?

Surely she would cry. Maybe we would both be too broken to leave this bed today. I had no idea how Marigold might react to that, but I somehow could not refuse my daughter anyway.

"It—it was a very sudden accident, honey." I tried to abbreviate if she'd let me. "It didn't hurt just his finger and it wasn't just a door. It hurt much more of his body, so much that he couldn't get better."

"But what kind of accident? How'd he be a hero?"

I sighed, knowing she'd persist. And I hugged her tight, hoping I was doing the right thing.

"Near a loud, busy station with a lot of tracks and trains, an—an old man was moving his cart of boxes across the tracks. It was a heavy load and he had a lot of trouble. Your daddy was waiting for a train and he went to help that old man."

I stopped and drew a deep breath. She was watching me

closely with a hint of tears rimming her shining eyes, but the tears didn't fall.

"A train car started moving on a track where it wasn't supposed to be," I continued. "They never heard it because of all the other train noise. It would have crushed that old man if it hadn't been for your father. That's what they told me. Even though the man was hurt and had to go to the hospital, he was able to go home later and care for his sick wife and grandbabies. Your daddy saved his life."

To think again of the gift John had given to that family made me weak inside. It still seemed utterly unfair that my young, strong husband had not come home.

"Did the train hit my daddy?"

I nodded. Though the slow-moving train car had only knocked him aside into the pushcart along the tracks, he had lived just six hours in the hospital emergency ward, with internal bleeding that could not be controlled. It was wrong. Senseless. He should have lived. He would have lived, the doctors said, if he hadn't both hit his head and ruptured a blood vessel in the impact.

Eliza's tears rolled softly, soundlessly, down one cheek. "Did the old man have lots of grandbabies?"

I would never in a thousand years have expected that question. "Yes. I think someone told me there were five children in his home who'd lost their mother a year or two before."

"Then they needed him. Daddy helped them."

She didn't seem to see the inconsistency of her own statements. She needed her daddy too. We both did. Why hadn't that mattered to the Almighty God?

"Yes," I was able to tell her, despite my selfish thoughts. "He helped them very much."

"Then God made a bad thing be a good thing," she reasoned. "Because those people needed their grandpa and Johnny James was gonna need his daddy to hold him as soon as he got to heaven. I miss him, but it wouldn't be right for baby Johnny if Daddy wasn't there."

"But there's nothing to fear there and no one is alone," I

protested. "There are angels, and the Lord himself. Johnny would have been—" I suddenly couldn't go on.

"If it was me that went to heaven, I wouldn't want to go first of anybody I knew," Eliza told me. "I'd be glad for somebody to be right up there waiting for me. We could have a party when I come in the door. That's what Aunt Marigold says it's like in heaven when somebody gets saved. The angels have a party, and then everybody has a big party all over again when the person gets to come right up there to be with them and God."

"Yes," I muttered uncomfortably. "Maybe that's so."

"Daddy and Johnny is waiting to have a party for us, isn't they?"

I raised my head from the pillow and propped on one elbow. "We really should be getting up in a few minutes . . . see? It's daylight outside."

She hugged me again. "Okay."

We both sat up slowly, and I was relieved for her attention to be turned to the start of our day. I could not have borne another moment of talk about death and heaven. Though such things seemed to be a comfort to Eliza, who'd brought up the subject more than once with Marigold, I could barely manage, and this time had been the worst. I felt wobbly in the knees and entirely drained of stamina. How could I make it through a morning that might require even more strength than usual? I'd be facing church for the first time in so long. And Josiah again, and who could know how he'd react to me today?

The horror of my dream stuck to my mind like a haunting phantom, and worst of all, I could see the tears still in Eliza's eyes. Though her countenance had brightened, I knew she couldn't help but be affected by the things she'd learned. Had I told her too much? I did not want her to be fearful as I was, or mournful and glum.

I could not eat anything at breakfast, especially when Eliza decided to tell Marigold every word she'd heard about her father's death. I could not even bear to listen but had to step outside to catch my breath.

And that was a mistake. Apparently Josiah'd had the same idea in order to avoid encountering us at the breakfast table. He was sitting on the slant of the cellar door, and I didn't see him until it was too late.

"Did Mari send you out to fetch me?"

"No," I said, far more snappily than I should have. "I guess she figures if you want to skip breakfast that's your privilege. She didn't say a word about it."

"Fine. What are you doing then?"

"Nothing. Just getting some fresh air." I was feeling rather peevish that he would ask about my business again, but at least I had the sense not to say so. I turned from him and walked to the garden, wishing he would go inside. I didn't like knowing he would be where he could see me. I only wanted to be alone while Eliza and Marigold finished their jelly toast and cambric tea.

In a few moments I heard him get up from the cellar door. But I didn't hear the porch door and wasn't sure where he went. I turned, afraid he'd be right behind me, but he was nowhere in sight. I sunk to my knees on the garden path, feeling suddenly guilty. Had he been outside all night? I wasn't sure, but those might have been the same clothes he'd been wearing. Should I have been more gracious and told him that indeed Marigold did wish him to come in?

She'd said nothing about him this morning. I hadn't asked. I'd only assumed he must have come in sometime after I went to sleep, but had he? Where had he gone? Had he succumbed to drinking again? What must it be like to carry the guilt that he bore?

I remembered my thoughts last night that if I were a praying person, I should pray for him. Someone should. And someone should pray for my daughter too, who despite her cheerful reasoning still carried the lonely ache of missing the father she dearly loved. But Aunt Marigold was praying for all of us. I was sure about that, and as long as there were prayers being said, it didn't matter where they came from. Or where they didn't.

I tried to comfort myself with that logic but knew nonetheless that it was dead, empty, and utterly selfish. I was being stubborn and spiteful. Far less than the person John and my mother would have wanted me to be. Over and over my own heart tried to tell me that prayer could help bring peace, but I was still waiting for God to satisfy my own personal demands. Yet at what cost?

What benefit might there be to Eliza through her mother's faith? And might others benefit as well? Marigold or Josiah? How might I be different if I chose to tell God I would honor him regardless of whether I understood the things that had happened? Mother had said it helped to trust him, to give everything over to him, and relinquish your own desire for retribution, elucidation, or control. How had I become so stubborn that I still refused to do that?

My father had ridiculed her terribly for her faith. When she spoke of prayer, or trusting for answers, he would shake his head and scoff. "How do you know he'll lift a finger just 'cause you ask him to? He ain't been all that careful to keep things painless before."

How had I not realized that my father's sentiments had become so nearly echoed in me?

I heard the porch door and looked up, for some reason thinking that I would see Josiah heading in my direction with a frown on his face, ready to rebuke me. But instead it was Eliza standing on the back steps, looking across the yard at me with a worried expression.

"Did you fall down, Mommy?"

I had forgotten. Here I still knelt on the garden path. That must have looked strange indeed.

"No, honey, I'm fine." I rose and dusted myself off, tempted to think of some quick lie to explain myself. But maybe it would be better to offer no explanation at all.

"Aunt Marigold says it's almost time to go to church," Ellie told me. "Rosie Batey'll be here in a few minutes because she likes to be early."

I'd almost forgotten about the ride Marigold had told us about. Every week the same dear friend came by in her jalopy and picked her up for church. Marigold was certain she wouldn't mind the extra passengers. I'd asked if Josiah rode along too, but no. When he attended, he always walked. Rain or shine. I wondered if he'd attend today.

"It does seem early," I observed, more to have something to say to put Eliza at ease than anything else.

"Aunt Marigold says they have a good Sunday school before the regular church and I'll like it."

"I'm sure you will."

I looked down at my clothes, hoping I hadn't carelessly soiled my skirt. There might be little time to change, and the other things I had were for everyday and not for church anyway. I didn't see any stains, but Eliza's hair was mussed, and I decided to turn my attention in that direction. I had no idea whether anyone at Marigold's church knew of us yet, but whether they did or not I hoped to not leave too bad an impression.

Marigold seemed worried about me being distant this morning. Eliza had told her about our conversation and even that I'd had a difficult dream.

"Would you like to talk about it, dear?" she asked me when we came inside. "Or have special prayers in church?"

I shook my head. There was no way I wanted attention drawn to myself in such a way. She gave me a hug and said I looked wonderful, which I took to be more her effort at encouragement than actual fact.

"Don't worry about Josiah," she told me then. "I talked to him early this morning, and he assured me he was fine despite the struggle he was going through yesterday. He'll meet us at church later."

I wondered if she thought I was troubled for him, or "burdened," as John and his minister friend would have said, with a need to intercede. Perhaps I should have been and would have been if my own hard head had not stood in the way.

17

Leah

Rosie Batey was a lovely woman nearly as old as Aunt Marigold but considerably more spry. She drove an old model A splashed with green paint and made me nervous by scarcely slowing down around corners. Fortunately, Marigold's church was only a few blocks away and we only had to make three turns. Two young men stepped out as soon as we parked to help Marigold up the steps, and I knew this was a place where she was deeply loved and respected.

I would have preferred to wait until the worship service to come to church and not have to sit through Sunday school. That was what I expected Josiah would do. But after everyone was directed to one of four class groups—young children, older children, young adults, and older adults—he walked into my classroom two or three minutes late.

Several people, including the man who was teaching, greeted him, and he sat at the far side of the room, never turning his eyes in my direction.

The lesson was about forgiveness. I'd heard the like before and didn't think I needed to hear it again. But a number of the people responded as though it were exactly what they'd been longing to listen to. The class got into a lively discussion about what Jesus meant by "seventy times seven" and how a person should behave toward someone he claims to have forgiven.

When one man suggested that believers should treat people as though their transgression had never happened, Josiah stopped the entire class with one word.

"Impossible."

"What do you mean?" the teacher asked. "When we've repented, God no longer remembers our sin."

I held my breath, waiting for Josiah's answer.

"I understand that. God wipes away the past and we're reborn with a clean slate. But just because God can do that doesn't mean men can."

Every eye in the room was on him as he continued. "If a man killed my wife or child, I couldn't act like it never happened. My whole life is changed because somebody important to me is gone. You can't pretend something bad didn't happen when you live with the consequences every day. Pray for the killer's soul, maybe, but to behave the same as before is impossible. We can't go back and put things the way they were. No one can."

The room was silent for a moment, and I wondered how on earth anyone could respond. Finally the study leader, with a deep sigh, made his attempt to address Josiah's words.

"I'm glad you said about praying for a killer's soul. You're right that evil deeds can change the whole course of life for victims and their families. Sometimes people can't go on the way things were before. And that's not really what we meant by the suggestion to forgive and forget. What we're saying is we don't continue to hold on to blame against the one who did wrong. We release that into the hands of God, pray for the person as you said, and become free from the burden of that bitterness."

Josiah said nothing. I almost wished he would say something. But a woman in the room spoke up with words that probably were devastating for him to hear. "Perhaps the hardest person to forgive is yourself."

Did she know about Josiah's family? If she did, it seemed a callous moment to bring it up before everyone like this. It made me mad. But the words of a man in the back corner of the room shook me even further.

"Maybe so. But an even rougher predicament is holding unforgiveness 'gainst God."

No one in this room could know the thoughts of my heart. Maybe I'd given Josiah a tiny peek, but I couldn't imagine that he'd run to tell anyone. He wanted nothing more to do with me. He wouldn't bother. But God himself might be trying to speak through these people, to work over my heart. And that was such an unnerving notion that I wished I could flee the room.

The Sunday school teacher talked on as one might expect, about understanding God's forgiveness for us, and learning to accept and extend such grace to ourselves. And about not blaming God for the unexplained hardships of this fallen world. Better to trust God's goodness and believe that he'd bring us through every trial into joy again.

These were words that had found their way into my ears before. But not into my heart. I still felt like fleeing the room. I was too tired of the struggle to have all of this shoved at me again. Why would the Lord take my husband and son, exhaust me with poverty and nightmares, and then try to insist that I acknowledge everything to be all right? Maybe it would be better if he just left me alone.

Josiah was quiet for the rest of the class until someone asked toward the end if he were all right or needed prayer for anything. I expected continued silence from him or maybe a dismissive shake of the head, but instead he lowered his eyes and answered honestly. "I've been struggling. I guess you can tell."

"Is there anything we can do?" someone asked.

"Just pray for me."

For some reason it made me shake inside to see him so humbly acknowledge his need. And it made me feel guilty because I'd been aware of it, I'd thought of doing exactly what he was asking for, yet talked myself out of it for no better reason than I still didn't wish to pray whether I knew of a need or not.

Even worse, Josiah prayed for other needs and to dismiss the class after the Sunday school leader finished praying for him.

We were opposites, plain and simple. He was responsible for what had happened to his family, whereas I could not have done anything to change the outcome for mine. It had been completely out of my hands. And yet I knew that he was justified before the Spirit of the Almighty far more than I. Because I blamed God. And he laid a charge against no one but himself. My mind warred with my heart, trying to reconcile the matter.

The church service itself started out worse than Sunday school. They sang "Have Thine Own Way, Lord" followed by "What a Friend We Have in Jesus" with its repetitive admonition to "take it to the Lord in prayer." I did not want to be affected by anything that happened in this place, yet I could feel God's drawing on my heart, ever stronger.

Why do you keep meddling at me? I asked him. *I'm not sure I can ever change. Why don't you give up and leave me alone?*

"I will never leave thee, nor forsake thee," the preacher suddenly said. "Jesus Christ the same yesterday, and today, and forever. As the Lord told Joshua of old, so is his word for us today: Be strong and of a good courage; be not afraid, neither be thou dismayed: for the Lord thy God is with thee whithersoever thou goest."

The preacher's words called to my mind the psalm Josiah had read to Marigold on our very first day here. "*Whither shall I go from thy spirit? Or whither shall I flee from thy presence? If I ascend up into heaven, thou art there: if I make my bed in hell, behold thou art there. If I take the wings of the morning, and dwell in the uttermost parts of the sea; even there shall thy hand lead me, and thy right hand shall hold me.*"

I'd been running in anger like a distressed child, rebelling, arguing, crying out, as ill-mannered youth are wont to do. But he remained patient, reminding me of his presence, gently calling me to return to him.

I'd given my life to God when I was fifteen. And my mother had told me then that nothing, nothing but my own heart, could ever separate me from his great love. She'd read me a Scripture about that, and I tried to remember it even as the preacher went on talking. Not height nor depth. Nor principalities nor powers. Nothing can separate us from the love of God that is in Christ Jesus. I wasn't remembering the words perfectly, but I knew they were in the book of Romans and I at least had the basic idea.

You're stubborn, Lord, I suddenly thought. *Even more stubborn than I am, but in a good way. You don't quit. You don't back down. You stay right with me, refusing to give up, even though I don't deserve you.*

My eyes filled with tears, thinking of the cosmos suddenly being brought into existence by the spoken word of God. He who hung the stars and set the earth in its orbit, he who formed the ocean and the dry land and all the mysteries of life, chose to love people. Vehemently, unabashedly, unconditionally. And I would turn my back? Puny little me?

I don't know all of what the pastor's message was. I heard him turn to the book of Matthew in the New Testament and tell his church more of the words of Jesus: "Lo, I am with you always, even unto the end of the world." But I could not concentrate on the rest. The tears got in the way. I sat and cried through the remainder of the service. And strangely, though I thought I would wish myself invisible, it suddenly did not seem so bad if my daughter and Marigold, nor even Josiah and the whole world, should see me crying.

I don't think the pastor had any idea what to do. At the end of his sermon when he was about to dismiss the congregation, he paused in front of me and then finally said, "Dear lady, do you have special need for prayer?"

I nodded my head in acknowledgment but could not tell him anything more. By this time, both Eliza and Marigold were in tears too, though I wasn't sure why.

That pastor tried to pray, though clearly he had no way of

knowing which direction to take. Then he dismissed the service, and several ladies of the church gathered around, I suppose to be a comfort and at the same time find out what in the world was troubling this stranger in their midst. But I could give no explanation. I didn't want to speak to anyone at all. If I could've had the sanctuary completely to myself right then, I would've preferred it, but no one seemed to be in any great hurry to go. Except Josiah. With a pained expression, he left abruptly without another word to anyone.

For a moment I wondered if I might have done something wrong. But Eliza was clinging to me, Marigold was asking her friends to continue their prayers, and despite my misgivings about coming here, I knew that my heart had made an important stride in the right direction.

"Are you all right, dear?" Marigold asked me as we were finally getting ready to leave.

I managed a nod. Eliza held tight to my hand. "Did you cry the sad away, Mommy?"

The tender question brought tears to my eyes again, and I hugged her. "I've been needing some time in the Lord's house, I guess."

Marigold smiled. "We all need to lay our hearts bare before the Lord sometimes. Would you like to talk about it?"

"No, thank you, ma'am," I said rather shakily. "Not yet, at least."

She accepted my words without a hint of offense, gathered her shawl and Bible, and started for the door.

For some reason I was watching for Josiah as we left the building. It should have been no concern that a grown man would choose to leave church promptly and walk across town on his own. Yet it did concern me. Almost as though as soon as Josiah had asked me not to try to be his friend or help him, I had a heightened desire to do both. Maybe I was just contrary, like he said.

"He'll surely join us for Sunday dinner," Marigold whispered to me, and I wondered how it could be so obvious to her what

I was thinking. She squeezed my hand and smiled, and I felt like asking her if my thoughts during the church service had been transparent too.

Thanks for not giving up on me even when I wanted you to, I said to the Lord in my head. *Thank you for Marigold.*

Suddenly I was exhausted. It seemed that opening myself up just a little to acknowledge the God of the universe, or perhaps breaking through the wall that had kept me from it, had drained away all my strength. Walking to Rosie Batey's car was an unexpected struggle that I tried my best not to show.

Marigold invited Rosie in to dinner, but Rosie was already planning to go and meet with grandchildren across town. So Eliza and I alone accompanied Marigold along the front walk to her house. Again I thought it would be nice to be by myself to collect my thoughts for a while, to set in order all the things I'd been feeling toward the Almighty. Marigold might understand, but I did not want to push Eliza away. She was careful to keep hold of my hand and stay right at my side.

I looked around a bit for Josiah now that we were home again. I had mixed feelings about that for sure. If he wasn't here, Marigold and I would both wonder. If he was, he might ask me questions I wasn't yet ready to answer. Like, what happened at church today? Why the tears? What exactly were my feelings toward God?

He probably wouldn't ask, not out loud at least. But I would probably think I saw the questions in his face and have to struggle with them anyway. When I would rather busy myself with something and try to put it out of my mind, at least till I could be alone.

Marigold took my arm as we climbed the porch steps. There was no sign of Josiah, though perhaps he was inside.

She glanced toward Mr. Abraham's house wistfully and spoke almost under her breath. "Wouldn't it be dandy if we could invite the neighbor to Sunday dinner?"

"Oh, Aunt Marigold, why don't you?" I replied immediately. "It would be dandy."

"He wouldn't come. Not with his father in the house. The old man does not approve of me."

That was plainly put. I had thought his father's poor health was the only reason we'd scarcely seen Mr. Abraham for days. "He's far from a child," I ventured to say. "Must he allow his father to keep him from friends?"

"He wouldn't have to," Marigold conceded. "But he made a promise years ago, and he has chosen to abide by it, much to his own detriment, in my opinion. But I certainly respect his fidelity in the situation."

"What promise?"

"That he wouldn't consort too closely with a Christian woman as long as his father was alive."

"Oh, Aunt Marigold."

"I know," she answered solemnly. "I might not have remained a widow for nearly so long had the neighbor refused his father such a maddening pledge, but there's nothing to be done but take the matter to prayer. We can hardly wish a man dead. There'd be such sadness in that family."

I was rather stunned. "Then you really have considered marriage, quite seriously, with only this to hold you back?"

"I wouldn't say that," she said. "Nor venture to answer for Saul in the matter. I can't accuse him of impropriety in his father's eyes. But he did tell me once that his heart skates a rather fine line."

I'm sure my eyes grew wide. "What did you say to that?"

"I told him I like to skate."

Eliza may not have purely understood such a conversation, but I was left with my heart rather in a flutter about it, especially when three separate automobiles pulled up outside the Abrahams' house before we even got dinner on the table. What if the old man lay dying already and they had called the family in to be at his side in the final moments? It just wasn't right to think of it, and I'm sure it must have been a struggle for Marigold when she noticed. But she bowed her head and said a prayer for the man's soul as well as his body, and I wished that I could one day stand with my heart so blameless before the Lord.

"Do you really love Mr. Abraham?" I dared to ask her.

"Of course I do," she said abruptly. "Or there'd be no use discussing it."

"Do you think he will come to know the Lord?"

"Perhaps. One day." She glanced out the window at an unfamiliar young man standing on Mr. Abraham's porch, but then turned her attention back to the mashed potatoes. "What do you think? Do these need more butter?"

I didn't bother to taste them. "Surely they're fine. You seem to season everything to suit my taste."

"You're just easy to please."

Josiah hadn't shown himself, and I wasn't sure he'd come home, but Marigold asked me to call him down from his room, if he was there.

I half expected not to find him but he was upstairs, barefoot again, in an undershirt, and with his hair even more disheveled than the last time. He must have been lying down.

Once again he asked me if I'd rather take dinner without him.

"No," I said. "Because Marigold wants you to come now."

He shrugged. "It's her house."

He turned and shut the door to his room without another word, and I knew he would be getting himself dressed appropriately for Marigold's dinner table. I thought of the things he'd told me, that he was a distant relative of Marigold's late husband. No wonder John had never mentioned him. They were no kin at all. Josiah was just an old acquaintance who had gotten him in trouble with his mother one summer.

Marigold had amazing patience. Waiting for Mr. Abraham. Enduring her husband's moody relative, Josiah, all this time. And me. How did she see me? Teary. A charity case or mission project. Such thinking had me a little testy as I descended the stairs and returned to the kitchen.

Eliza was singing beside the table, carefully laying napkins beside each place setting. Marigold was arranging carameled carrots around the roast beef on a platter. This was a meal fit for company to be sure. Too bad she could not have the guest she wanted, at least not yet. Watching her, I thought of how comfortably we'd worked together for the last few days. I'd thought of her as a pleasant grandmotherly type, simple and easy to become acquainted with. But did I really know Marigold at all? How could I, in less than a week? There was certainly far more to her than the limp and the fruit harvest.

I sat at the table and felt like crying again. Somehow the tears at church had been cleansing, maybe even healing in a way, and I'd felt that perhaps I could start over with God and find solid ground again in my heart and my thinking. But this, these feelings now—it was as if some invisible thief had snuck in and stolen away the peace and hope I had found. We were stranded here. Penniless. With strangers who would not necessarily care to cope with us for much longer. Marigold's heart was not in her boardinghouse at all, but next door with the neighbor. And Josiah. His heart was simply lost with the grief and the guilt he would probably never come to terms with.

I'd been awed by thoughts of God's creation, his majesty, the very bigness of all he'd made and all he was. But how could I translate such feelings into the small space of my life, which looked so bleak and pointless? What did it matter that I could respect the Maker of the universe, when I still failed to truly trust him for tomorrow?

Surely it was my own failing, my own finite view of things and pessimistic attitude causing my unrest. But it was far too easy to let the old bitterness creep back in.

If you can create the world, Lord, if you can make the stars, why can't you give me any assurances? Why can't you show me why the things you do make sense, and help me find a way to make a decent life for my daughter? We can't stay here! Not for very long. Can we?

Eliza stopped what she was doing and gave me a hug. "Feel

better?" she asked. I nodded, unable to tell her that the truth was quite the opposite.

Josiah came in behind her, looking like he was dreadfully unhappy to have been disturbed. I knew he was still upset with me, though the reasoning was bizarre enough that my daughter would never understand. I wouldn't promise to despise him as he apparently despised me. I wouldn't pledge to refuse him any potential help or possibility of friendship. What an absurd place to be in.

Of course, Marigold's wonderful meal was eaten mostly in silence. She surely noticed, but I know her attention was distracted by whatever might be taking place at Mr. Abraham's house. We heard the door several times. Two automobiles pulled away only to be replaced by two more.

She said nothing of it. And when we were finished with the meal, she surprised me by inviting Eliza to her room to listen to the Victrola. "I'm not feeling all that chipper right now," she told me. "Would you mind cleaning up without me?"

"No, of course not. Not at all."

She took Eliza's hand and started away. I expected that Josiah would simply go and seclude himself in his room again. He probably expected that too, but as she was leaving, she turned her head suddenly and addressed him with a somber expression. "Josiah, every single knife in this kitchen is dull as an old sugar spoon. I would appreciate it if you would sharpen them for me."

He sat and stared. He didn't say a word. And then when she and Eliza were gone from the room he slapped his hand against the table with enough force to rattle the dishes. I carried the platter to the stove top, careful not to look at him. Was he angry at Marigold? Probably. Her words had certainly seemed designed to prevent him from separating himself this afternoon. Maybe even to make him work alongside me, or at least tolerate my presence for a few minutes as he gathered whatever he needed to work elsewhere.

I thought he'd jump up, grab every knife he could find, and

go outside. But he surprised me completely. He didn't move again as I cleared the table, except to lean forward and put his head in his hands. And then as I began running water for the dishes, he thumbed through Marigold's old Bible, apparently found what he was looking for, and read it in silence. Finally I could hear him behind me, closing the big book, rising to his feet, and pushing the chair back.

"How many knives to be washed?"

I was so startled at his voice that I didn't catch the words. "What?"

"How many knives need to be washed? Lay them aside when you're finished, and I'll get them when I'm done with the rest."

"Um, it looks like two."

"Steak knives?"

"Oh, four more then. I meant the carving and paring ones."

"Yeah. Okay."

He walked closer and opened a drawer. "I guess she's probably got more than a dozen if you count every type. And she did say every."

I found his mellow compliance somehow disconcerting. Too bad he hadn't stood up to Marigold and insisted that he could do his job later, after I was done in the kitchen. But his next words confirmed to me the condition of his heart in the midst of the outward obedience.

"It's her house. Bottom line."

Noisily, he filled his hands with the knives from the drawer and plopped them all onto the newly cleared table. Then he pulled something wrapped in cloth from the very back of the dishtowel drawer.

"It's only been about six months. They can't be all that bad. Course I didn't do them *all* then."

I wished he would stop talking and take everything outside. But he sat at a kitchen chair, unwrapped the knife sharpener, and began the steady *skritch-skritch* sound of the polishing stone on metal.

"I've done this twice for Aunt Mari," he said with a strange calm in his voice. "Both of the other times she was looking for a way to busy my hands while she tried her durndest to talk some sense in my direction. Wonder what she's up to this time. It's been a long spell since she's played her Victrola."

"Maybe it's because she has a child here with her," I dared to say. "She tries very hard to make Eliza comfortable."

"Yeah. Maybe."

Why was he talking to me? Even more, why was I responding? Was that what Marigold had in mind? I bumped one drinking glass into another and had to carefully inspect them both to make sure they weren't chipped. Behind me, the *skritch-skritch* continued.

We were both quiet for several minutes, and I was beginning to hope that I could finish my job and leave the room before any more words were spoken. But he callously shattered the silence before I even finished with the silverware.

"Why are you here, anyway?"

"Excuse me?" I asked, immediately feeling hurt and defensive.

"Why are you here? I mean in Andersonville and not some other place."

"I told you, your—um—Marigold invited us."

"I know you said that. But why'd she invite you? What'd you say to give her the idea that she should? And why'd you take her up on it?"

How could he ask such a thing? He knew of John's death. Did he think I had abundant means, abundant options?

"I . . . uh . . ."

How could I answer? By spilling out the woeful story of selling our household goods bit by bit, losing our home, sleeping in the park? My eyes filled with tears. Maybe he was trying to drive me away. But where could we go? I still had nothing.

"You got family of your own?"

I choked down what I could of the anger and despair rising in me. "Very little."

"'Nuff to write letters to, I guess."

Words spilled out before I could stop them. "Isn't it my business if I choose to write letters, and none of yours what Marigold and I agree upon?"

"Yeah," he acknowledged. "But I'm a prying cuss that wants to know why you didn't just go and stay with those other folks you're close enough with to be writing letters back and forth."

I dropped a fork and left it where it lay as I made an attempt to answer him. "I wrote to an old neighbor in St. Louis. I did ask her once if we could stay with them. She . . . she said she didn't have room and her husband wouldn't allow it."

He was quiet for a moment. A solitary tear dropped to my cheek as I swirled the dishcloth around a bowl in the dishwater.

Maybe he was thinking. But he was just hardheaded enough to push me a little farther. "What about the other letter?"

"I—I wrote to my father. Anna—the neighbor—said he hadn't been well. But we can't stay there. And—and I'd appreciate it if you'd stop asking me questions."

Skritch-skritch. There was no other sound from him as I hurried with the rest of the regular dishes. And then again as I was just getting started with the pans, he broke the silence.

"See what I was telling you last night? There's no help in a conversation with me. Nothing particularly friendly, either."

I didn't answer. I prayed he'd go away.

Skritch-skritch.

"So why can't you stay with your father?"

Skritch.

"It's none of your business! None at all! We just can't!"

"Is he a hateful drunk like mine?"

I set the pot I was holding upside down in the wire drying rack, took a dishtowel with me, and headed straight for the back door. I didn't need his questions, didn't need the onslaught of suspicion and spiteful distrust. I'd gotten most things washed. I'd finish later. When Josiah was out of the kitchen.

I sat on the back step for a moment with the towel in my

hands. A dark-haired woman was walking with a tiny child in Mr. Abraham's backyard. She glanced my way and then turned her head.

Why, Lord? Why am I here where I'm unwanted? What does Josiah have against me and who gave him the right to question me anyway? What should I do now? And why are you so silent—every time I need you?

The woman and her child next door went into the house, and I glanced toward Marigold's garden. I could weed a little more. Of course it needed it. But I really didn't feel like doing anything. The tears blurred my vision, and I wiped at them with a corner of the dishtowel. We should move on. I would, if there were any way possible.

Behind me the door opened slowly, and I hoped it was Marigold, or perhaps Eliza ready to place her comforting arm across my shoulders as she'd done before. But I could tell by the footfalls that it was Josiah. Following me. I rose to my feet.

"Please don't walk away," he said, his voice strangely sad.

"Why shouldn't I? You don't want a conversation, at least not a friendly one."

"I need to tell you something."

I almost wheeled around. "What? What else? That you think I'm some kind of cheat taking advantage of John's aunt? Taking whatever I can get? I promise you—we'll move on when we can! And in the meantime I'll make sure I'm no burden. I'll stay out of your way if you'll let me, and I'll do everything, anything that Marigold needs—"

"Stop. Okay?"

He sounded broken. So much that I turned. To my surprise, there were tears in his eyes.

"When I said I couldn't help you, I didn't mean I wanted to be hurtful. Okay? I want you to know that."

"I—I don't know what I know! Or what you mean. You're two different ways and I don't understand you. But I think—I think you may be right. At least I think it's useless to try to talk any further."

"Maybe. Just let me explain myself. Your crying in church—it got my ire. I got the idea you were putting it on for show—for Marigold's benefit, and maybe snowing the whole congregation to get on everybody's good side. Maybe people used to think that of me. But what all else of a mess I am, I'm not a phony—not in church. And I couldn't stomach it too well."

I could scarcely speak in the face of such a confusing accusation. Could he really think I'd been pretending? "I didn't plan to cry, Mr. Walsh. I . . . I didn't wish to."

"Okay. Thanks for saying so. I'm just telling you why I was cross with you. Skeptical. I saw a woman pull out tears once and snooker a whole roomful of people out of their hard-earned cash. Not saying you'd do that. I was just—just checking where you stood."

"On shaky ground in your eyes, apparently."

"I'm sorry."

I took a step away from him. "Don't bother saying that or anything else. I have no way of knowing the next thing I'll hear. Please just leave me alone."

He stood silent. For a moment I was sure he'd respond. But he only turned and went back into the house. And I sunk to the step and cried.

18

Josiah

What kind of man was I? I'd hit a grieving widow over the head with my foolish suspicions, chased her out of the house, driven her to tears. John's wife. After all she'd been through.

The sound of her voice plagued me now, the look of her when she'd said, "I promise you we'll move on when we can . . ."

I was the one who should move on. A grown man acting like a child. Dependent on an old woman for the stability I should have been able to find on my own.

When will you stand on your own two feet and quit leaning on Marigold McSweeney like a crutch?

"She needs me," I railed against the familiar voice of accusation in my head. "She's got no other income and no way to do so many of the things that need done around here."

But I really did lean on Marigold. There was no way I could deny that. I counted on her to keep me on track when I couldn't trust myself. And she should have known not to leave me alone with Leah. I'd done damage that it might not be possible to repair.

I wanted to go and tell Mari how badly I'd messed up, but it might not be right to interrupt her and Eliza if there was a need being met in that little girl's life. Better for the child to be enjoying the old Victrola than to go and find her mother in tears yet again.

I didn't know how to make this better. Leah had not received my apology very well, and I couldn't blame her. I wished *I* could move for her sake. And still find a way to be here for Aunt Mari. The answer would not be as easy as taking biscuits to the Kurchers.

I finished in the kitchen quickly, my mind racing over the disastrous conversation with Leah. At least now she could see that in my own stupid way I'd been right. There was no chance I could be any help to her. Far better that we make the agreement I'd proposed and avoid each other completely just to minimize the hurt.

Glancing about, I was careful to be sure all the work was done and everything was back as it should be. Then I headed for my room upstairs so I would not be in the way when Leah came back inside.

Rein me in, Lord. Help me not to be a plague to anyone. If she's really got no place else to go, she doesn't need me attacking her chance at peace.

In the front hall, at the base of the stairs, I had to stop, almost overcome by a sudden memory. John had come flying down these stairs, two by two. "*Joe Walsh is a stinky old horse pie!*"

Of course, he'd just been teasing. We'd teased each other constantly, fought about half the time, and loved every minute of it. What would he think of me now? I could imagine him big and strong, and knocking me flat on the floor with one solid punch.

"I'm sorry," I whispered to the air. "Guess I disappoint you along with everybody else."

I'd had a Scripture in mind earlier, in Romans, chapter 7. It hadn't been hard to find because we'd gone over it in Sunday school not long ago. "For I know that in me (that is, in my flesh,) dwelleth no good thing: for to will is present with me; but how to perform that which is good I find not."

Pretty depressing, standing alone. But God had given the whole next chapter to show us things set aright again. "If the Spirit of him that raised up Jesus from the dead dwell in you . . ."

His love was supposed to work all things for good for those that love him. That was what the chapter said, and a whole lot more. Would things work for good with all the ways I'd found of messing things up for people?

I want to love you truly, Lord. I want to walk after the spirit and not after the flesh. But over and over, time and again, I fall. Oh, wretched man.

19

Leah

What should I do? Mr. Walsh seemed determined to keep me ill at ease. I leaned back against the porch door, shutting my teary eyes and wishing this emotionally trying day to a speedy close. Had he meant to accuse me, or to just see how I'd react? Could he really think I was here under false pretenses, trying to deceive Marigold and her church?

Perhaps it didn't matter. I would never ask for money, nor take anything I didn't work for. He could not shove his guilty conscience onto me.

I thought I heard the sound of a door again from Mr. Abraham's house but didn't move my head or open my eyes. He must be having a family gathering of some sort, for there to be all those people in and out.

My mind was soon far away, revisiting the horror of last night's nightmare. My pulse raced a little faster, and I clamped my eyes tighter. Why did I have to dream such things? It was nothing but nonsense, really. I hadn't been there when John was hit. And what I'd been told was nothing like the scene I'd dreamed. None of it made any sense. The nightmare kept jumping back at me, but it kept changing. Only certain things stayed the same: myself as a child, the train, the terror . . .

"Ma'am, excuse me."

I jumped so forcefully I nearly fell off the step, eyes popping open to meet the source of the unexpected voice. A thin young man in a cap stood before me, his dark eyes shadowed with concern.

"So sorry to startle you, ma'am. Tell me, please. Are you boarding with Mrs. McSweeney?"

It took me a moment to register what he was asking. "Yes."

"My father asked that I please inform the neighbor. Could you take the message for him that Rabbi Josef Abraham has passed from this world? This morning."

"Oh. Oh, yes of course. I'm so sorry for your loss. Please tell Mr. Abraham that we're so sorry."

"I will do that," the young man said. "Thank you."

He turned and walked away, and I sat in a stunned silence for a while. This news, oh, this was bound to change everything. I stood to my feet, feeling shaky.

I felt odd going back into the house, as though the newly familiar had become strange to me all over again. What could I do? Where would we go?

Marigold was in a rocking chair beside the solitary window in her room, and Eliza sat on the edge of her bed. They were listening to voices, singing vigorously in a language I couldn't begin to decipher.

"What do you think?" Marigold asked immediately. "I think it's an Italian opera. Rosie Batey gave it to me."

I sat beside Eliza. "I always liked flowing violins. The same as my mother." I looked down at the lovely woven rug beneath our feet.

"Oh, I like violins too," Marigold said and stopped rocking. She waited in silence, apparently knowing that I had come to say something to her.

"Aunt Mari," I started slowly. "A relative . . . a young man . . . just came from Mr. Abraham's house to tell us—he wanted—I mean he said Mr. Abraham wanted you to know that . . . that Rabbi Josef has passed away."

I had no idea how she would react. She was quiet, only sitting for a moment, as if the news took time to sink in. Then she nodded and bowed her head. "Dear Lord, comfort that family and give them peace."

I bowed my head with her, and so did Eliza. Then when Mari was done with her prayer, she thanked me for relaying the words and rose to her feet. "I think we have time before the dinner hour to bake a couple of cakes and put together a decent meal. How many people do you think are over there?"

"Oh my. I don't know. There have been several in and out, and I have no idea how many may have come with each car."

"We'll need plenty, just in case. Least we can do is share a meal. There'll be nobody wanting to cook over there, but they still need to eat."

I smiled at the kindness, at the natural way it flowed from her thinking. Again I couldn't think of a time my parents had made such a gesture. Maybe Mother would have if Father had let her. Maybe they never had the means.

We spent the rest of the afternoon cooking and baking for the Abraham family. Marigold didn't ask me anything about Josiah, and I didn't volunteer a word about our unpleasant conversation.

"Thank you for finishing the pots and pans while I was outside," I told her while we worked. "I'm sorry I was taking a little break. But I meant to get back to them."

"I didn't do a thing with pots and pans," she said without looking up from her batter bowl. "Maybe it was Josiah."

I could not picture him doing dishes, especially for my benefit, but it must have been so. He was a puzzle, two ways just like I'd told him. Prone to a moment's kindness and then to be confusingly difficult afterward. I wondered how Marigold had managed with him all this time. But I didn't ask.

She had her head full of the neighbors' needs and the menu

she was planning. "Step down to the basement for me and bring up some green beans. Two or three quarts, I think. And a couple of pints of pickles. Let's make candied apples, what do you think of that? I wish we had more bread made. We'll have to start a quick bread in addition to this cake."

Eliza followed me down the basement stairs. "Mommy? Who died?"

I took her hand for a moment. "It was Mr. Abraham's father, honey. He'd been very sick."

She was quiet as we walked to the storage shelves. I began selecting the jars we'd need, and she suddenly had a question. "Isn't Mr. Abraham an old man?"

"Yes. I would say so."

"Then his father must've been a very, very old man, right?"

"Yes. But I'm not really sure how old."

"Then is it okay that he went away to heaven?"

I turned from the shelves to look at her. Perhaps I should have said that God would always make things okay when we lose a loved one, but I couldn't quite manage such words. "Maybe it's not entirely so hard when an old person dies," I told her. "Because at least it's not such a shock and they've a full life behind them. But it's still a sad time for the family, because they will miss him so much."

"I'm sorry that Mr. Abraham is sad."

"So am I."

The rest of the day seemed unreal. We finished a feast for the Abraham family, with Marigold still wondering if it would all be enough. Josiah carried everything over for us and then walked down the street in the other direction and did not come back until late into the evening. We ate our own supper in solemnity without him.

20

Leah

I was nervous for days that I would have to find a job very quickly or end up homeless again. But I was careful not to share my nervousness with Eliza, and she adjusted very well to her first week of school. On the very first day, we'd made new friends. Dorothy Humphrey was a delightful woman who lived catty-cornered across the street from Marigold. Her daughter, Betty, was in Eliza's class, and almost immediately we took to walking together to the school and back. That Eliza now had a friend and playmate so close seemed a wonderful thing, but still I worried about the possibility of having to move.

Marigold attended Rabbi Abraham's funeral, though I wasn't sure whether the family had intended her to. She simply felt she must, which I could very well understand. I asked her afterward if she'd had an opportunity to speak with Saul, but she said he was far too busy with family and the affairs of his father's estate for that.

"He needn't concern himself right now with being a neighbor when he's got so much else to think about," she told me.

"But he's more than that," I protested. "More than even a very good neighbor."

"Right now he's being a good son." She left it at that, and I knew it was only right that she should do so.

While Eliza was in school, I walked about town, getting acquainted with the other businesses and attempting unsuccessfully to find work at one of them. Most of them came right out and told me that if they were looking for help they'd be looking for a man. But they weren't looking for help. None that I found. Marigold had lost two boarders who had to go elsewhere to look for work. And even though she usually had more than that, she'd told me that she might not get more till things picked up a bit in town.

Josiah kept to himself so much that I scarcely saw him. Marigold told me that he was spending a lot of time with a friend across town. I wondered if she worried that they might be drinking. I did.

Not only did dreams of trains continue to plague me but the waking sound of them going through town began to bother me more again as well. Walking through the business streets not far from the tracks, I would jump when I heard the piercing whistle and sometimes start to tremble, even when I'd known the train was coming. Such a foolish plague, but I could not be rid of it, no matter how I tried.

"No way it could possibly hurt you four blocks away," I tried telling myself, just as I had at first. But the sound would still stop me in my tracks every time. I began to worry that Eliza would notice these things when she was with me and begin to be afraid, thinking that something was wrong. Sometimes she got very quiet, watching me. But she only asked me once what was the matter, and I managed to dodge the subject, telling her I'd noticed the first chill in the air and had grown concerned that she might need more clothes before winter.

"Don't worry, Mommy. God will give us clothes just like he gave us an orange and Aunt Marigold."

There was a peace in my mind about her words. *She may be right. Somehow I can believe that God will not disappoint her.*

After Mr. Abraham's family had all gone away again, Josiah took to going there when he got off work and within a week told us that he would be moving next door, as long as Marigold was willing to agree on the neighbor's conditions. If Marigold would provide meals, except breakfasts, and see to washing for them both, with my help, then Mr. Abraham would see that Josiah's rent money still went to her. And either of them were allowed to check on Marigold or her house and help with things when they saw the need. I thought it a rather odd arrangement, but Marigold was perfectly happy with it. She seemed to like Josiah spending so much time with Mr. Abraham, though I would have thought she might like more of that herself.

We still rarely saw Mr. Abraham. Marigold said that he was going to need some time and that was perfectly all right. Sometimes I took food next door, and sometimes Josiah came and got it. And he always came on Tuesday and Friday mornings to pick up Marigold's biscuits for the Kurchers.

The house seemed a little strange without the sound of large feet on the hardwood stairs and hallway floor. But at least I didn't have to worry about chance encounters with Josiah's sullen eyes and unpredictable tongue.

Eliza missed him, but thoughts of that were soon swallowed up in her excitement over her new friends at school, especially Betty Humphrey. They became so attached that they were soon arm in arm on the way home from school nearly every day. The whole Humphrey family was very nice. Sometimes I let Eliza play at their house after school or on Saturday.

We continued to attend Marigold's church, though I tried very hard not to make another spectacle. I spoke as little as I could get by with to anyone there, and mostly they gave me plenty of space. Marigold liked to discuss the service with me afterward, and I would listen and try to comment when I should, but I always wished she would let it all alone. Deep inside, I knew I needed to think things through more thoroughly, but I still did not want to fill my mind with it all. God's Word still made me uncomfortable, because it always seemed that he was expecting something from me that I might never be able to give.

Nonetheless, Marigold had me be her eyes to read the Bible to her every morning, now that Josiah was scarcely available. And though she usually did it herself, sometimes she asked me to pray at meals too. I didn't refuse. I didn't think that I could, but it gave me an uneasy feeling, as though she'd suddenly caught me at something and I had to try to set things right.

Plenty of time had passed for my mail to have reached its destinations. I wondered about my father off and on, if he were already feeling better and how he might have reacted to my brief letter. There must have been something unusual going on for him to have made any effort to contact me. I wished I knew what it was, yet at the same time almost hoped that he would not feel the need to write back. I was still desperately looking for any work I could find to bring in a little money. And helping Marigold with the cooking and chores in her big old house still kept me busy for hours every day. I had enough to handle here without him heaping agonizing words on top of it all.

I didn't get any more mail from Anna, but we'd been in Andersonville a little more than a month when the letter finally came that I had begun to dread. From Walter Wiskirk, my father.

Leah,

Should have told me you were moving. I could have died trying to figure out where you are. Doctor tells me heart's gone bad, said I should ask you to come. Don't bring the girl if you got a place to leave her. Don't want the noise in my house.

He didn't even sign his name. I sat on Marigold's front step staring at the page. How could he do this? Was he dying? How could he not wish to see his granddaughter? He didn't even say that he wanted to see me.

His attitude in the letter angered me so much that I almost wanted to march in the house, throw it in the trash basket, and forget about it. But the doctor thought I should be there? That thought was dizzying. Surely something was seriously wrong.

Marigold's mail lay in my lap and I would have to take it in to her. But maybe I needed to sit a moment and rein in my emotions first.

I hadn't really wanted Marigold to know about this letter, about my problems with my father and his headstrong, uncaring ways. But I couldn't simply forget this. If I didn't answer him in some way, I would probably be plagued with guilt, despite his less-than-inviting overture. I wasn't sure what to do and thought it might help to talk the matter through with someone.

So I carried the mail inside, found Marigold in the kitchen, and told her everything.

"What should I do? I can't go."

"Why not?" She looked at me rather sharply.

"First of all, I don't have the money. But even if I did, I couldn't leave without Eliza."

She looked into the pot she was stirring. "You need to at least consider it, Leah, dear. It seems he needs you."

"More like he wrote that letter under duress. It doesn't sound like he wants me there at all. It was the doctor's idea."

"Maybe the doctor pushed him to it," she acknowledged. "But believe me, if your father is as hardheaded as you say he is, if he didn't want you, there'd be no letter in your hand. Doctors can give advice, but they sure can't make any bullheaded man act on it unless he's decided that he wants to."

I stood in silence.

"You need to pray about going. The Lord will make a way. Maybe your father's feeling that his time is short. He wants to see you, even if he can't admit it outright. He needs you there, or he wouldn't be pleading."

"Pleading? He seems to be rebuking me more than anything."

"Maybe you read a rebuke in that letter. But believe me, between the lines, he's pleading. I can feel it—all the sorrow, and the hope that his little girl will come home for him, at least one more time."

I sat in a chair, stunned with her interpretation.

"Sometimes when a person gets older and the strength of his body fades, the heart has a chance to speak," she continued. "I've seen men desperate for restoration, for the love of their loved ones, if they can find any way to claim it. It's a sad thing, but it can be beautiful if families are willing to forgive and let love be."

"But . . . he . . . he doesn't want my love. He doesn't want anything from me."

"If he didn't, he wouldn't have written."

It seemed so simple. In Marigold's mind. But I didn't know how to reconcile her words with all the hurt inside me, so I went outside to rake the leaves.

When it came time to walk Eliza home from school, I met Dorothy Humphrey on the sidewalk as usual and we walked together.

I would never have thought to mention the whole matter to anyone else, but it must have been plain on my face that something was troubling my mind. She asked me right away what was wrong.

I almost told her nothing, but maybe because of Marigold and the way the Lord kept trying to soften my heart, honest words came pouring out instead.

"I'm so confused about what to do. I've never had a good relationship with my father. But now he's sick with some kind of heart ailment and he's written to tell me that the doctor said I should come. He doesn't want Eliza to come with me.

It makes me angry. And I think I may just have to write to him and tell him I'm not able."

Dorothy shook her head. "But it sounds serious. Maybe the doctor advised against having a young child present. Sometimes they do that, even with the child's own mother if she's ailing with certain things. It would be hard for Eliza to miss school and see her grandfather looking poorly anyway. You really should consider going. Couldn't Eliza continue to stay with your aunt?"

I didn't think I'd told Dorothy that Marigold was my aunt, but I might have mentioned "Aunt Marigold" in our casual talking, or perhaps such things were generally discussed around this small town. "I don't know," I told her. "She said the Lord would make a way for me to go if I wished it, but we didn't really talk about Eliza staying. Marigold has such trouble with her legs, I hate to leave her with the responsibility, especially of seeing her off to school in the morning. Eliza's been very good, and loves to help her, but it might still be a bit much."

Dorothy smiled. "Marigold's probably tougher than you give her credit for. Besides, I could help. I could just start a little earlier in the morning and come right to Marigold's house to help if she needs me to. That way Betty and I could walk Eliza every step of the way. Maybe she could even sleep over part of the time. Betty would love that."

I didn't love that. The thought of leaving my daughter and going back into Missouri without her was simply terrifying. I was glad I didn't have the money. But I didn't want to mention that. "Thank you so much for your kind offer. I will consider it."

Betty and Eliza came out of the school arm in arm again, and I thought about all the things Dorothy had said. Might the doctor have asked that a young child not be brought in, as she had suggested? If that were the case, why wouldn't my father say so? Could it be possible that he'd tried to hide from me just how serious this really was?

Eliza showed me a drawing she'd done, and I tried to shove

thoughts of Father from my mind. None of it mattered anyway. Without money, there was no way I could go. It was as simple as that.

On the way home Dorothy said that she would be praying for my father and would ask her church to do so as well.

I cannot remember praying for my father, I thought guiltily. Maybe I had when I was little, along with my mother and with her guidance, but I certainly couldn't remember ever doing it on my own. "Thank you," I told her, and walked on.

The next morning, Eliza and I woke very early to the thunderous sound of a rainstorm. We huddled together for a moment and I tried to keep her fairly quiet, but then I remembered there was no one in the room next door and let her bounce about and sing to the rain. She hadn't done that since she was three. I was stunned that she remembered. But maybe she didn't. Maybe it was just part of her nature to celebrate some of the moments of life.

"Let's pray for Grandpa like the Humphreys," she suddenly said.

Like always, I couldn't tell her no about something like this. So as she sank to her knees beside the bed, I nodded and sank beside her.

I thought she might be satisfied with both of our heads bowed in silence. But that was not good enough. "You pray, Mommy. Bless Grandpa."

I'd never seen her so insistent. Such a simple request should have been easy, but I could scarcely manage the barest minimum.

"Bless Grandpa," I muttered, feeling suddenly sick in the pit of my stomach. Why did she have to be this way? What if he died? What if he were already dead? How would she feel then?

"Help him feel better, Mommy. Say that too."

"Honey, you can pray for him."

"Please, Mommy, *you* pray."

I didn't know why it was so important to her. Some angry,

broken part of me wanted to refuse any prayer for my father. *He doesn't deserve it*, the hurt in my heart wanted to scream. *He doesn't care about you, about God, or anyone!*

For a second or two, a battle raged within my mind. But despite all the bitterness I held for my father, love for Eliza and for my mother finally won out. Mother had shown me how to be a good example. She was the best she could have been in her circumstance, and I would be wrong not to at least try to emulate her for my daughter's sake. So many times I'd done poorly in that area, but now she was waiting expectantly, head still bowed.

"Help him feel better," I said, barely above a whisper. "Thank you, heavenly Father. Amen."

Still on her knees, Eliza smiled up at me. "I like when you pray, Mommy. It makes me feel all warm and *believy* inside."

21

Josiah

I hadn't planned to move in with Mr. Abraham. I went over first just to talk, then to try to help him get his clatter-trap car running again, without much success. The idea came up all of a sudden, and while we were both a little surprised, it seemed like a natural fit. I needed to be away from the women a while, and he needed to not be so alone.

Marigold wasn't upset when I moved out, even though I'd thought she might be. She said it was probably the most appropriate thing to do and apologized for thrusting Leah and me together the way she'd done.

"Can't push you to be good for each other just because I think you could be," she said, and then thanked me for spending time with Mr. Abraham in his grief.

She must have had it through her head that I thought like she did, about doing for the man, just for the doing's sake. But it wasn't like that at all. I'd moved next door because I couldn't stand another night with just one thin wall between me and Leah. And her humming daughter.

The last week there I'd hardly been able to sleep, just hearing them had bothered me so badly. *Why, God? Why them? They didn't do anything to deserve heartache. Why don't you punish only the guilty and let everybody else stay with their loved ones until they're old and gray?*

Of course, even my finite mind understood that such a thing would be impossible. No adult in this world was purely innocent. I'd been around enough to know that. And there'd be no way to keep one person's blessings or trials from affecting a multitude of others unless we were all hermits. I had no reason to struggle with God over the injustices of this world. As long as sin remained, bad things would happen. Until he brought an end to everything. It was as simple as that.

Mr. Abraham's home was almost as large as Marigold's but did not have so many bedrooms. He gave me a room down the hall from his own, the only other room in the house with a bed already in it. He was terribly quiet compared to the jesting and talking Marigold and I had done when no one else was around. It was almost like being alone. I'd thought I'd love it, but after only two days the silence was about to drive me insane. I'd talked to him plenty of times, I'd even seen a little mischief out of him now and then, at least in Marigold's direction. So this was not characteristic surely. Finally one morning in the midst of flapjacks, I decided to ask.

"Has everything been all right with you? Since the funeral?"

"Yes. I suppose so."

"Really?" I questioned, not willing to let him slip back to silence that easily.

"Much to think about right now," he said. "Much to pray about."

"Like what?" I pushed, knowing full well it was none of my business. But I was going to be nosy whether he liked it or not.

"Da," he said. And for a moment I thought he'd stopped, but then he spoke again with a solemn voice. "He told me many things before his final journey, and I must consider them all very well."

"You mean your father?" I continued to prompt, hoping I

wasn't somehow stepping over a line. Sometimes my mouth rushed ahead of tact or common sense, and I didn't usually care. But I'd been insensitive and offensive with Leah and just made matters worse. Better for that not to happen again.

"Yes. He was strong in his teaching. Strong in his opinions."

"Did he preach? Like in a church? I mean, I've never really been sure what a rabbi does."

Mr. Abraham passed me the plate of flapjacks for the fourth time, and I took what was left on it. "He was a teacher. In a big city he would probably already have had a building similar to a church because people would come to be taught and to worship. But the town where he lived was small, larger than this one, but with not very many Jews. They do not have a building yet but met every Sabbath in his home."

"What do they do now?" I really wanted to know.

"Now they meet in my son's home, or another of the families'. They are making plans for a building, especially since they expect several more families to join us in this area. And my son is the teacher now."

I would have expected some kind of pride in that, but he seemed only far away, and sad. "Mr. Abraham, do you go and worship with them?"

"Call me Saul. You may as well, since we are housemates now. Why so many questions this morning?"

"I miss a good conversation. And I'd like to know. It's not very far, right? Do you go there for the Sabbath?"

He sighed. "Sometimes. But many times I use an excuse, like the condition of my car or even the weather, to stay away, sometimes for weeks at a time. Then I try to worship and seek teaching right here in my own home."

"You could come to church with Marigold and me. If you want. Maybe on a week when the weather's not so good for leaving town."

He smiled, just a little. "I think were I ever to do that, you might lose half your congregation."

The words shocked me completely. "Why?"

He looked down a moment. “This town knows I am a Jew. And they don’t mind, if I stay in my home or use my cash in their stores. But if I came into one of the churches, I think many would be afraid.”

“You’ve got to be kidding,” I blurted out, though his face showed no sign of kidding at all.

“No. You would see it.”

“I can understand people being uneasy about *me* showing up in church. I nearly set the place on fire when I was thirteen messing around with a box of stolen cigars in the crawl space that used to be under the front steps. But you? You don’t have a hooligan’s reputation, a record of drunkenness, or anything like that.”

“I’m a Jew. That’s enough.”

The words made me angry, but he wouldn’t discuss it any further.

“Take every egg you can find to the Kurchers’,” he said. “I have half a dozen in the icebox and that is plenty. Marigold is probably ready with her biscuits. You’d better go.”

“What if *I’m* part Jewish?” I insisted. “Who would know? I don’t know where my people are from. And what the heck difference would it make anyway?”

“Josiah.” He smiled. “With a good Jewish name. Stop thinking and go to work.”

Right and wrong. Blessings and cursings. I couldn’t have stopped thinking that day any more than I could have stopped breathing. So many situations frustrated me. So many things just seemed out of place. Marigold had told me once that I was discontent because I hadn’t stepped into the place God had for me yet. Well, who had? Wasn’t the whole world discontent? Even Marigold herself, because she loved a Jew, an old man who still hadn’t proposed and maybe never would. Maybe never should if it meant either of them would have to change more than their heart wanted.

“You’re called, sure as I’m born,” Marigold had told me once, not long after I'd come from the jailhouse to her boardinghouse. "That's why things touch you so deeply. He's already got hold of a good piece of your heart."

Called. To minister, she'd meant. And that thought was still almost as ridiculous now as it had been then. I just had a pitiful habit of getting my mind so wrapped around things it was hard to let loose again. Kept me frustrated much of the time, but it did nobody else any good.

When we pulled into the Brighton station, I knew immediately that there must be a problem with the Kurchers. Dodie was not waiting on the platform as she usually did, the way it had been since Marigold had started sending biscuits over a year ago. At first I didn't see anyone, but then scrawny little Bobby came racing like Man o' War from behind a building to be in time to meet the train. He couldn't have been more than nine or ten. The brakeman stopped us and I stepped to the platform with the biscuits and eggs. Poor Bobby was breathless.

"Mama's sick," he said immediately, sucking wind to get the words out. "Dodie too. Almost everybody. Been hittin' pretty hard."

"What has? What kind of sick are they?"

"Fever and spots. Measles, Mama says. I hope to never catch 'em. Mama's got me doin' the outside fetchin' and we's hopin' I'll stay clear."

"Are all the older children ill, then?"

"Yeah. 'Cept Beth Ann, an' she's tending the younger ones. Mama wanted to know if Mrs. McSweeney might come out a few days and lend a hand. If she's done had 'em, that is. Wouldn't want her pickin' up the measles herself."

"No. You're right," I said. "We wouldn't. She's a pretty strong woman for the most part but with a lot of trouble with the rheumatism in her knees lately. I'm not sure she could do what you all have need of, or ought to even try. But I could ask her if she thinks somebody from our church would be willing."

"Thank you. That's good enough that you'll ask." He took

the bundle of biscuits from my hand. "We sure thank you for bringing the food again. We sure need it, 'specially now with all the cookin' and harvestin' slowed down." He reached for the basket of eggs. "I'm sorry I forgot to bring a basket to swap everything into. Can I bring yours back the next time?"

"I think we can manage without it. Can you carry it by yourself?"

"I'm going to. I sure will. Slow and gentle, Mama said. So I don't break a one."

"That's right."

He nodded to me and was on his way, leaving me with a sour feeling. The widow Kurcher and most of the kids down with measles? Harvest slowed down? Oh, Lord! Marigold would want to do everything she could for her old friend, which was a huge problem because she couldn't, and surely shouldn't, try to do much of anything at all.

I fed the flames beneath the locomotive's steam boiler the rest of that day with my mind on the Kurchers' troubles. Surely Marigold wouldn't think to go. I could help her find somebody else.

What a pickle, exactly what we didn't need right now!

At least I'd have tomorrow to try to help find a solution. Mr. Behrens had put his nephew on the train as fire man on Saturdays. It was an odd arrangement, which made me wonder a bit, but it gave me an extra day to take care of other things.

When I got back to Andersonville, I went right to Marigold's with the news.

"Oh, that Hilda!" she exclaimed. "I wish to goodness she was in church over there regular. With church folks hardly knowing them, they don't know to look in on her like a church family should."

"Could we ask someone from our church?" I wanted to know.

"None of them know her, and I've got to think about who could go without having little ones of their own to keep them from it. I'd say Minnie Fromm, but she's away visiting this week. Has the doctor been out?"

"Bobby didn't say, but from what I know of that family, I doubt it."

She nodded. "Surely right."

"What about the Richlers?"

"Oh, Josiah, they're older than I am."

"Reverend Pierce?"

"They need somebody to go tomorrow and stay a few days. He'd not be here to fulfill his own responsibilities to the church. We can't ask him unless there's no one else."

"Mrs. Bower?"

"She's got company this weekend. Clear from Peoria."

It amazed me how Aunt Marigold always knew so much about so many people, especially since she saw most of them only on Sundays.

"Mrs. Batey?"

"She may act like she's got sass, but she's not got the constitution for that rip-roaring house of youngsters, especially when they're sick. Three years ago she went to nurse her sister and took a lung infection so bad she nearly died."

"Well, you can't go!"

"Why not? I'm not bad as a nursemaid."

I couldn't believe I had to point out the obvious. "You can't climb stairs anymore, Mari. You have trouble enough just going from one room to the next."

"I'm doing better the last few weeks, haven't you noticed? Maybe it's the hot oil rub. Or maybe it's having Leah here to lighten my load a little."

"I have noticed. And I'm glad. But it's not better enough. Not for this."

"Well, then you think on it and I'll think on it and between us maybe we'll come up with a solution. They're going to understand, Josiah, if nobody comes right away. It's awfully short notice to ask somebody after dark tonight and expect them to be there tomorrow. If we have to wait and get a volunteer at church Sunday and put them on the train the next day, it'd still be a help. Believe me."

We left it at that. But I didn't like it. I thought about Mel and Dotty, but knew they wouldn't go for strangers they'd never met. They just weren't that way.

I should have been able to let it go. After all, measles weren't like the typhoid fever, or even the killing influenza that had taken Leah's baby. The Kurchers would weather this soon enough and be none the worse for it.

If they got their harvest in before it went to waste. Pumpkins, I think they grew, for a local cannery. Corn for market too. Maybe other things.

I used Mr. Abraham's telephone to speak to a few people about the problem but didn't get a definite answer. So he and I prayed together about it over a late pot of Marigold's stew. I watched him in the midst of the prayer as he sat almost tearful, clearly touched by the plight of Marigold's friends.

It was a foolish moment to bring up another subject, but once again my mouth got ahead of all reason. "You're a good man. And Marigold's a good woman. You care about each other. So are you ever going to ask her to marry you?"

He paled in front of me. "Do not ask me that again."

"But you haven't answered."

He put his elbows on the table and his head in his hands. "There is more to that than you can see from where you stand."

"Like what?" I knew I was pushing boundaries this time, absolutely stepping across a line of what was proper to pry into. And to my surprise, he laughed.

"God works in mysterious ways, Josiah. When we talked about you staying here, I didn't know he'd be stirring me so."

"What do you mean?"

"You ask and I have to face this, put all my reasons together on one side or the other and come to a decision."

"Is it that hard?" I asked, with considerable surprise.

"Yes. More than you know."

"Why?"

He looked up at me in silence for a moment and I could tell his mind was far away.

"My father asked me to promise I'd not attach myself to a Christian woman so long as he lived. He wanted me to be faithful and not shame him before his people because he knew they wouldn't approve. A Christian would want to pull me away into the apostasy."

I almost objected to his use of that term, but thought I'd better not if I wanted to hear more.

"I obeyed him because it was my duty as a son to respect my father. And I kept that promise because it is a sin in the eyes of God to break a solemn vow."

"I understand."

He nodded. "So you're thinking I am free. I could marry her tomorrow if she agreed, because now my father sleeps with his fathers and I am released. But it's not as simple as that."

"Maybe not, but I still don't understand."

He smiled. "You're a young man, Josiah. One day you'll love again, even if you can't see that now. And a young man doesn't always see the consequences of his young love. But I see what could be because of mine, and it may be too high a price to pay."

"What price? You and Mari'd have to decide which house you'd live in and what to do with the other one. Not much more to it than that. Especially since you're already sharing things back and forth."

"It has nothing to do with our material goods. It's the people we respect and love. And how far I am bound by duty to respect my father's feelings even after he's gone."

"I don't think it's right for a man to bind another, kin or not. He ought to let you follow your own heart."

"He said as much. That I would be free to make my choice. We talked frankly because he'd known of my feelings for Marigold. But he wanted me to remember my son and his position. And especially my grandchildren, whether I'd be the kind of example that they need me to be."

I got riled over that and almost knocked over the stew. "Good example, huh? What's a better example than being your own man? Not letting anything hold you back from loving somebody just because of what somebody else might think! What kind of an example would you be if you denied your own heart? Do you want that kind of bondage for them? Or would you rather they see you really free?"

He gathered a few of the dishes out of my way and didn't answer immediately. I had no idea how he'd react.

"I understand what you're saying," he finally said. "It's the cry of at least one of the voices within me. But there's more. I wouldn't want my grandchildren to believe that *feelings* are the most important thing, to be catered to and acted upon at the expense of family and all else. We're not put here to oblige our own desires, after all. Solomon tells us that the ultimate duty of man is unto God."

"Okay. But I don't see how it would hurt him for you and Mari to be together. He's practically put you together already. You're the closest neighbors I've ever met, if you know what I mean."

"Yes. Of course it couldn't hurt him. But does it serve his purpose?"

"You're serious. Wanting to know that?"

"Of course I'm serious."

He didn't seem to understand what I was getting at. "I've never in my life heard of anybody taking that into consideration. Not even believers. I mean, a man falls in love with a girl, he decides on being with her, and they go from there."

"That's the way of the world. But we're not called to be ordinary but a holy people."

"Are you telling me Jews only marry when it's God's will?"

"I'm not saying Jews. I'm not saying that's the way it always is, but that it's the way it should be for any follower of Almighty God."

"Well, how do you find out?"

"Seek him," he said with a hint of a smile. "That's what I'm trying to do. I don't know how long it will take."

"If you ask me, I'd say the Lord's already stamped his approval. And I wouldn't be surprised if Marigold agreed."

"But I must consider what it could cost her, among her friends and church, to marry a Jew."

"You don't think they already know you're close? If they're real friends, it won't matter."

"It will if they think I will pull her from faith, just as it would matter to my family if they feel I will lose my identity as a Jew."

I crumpled up my napkin. "I'd say they all have a problem then. You're in God's hands, and they can leave *him* to work it out to his own satisfaction."

He smiled again. "Yes. Josiah. Named for the king who purged idolatry from Israel. Purging now the idol of religious prejudices."

I scoffed immediately. "I was named for some singer my mother met in a tavern while she was carrying me. Years later when my father found out, he beat her. And he never called me by my first name again."

"I'm saying you have wisdom about you, Josiah. An uncommon wisdom, unfortunately."

I didn't know how to answer that, so I just got up to clear the rest of the table and help with the dishes. "Would you mind if I read the Bible aloud some mornings?" I asked him eventually. "I used to do that for Mari and I kind of miss it."

"What part of the Bible?"

"We finished Psalms together and got started in Proverbs. But on my own I've started in Romans."

Only after I said it did I realize he was almost surely not familiar with a New Testament book. But he surprised me.

"One of the Epistles?"

"Yes. Written by Paul."

"The Paul who was Saul?"

"I think you're right."

He gave me a wry sort of smile. "I might be interested in hearing a bit of that."

22

Leah

I could not believe what Marigold was asking of me.

"It would only be a couple of days. You could take the train over in the morning and then ride the same one Monday that Josiah takes to get home. Or if we could get a driver that would be so much better! We could get you over there as soon as possible and back as soon as we find someone else to take over for a while. Oh, I wish Mr. Abraham's automobile was working again! You've had the measles, haven't you?"

"Yes, but what about Eliza? I can't take her among all of those sick children. She hasn't."

"She'll be fine right here with me. I'm even sure that if you weren't back on Monday morning, Mrs. Humphrey wouldn't mind walking her to school. She gets along so well with the Humphreys."

Tension boiled in me and I wished I could let it explode. How could she do this? "Marigold, I don't even know these people."

"*I* know them. And believe me, I want to go. But I daresay Josiah may be right that it would be too much for me. There's a passel of stairs just getting into the house, and the bedrooms are upstairs too, as I recall. I might be all right if you were there with me, but it would surely be better for me to stay here for Eliza while you're gone."

"I didn't say—"

"I know, dear." She answered my protest before I could voice it. "You're still considering. Remember that the good Lord blesses those who bless others, and the Kurchers sorely need you. I've been racking my brain through our little church family to decide who I might ask, and even if I do come up with someone able who doesn't have family needing them, I can't say for sure when they could go. Wouldn't want to wait till Monday. They need help *now*. And this is the quickest thing I can think of. You'd be a godsend, Leah. Hilda wouldn't send her boy to ask for help if it weren't serious. I know her that well. She's pretty independent about anybody coming in her house to lend a hand."

"Maybe she wouldn't want a stranger then. And I've got Eliza to think about."

"Eliza's used to me by now. We'd be just fine."

"But Marigold . . ."

We both let her name hang in the air. What else could I say? How dare she put me in such a spot? Go and help a sick family? I didn't even know that I could find the right house, or that I could be any real help if I got there. What was she thinking? Was this the sort of thing that Josiah had meant about her pushing him to help people? Maybe I'd been here long enough that she was beginning to push *me*.

I just can't . . . I wanted to say it aloud, just refuse her request and be done with it. But her voice rang in my head. *Why not?*

I didn't have a ready answer. Was I really unable, or just unwilling and reaching for a reasonable excuse? Would Eliza really be all right without me for two or three days? Or would she be scared, especially at night?

I'd not been able to seriously consider going to see my father because of the horrible thought of leaving my daughter behind. And now a completely different situation with the same uncomfortable request.

I left Marigold in the kitchen and walked to my daughter, who was drawing a picture beside the lamp in the sitting room. "Eliza?"

She looked up at me with a bright smile.

"We've always been together, haven't we?"

She nodded.

"Does it bother you to be at school away from your mommy?"

She frowned a little. "It did on the first day because I didn't know anybody yet. But not anymore 'cause I have fun with my friends. And the teacher's nice too. I thought she might be scary, but she's not a problem at all."

"That's wonderful." I put my arm around her. "I'm glad you like it."

Her bright smile was back. "I knew Ill'nois would be lovely."

"Yes, you did. And I should have known too, that you'd have no trouble at all making friends. It's your nature to love being around people."

She looked down at her drawing and added a line. "This is me in the apple tree and Aunt Marigold in the chair outside. I wanna make a ladder with you on the very top."

"The second rung would be good enough. I'm not brave enough for the top."

"I think you're brave."

I suppose she did. Simply because I was her mother. But I knew the truth. I'd been more afraid sending her to school than she was. And far more afraid about the trip coming here. I was terrified of leaving her for even a few hours, let alone two or three days to go to the Kurchers', or maybe even more if I should visit my father. What if something should happen? She was all I had left. Tears filled my eyes, and I almost wished I hadn't come in to talk to her.

"Mommy, what's wrong?"

"I don't feel very brave, honey. So often it seems you're braver than I am."

"That's 'cause I'm not growed up so I don't have to think so much."

I smiled a little. "Maybe you're right."

"Do you miss me when I'm in the school?"

"Yes. I do. Enough to make me wish I could go right in your classroom with you sometimes."

"That would look silly, Mommy."

"I know."

She hugged me. "I still gots time at home every day and for the whole weekend. I'm not at school *all* the time."

"I know. It's really not so bad."

"I bet you'll get used to it. Just like me."

"I'm sure I will." I looked her picture over more closely. She'd drawn herself reaching down out of the tree and holding Marigold's hand. She had a ready explanation when I pointed it out to her.

"That's in case she needs help gettin' up, or I need help gettin' down. I haven't decided which yet."

"You really like Marigold, don't you?"

"Lots and lots."

I took a deep breath. "Do you think it would be scary if I had to leave you with her overnight?"

She looked a little worried suddenly. "Are you going away?"

I almost panicked. "Oh, honey, don't worry. I might never. But if I do, it would only be for a little while to help somebody or to go see Grandpa."

"If you go away on a trip, I would like bestest to come too. But if I hafta stay an' go to school, would I hafta still sleep in our bed? I don't wanna be the only one upstairs."

"I don't know, honey. Maybe Marigold would make a bed for you somewhere down here."

"I bet she would!" Eliza jumped to her feet with sudden excitement. "It would be like a sleepover, me an' her. We could eat popcorn an' listen to the Victrola and sing and everything!"

Her enthusiasm made my insides knot. "That would really be all right with you?"

"Yeah! If you come back pretty soon."

I remembered the first time I'd slept over with a friend. I'd thought the whole thing would be the most fun I'd ever had. And it was, until night came and I was nowhere near my mother.

How would my absence affect her nightly ritual or her already wounded heart? My mother had been reluctant to let me go, rightly considering the nightmares that still bothered me sometimes. But she'd consented because, as she'd put it, "a child's got to learn to walk without holding Mama's hand." And I'd weathered the difficult night, fortunately without nightmares, and been ready to do it all again.

Maybe it would be okay.

Maybe. But of course there were no guarantees. And my mind raged with the thought. *You cannot leave your baby! You can't go! You just can't!*

Marigold was making cambric tea for herself and Eliza, and regular for me. We rejoined her in the kitchen and I sat in silence, trying to reconcile the thoughts churning in my head. *They're in need. They're strangers. And I might have to ride the train . . .*

"A ticket for such a short ride isn't going to cost very much," Marigold suddenly said, as if addressing my thought. "Surely we could find a driver. But if we can't, I could pay that much out of that last rent money—I mean food and wash money—that Josiah gave me."

"Marigold, I just don't know—"

"Pray on it, child. That's all I ask."

By morning I was all in a stew, but I couldn't just let it go. I *had* prayed about it, not wanting to feel anything, but instead I'd felt strangely compelled not to turn my back when I really might be able to answer a need. Maybe Marigold was rubbing off on me. Or at least heaping my conscience with guilt. Whichever it was, I agreed to go. But I did tell her I'd rather not take the train. She thought it was because I feared getting lost on my own.

"I know right where the house is, and I can sure be of help getting you there."

Marigold sent me over to use Mr. Abraham's telephone to invite Rosie Batey over for a breakfast pastry and tea. While we waited for her, I packed a bag and we explained everything to Eliza, who seemed very pleased that I would be willing to help a family in need.

Then while Rosie was enjoying the treats, Marigold shared the problem and got an immediate agreement to drive me all the way to the Kurchers'.

"I can't be going inside now," Rosie insisted. "I take sick awful bad around ailing folks. There might be somethin' brewing there along with those measles. Can't take that chance. My doctor'd never let me hear the end of it."

"That's all right," Marigold assured her. "All we need is a ride over there. I'll show you exactly where the house is, and Eliza and I can keep you company on the drive back."

"I'm going too?" Eliza piped up.

"Only to see the place and see your mama off. I'm sorry to say you can't go inside because you could catch the measles from those poor children and your mama wants to keep you well."

"Will Mommy get sick?"

"No, honey," I promised. "I had measles when I was little, so I can't get them again."

I don't think she understood that, but she didn't ask for an explanation and I probably wouldn't have been able to provide a very good one if she had. We finished our breakfast, I fetched my bag, and we were soon ready to go.

Riding with Mrs. Batey farther than the church might have been alarming, but I'd become more used to her driving in the weeks since we first came, and I'd even convinced her to try slowing down more while turning. I was confident that she did all right most of the time, and her automobile was certainly not as frightening as a train. It turned out to be a lovely day for a drive, and though my stomach felt tight and almost sick with the thought of sending Eliza back home without me, I was glad that they'd been able to accompany me on the way.

"Are you sure you'll be able to come back and get me tomorrow afternoon?" I asked, just for the assurance. I didn't want to be away from Eliza more than one night if possible, and Marigold thought that by then she would be able to find someone else from the church to take my place for a few days.

"I don't see why not. As long as it's not storming. I don't drive in storms."

"I'll find someone else if I have to," Marigold promised me. "And you can call Rosie or Mr. Abraham from Hilda's neighbor's phone if you need to."

It seemed to be all settled, and I tried to feel comfortable about it. I watched Eliza, hoping she wasn't scared or worried, but she seemed to be taking it all in stride. Of course, I had no way of knowing how she'd be on the ride home.

Perhaps we were a sight, three women and a child driving across the countryside. Every time we passed anyone, they turned their heads to look at us. But of course, Mrs. Batey did have an oddly painted car.

Marigold did her best at making the trip merry, singing hymns and telling stories about her and Rosie when they were younger. "Oh, we were the corkers," she told us. "A wonder we didn't one of us end up in a vaudeville show."

I held Eliza's hand and she leaned into me as we got closer to the destination, but she was laughing at Marigold's stories and seemed to be thoroughly enjoying the outing. I would have too, if it weren't for my worry over Eliza's feelings later.

At the nearest town before the Kurchers', Marigold pointed out a little corner restaurant. "That would be the perfect place to stop and get an ice cream on the way home. If you don't think it's too cold."

"It's not cold," Eliza said immediately. "We only needed one sweater."

"Quite right," Marigold agreed. "So that would be the perfect time for ice cream. If it's all right with your mother."

"Oh yes. That would be fine with me." I really appreciated Marigold already finding a way to give Eliza something to look forward to and think about, other than missing me.

Kurchers' farmhouse was nearly as big as Marigold's house, but older, in far worse shape, and surely bursting at the seams with all the children they'd told me about.

Mrs. Batey drove as close as she could, but the driveway was full of too many dips and hollows to take it all the way beside the house where it looked like it used to go.

I was so nervous I was almost sick to my stomach and wished I'd never agreed to this. Until Eliza squeezed me tight and gave me a kiss on the cheek.

"Make all those children all better, Mommy. And their mama too. You're a real alive hero!"

My eyes filled with tears and I almost couldn't get out of the car. Was she thinking of her father the way I did as soon as she'd said those words? Was she afraid that I might not come back?

If so, it certainly wasn't apparent. She smiled a huge smile. "See you tomorrow, Mommy! I'm gonna say a prayer in church that God make everybody better really fast. An' I'm also gonna tell people they oughta come an' help, just like you."

"Thank you, honey."

Two Kurcher children ventured out to greet us, a girl of about thirteen and a little boy smaller than Ellie. The girl knew Aunt Mari.

"Oh, Mrs. McSweeney! Thank you, thank you for coming."

"I fear I can't stay, but I've brought you good hands in my stead. Tell your mother this is Leah Breckenridge, wife of my dear nephew. She's a blessing to me and I know she'll be to you as well. She can stay until tomorrow when I hope to have some more coming."

The girl thanked her again, and I hugged on Eliza.

"Is there babies inside?" she asked.

"There's two wee smaller'n this'un," the girl answered, indicating her younger brother.

"Sick?" Ellie asked on.

"Whole house is sick but us two here and Bobby," she said.

I groaned inside. What had I gotten myself into?

"Will you kiss them little ones for me, Mommy?"

"I'll do that," I promised, kissing her first.

"I would love to visit with your mother," Marigold told the big girl. "But I suppose that'd best wait until another time. Is she sick in bed?"

"Yes, ma'am. She's been pretty poorly."

"Give her a hug from me. I'm not sure I could manage the stairs going into your house without help, and I'm not going to ask her to come out. I'll be back when the family's feeling better."

The big girl nodded, and then, that quickly, Rosie was ready to distance herself from the house of illness. I grabbed my bag, and she started the car going again. Eliza turned around three times to wave to me as they drove away.

I suddenly wondered how I could muster the strength to climb the porch stairs and meet the rest of the family. This woman had twenty-one children? How many were still at home? And all sick, except for three?

The big girl's name was Beth Ann, and she was ready immediately to take me in to meet her mother, so I took a deep breath and mustered the determination. There was nothing else I could do now. Eliza was on her way home without me. I had to trust her in Marigold's hands. And God's.

Hilda Kurcher cried in gratitude to have someone here to help. "I sent Bobby out again to meet the train," she told me. "In case Marigold was to send somebody thataway. Don't suppose he'll find nobody today then, but that's all right. You're here now, and he won't be gone long."

Apparently there were eighteen still at home, most of whom had been sent to bed and told to stay there. She told me all their names and ages, and I asked her what was her most immediate need. "Laundry. Oh, my stars, we ain't been able to keep up with the laundry. And we need more a' the medicine tea boilt. I got three with their eyes sore and needin' bathed. An' those that's got appetite ain't been fed a decent meal neither. Thank you again so much for being here. Whatever you can put a hand to will be a help. I don't know why I feel so weak. Seems to have hit me harder than the children."

"Could be exactly that, Mrs. Kurcher. Adults don't take measles often, but when they do, I suppose they make up for lost time."

"I usually keep the children home from school when there's anything going around so they don't catch it. But this time—I don't even know how this got started. We don't know anyone else with measles."

"What's surprising to me, Mrs. Kurcher," I admitted, "is how you got this far with none of them having it before."

"That's the funny thing. My oldest ones did have it, years ago. Three of them are on their own now, but of the other four, they're all down sick except Beth Ann. I was expecting my eighth then. Mother made me stay away so I'd not take it then and put the baby at risk."

I was immediately frightened to hear this. We might not be dealing with measles at all, though it did look like it in the mother. So if measles was in the house, there was probably something else along with it. Or how could the older three be sick again? Not with measles, surely.

"Do their spots look like the others?" I asked.

"Rafe and Ida don't even have spots. But they've been feverin' with the rest. Dodie's got some, but they're peculiar, I think."

"May I go and look at your children?" I asked Mrs. Kurcher.

"Lordy, yes," she answered me. "Do what you can."

I had little doubt about the measles in all but the oldest three of the sick children. They all had fever and chills like the others, but they were the only ones with sore throats. And Dodie's spots were only on the arms, not typical at all. I'd come to be just an extra pair of hands, and Marigold had thought that would be all that was needed. I was sorry now that I hadn't asked them to summon a doctor.

I had my work cut out for me, to say the least. Nobody was dreadfully sick, and most of the children seemed to be at least a little hungry, so I decided that the first priorities would be a little food and the medicine tea Mrs. Kurcher had mentioned. I got her directions and got started in the kitchen.

Half an hour later, I had a nutritious brunch well under way and Mrs. Kurcher's catnip and peppermint steeped into tea and distributed around the house. It was familiar, cooking on a woodstove again, though I needed wood brought in and wasn't sure who to ask. Beth Ann was better needed helping with the younger siblings, and Dougy, the little boy who had greeted me along with her, was too little for a job like that. Maybe I'd find the woodpile myself after a bit.

I was almost ready to begin feeding whoever felt like eating when Dougy yelled that Bobby was on his way back across the field.

"An' he's got somebody with him!"

Someone from the town, maybe. Or a neighbor. It didn't really matter, as long as they'd come to help. That would be a tremendous relief. There was far more work here than only my hands could manage.

I heard the heavy footfalls on the porch, the hint of his voice outside, but I didn't make any connection until Bobby Kurcher proudly brought his guest right into the kitchen. I turned, hoping for a doctor or maybe a knowledgeable neighboring farmer and his wife. And then I nearly fell against the stove, so great was my shock.

Josiah Walsh.

23

Josiah

My first impulse was anger. Had Marigold done this? Could she have devised it on purpose, getting Leah and me both here at the same time? I couldn't be sure. I'd told Mr. Abraham of my intentions, but not Marigold. And he'd said that Marigold would be asking several people, hoping to send someone tomorrow. He'd said not a word of this.

Leah seemed as stunned as I. She didn't speak or turn to the pot behind her on the stove. She looked afraid, like she'd been trapped in a snare. I didn't want her thinking it was by my design.

"I promise you, I did not know you would be here."

"Th-that's a little hard to believe," she managed to answer me.

"Maybe so. But it's the gospel truth."

The incongruity of her presence sunk in slowly. I would never have imagined that she would even consider this, whether she'd brought her child into this sick house or left her at home. And how had she gotten here? She must have left at almost the same time I did but had someone bring her directly by car.

Bobby stood staring at us. "How'd you get here?" He asked the question for me.

"Mrs. Rosie Batey drove me," Leah replied. "At Mrs. McSweeney's request."

She turned, found a stirring spoon, and gazed down into a pot of something on the woodstove. "There'll be food in a moment if you all are hungry."

I needed to think. I needed to put my hands to helping. I did not need to sit and have her waiting on me first thing. "I believe I'll step on out to the field," I told her. "Since you've got things taken care of in the house. This boy's been telling me how badly they need to bring in the harvest. Bobby, get yourself something to eat before you join me. Put some meat on those bones."

"I—I'll need wood soon," Leah said.

Bobby jumped at the spoken need. "I'll fetch you some."

And I followed; the quicker we filled the wood box, the quicker we could move on to something else.

She offered me food again after we'd brought in wood, but I went right back outside. It seemed the easiest way to handle the situation, at least for now.

There were so many things I would have liked to ask her. Why had she come? Had she brought Eliza along? Did Marigold have such a strong influence over her that she now felt obligated to come and serve? I could almost imagine Mari's words: *"We're here to help one another. That's why God put us on this earth, whether we realize it or not."*

I hated field work. I hated gardening even worse. But these people needed their corn brought in and their potatoes dug. There were tomatoes and other vegetables in a sizeable patch, and a field full of pumpkins, all sizes. Most of the vines were shriveling and the fruits were almost all plump and orange. The nearest end of the field was downhill and soggier than the rest. I could see a few of the closer pumpkins sunken on one side, infested with squash bugs and rotting on the damp ground. Hopefully there wouldn't be much of that problem in the rest of the field. But they ought to be harvested promptly and hauled to market to get as much gain out of them as possible.

The corn was ready too, but I started with the pumpkins because it was their peak market time and I was concerned over losing more of the crop. I pulled one of the closest pumpkins first and then decided I might want a way to carry more than one at a time. A quick check in the barn revealed a rickety wheelbarrow I could use immediately. And a truck which they surely used to haul the crop to market, but I dreaded that idea.

Before Bobby came back outside, I'd already picked more pumpkins than I'd ever handled in my entire life. Because I'd not been sure how they might select for market, I'd just been setting them all together along the nearest side of the barn.

"Sure you don't wanna go eat?" Bobby asked me as he reached my side. "That woman made some pretty good soup."

"Later. Need to keep making progress first. Do you sell right in town? And would your market be open today?"

"Should be. Grocer and canner both. And they'll prob'ly be glad to see 'em. Mama's been telling me all week we need to pick punkins, but I ain't been able for doin' t'other stuff needing attention first. Probably weren't much use to it anyhow without somebody to drive 'em in."

He eyed my pile rather critically. "You know we gotta sort, don't you? The biggest and prettiest goes to Fletcher's Grocery. The smaller and not quite so nice goes to the cannery, and the ones that ain't fit for neither goes to Mr. Hawkins for his pigs. He'll give us a side a' bacon later. Best trade I ever knowed."

"Couldn't argue with you there."

"We gets to pick out and save a bunch for our own eatin' too. Many as we want. Mama lets everybody handpick their own." He gazed around the field and frowned. "The littler kids loves pickin' their own punkin. It's good fun and they ain't allowed in the field otherwise. I s'pose we'd better leave some for when they're feelin' better. Wouldn't wanna pick everything an' spoil things for 'em."

I looked at the massive field. "Not much chance of that. Let's just get a start for a first load to market and try to get some corn in too."

He began sorting through the harvested pumpkins and I started to go back to picking. But the thought of getting these to market today, if possible, wouldn't leave me.

"Is your mother the only one that drives?"

"Lowell, Dodie, and Rafe, but they's all sick. An' Buck and Junie, but they went with Buck's pa to Effingham for some kind of reunion. Sure wish they'd get back. We been in need a' their help."

I knew he was referring to an older daughter who had married a neighbor's son. I'd planned to ask him about getting their help. But maybe there were others available. "What about Dodie's beau and your other older sister and brother?"

"Dodie's fella broke his leg 'bout three weeks ago. Ben's gone away to the army. An' Mama said we wasn't to mention nothing to Verna's husband even if we see him. On account that he said he wasn't going to be burdened with us."

I gave a grunt of disgust and glanced over at the boy. "That's a shame. He's missing out on a blessing."

He picked up a giant pumpkin and set it to one side away from the others. "You think it's a blessing, helpin' us?"

"I'm sure it will be. And since he's your family now, it seems to me that working alongside you and knowing you a little better would be a double blessing for him."

He whistled. "You got a pretty way a' lookin' at things, mister. Bet he's never took no thought on blessings at all, lest they's the kind you can jingle in your pocket."

"Maybe not. Some people are like that."

That boy and I worked until my back ached and I was so empty that my belly ached just as badly. "You need a break," I told him.

He laughed. "You're the one that looks done in. But that's 'cause you didn't get none of your sister's soup."

"Sister? You mean Leah? She's not my sister."

"Oh. Your cousin, then. I noticed you both call Mrs. McSweeney Aunt Marigold."

"Long story." I didn't see any point in explaining to him that we were both related to Mari through marriage but neither of us was actually blood kin to her or to each other.

"But you are kin?"

"After a fashion."

"That's what I thought."

He helped empty another wheelbarrow of pumpkins beside the barn, and together we walked to the house.

"Wish we could take a load to town today," he said. "Sure would be nice to have the cash. And the longer they sit, the greater the chance I have to sort 'em twice."

We almost had enough to fill the old pickup already. It would be nice to get at least some to market. But the thought of it sent a chill through me. I did *not* want to drive that truck. "Maybe Leah can drive." I spoke the sudden idea aloud.

"Don't you?"

I swallowed hard. "Maybe. If I have to. But I'd rather take a train or walk."

He looked at me with a bit of concern. "You takin' the train goin' back through tonight?"

"No. I'd rather take the train home, but I didn't want to have to leave that soon if you need the help. A friend of mine is driving over to get me tomorrow night so I'll be back in time to catch the train again in Andersonville early Monday."

Leah wasn't in the kitchen when we went in, so I determined with some relief to gather something to eat on my own. Didn't take me long to notice that there were plenty of herbs and tomatoes, and a few other garden vegetables, but not much else to be found.

"We's sure thankful for the biscuits and things you send," Bobby said. "Got no cash for the grocer till we get the crop money in. That's another reason I'm wishin' we can haul what we picked. Be nice to have some flour for bread around here on what ain't biscuit days."

I hadn't realized they were in quite that bad of shape. But a little more looking around confirmed it. There was no flour in that kitchen, nor sugar, coffee, butter, or anything that couldn't be produced in their fields, except maybe a tablespoon of salt in the bottom of the shaker. "How long have you managed like this?"

"Most all summer. The money from last year run out back in April. Mama said to be thankful we had enough on the shelves to last till the garden come on, and that'd take us to the fall cash harvest. Ain't been easy, though. Some days all we had was greens." He made a face.

I looked at Leah's pot. "What did she put in that soup?"

"Oh, this and that a' what was around. A tater or two an' some carrots an' such. I reckon she's done this kinda thing before."

I turned back to him. "Got a milk cow?"

"Not no more."

"Chickens?"

"A few. Not enough laying to keep us in enough eggs. So Mama called what come from you a gift from heaven."

Marigold had known. The need was great, and she'd determined to do what she could. "How long since you had meat?"

"I went out with Buck an' got a rabbit. 'Bout three weeks ago. Rafe an' Lowell've done that too. Been too much doin' around here to go again. Sure would be nice, though."

I sat at the table with a cup of the broth from Leah's pot, a plate of tomatoes, and half a bell pepper sprinkled with a few grains of salt. Bobby joined me with pretty much the same thing.

"Sure would be nice to have pot roast again. And chocolate pie. Oh, what a dandy!"

I smiled. "You're a dandy, yourself. Do you know where the grocer is?"

"Sure do."

"If we can get some pumpkins sold this afternoon, do you think your mother would mind us taking the time to get some groceries before we come home?"

"Mind?" he asked. "I think she'd wanna kiss ya!"

24

Leah

Fifteen sick children. It was enough to drive anyone insane.

Most of the children had only mild cases of what I was sure really was measles. They were restless and cranky and out of sorts about staying in their rooms as their mother had told them to do. But I was so glad she had. I'd never have been able to keep track of them all otherwise.

The mother seemed weakest, which concerned me quite a bit. If that had been all, they might have fared all right without help. But both of the older girls as well as the oldest boys being down sick really complicated things. Especially since it still seemed to me that there must be something in addition to measles going around among them. Several of the children had coughs. At least two had upset stomachs. The oldest boy, who looked nearly as big as a man, had the worst fever among them. The youngest two were pouty almost all the time and wanted nothing to do with me. Finally Ida, the oldest girl, told me just to let them on her bed with her, and that helped.

At least nobody seemed to be in serious shape. In fact, several said they were feeling some better than they had been. The big girl called Dodie puzzled me, with the worst cough of anyone and a rash that looked more like a reaction to something in the yard than to a disease.

Beth Ann was a great help. She seemed a little tired, but otherwise sturdy and willing. Dougy didn't know what to think of all this. He was frustrated that their normal routine was disrupted and told me twice that he wanted crackers. I'd looked, but there were none to be found. None of the children had as strong of appetites as I'd hoped when they first told me they were hungry. But at least they'd been able to eat a little. Maybe it was a good thing that they weren't ravenous for more until I figured out how to make something passable in a large enough quantity from what little I could find around.

"Don't worry," Beth Ann had told me as we took soup to some of the younger ones. "I'll go an' help Bobby dig more potatoes enough for supper. There's pumpkins and plenty of tomatoes too. And if Mr. Walsh'd pull us some of the field corn, I could grind it for meal for the morning."

Eliza and I had been destitute in the city, and hungry, true enough. But this number of children? Trying to do for so many—just thinking about finding enough of anything to go around—it was overwhelming. I didn't know how they could manage even when the mother and the older children were well.

I bathed foreheads, gave cool compresses to the ones with sore eyes, and tried to coax everybody to drink what they could. Maybe there'd be a way to get a doctor here. I could use the advice. I didn't think anyone's measles were a real problem, but the soreness in the eyes did concern me. And I most needed to know if there was another sickness involved. Hopefully nothing I'd need worry over catching.

Even with all of that to think about, my mind still strayed to Josiah Walsh's sudden appearance. Why hadn't Marigold told me he was coming? It would be astounding for her not to know. I might have backed out if I'd learned that he would be here to help. Surely she would have known that. So had she planned it this way on purpose?

They could use both of us here, that was certain. They could have used six more helpers, truth be told. But would Marigold really deceive me intentionally? Or had Josiah come here simply by chance? It was a little hard to believe either way.

I returned to the kitchen for more tea and found Josiah and Bobby at the table eating tomatoes. They both looked considerably dirtier than they had before, and I knew they'd been working, though I wasn't sure at what. I wouldn't have said anything, but the Kurchers had no pump or faucet in the house and I wasn't sure where the well was.

"I'm going to need plenty more water, if one of you could bring it in, please."

Bobby hopped right up again. "Sure. That's one of my jobs anyway. I'll get it."

He was out the door to meet the new need in a surprising hurry. Was he always this quick to help? Or maybe strangers and the dire circumstances had him doing everything he could.

I would've rather Josiah had hurried to fetch the water, so I'd not have to be alone with him.

"Are you able to drive?" he suddenly asked.

"Why in the world do you need to know?"

"Because that hard-working boy and I have harvested stacks of pumpkins out there. We need to haul them to market. I guess you've noticed they're in sore need of grocery money in this house."

My mind started racing with all this need. "Is there a vehicle?"

"Farm truck parked in the barn. I'm in high hopes it's running well. Bobby says it should. Think you could drive it?"

Maybe because of the whole situation, or maybe because it was him asking, my muscles tightened and I got hot under the collar. "Are you going to stay here and tend to fifteen children and their poor mother? Why do you want to send me?"

He looked helpless. "I'm not sure I'd do as well at tending, and I'm not keen on you and that little fellow doing all the unloading, either. So if we have to leave these here alone a while, maybe it wouldn't take long. I want to be sure the boy gets paid today and paid fair. Then we could pick out a few necessities from the grocer."

I couldn't believe he'd come up with such an idea, and I'm sure he didn't expect the earful he got.

"Marigold did not send me here to leave these people alone and run to the market with you! Why don't *you* drive? I could make a list for the grocer and stay here where I'm needed."

He stared at his boots. "I . . . um . . . I'm not sure I can."

"You've driven before."

"Not since . . . I haven't even *ridden* since . . ." He rose to his feet, and I thought he might just walk out.

"Listen to me!" I called to him. "Is there a physical reason that you can't drive?"

He turned, looking whipped.

"If there isn't, then you *have* to. Do you understand? And while you're in town, see if you can find a doctor. I not only shouldn't leave, I need help here."

Whatever was at work in him made his eyes a little wild and his face two shades paler. "Make your list," he told me. And then walked out.

25

Josiah

She was right. I knew without question that she was right, but the very physical reaction in me to the idea of driving again was immediate and painful. Throbbing head. Aching gut. Sweaty, shaking hands. *Lord, please help.*

I went to look at the truck again first, praying that it would start and afraid that it would, all at the same time. Bobby hauled the water bucket across the yard to the house and then came running back out to join me.

"When was the last time anybody started this thing?" I asked him.

"No more'n a couple of weeks, I don't think. Shouldn't be no problem. 'Cept it's been poppin' and sputterin' some."

"Got plenty of gas and oil?"

"Don't know."

I checked both and they were low, but Mrs. Kurcher, or someone, had had the foresight to have gas and oil cans, with a little in each, close by on a barn shelf.

"Let's see if it starts. If it doesn't, we hoof it to town for the doctor and then see what we can harvest or work on here that'll do the most good."

"Mama ain't wantin' the doctor. She tol' us that. Can't pay him, and he don't contribute more'n common sense gives ya anyhow, most times."

"I understand. But Leah needs the extra pair of hands and maybe a word of advice and I'm not about to argue. If he wants money, I'll guarantee it to him, since I'm the one fetchin' him. I'll drop it off to you from my next pay."

"Mister! You ain't gotta do that!"

"Ain't gotta be here at all, but I couldn't do otherwise. Some things need to be done, and that's all there is to it."

The truck started, and it rumbled rough, just like he'd said. But it'd surely get us there, and that was good enough.

Bobby thought we'd have room to haul for both the canner and the grocer since we didn't have a full load for either one. I agreed, thinking it was worth a try at selling what we'd picked. Harvest for the rest would come soon enough. He helped me load everything, starting with the pumpkins for the grocer. Then we covered them with gunnysacks and added the rest.

I sent Bobby to the house for Leah's list, gladly anticipating a moment alone. I'd intended to pray, but my mind wandered to puzzling about why Marigold would send Leah. Hadn't Mr. Abraham told her I was planning to help? Maybe not, because the only reason I'd determined to come here was to get somebody to the Kurchers' *today*. If I'd known anybody else had agreed, I would have stayed in Andersonville.

Bobby came running back out with Leah's paper, pleased as he could be. "Mama's gonna be proud," he said.

"Rightly so."

He climbed in the passenger seat, excited to be on our way. I took a deep breath and turned the crank again. The truck started with a sputter and a cough, and I moved quickly to the driver's seat. And just sat.

"What's the matter?" Bobby asked.

I stretched my hand to the steering wheel, my eyes to the long, rutted driveway. "Nothing." *Help me, Lord.*

My heart pounded viciously as I put the truck in gear and it lurched forward. It seemed so familiar, so terribly, terrifyingly the same. Several times I'd dreamed of driving again. And it had always ended badly.

"You'll have to direct me. I don't know the area," I told Bob, hoping he wouldn't discern the tension in my voice.

"I know," he said cheerfully. "Otherwise, I might a' stayed home to dig taters. 'Cept that Francis at the cannery might like seeing a Kurcher over a stranger. He's already agreed to take most all we can bring him."

"Good. But to the doctor first. Do you know where to find him?"

"I think so. I think it's a little brick house behind the milliner."

We didn't talk much on the way, which was good. My mind was too distracted to have responded much to him anyway. I kept picturing myself swerving, crashing this truck and killing this precious child. My grip on the wheel was tight, and I could feel a surge of panic every time I even saw another vehicle on the road, even if it didn't come near us.

God, please. Help me not to mess this up and hurt anyone. Calm me, please. It's going to be okay.

Bobby's directions took us to the only doctor in the area, a balding man named Harold Flatt who knew exactly the farm we meant and was willing to drive himself there as we went on to our other necessary business.

"I wouldn't mind having a nice big pumpkin for my services," he told us.

Bobby smiled. "Whichever one you want."

Francis at the cannery took the pumpkins as Bobby had predicted and paid cash for them. But the grocer was a good deal pickier. He took only about half of what we'd selected for him but said he'd probably have plenty of room for more later. "Check with me every couple of days," he said. "I'd keep a steady supply clear past Thanksgiving if I could."

"We'll do the best we can, Mr. Fletcher. Thank you very

much," Bobby told him politely. I'd have to tell his mother how well he'd done, nicely introducing me and everything. She should be proud of her boy.

"I ain't never got to sell before," he whispered to me as we began picking out the things on Leah's list. "That was great."

"I'd have thought you did it every time," I told him.

"I only just watched."

It was a bare bones list of groceries we filled. Bobby told me that Leah had consulted his mother and she'd advised what she called a "working minimum" for now, until they knew how much the crop would bring and what other needs there might be. But I was sure the addition to garden vegetables, especially the flour, baking powder, and sugar, would be greatly appreciated in that household. Might even help stir the appetites of some of those children to smell something baking again.

The drive back to the farm wasn't such a battle; the tension in me had subsided and I could breathe a little easier. This was not so bad after all. And that gave me a very good feeling. I'd told myself that I would never drive again, *should* never drive again, because of the harm I could do to someone else. It'd been a double binding—guilt and fear—and I'd broken through it to help a family in need. That felt like a considerable victory, and whether she knew it or not, Leah was largely responsible. She'd been angry. She probably wouldn't want to speak to me. Yet now I felt that I ought to thank her.

Maybe she'd be able to hear it and not think me a coldhearted imbecile for suggesting that she leave the house. Maybe. But she'd probably just turn her back and tell me to leave her alone again.

26

Leah

In the midst of everything, annoyingly persistent thoughts of Josiah kept creeping up on me. He could be giving and kind. Or terribly thoughtless and abrupt. Depending on the circumstance.

And here at the Kurchers', I'd seen something else. A scared child looking through his eyes. He'd driven again, despite considerable turmoil. I'd pushed him to it, and I hoped there wouldn't be resentment to complicate things in front of these children.

I truly didn't want a continuing conflict with Josiah, but there seemed no real way to avoid it, as though we'd been set as roadblocks in each other's paths. At least I could be certain that the sheer volume of need here would keep us both busy. There simply wouldn't be time for words.

I was very grateful for that, because I wasn't sure I'd be any good at controlling my own emotions right now. One of the Kurcher girls was about Ellie's size, and I grew teary seeing her sick, thinking of my own little girl and missing her badly.

What would I ever do without her? What if something were to happen to keep us apart? Was she missing me, tearful and afraid? And if so, how could Marigold console her?

It was hard to concentrate on the tasks at hand as long as my mind was on Eliza, but if I forced my thinking away from her, then it wandered back to the strange vulnerability I'd seen in Josiah, and that was no better.

At last, a doctor arrived, and I could feel at least a little more ease. Mrs. Kurcher was terribly troubled at first that he'd come, until he told her he'd made an agreement with her son for a pumpkin. It made me smile that the boy would be willing to bargain for his family's sake, and that this doctor was kindhearted enough to happily accept such payment for his services.

I was glad when I saw the truck returning down the lane later with much of its burden gone. Surely Josiah and Bobby would be bringing the groceries I'd sorely need to prepare the next meal. But I was still apprehensive. At Marigold's house I'd seen Josiah storming off or shutting himself away when something upset him. Would he react that way to me here because of the way I'd pushed him? I was afraid he might, and for that reason I made sure to be upstairs when he and Bobby carried the groceries in.

I soon heard the boy run to speak to his mother. From the energy of his footfalls, I assumed that he must have been pleased with what they had accomplished. I wasn't sure where Josiah had gone, but I was glad not to have to face him.

Doctor Flatt confirmed my thought that something besides measles was at work among at least some of the Kurchers. "Could be just a touch of la grippe," he told me. "There's a bit of it going around the area. Three or four other families are dealing with measles in the county as well, though I've not seen any with a plague of both like this."

"Could it be serious?"

"I don't think so. They all seem to be coming around all right. I'd expect a great improvement in just a few days. They'll probably be full of energy and appetite again before you know it. Except perhaps your mother."

"Oh!" I exclaimed in surprise. "I'm not one of the Kurcher

children, sir. I'm a visitor, come to help for a couple of days because they're sick. But why are you worried for Mrs. Kurcher? What's wrong?"

"Nothing to fret over. She just needs to know that too much too soon will wear her down weak again. She'll have to get as much help as she can even after she begins to feel better to make sure she isn't worn to a frazzle taking care of a household this size. I hope you can stay a while. It's very kind of you to help." He glanced out the window and then back at me. "That must have been your husband I met in town with the Kurcher boy and that load of pumpkins then. Are they back yet?"

"They're back," I offered soberly. "But he's not my husband."

"Oh." He had an odd look on his face.

I tried to ignore it. "What about Dodie's spots? They're not the same as the measles, surely?"

He shook his head. "It looks like a contact rash more than anything else. Something she got into outside on top of everything else."

I suppose there was no reason to be surprised. And at least he didn't expect anyone to worsen. But la grippe? That was almost the same as influenza, wasn't it? That plague again? I asked him if I was in danger of becoming sick myself, or carrying the illness with me to others after I left.

"I don't think that will happen." He tried to calm my worries. "This is not like what we saw a couple of years ago. I'm just glad it's not the dead of winter. Doesn't seem so virulent in the fall for some reason."

Doctor Flatt stayed for several hours, helping me with compresses and taking the time to observe each child long enough to be sure of his diagnosis. I was not the only one who had worried that things might worsen, so he set minds to ease while he was there, and took two pumpkins with him when he left. He'd administered medicine to the patients who needed it most, and since there was very little remaining in the bottle, he promised to return and bring more.

I guess it was a natural mistake for him to think that Josiah could be my husband. A couple of the Kurcher children had asked me about that too, even though we hadn't arrived together. It was an embarrassing spot to be in, and I was careful to make sure they knew the truth.

Some of the children already had improving appetites so I decided a treat of some kind was in order. Some simple cake, not too thick, nor too sweet, might be just the thing.

Beth Ann asked Bobby and Josiah to dig more potatoes. I thought I'd use some of those to make a nourishing potato soup with some of the milk and butter they'd brought from town. That might be more appealing than the assorted vegetable soup and broth I'd made earlier with scarcely anything to season it.

For now, soups were an easy way to make a large quantity and to satisfy the varying appetites in the household. Some might be able to take only a bit of broth like earlier in the day. Others were hungry already and anxious for a full, hearty bowlful. Mrs. Kurcher had made sure to put crackers on the grocery list, especially for those whose stomachs were a bit unsettled, and for Dougy, who'd apparently been wanting some for weeks.

Both the soup and the cake went over better than I'd expected. Especially the cake. I had to limit some of the children and admonish them to eat it slowly, so they'd not tax their stomachs so soon and end up with a bellyache. Apparently, it'd been weeks since they'd had anything of the sort, and it seemed to lift everyone's spirits.

I was completely exhausted by nightfall, but I helped Beth Ann get all the younger children cleaned up and tucked in. It was heartening to be asked by more than one if they'd have to spend the whole day in their rooms tomorrow too. Hankering to be moving about was definitely a good sign. Tomorrow might be even more of a wild and chaotic day than this one had been if more of the children were up. But having them so quickly on the mend would be well worth it.

I hadn't given much thought to where I might sleep. Beth Ann offered her bed, which she shared with a younger sister, but I accepted instead the pallet on the floor she was going to make for herself.

I don't even know where Josiah slept. He'd continued at the harvest work as long as he had daylight. After that, I'd thought he might say something to me about how it had been for him to drive again, but I stayed busy with the children's needs and he didn't interrupt. He went outside after claiming a bit of supper, and I didn't see him come back in.

I lay for a long time that night, staring up at the chipped paint on the ceiling of the Kurchers' sitting room. Though I'd had so much trouble praying before, it seemed considerably more possible now. Because I missed Eliza and worried for her, my first feeble prayer was for her. Then I made the simple plea for the Kurchers all to be well.

My father came to mind. Might he be much improved already? He seemed entirely too stubborn to be sick for long, but there was really no way for me to know. Then I thought of Josiah, maybe sleeping in the barn. I was sure I wasn't mistaken about the fear I'd seen in him earlier. Yet he'd not shown any sign of the resentment I'd expected when he got back. He'd been civil, what little I'd seen of him. But he'd seemed to be watching me. A little too much for my comfort's sake.

I should have been able to sleep. I felt physically, emotionally drained. But instead, I just stared at the ceiling for what seemed like hours, piecing this whole day together in my mind, along with all the time I'd spent with Marigold. What if she'd sent me here on purpose to be here when Josiah was here? What if it was her intention to make sure we continued to encounter each other and work together, even though he'd tried so hard to separate himself by moving out of her house?

Maybe I should ask her why it seemed important to her. And then ask him why he had such a problem with me. Or maybe with John. Or the very idea of someone with a claim of kinship coming to occupy space in Marigold's home and heart.

But it didn't seem right to accuse Marigold without knowing the matter fully. Or to dismiss Josiah's behavior as simple jealousy. I didn't know how to analyze either of them in this situation and I wished I could just stop trying.

Had Josiah really not ridden in a car since his accident? Was it so much fear in him? A way of punishing himself? Or both?

Only thoughts of Eliza could tear my mind away, and so I came full circle to worry for her again as I lay hoping for a few hours of sleep. Was she lying awake like I was? Thinking of me right now? Scared for me not to be there? I could only try to picture her sleeping peacefully on the cot I'd helped prepare for her beside the window in Marigold's room. Maybe Marigold had even played some Victrola music for her.

I could be sure she'd prayed. I could even picture Marigold up and praying still, for all of us here. The image gave me peace, and finally my eyelids grew heavy. With another tiny prayer for my daughter, I drifted off to sleep.

27

Josiah

Leah Breckenridge had begun to haunt me. I'd tried to distance myself. But Marigold finagled ways to make that impossible. And Leah kept finding ways to show herself a better woman than I'd ever expected.

She could cook. For a crowd. Passable meals with a little of nothing.

She was definitely a willing worker, helping where there was a need, both here and at Marigold's house.

She'd refused my stupid pledge, insisting that she couldn't make a promise to preclude friendship. Even though I knew she wasn't interested in being friends.

And now she'd gone a step further. I'd known this trip would force me out of my self-imposed shunning of automobiles, because I'd have to accept a ride back to Andersonville with Mel and Dotty just to keep my job. But Leah'd made me lay those fetters aside more completely. And that was good. But also terrifying.

Leah had gotten under my skin, no doubt. What was Marigold trying to accomplish? If I were back at Mr. Abraham's house, I'd ask him.

The hay beneath my head was a little scratchy, but all in all, I found the barn loft a comfortable place to keep me away from the crowd in the house. But sleep came hard.

"You were born to minister," Marigold had told me once. "Maybe not preach, but who knows? I can see the heart for people about you. I know you want to help when folks are needy. And that's nothing to be ashamed of."

A missionary's story had touched me in church one Sunday, his tales a little too vivid for my injured emotions so soon after coming to Marigold's. She'd seen the tears I'd tried to hide, and she'd been sure ever since that I was moldable material for the Lord's work.

Hauling biscuits and doing field work I supposed I could handle. Plunking money into a missions basket wasn't hard either. The problem came when she expected something more. Words that made a difference. Closeness with another soul. One-on-one fellowship and touching of hearts.

Maybe I'd shunned that too. Wisely so. Far worse than driving, the risk of wreckage was very real.

How did Leah do it? How could she come all the way over here, selflessly serve and give her heart to this family, and seem so downright comfortable at it?

I found myself wanting to ask her things. Like whether she dreamed of John, and if the grieving ever made her feel like staying in bed and wishing the world away. Was there consolation in having Eliza still with her, or more heartache for the child growing up without a father? I wished I knew how she could seem so poised and sure of herself.

Barn cats and creatures unnamed lent the night a collection of unfamiliar sounds. I lay listening, wishing the morning would come and tomorrow could speed by quickly. I didn't think I'd ever get any rest.

But finally, in the wee hours, I lifted my heart in prayer, and solace began to come.

Lord, there's so much I don't understand. But maybe I just need to rest in your arms like I'm trying to rest in this hay. Not worrying so much about my own understanding, or my own feelings, just leaving things up to you. I promise to try, Lord. Thank you . . .

28

Leah

Morning arrived with the call of a rooster I hadn't realized they owned. So much awaited my attention already with so many in this household. I was still deeply needed here, but before I'd even made breakfast, I was anxious to leave and get back to my daughter.

Some of the Kurchers were feeling a little better and some were about the same, but I had difficulty concentrating on any of that. Mrs. Batey wouldn't be starting out before the afternoon. As I worked at the things that I needed to put my hands to, a nagging worry rode over everything. What if something happened to delay her? What if she couldn't come at all?

Finally I thought of an excuse to communicate with the people in Andersonville, just to seek the confirmation I needed. We'd sent apples to the Kurchers weeks ago, and as far as I could tell there was not a one left. Yet there were still plenty in Marigold's basement. So I persuaded Bobby to run to the neighbor and borrow the use of the telephone to call Mr. Abraham's house.

"Tell him I'd like him to please load a basket of apples into

Mrs. Batey's car before she comes," I instructed. "Surely he'll be able to tell us if she's leaving on schedule."

"Will he be home on a Sunday morning, ma'am, and not at church?" Bobby questioned.

"Yes," I assured him. "He keeps a Saturday Sabbath."

I knew the boy did not understand that, but he was trusting and obedient anyway. Maybe for the sake of the apples. But he came back with shocking news.

"He says Mrs. Batey's not coming."

"What?" My mind raced into a panic.

"When they found out you was both here, she decided there weren't no need of her driving when there was already a ride arranged. So they's figuring you to ride back with Mr. Josiah's friends. Don't worry, though. I tol' him to load the apples in their car if they'll let him."

I'd hoped Marigold and Eliza would ride along with Mrs. Batey again. That way I'd see Eliza so much more quickly. But now I'd be riding back with people I'd probably never met. With Josiah. At least it was better than not having a ride at all.

I should have had Bobby ask who might be coming to help today so there would be someone after I'd gone. But Mr. Abraham might not have known that yet. And what if Marigold found no one? It was a strange request, to expect someone to drive and tend a sick family they probably didn't know. I could imagine people asking Marigold if there weren't anyone closer who could help.

And maybe there was. I asked Mrs. Kurcher about it, but she couldn't come up with anyone she thought would be willing, at least that she would be willing to ask. Some from the church down the road had helped them before, but she just couldn't bear to lean on the same people again.

"The Lord'll provide," she told me. "When he sets you on a path, he'll make a way. I can't complain. Look what he's done for us so far."

Amazing words from a woman in her position. Widowed, with such a vast burden of responsibility. I felt small in comparison, complaining the way I'd done, and yet God had provided for Eliza and me too.

I did a lot of thinking about Hilda Kurcher and her enterprise here. Running a farm and raising eighteen children still at home without the help of a husband. Of course, they'd gotten in a bind with all this illness, but she and I talked about how they did things here on a normal basis, and I was impressed. Everybody had their assigned chores. The house and farm work was all carefully scheduled.

"We'll be back to that soon enough," she assured me. "It's been such a blessing for you to come and help us weather this little storm. Ida's feeling better already. When she's back at things again, she's the house manager as much as I am. And Rafe's the farm foreman. When those two are outta bed, and then the next, Dodie and Lowell, everything'll turn a little easier again."

I reminded her of what the doctor had said, that she was to maintain her rest even after they all started feeling better, and she promised she would.

By midafternoon I was so anxious to get back to Eliza that I could hardly function, but I was feeling a very mixed array of emotion. A piece of me was reluctant to leave, especially if I weren't assured of some additional help here for at least a couple more days. But I could barely wait for my ride to get here. I'd only been here one night and much of two days, but it seemed far longer since I'd held my girl in my arms. Yet despite that, I was apprehensive about the drive home. What would it be like riding with Josiah and his friends?

To my great relief, Charles and Lydia Casewalter from Marigold's church drove in and told us they could stay until Monday evening. Shortly after that, an incredibly dusty little Ford came chugging up the lane behind the Casewalters' truck. Josiah's friends were here already.

I collected my things and said good-byes all over the house. Most of the children asked me to come back.

"I'd like to," I told them. "When you're all better and I can bring my daughter to meet you."

One of the girls gave me a little cornhusk doll to give to Eliza. "Did you make this?" I asked her.

She nodded. "Mama showed me how."

"It's wonderful. You're an amazing family."

Josiah's friends introduced themselves as Mel and Dotty Reiner. They had a basket of Marigold's apples with them. Hilda insisted that I take a pumpkin back with me, and I obliged, thinking of the fun Eliza would have making pumpkin pies with me and Marigold.

She offered a pumpkin to Josiah too, but he turned her down. "Sell mine," he told her with the hint of a smile. "I'll make sure Leah gets a big pumpkin and maybe she'll see fit to spare enough for a pie for Mr. Abraham and me."

Mrs. Kurcher smiled back at him. I'm sure she thought there must be some sort of relationship between Josiah and me, and he certainly did nothing to dissuade such an idea. But for me to protest aloud would be quite awkward and might produce an opposite effect, so I kept quiet.

I'd hoped Mrs. Reiner would sit in the backseat with me and let the men ride in the front. It would have been more proper, especially for the eyes of any of the Kurcher children who might see us depart. But she merrily plunked herself in the front seat with her husband, leaving me no choice but to share the only seat left with Josiah. For a moment I was extra grateful for that pumpkin, thinking I'd set it conveniently between us, but to my dismay, there was no room for that. We were forced to ride nearly touching, me with my bag on my lap, and he with the pumpkin on his.

"Glad to be going home?" Mr. Reiner asked as we turned onto the main road.

Josiah's answer was strange. "Not sure where home is right now."

Did that mean he was planning to move back into Marigold's? Or somewhere else? I wanted to know, but I was afraid to ask.

"How did you manage things over here?" Mel asked on.

"All right," Josiah answered simply. He looked away across the fields to our left, and it seemed obvious that he wanted to retreat from us somehow, even in these close quarters, and not have to say anything. He seemed to barely tolerate making a response.

"Seems all wrong," Mr. Reiner talked on, loudly, over his engine's roar. "One woman having so many children to see to. And not all of 'em born to her. Don't the state have an orphan home? Seems like they'd be better off if about half of 'em was trucked over there. Wouldn't need to be calling on charity that way."

I'd seen Josiah in various states of emotion. Several times. But not with the fire of anger that flashed in his eyes now. "That's stupid, Mel. They're family. Even the ones that've been taken in. Love's stronger than blood, and they belong together."

I was looking his way, strangely interested in the depth of feeling so plain on his face. But he turned his head toward the field again.

"Didn't mean to spark nothing, Joe," Reiner went on. "Just thinking practical."

"Kids belong where somebody cares," Josiah answered bitterly. "That's better than practical."

"You don't think nobody cares at the state home?" his friend persisted, and then laughed a little. "They really got to you, didn't they? You gotta be thinking about finding you a woman again, Joe. Maybe you need a son or two running around."

"Shut up."

"Leave him alone, Mel," his wife agreed. "It's bound to have been a trying couple of days."

Everyone was quiet for a few miles after that and I was glad. I couldn't quite picture why these people were Josiah's friends at all. The man didn't seem to be very considerate. And Josiah hadn't volunteered a word to them on his own. But maybe he was just out of sorts and didn't feel like talking to anybody. Maybe it was somehow because of me.

But then it dawned on me what was much more likely to be the problem. Here we were in an automobile when he hadn't been a passenger in one since before the accident. He must be having a terrible struggle with this today. Maybe having to drive yesterday had only made it worse.

I tried to imagine the swirling emotion that facing a car again might be bringing him. Was he afraid? Or plagued with his burden of guilt? Either way seemed completely plausible to me. I was willing to give him plenty of space. But Mel and Dotty were soon trying to make conversation again, and it seemed to irritate him terribly. Why didn't they know him well enough to understand?

29

Josiah

I was being rude to Mel and Dotty, but I didn't care. I didn't want to talk in front of Leah. Not about anything, no matter how they pushed. She'd invaded my dreams, sounding like Marigold: "*We've got to help these children . . .*"

I'd tried to tell her that we already were, but she didn't seem to hear me. And now I wondered what business I had dreaming of her anyway.

But that really wasn't all. Maybe Mel was right about the Kurcher kids getting to me. Maybe I was envious. Not that they'd been sick, of course. Or that they'd gone weeks without store-bought groceries. They wouldn't be hurt in the long run by either of those things. But what I envied was the very thing that Mel didn't seem to see. They accepted life the way it was. They accepted each other, and didn't seem to want things any other way. Mrs. Kurcher loved all the kids enough that there'd been no way I could tell which ones were her birth kids and which ones weren't. They all belonged.

No wonder she was Marigold's friend. In some ways they were much alike. In the accepting of waifs, at least.

When I was a child, I'd wished Marigold was my mother because she didn't seem to mind my presence. My own mother'd always had things to do and would rather have not been bothered by me. And my father'd been downright hostile till the day he wanted nothing more to do with us, and then he was just gone. I was only one child. But for them, I'd been too many. Mrs. Kurcher could love a houseful.

I sat with Leah's pumpkin on my lap, wishing I could disappear. I was no good to be around when I felt morose like this. My lows weren't nearly as low as they'd been before I got saved, but when I struggled I'm sure it wasn't pretty, and I only wanted to withdraw.

Marigold had pulled me out of such depressive pits more than once, got me joking with her and feeling all right again. Now I questioned if it'd really been right to move out. If I went back to Mr. Abraham's house, it might be too easy to close off for days.

Leah seemed to be watching me, and I hated having to sit in a car with her. In some ways this was worse than driving with Bobby. The day of the accident, Rosemary'd been sitting beside me, watching me, afraid I'd drunk too much. Now it was Leah watching. I didn't know what she was thinking, but she seemed a little afraid too. And the sound, the feel, of the car under me was giving me a headache.

Finally, I crossed my arms over the top of the pumpkin and lay my head to rest on them. If anyone asked if I was sick, I'd tell them yes.

And then maybe they'd leave me alone.

Mel and Dotty might be angry. They'd never understand. I'd probably never even try to explain all this to them. And like so many times before, they'd eventually dismiss my behavior as another of my "loony spells" and leave it at that. But I wouldn't talk, couldn't talk, for the rest of this ride. Leah seemed too much like Rosemary, this car too much like my own. Everything seemed to be swirling at me at once. The wreck. The Kurchers. Marigold's expectations. I needed to close off from it all or risk falling to pieces.

30

Leah

I'd never been so glad to get anywhere. Eliza must have been watching for us, because she ran out of the house before the car even stopped and bounced up and down waiting for me to get where she could grab me in a hug.

Josiah seemed annoyed by her exuberant welcome. He gave his friends one word of thanks, turned his back, and then carried my pumpkin into the house.

"Thank you very much for the ride," I told the Reiners then, hoping they wouldn't be dismayed by any perceived lack of gratitude. "I wish I could ask you in for tea, but I'll have to check with Marigold first."

"No, that's all right," Dotty told me. "We've got other plans. Tell Josiah to come over again when he settles down. He's not a bad fella, you know, if you can get past all the crazy briars."

They drove away and I turned to the house.

"What's that mean?" Ellie asked me.

"What?"

"'Bout Mr. Josiah havin' briars?"

"Oh. Maybe she meant that he seems a little rough or unpleasant on the outside sometimes. But not bad on the inside."

"So he's got a good heart?"

I sighed. "I guess so."

She smiled and took my hand. "I already knew that. And you got a good heart too, Mommy. You went to help those people. I sure am glad you're back, but I wanted to help too, so me an' Marigold's been prayin'."

"Good. Thank you so much." I hugged her again, petted her wonderful curls. "Mommy missed her good girl."

"I missed you too."

It was a great relief to walk back into Marigold's house and know that the Kurchers still had capable hands to help them. And it was joyous to be holding my daughter's hand. I looked forward to sitting with her and Marigold over tea, relaxing a moment and talking over the things that had happened.

I'd expected Josiah to lay the pumpkin on the porch and be gone almost as quickly as he'd come in. After that ride, I couldn't imagine that he'd linger, but he was talking to Marigold in the kitchen when we entered. And they were not pleasant words.

"Forget it! I don't want to hear your fancy explanations."

"Now, Josiah, it was an accident, a simple lack of communication—"

"Working exactly for your ends. Fine."

"Josiah—"

He glanced suddenly at me but then turned back to her. "Don't talk to me right now. Please. Just let me leave."

If I were Marigold, I wouldn't have said a thing. I would have let him go and been glad to have him gone when he was being so difficult again. But Marigold reached for his arm before he could pull away and stepped close enough to embrace him.

He stood stiff for a moment but then slowly put his arms around her and seemed to tremble a little. "You are loved," she whispered. "Don't ever forget that. You can get mad at me all you want, but that'll never change."

"I'm not mad," he managed to say, and then pulled away abruptly and walked out.

Marigold sat at a kitchen chair. "God love him."

"What's wrong?"

She sighed. "There's probably more to it. But I guess he thought I put the two of you there together on purpose. Saul and I just failed to communicate, that's all. We didn't tell him when we invited Rosie to breakfast that we were going to ask a ride for you. And he thought I already knew Josiah was leaving. He just realized later that he was supposed to tell me."

She reached her hand in my direction, and I took it. "I hope you're not dismayed with me too. I really didn't mean for it to happen that way."

"It's all right," I assured her. "They really did need two sets of hands."

She smiled. "Thank you so much for being gracious. I've appreciated your willingness, and I've worried that things might have been pretty sour, finding yourself together there when you most clearly don't like to be."

Eliza looked up at me.

"It wasn't so bad. We were both very busy."

"Sit down. Please," Marigold said. "Tell me all about it. How is Hilda? What all happened? Maybe you can answer better than I can what's wrong with Josiah today."

I couldn't, not really. But I told her everything I knew about the Kurchers, their illness, their farm, and the doctor. I even went so far as telling her about Josiah driving Bobby's pumpkins to market after what he'd admitted to me, and the uncomfortable ride home.

"He's hurting." She bowed her head a moment. "Sometimes it seems that a strong man should just be strong. But it's not as easy as that. A big heart takes a lot of time at healing when it's been ripped in pieces." Her eyes filled with tears. "Sometimes a woman can put things back together more quickly . . ."

She glanced at Eliza and continued. "Especially for the sake of her child. You've done well, Leah, having the peace you do. He struggles terribly, but it doesn't mean he's weak. Do you understand? He thinks he is, but he'd never have sacrificed to go there this weekend if that were the case."

Once again Marigold seemed to be telling me she thought me strong. Maybe stronger than Josiah, and she seemed to be asking me not to look down on him. It was a little much, knowing that I still hid my own debilitating doubts, fears, and even anger under a busy and proper façade. Maybe Josiah was simply not so good at hiding, which meant that of the two of us he was the more honest.

"Oh, Marigold—"

"Please just pray for him. Put your feet up. You must be exhausted. Let me get you some tea."

She wouldn't let me lend a hand at anything that night, insisting that I rest. But I felt like crying and could barely keep myself from it. Eliza stayed at my side, and I wouldn't have wanted it otherwise. I was so very glad to be back with her again. But the house seemed empty, as though it were a sad lack that there were not children enough to fill the place. I found my heart aching again for the baby I'd lost.

And wondering over Josiah. Again. Why couldn't I just stop thinking about him? His volatile ways were grievous to deal with, to say the least, yet I could deeply respect the spark of anger I'd seen in him on behalf of the Kurcher children. Not a bad fellow if you can get past the crazy briars, as Mrs. Reiner had said.

The next day was unexpectedly cool, and I dressed Eliza in double layers the best I could against the chill.

"Could Eliza use more stockings?" Dorothy Humphrey asked me as we were walking together to the school. "I've a sister who has a daughter a year older than Betty. They're rather well off, and they buy more than any child needs. She keeps giving me hand-me-downs, and it's a blessing, but we haven't room for it all. A little girl only needs so much."

Such a timely, unexpected blessing! Eliza only owned three pairs of stockings. One was full of runs and the other two were so thin, I'd had her wear them both. "We could sure use them. Thank you so much."

"What about a paisley blouse and a little brown coat? Would you take them too?"

I almost hugged her. "Yes, thank you."

"There'll be more, I'm sure. Especially since your Eliza's a little slimmer than Betty. We could probably give you plenty more that are a little too tight on her. If you only had boys, we could give you all the clothes you need. She's got two sons, and they have as many clothes as their sister."

I had a sudden idea. "I know who'd take them! And I'm sure they'd be so grateful."

Mrs. Kurcher had told me that lack of good clothes was one of the reasons they seldom made it to church. Surely if Josiah would carry biscuits, apples, or eggs, he wouldn't mind taking a bundle of clothes sometime as well. They had boys in multiple sizes. And even if some of the things didn't fit anyone, maybe Mrs. Kurcher or her daughters could alter them or use the fabric for something else. I was so pleased to have found a way to help again, and Mrs. Humphrey was just as pleased when I explained to her about it. Eliza's faith had been answered yet again. And instead of feeling resentful, this time I felt jubilant. It was amazing.

But the joy of having a need provided, for me and for the Kurcher children, was short-lived as thoughts of my father began to wear at my mind that day. Would I hear from him again? And if I didn't, would it mean he'd become well? Or died? Or was simply too stubborn to write again if I didn't jump in response to his first letter?

I'd managed one night away. Eliza had been all right with me gone. She told me about Marigold playing games with her and singing songs. It had all come out very well, but going to see Father was another matter. That was farther. With no guarantee of how long I'd be gone.

I tried to push the thought away, telling myself there was no use considering it. I must simply write him back and explain that I had no money for the trip. But I couldn't quite bring myself to do it. My heart seemed to think that if I were only willing, somehow there would be a way.

So I told myself I was unwilling. I didn't wish to consider it further. I couldn't leave Eliza again, nor take her along when he'd told me not to. I certainly didn't want to have to face his tumultuous ways. Why should I? In all these years, he'd never showed me that he cared. He'd never chosen to receive the love I'd tried to give. So what did he want from me now?

Despite such attempts at logic, thoughts of my father would not leave me alone. I didn't expect to get a second letter. He might have gotten better. He might be too stubborn to make his request a second time. But if he died, would I ever even know? Was there someone there that would know to contact me? Or care to do that much?

I was having such a struggle in my heart that I finally decided to explain it all to Marigold and ask her to pray about it for me. I should have known how she might react.

"Oh, dear, Leah, of course there's a reason this won't let you alone. He needs you. You really should go to him."

"But I can't leave Eliza again."

"Nonsense. We were fine. You can consider the first time to be practice. Like trying out a new recipe before sharing it with company. Now you know it works. Eliza was fine, and she'll be fine again, so you needn't worry."

"But it's silly even to think about. Even if I had no concerns for Eliza, I couldn't go. I've no money for the train, and no way to get any money."

"The Lord will provide, Leah dear," she said confidently. "You go next door and ask Mr. Abraham to send Josiah when he gets home from work."

"No. I don't want to concern anyone else with this. I certainly don't want to ask him for money."

"I just want him to find out for me what the ticket would cost. That way I can pray on the exact amount. I'll tell him it's for a friend and that'll be the end of it."

I didn't want to do as she said, but she threatened to struggle across the yard herself if I didn't, so I hurried over and gave Mr. Abraham the message.

"Marigold is well?" he asked me.

"Yes. But missing you, I think. Why don't you come over for tea again soon?"

He smiled. "Is that you asking, ma'am? Or her?"

"Well. It's me. But I know she'd love to have you. She says she needs to give you space, but I think too much space is lonely for both of you."

He nodded. "I'll think about it. If you'll ask her. Perhaps tonight Josiah could bring me back the response."

At first I thought nothing of talking to Mr. Abraham as I'd done. But then I worried that I'd meddled in Marigold's affairs without her permission, just as she was about to do with mine. I still didn't want her to mention the idea of train tickets to Josiah. She seemed to be taking liberties with my situation, but how had I come to feel so comfortable that I could take liberties with hers? It was none of my business to get Mr. Abraham over for tea again.

But maybe it was not so bad. Friends and family were supposed to get in the middle of each other's lives and know each other's business, pleasant or not. Except for Mother and John, I'd never had that with anyone. But maybe I was supposed to again.

I confessed to Marigold what I'd asked Mr. Abraham, hoping she'd be thrilled with the idea of having him over again. She didn't seem to be, but she wasn't upset with me either.

"Things have changed," she said. "We must not be in any hurry and we must certainly not throw caution to the wind."

"What do you mean?"

"I mean, Saul answers only to God. He's not just my kindly neighbor anymore. Now he's free to be my friend."

"Wasn't he always your friend?"

"Oh, of course. But he's not the same. He doesn't have to be the same."

I thought I understood what she meant, despite the strangeness of how it sounded. She wasn't sure what to expect now. He wasn't either. So neither of them knew what to do. But Marigold would let him find his way. It was really up to him.

Josiah promised to find the ticket price, though he seemed a little puzzled when he heard the destination.

"Round-trip," Marigold told him. "Of course my friend will want to come back to Andersonville."

He'd brought the supper dishes back with him from Mr. Abraham's house and I was washing them while they talked. He looked my way.

"Did you enjoy the pumpkin pie?" I asked.

"Very much. Thank you." He turned quickly to Marigold again. "I'll be back over tomorrow with what I found out."

"Wonderful. Thank you very much. And I'm pleased to find you more yourself this evening."

"Are you sure you know what 'myself' is?"

She smiled. "That's far easier than you think, Josiah. It's the kindhearted soul willing to help a neighbor, do for a child in need, or put up with the notions of an old woman the way you've done. I know you by now. I see so much in you that sometimes you refuse to see in yourself."

"You never give up, do you?"

"You may never preach," Marigold persisted. "Don't worry about that. But a servant of God you are. A minister you are. With more love than you're willing to put on display."

He turned to me with a wry look. "Be careful. She'll be calling you a minister next. Or maybe she already has. Marigold's Ministry Boardinghouse. Come homeless. Stay and give your soul to the needs of the world."

The words could have been ugly, spiteful. But instead they were gently teasing, and Marigold smiled. "Go on and get yourself some rest for the night. Pray about my words, that's all I want you to do. You're precious in the sight of the Lord. And here for his purpose. Stop being so hard on yourself."

It was a relief to find Josiah considerably more peaceful and accepting tonight. He didn't protest such talk as I might have expected. Instead, he rose to his feet with a gentle nod in Marigold's direction. Then he walked past me and on to the door.

"Please tell Saul that I would love to have him over for tea tomorrow," Marigold called as he was almost gone.

And Josiah glanced back with a smile.

31

Josiah

Sugar Creek, Missouri. That had been the address on an envelope I'd mailed for Leah weeks ago, I was sure of it. And now Marigold was asking what it would cost to take the train there. At first I'd thought Leah was leaving, moving out to be gone for good. But then Marigold said *round-trip*. So she wasn't leaving at all, only visiting someone.

It must be her father, since the old neighbor was in St. Louis. The father she simply couldn't go to but hadn't told me why. Fine. Let her go on and go. Maybe she'd change her mind entirely and decide to move there after all.

I wasn't sure what bothered me about it. Whether it was the idea that Leah might have a reasonable relationship with her father after all, destroying some vague commonality between us, or the notion that she may have been less than honest, for whatever reason.

I could have given a pretty fair estimate of the ticket price based on the distance, if I'd known how far past St. Louis Sugar Creek might be. But I didn't want to ask. Marigold didn't seem to think I'd know the "friend" she was talking about. She must have assumed I'd have the scruples not to read anything on a pair of envelopes entrusted to my hands.

Saul was waiting up for me in the kitchen of his house.

"Marigold would like you to come to tea tomorrow," I told him immediately.

I'd expected a smile but didn't get one.

"What's wrong? You've had tea with Marigold plenty of times."

"I know. But now I could hurt her feelings."

He was probably thinking like he'd been before, but it didn't set any better with me than it had the first time. "Why would you do that? Forget what other people think. It's between you and Marigold and God. That's it. Don't consider anybody else."

"That's impossible."

"Maybe so," I conceded. "But you know what I'm getting at."

"She could be ostracized."

"Whatever that means, do you think she'd care?"

"She might. About her church."

"But why would it matter to the church people?"

"There's a Scripture in your Testament, right? About being yoked with unbelievers?"

Maybe he was searching for a closed door, an insurmountable barrier he could blame on someone besides himself. I wasn't going to make it easy for him. "But you're not an unbeliever. Are you?"

He was quiet for moment. Finally he motioned to a chair. "Please. Sit."

I did, stricken by the pained expression on his face. "I'm not trying to be difficult," I told him. "I just don't think this Jew or Christian difference ought to matter."

"Ought to or not, it's a vast historical rift that runs far deeper than you realize. One or the other of us is bound to be shunned. Perhaps both."

"But you are a believer, aren't you?"

"Tell me what you mean by that."

"I guess one who believes that God's real. But not just that. Honors him. Trusts him."

"Tell me something, Josiah." He looked exhausted, beaten, as if he'd been in a long struggle that hadn't ended well.

"All right. If I'm able."

"Why are you a Christian? You do not have a deep heritage, am I right?"

"If you mean my parents weren't Christians, that's right."

"Then why do you believe? In Jesus?"

I took a deep breath and my heart raced. He was trusting me to give him an answer with soul-reaching depth. I knew he was, and I knew that the turn of this conversation could impact his future. And Marigold's. It made me want to run and hide.

"Mr. Abraham, I—"

"Please call me Saul."

"Saul. I don't have a nice way with words. I can't give you lots of Scriptures and fulfilled prophecies and all that like Marigold can. I know it's there, but I can't remember it all very well. It comes down to something different for me and it may seem pretty weak, but it's the best I can do."

He was watching, silent. Waiting.

"I'm a mess. No good on my own. Do you understand? I can't get things right even when I want to. There's always some bad thought or stupid thing I've done when I should've known better. I killed the only person that ever loved me, except maybe Marigold."

My eyes misted. And then I noticed that his did too, and I tried to go on. "If I had to depend on what I could do, I'd be in deep water. You know what I'm saying? If we had to sacrifice for our sins every year like they did in the old days, I'd probably mess that up too. I'm a hopeless case without Jesus. I can't be enough. I never could be."

He looked down at the floor.

"Does this make any sense? Maybe not to you. But he became the sacrifice. Once for all. He took away all that I did wrong and gave me his rightness. I still mess up, but now I can say,

'I'm sorry. Look at what he did for me. He paid what I owed. He took the penalty. He made it right again, as much as things can ever be right in this world.' "

I took another deep breath. "With hope for the next. Do you understand? I don't have to think that God'll throw me out for doing the things I've done, because he wiped all that away. I don't have to try to be perfect because I know I can't be, except in believing what he's done for me. And I don't care what anybody thinks of themselves. It all comes down the same. Nobody can be good enough. Nobody but God. Everybody fails. Everybody hurts somebody else, whether they meant to or not. Everybody breaks the laws of God. So we're all in the same wretched trouble. Without his sacrifice."

Saul was still looking down at the floor. "There is none righteous. No, not one."

"There is now. Jesus. And the ones he's cleansed."

"He had done no violence, neither was any deceit in his mouth."

"Right," I answered, a little surprised.

"That is from the prophet Isaiah. Marigold shared it with me, but I was already aware. And I am also aware that God has instructed his people to keep his commandments and to make sacrifices daily to atone for our transgressions. But we are not able to keep the commandments faithfully. No one is, as you've said. And we no longer have a temple or any way to properly present a sacrifice to Almighty God. We cry out in our hearts and with our lips, but it is not good enough. Because it is not the order that he has set."

Saul took hold of the front of his shirt and tore it open. Two buttons hit the floor with a plink and rolled in opposite directions. "My father said we must now rely on the mercy of God upon his scattered people. But how do we receive such mercy with iniquity in our hearts?"

Believe in the One God has sent. I knew the answer, but I couldn't say it. I couldn't speak another word in the face of his obvious anguish, and I felt like a failure.

"Josiah, do you know how many prophecies of Messiah are contained in the Books of God?"

"No."

"Maybe hundreds. I've studied many of them. I've meditated much on what Marigold has told me. But you've brought all of the word down to one thought. We need him. There's nothing else that needs to be understood as well as that. We need him. I cannot serve God perfectly. I cannot live sinlessly. You're not the only one, Josiah. And I do not have a remedy."

"You do. You could. You know exactly what I mean."

Tears hit his cheeks. "If I claim the Nazarene to be Messiah, my family may never speak to me again."

I swallowed hard. "That would be a shame. A loss. For them, especially. But what would you gain?"

He looked at me, the tears still flowing. "Peace. If it's there for me. Do you have peace?"

I sighed over that. "Yes. When I put my mind on him and not my own feelings and problems. I know I'm not condemned anymore. I don't have a stupid hammer over my head waiting to fall. He actually loves me. If he died for me, how could I doubt it? That's peace."

He nodded. "Do you know this is why I've avoided Marigold these last few weeks? I'd like peace. I've felt her Messiah chasing me and haunting me, calling out all the prophecies I am supposed to see. Born in Bethlehem. Betrayed by a friend. Pierced in hands and feet."

He pulled a handkerchief from his back pocket. "Those things chase my mind. But none grips my heart like the simple understanding: we need him."

I was suddenly scared. What was I supposed to do? *Oh, Lord, what now?*

"Josiah, please pray for me. Teach me to trust Messiah. Please."

"Um . . ." *Lord, help.* What was I supposed to say? "You just talk to him. Tell him you believe in him. Tell him you want him to save you . . ."

Saul Abraham prayed. We prayed together. We were up half the night praying. And then laughing, oddly enough. Because when Saul finally found his peace, he started laughing. That got me started. And then we could hardly stop. I think we both felt reborn.

32

Leah

I dreamed of my father. Dying. Reaching his hand to me. And then, like the gripping hand of evil, a screaming locomotive tore between us and I saw him no more.

"You should go to him," Marigold had said. And I didn't want it. But I knew the compulsion would not leave me. So I began to speak to Eliza about it, and I planned to mention the possibility to Dorothy Humphrey again as well.

"The Lord will make a way," Marigold had said. If it was to be, somehow I'd be able to afford the ticket.

I could scarcely believe my eyes when Josiah came in to Marigold's kitchen that morning and laid money on the table. His eyes twinkled with a strange delight that I'd never seen in him.

"Aunt Marigold—Mr. Abraham received Jesus as Messiah last night. We felt like giving a gift to celebrate and figured you'd know some dandy places to put a few dollars."

Marigold grabbed Josiah quicker than I'd ever seen her move and squeezed him in a huge embrace.

Eliza, sitting with me at the table, stared and then giggled.

"Oh, Josiah! Oh!" Marigold exclaimed. "I just knew that

you staying there—I just knew he'd hear you. Oh, thank you! Thank you!"

"I—it wasn't me," he started to protest.

"Oh, I know. The good Lord draws, and he saves. But you were his instrument. A tool in his hand."

He smiled, he hugged her back with real tears in his eyes. But then he pulled away just a little. "I've got to be going to work."

"Let me kiss you first," Marigold asked. "You wonderful tool of God."

Josiah's smile grew, making his face brighter and more handsome than I'd ever noticed before. He kissed Marigold's cheek before she got a chance at his. "You're a tool of God yourself. A blessing. Thank you."

He motioned to the money on the table. "Use that to meet a need, bless someone, whatever is on your heart for the glory of God. That's what Saul and I decided we wanted."

He hurried to the door, as though he thought he must be running late. But he turned to Marigold one last time. "He also said to tell you he'd be happy to join you for tea. The usual time."

When Josiah was gone, Marigold spun once around and then plopped into her seat. "Oh, praise the Lord! Thank you, thank you, precious Jesus!"

"Mr. Abraham knows the Lord?" Eliza asked, as if seeking to affirm what she thought she'd heard.

"Oh yes! Thank you, Jesus!" Marigold's eyes filled with tears, and she fumbled in a pocket. "Oh, Leah, darling. Can you please fetch a hanky? I thought I had one, but it seems to have disappeared."

I ran to pull one from a drawer for her, my heart pounding with the wonder of this news.

"It's a great day that makes all the angels happy," Eliza said when I got back in the room. "Right, Mommy?"

"Yes," I told her. "Absolutely."

"I bet Daddy and Johnny James are havin' a party too."

The mention of them jabbed at my heart, but not as badly as it once would have. I gave Marigold a little hug when I brought her the hanky. "I am so glad."

Beyond walking Eliza to school that day, it was difficult to get anything done. Marigold wanted me to work with her in the kitchen, but every time we started, she would stop and exclaim her thankfulness, or just sit down and cry. Happy tears. Of course. I expected her to be happy. But I'd had no idea that her reaction would be this profound. No question that Saul Abraham was deeply entwined in her heart.

Finally she motioned me to sit beside her. We were silent for a moment, then she took my hand. "They said the money was at my discretion. I want to use some of it to send you to see your father."

"But that wouldn't be right," I protested. "He said it should be for God's glory."

"You don't think there's glory to God in relationships being restored that the devil has taken? Tell that man you love him. Tell him God loves him, and that will be glory to him. Believe me."

I couldn't argue. I knew she wouldn't hear it. But the idea gave me a dreadful pinched feeling inside.

"There's enough here to do more good besides. Don't you worry over a piece of it being put to use on your behalf. It's an answer to prayer."

"Would you like me to make the scones?" I asked her, hoping to busy my hands and keep my mind from racing frantically about the details of a trip. "You said you'd like some fresh for the tea." I gave her a smile.

She returned one. And I hurried into the baking with a will. But when it came time for Saul's visit, I grabbed my shawl and started for the front door. "I need to visit Mrs. Humphrey."

"All right, dear," Marigold answered with a sparkle in her eye. "Tell her I said hello."

I ended up crying at the Humphreys' dining table, dreadfully embarrassed and yet unable to hide my apprehension at going to see my father.

"It's something you need to do," Dorothy agreed with Marigold. "But you're right. If he's this difficult to face, it's better that he told you not to take your daughter. It wouldn't be wise to have her there. At least not yet. Perhaps the two of you can come to peace, and then she could go on a later visit."

I found it nearly impossible to imagine that happening, but I tried to get hold of myself and talk to her about details. She was happy to see Eliza back and forth to school, and even let her sleep over some of the nights. I wished I could tell her how long I'd be gone, but I had no idea what my father's need might be. Finally I decided that I'd have to determine a time frame, for my daughter's sake, whether it suited my father or not.

"I'll be gone from here one week, including travel time. No more. He'll just have to accept that. Of course, he might not be able to tolerate me in his house for more than a day."

"Surely he'll not be that bad."

"I have no idea what to expect."

Dorothy said she'd pray for me, both before the trip and after I'd gone. And then I felt I should share with her our good news.

"Mr. Abraham received the Lord last night."

I did not expect the strange look on her face. "But he's a Jew."

"He's a child of God. It's a wonderful thing."

She nodded her head, but her expression didn't change. She glanced quickly at the wall clock. "It's time to get the children."

We walked together quietly. She'd become a good friend in a short time, but I'd seen something I didn't really understand. Did she mistrust Mr. Abraham? Or simply the idea of his conversion? Neither made much sense to me.

Eliza was joyous on the way home from school. Marigold was equally joyous, if not more so, when we came into her house.

But in the midst of that joy, I felt a heavy weight of dread. I was going to see my father.

I prepared Eliza carefully, scared that she would be far more apprehensive about this trip because it would be longer. But she didn't seem to be bothered much at all.

"It's going to be okay, Mommy. I miss you at night, but I know you need to see Grandpa, and you'll come back just like you did when you were helping all those sick people."

"I really wish I didn't need to go."

"But Grandpa's sick too, so he needs your help now. And I gotta stay here in school. That's the way it is for big kids. If I was little, then I'd have to go where you go."

That thought made me smile. She was only six, and one of the smallest in her first grade class. But in her mind's eye, she was "big."

She took my hand. "Do you want me to teach you the moon song so we can both sing it if we miss each other?"

"The moon song?"

"Yeah. Marigold taught me. When I couldn't sleep so good. She gave me that cot beside her window, remember? And we looked out at the moon and she said that same moon was looking at you."

I wasn't sure I quite understood.

Then she taught me the song, just a cute little ditty about the moon seeing the person we miss. "Isn't that pretty, Mommy? Isn't that a good song?"

It certainly was pretty, especially with her angel voice. I wasn't so sure of all that about the moon, but I supposed there was no harm in it, especially if it gave a child peace. "It's pretty. Thank you for sharing it with me."

"I'll be used to things this time," she said. "So I won't be scared at all now. Can I make Grandpa a picture?"

I nodded my head. The admission that she must have been a little frightened last time made me reluctant to proceed with my plans to leave again. Yet I knew if I didn't, regret for not making the effort would follow me for the rest of my life.

With so many of the other details beginning to be resolved in my mind, a familiar dread jumped in with everything else. I'd have to take the train. Alone. I'd have to ride that belching, murderous monster again.

The nightmares jumped at me with a renewed vengeance. And even in the waking hours, thoughts of the train plagued me worse than before. What if I couldn't go through with it?

It wasn't hard to prepare everything else that needed to be prepared that week. Marigold had plenty of groceries in, and Josiah and Saul would be checking every day anyway to see if she needed anything. Dorothy would come to the door and escort Eliza to school and bring her back to the door again. Except for two of the nights, when Eliza would get to sleep over with Betty.

We even had an arrangement for seeing me off. Josiah had finally gotten Mr. Abraham's car in good repair, so Saul planned to drive Marigold and Eliza to the station with me so they could wave me on my way.

But before then, I wanted to make sure I didn't leave anything undone. So I washed up all the laundry, for myself and Eliza, as well as for Marigold and the men next door. That way, Marigold would only need to cook while I was gone to fulfill her agreement with them. And she loved doing that anyway.

But it was not so easy to prepare my mind. Over and over I went through the trip mentally, telling myself that I'd ridden the train once and I could certainly do it again. But somehow this time seemed so different. Whether it was because I was going home, or because I'd be without Eliza's childlike faith, I didn't know. But I could feel my heart swirling in near panic.

The night before I was to leave, I'd put Eliza to bed early as I'd been doing whenever possible since school began. I'd been shaking rugs and sweeping and mopping floors nearly all day so Marigold could be caught up and not have to think about such things while I was gone. Now I had only the kitchen floor left to scrub because I'd planned to leave it for last. But my wash bucket and brush blurred before my eyes several times, and finally I just crumpled to my knees and wept.

Unfortunately, Marigold caught me at it. I tried to brush it off, pretend that there wasn't any problem, but of course she knew better.

"Talk to me, Leah. Are you so afraid of your father? Has he hurt you?"

I almost couldn't answer. Of course, he'd hurt me, probably more than even he could realize. But not physically. Not like she meant. "It's the train . . ."

"What? What about the train?"

In all this time, I'd not confessed the immense fear that haunted me so. Of course my parents had known. There was no hiding it from them when I was a child. And John had known. He knew I had nightmares, and I'd told him trains made me nervous. But many things did, so he'd lumped that fear along with the others into one bundle to carry before the Lord in prayer. And it'd been better as long as I had him and his prayers to lean on.

But after his death, the terror of my childhood had rushed back with an overwhelming power. Now I was nearly paralyzed. And though Marigold didn't understand, she could plainly see the depth of my dismay.

"Please, Leah. Try to explain. I want to help."

"Th-the train. I . . . I can't face the train."

"But you rode a train to get here, child. Was it that bad?"

I shook my head.

"You're just in a tizzy over facing your father after all this time. But I assure you he'll be so glad you've come. You'll be glad too. And that's all it is. Just fear over how he'll receive you. But it's nothing to worry about. He needs you. It's the right thing to do."

I shook my head again. "The train . . ."

"What about the train?"

I struggled to catch my breath away from the tears trying to take hold. "Father scares me," I managed to admit. "I—I don't know what to expect. But he doesn't scare me as badly as the train . . ."

I started shaking, and though it was surely going to be hard for her to get back up, Marigold sank to the floor beside me and held me in her arms. Then everything came pouring out. The nightmares, the panic of my childhood, the depth of my terror that seemed to be gripping me with new vigor.

She held me and let me cry and bare my soul of this pain. And then she prayed. She didn't try to tell me my fear was foolish. That I was an adult and I should lay this nonsense aside and act like one. She only prayed, until I grew calm again. And then we sat for a long time in each other's arms.

I don't know how long. Finally, she said, "You need to conquer this, you understand, don't you? You must not let this keep you from your trip."

I nodded my head.

"I know you don't understand the source of this fear, and I don't either, except that it's a weapon of the devil to torment you and keep you from doing what you need to do." She smoothed my hair back from my face. "You had one safe train ride, and you're about to have another. There'll be no difficulty in it. And a blessing of God at your destination for the renewed relationship you need with your father. It'll be all right."

"Yes," I managed to agree.

"Leave the floor the way it is. You need to get your rest."

I sniffed. "All right."

"Go on," she prodded. "Get up."

So I got up. And then I helped her up. I wiped my eyes and hugged her, and thought I was all right. So we both went to bed.

But the terror of my dreams was back, chasing me down, tearing in pieces all that I knew and everyone I knew. It was the longest, cruelest, bloodiest train dream I could ever remember. And I woke before light, trembling.

This was a Saturday, and I'd be getting on the early train.

I'd planned this on purpose so Eliza could sew with Marigold and then go and play at the Humphreys' instead of having to concentrate on her studies as she thought about me going far away. I'd thought it would be better for her to have Marigold at her side, or Dorothy Humphrey, so one of them could give her a hug and a listening ear if it was necessary.

I'd also thought it would be better to leave on a day when Josiah would not be on a train, lest people get the erroneous idea that we always traveled together.

But I could not seem to stop shaking. I tried to push the awful dream from my mind, but that only served to remind me of previous ones. So many of them. Of John. Or my parents. Myself, or the brother I couldn't remember, being chased by trains. I made myself get dressed, and then I walked to the kitchen, feeling almost too weak to stand.

Marigold was already up, and when she saw me, it was immediately plain how awful I looked. "Oh, child. Sit down."

Immediately I burst into tears and almost fell. She hurried to my side, not letting her still-pronounced limp slow her, and helped me to a chair.

"Did you sleep?"

I nodded.

"But there were dreams again."

I didn't have to answer. She knew.

"Let me get you a cup of tea. You need to relax."

"I can't do it," I told her. "I'll write to my father. He won't understand, but it won't matter. He probably doesn't expect me anyway. I—I can't go, Mari—I just can't."

She poured my tea and set it in front of me. "I see you're all dressed. That's good. Is your bag packed?"

"I—I did that yesterday. But I can't go—"

"You will not let fear stop you, do you understand?"

I sat like a stone.

"You are stronger than that, Leah. I want you to say it. 'I'm strong.' "

"But I'm not—"

"I don't care if you think you are. Saying it will help. 'I'm strong.' "

I heard a stirring upstairs, and in a moment's time, Eliza came jaunting down in her pajamas. She looked utterly stunned to see me in tears.

"Mommy?"

I took a deep breath.

"She's all right, child," Marigold assured her. "Just a little worried. Run and get dressed and we can all sit down for oatmeal."

I was surprised that she would push Eliza away so quickly, and Eliza seemed to be too. But she trusted Marigold and hurried away in obedience.

"You have a very bright and very speedy daughter, Leah Breckenridge," she told me. "You may have less than five minutes to get hold of yourself before she's right back down here."

I tried. I thought I'd managed, sitting calmly and receiving a steaming bowl of cinnamon raisin porridge, just the way I liked it. But I couldn't eat. I could barely drink my tea. Silence filled the air around the table. Finally Marigold took Eliza's hand carefully. "Your mother's worried some about the trip, of course, dear. You'll miss each other. But it'll be so good when she's back, and so good for her to help your grandpa while she can. Please be a dear and go next door to fetch Josiah for me. It's almost time for your mother to be leaving for that train."

I lowered my head and put my hands in my lap, hoping to hide the renewed shaking from my daughter's sight. *Lord. Lord, I don't want to scare her! Please help me to calm down. Oh, please don't make me go today!*

Once again, Eliza obeyed Marigold. But to get Josiah? To fetch me to the train? *No!*

"Leah," Marigold spoke into the swirl of panic I was feeling again. "Leah, you may think me an old bear before this morning's done. But you are not yourself right now. You made a decision of what you knew to be right. You know your father needs you. He may be dying, and it's your duty to go to him while you still have that opportunity. You're getting on the train this morning, Leah. Your daughter will see her strong mother going to be a hero again for her grandpa's sake, and she'll be proud. You are not going to allow fear to cripple you, child. Because if you do, it will never stop."

Something in my heart mustered the courage to give her my nod. I knew she was right. I knew it deep inside where it really counts. But the panic tried to grip me still.

Oh, God, please help me!

I'd been trying to pray now. Off and on, because I knew it was right. I really was making an effort. And today, for Eliza especially, I had to cry out, because I had no strength to manage this on my own.

33

Josiah

Saul was almost ready to bring the car around and escort the women to the train station as they'd planned. But I'd not expected a summons myself.

"Marigold wants you to come over, please," Eliza told me, her bright eyes looking worried.

Puzzled, I grabbed my hat. "Maybe she has a chore for me while you all are gone."

"I'll have the car around front when your mother and Marigold are ready," Saul told Eliza. We all walked out together.

To my surprise, Eliza grabbed my hand to hurry me across the yard to Marigold's back porch. "Mommy's crying," she said. She looked like she could cry herself.

"Missing you already," I surmised. "But she won't be gone long. It'll be fine."

I couldn't conceive of anything else that would be the matter, and Leah looked all right when I entered Marigold's kitchen. A little pale, maybe. A little stiff.

"Where's your bag, Leah, dear?" Marigold prompted.

"Upstairs. Beside our bedroom door."

"Do you mind fetching it for me, Josiah?" Marigold asked.

And I didn't mind obliging. It was a small thing, but it seemed a little silly to ask me over for that. After all, the bag wasn't too terribly heavy, and I knew for a fact that Leah could handle it when she needed to.

But that wasn't the real issue that Marigold had wanted me here for. When I got back to the kitchen, Eliza had her arms around her mother, and Marigold drew me quickly to her side.

"I know you weren't planning on accompanying us to the train station, Josiah. But I need you to come along. Please don't ask questions. I need you to carry Leah's bag and to take her arm between here and the car, and again between the car and the train. Can you do that for me?"

At first, a shred of anger rose in me. She was at it again. Insisting on putting me with Leah. Insisting that we be friends. In front of people, this time. Making me take her arm. I almost protested. And she must have seen it in my eyes.

"I will explain later, if need be. But I'm not strong enough for this, Josiah. I don't walk steadily enough. I need you to help me."

This could be the most perplexing thing she'd ever asked of me. Why would special strength be required to escort Leah to the train? But Marigold was so in earnest that I didn't feel right to refuse her. With a deep sigh, I gave her my nod.

Leah looked at me, her face slightly paler than before. Her jaw was set. She grasped her daughter's hand and pushed herself to her feet. "I think I'm ready to go," she said in a quiet, even voice. But her eyes did not say the same. To my surprise, they spoke fear. Sheer, unadulterated terror.

She started in the direction of the front door, still holding Eliza's hand. I thought for a moment that she'd decided she didn't need my arm, despite Marigold's request. But then her knees started to buckle, and I hurried to her side and took her arm as I'd been told.

"What's the matter, Mommy?" Eliza cried. "Are you all right?"

"I think I just tripped," Leah lied.

I knew it was a lie, but I couldn't fault her at all. I didn't understand what the difficulty was, but I could definitely respect her effort not to frighten her daughter any more than she might already be.

"Oh! You didn't eat very much!" Eliza exclaimed. "Do you want cookies or scones for the train?" She looked at Marigold in expectation.

"Oh, that's a wonderful idea. Why didn't I think of it?" Marigold quickly fetched a paper bag and filled it with whatever baked goods were handy, then brought it to Eliza. "Carry it for your mother, dear, if you don't mind."

She smiled as though everything was right now that such an important detail had been taken care of.

Leah still held her daughter's hand and looked down at the girl with a tender smile. But at the same time, her fingers had grown tight on my arm, and when she glanced my way, I could almost imagine her eyes speaking to me.

"I'm sorry. I don't want it to be this way. But please don't let go."

She leaned on me more than I expected as we walked, and I began to think that surely she must be ill. Was she going away to hide that fact from her daughter? And if that were the case, could she be sure of being well enough to return in the time she'd said? I wished I could pry Marigold to explain, but she'd told me to ask no questions. And I figured I owed her that much, just for caring.

Leah's words were steady, her face was set. She even smiled as she spoke to her daughter and said the sort of things that make perfect sense to put a child at ease when her mother is going away. But Marigold knew as well as I did that something else was afoot. At the train station, she drew me aside again.

"Josiah. I know I ask an awful lot of you. And this time you might think it's just too much. Upon my honor, it was just a curious accident that you both ended up at the Kurchers' at the same time. I didn't try to do that. And I'm not trying to put you together now. But—"

She glanced over at Leah, standing stiff beside Mr. Abraham, one hand still holding Eliza's hand, the other white-knuckled around a rail.

"What? What on earth is going on?"

"You don't have to be anywhere else today, do you?"

"No. You can't be asking—"

"Josiah, you're allowed to ride the train free because of your job. I was hoping she'd be better and that I wouldn't have to ask any more of you. But couldn't you go as far as St. Louis? Then take the return and be back tonight. See her that far for me, could you, please? I'm just not sure she's going to manage very well alone."

"Why? Is she sick?"

"No. Not really."

"Then what's wrong? It's a straight ride to St. Louis. No changes until then. And she made the trip on the way out here."

"Thank the good Lord for that miracle of grace."

I could hear the train in the distance now. Leah seemed to tip for a moment toward the rail, but she steadied herself again.

"There's something wrong with her, isn't there?" My heart was heavy with the thought. She was young. Beautiful. With a beautiful fatherless daughter.

"Not in the usual manner," Marigold admitted. "You'll see. You'll understand soon enough. Only please agree for now, Josiah. For that little girl's sake over there. And hurry up about it. Before the train gets in sight."

I had no idea what she was talking about. But she persuaded me, like always. Somehow, for some reason, this was very important to her. She'd call it a ministry later. She'd say I was the tool of God again. I didn't care about any of that. But I did care about little Eliza being afraid. And somehow I knew that it wouldn't be so bad if I did what Marigold asked.

"I think I need to ride to St. Louis today," I announced when

Marigold and I rejoined the others. "Hope you won't mind having me along on the same train."

Leah looked confused for a moment, glancing first at me, and then at Marigold. I thought she might protest. She did not seem pleased. And yet she nodded her head placidly, accepting.

"Are you gonna see my grandpa too?" Eliza asked with wonder.

"No. I've got other business. I'll just be on the same train for part of the trip."

"That's good," Eliza decided. "I don't think my mommy likes trains. But you know everything about them. So you can help if she needs anything."

"Oh, it's not far," I said glibly. "Can't imagine what she'd need from me."

Leah looked long at me this time but didn't say anything. The knuckles of her one hand were still wrapped white around that railing. Then the train whistle blew shrill and loud, and she closed her eyes. I don't know why I felt she might pass out. Marigold hadn't told me what was wrong, but Leah seemed suddenly frail to me, utterly weak and broken. I put my arm behind her just to steady her, hoping she wouldn't be offended at me. I didn't want her to fall.

The good-byes were short and sweet because the train never lingered long in Andersonville. Leah smiled and waved for her daughter, at the same time fumbling to put one foot in front of the other on the metal steps. Finally we were onboard and she plopped into the nearest seat.

"What's wrong?"

She ignored me completely, looking out the window and waving for her daughter, a smile still on her face. Only when we began to move did the façade begin to crumble. I knew the moment when she could no longer see Eliza, because her face fell, her shoulders sagged, and she came apart in a mess of tears.

I had no idea what to do now. Joe Pesh, the weekend porter, was checking for tickets. He didn't bother looking at my worker's paper. He just pointed at Leah, surmising that we must be together. But I didn't know where her ticket was, and she was way beyond us in her sobs, so I asked him to come back in a while if he would. Of course he gave me a strange look.

Marigold had no idea what she'd asked of me. I'd not live this down in a long time. The men I worked with would all soon know that their fire man had hopped a train on Saturday with a hopelessly crying woman.

I sat beside her. "Leah. Don't mean to bother you, but the porter'll be back in about two minutes. He'll want to see your ticket."

At first I didn't think she'd heard me. But she fumbled with her bag and couldn't seem to open it, so I reached to help her. Our hands touched for a moment, and she pulled away. I realized she was shaking.

"Can you tell me what's wrong?"

She shook her head. "S-side p-pocket."

She seemed barely able to catch her breath. But she'd given me permission after a fashion, so I searched through the bag's side pocket and found the needed ticket. Then, so the porter wouldn't have to come back this way and see her like this again, I got up and took it to him.

He checked the ticket and gave me a wry smile. "She seems just thrilled to be traveling with you, champ."

"Shut up. I'm just doing a favor seeing her as far as St. Louis. She's ailing."

I left him and his stupid grin behind me and returned to Leah, not sure if I should sit beside her again or not. She was leaning against the wall looking scared and tiny, her crying stilled a little, though the tears were still wet on her cheeks. I stood in the aisle with my hand on the back of a seat, wondering what to do.

She looked up at me, and I could still see the fear in her eyes.

"Tell me about the train wreck," she said in a voice so soft I barely heard.

"Are you sure you want to hear that? Right now?"

She nodded, but tears clouded her eyes again.

"Um . . . a car was crossing the tracks, that's all. They didn't seem to see us comin' and just pulled out in front of us. A train can't stop fast, you know. No way for that. So the car got mangled pretty bad . . ."

I stopped, watching her eyes. "You don't really need to hear this."

She sniffed, fumbled with a hanky, and tried to wipe her eyes. "Two—two people died?"

"Yes, ma'am. I guess they were killed instant."

She took a deep breath, and her shaking hands tried to close together around the twisted hanky. I thought she might say something about John's death, or about what was making her seem so weak. But she didn't. She only laid her head against the wall and closed her eyes.

Just then the engineer sounded the whistle, which was nothing to me, but Leah gasped and jumped like a wild beast was threatening. Her arms flew up to cover her face and head.

I sat beside her. "Are you all right?"

She didn't move. She didn't answer. *Lord, what in the world is the matter with this woman?*

Suddenly it hit me. I'd seen a three-year-old child act like this on the train once, thrown into a panic every time the whistle blew.

"It's not really so bad."

She lowered her arms and looked at me.

"I can't say there's nothing to be afraid of. Because trains can be scary, sure. I might be scared myself if I wasn't so used to them, having to work on one and all. But if I'd never seen one, or if I dwelt too much in my head on things like that wreck—"

She lowered her eyes, but I knew she was still listening.

"I'm just saying they can be scary. Sure. Especially . . ."

I stopped to take a breath. Could I really talk to her like this? What if I was making a huge mistake? "Um . . . especially if you've lost somebody you love."

She closed her eyes.

"But they're not so bad, really. Nothing but a hunk of metal, if you get down to brass tacks. And there's accidents with this kind of hunk of metal just like any other."

She started crying, sobbing like a child, and I couldn't help myself. I took her in my arms, glad the train wasn't full and Joe Pesh wasn't in our car. The fewer eyes to see this, the better.

"It's all right to cry," I told her. "Whatever the matter is. Sometimes you just got to, that's all."

I'd seen her stuffy and snippy, smudged with garden dirt, buried in apples, and fiery bossy for the sake of the Kurchers' need. But I'd never expected to see her broken like this. I felt like crying too. I'd imagined her strong inside, healed already and moved on from the raw pain of grief. But here she was, showing me almost more than I could bear. Weak like me. Hurting like me. Right now, somehow, unable to cope with the world.

"Leah. It's okay. Don't feel bad for letting it show, all right? You're human. Like me. Kinda busted up inside over losing the one you love. But it's gonna be all right."

I expected her to pull away. I could not have been more surprised that she didn't. She sunk in my arms, like a child finding a haven, and I wondered if Marigold knew this was going to happen.

"Peace," I said softly. "Lord, give her peace."

My eyes filled with tears, recognizing those words from Marigold's lips. More than once she'd said them. "Lord, give him peace." And it had helped, even the times when I hadn't wanted to acknowledge that it could.

Finally, Leah was still. The shaking gone, the sobs erased. I thought she'd sit up then, to distance herself from me and act like this had never happened. But she didn't move. Neither did I, for a long time, until I just couldn't help wondering if she was really all right. Leaning close then I realized that she'd drifted into sleep.

It was a wonder, a marvel I could have never expected. I prayed that Joe Pesh would stay away and no one else would say a word to disturb her. And I sat as still as I could, afraid to move a muscle lest I wake her. For some reason I wanted her to sleep as long as possible, to stay just this way for the whole trip if the Lord willed it so I could hold her in my arms and know she was at peace.

I didn't expect to feel the way I felt. Like this moment had been specially arranged and I was blessed just to be with this beautiful and strong woman in her need. It made me wonder if there could ever be something between us, despite my coarse and foolish behavior. Hopefully Leah wouldn't be angry when she woke. I closed my eyes, thankful that I'd done what Marigold had told me to do.

Lord, you work in strange ways. You really surprised me here. And I can't ask for nothing special. Just that you help her. Whatever the problem is, whatever started all this, you know. Let your peace run down inside her and never go away . . .

34

Leah

I woke to the sound of a train whistle again, but it seemed to not roar quite so loudly nor so threateningly as before. At first I was surprised to find Josiah's arms around me, and then I remembered that he'd grabbed me and held me in my panic and tears. And instead of being afraid, I'd welcomed his touch, his reassuring strength.

But it wouldn't be right to linger when the tears were gone. I lifted my head, I moved my arm, and he jolted a little. He must have fallen asleep too.

"I'm sorry," I whispered and sat up, scooting just enough away that we were no longer touching.

"Don't be," he said. "We all gotta cry."

We sat in silence, the awkwardness of the moment hanging between us. I glanced out the train window. "Where are we?"

"Almost to St. Louis already. Makes a quick trip when you sleep through half of it."

"I—I didn't sleep well last night."

"I understand. I have that problem sometimes."

I stared out the window. Why in the world was I talking to him? Why especially was I longing to talk to him more? "I don't think you really understand," I began slowly. "Nightmares kept me from rest. A jumble of them this time, all about trains."

I glanced at him. He was looking at me with a softness, almost sadness, in his eyes. "Do you have nightmares often?"

"Yes. Very often. And always about trains."

"Since John died?"

"No. Way before then. Even before I was Eliza's age. I don't really remember not having them, except that it was better when I was with John. And so much worse since . . ."

He looked puzzled. "I can understand worse since. But do you know why all this started?"

I shook my head. Maybe there was no reason at all.

He let out a long sigh. "I've come to believe that whenever there's deep pain, there's a reason for it somewhere. Maybe the Lord will show you one of these days."

"What if I don't wish to know? Maybe that would just make things worse."

But he disagreed. "There's peace in knowing. I've seen panic before. Don't seem to be nothing rational to it. But there's a cause, there has to be. And when you get down to that, I'd betcha the panic'd go away."

"When it happened when I was a child, my father would say I was just a whiny baby grabbing for attention."

"Maybe he was hiding his head from the truth."

I let the remark remain unanswered. He didn't know my father or anything about this. I'd already told him too much. There was no point in any further words.

Before long, I saw the Mississippi River bridge and tensed, especially when the whistle blew again. To my surprise, Josiah took my arm, and that seemed to make it better. Soon we were arriving in the city, and I found myself reluctant for him to go.

"How soon is the train going back?" I asked a little nervously.

"I've got plenty of time. So if you'll let me, I'm going to check when the train going south to Sugar Creek is leaving. I aim to see you safely on it. Do you think you'd be all right from there?"

I'd have to be. I couldn't ask him to go with me any farther.

It would make it impossible for him to board his connection back home. And it wouldn't do for me to be showing up in my hometown with a strange man, anyhow. "Yes. I think I'll be fine now."

"Okay. Let me go see about your train."

He escorted me to a seat in the station house and went to the counter to make sure they'd told him right in Andersonville when the next train would be headed south. It turned out I had a two-hour wait, which I didn't relish in such close proximity to the tracks. But Josiah surprised me again by offering to buy me a meal at a restaurant just down the street.

"I don't know . . ."

"Oh, come on. I need something to eat before I get on that train headin' back. And I'd hate to leave a lady sitting here alone."

"We've still got the bag of Marigold's scones."

"I thought since they made it this far, you oughta go on and take 'em to your father. Besides, I've got a taste for something hot right now. But like I said, I don't wanna leave you alone."

I watched his expression, wondering what he was thinking. "Then would you stay and wait here if I refused to go with you?"

"Yeah. I guess I would. And make Marigold feed me up extra when I get back."

I took a deep breath. How should I react to this? His train would be arriving a few minutes after my own, but somehow I knew that he'd miss his train if he needed to, whatever the cost, to be here and make sure I got on mine safely. But Marigold didn't require that of him. It was a choice he'd made for himself.

"I suppose we'd better walk to the restaurant then," I told him lightly. "I wouldn't want to put Marigold through all that work."

He smiled. He took my arm again. It was a strange feeling. And though I didn't feel nearly as shaky and weak as I had before, I let it be.

35

Leah

Josiah put me on the Sugar Creek train, even though it nearly made him late catching his own. I found it hard to reconcile in my mind what had happened.

Why had I let him get so close to me, or accepted Marigold's notion that he come along at all? But how could I have managed if he hadn't? I'd not had such a panic come over me since I was a child. I'd felt like I couldn't even breathe, that the fear had a stranglehold over my body as well as my mind.

It wasn't rational, just as he'd said. But whether there was any cause I might never know.

I didn't come close to enjoying the final leg of my journey on the train, but it wasn't as bad as I'd thought it might be. The immensity of fear had seemed to melt away in Josiah's arms. And it hadn't returned.

Still I had my father to face. The little Sugar Creek station was even smaller than the one at Andersonville. Even in the daylight, there was no one around, and I had to walk a block and a half to the filling station to ask to use the phone. Father didn't have a phone at the farm. But a neighbor did, and I'd already told him what day I would arrive. Rather than planning to wait at the station, Mr. Rafferty had said to call again when I got here, that he'd drive in and pick me up.

Maybe he'd thought I'd change my mind at the last minute. It really wasn't far from the truth. I stood outside of Buck and Bill's Gas and Service after the phone call, watching for Mr. Rafferty's truck on the road running east out of town. I didn't know if he'd told my father I was coming. I hadn't told him to, nor told him not to. Either way, I couldn't picture how Father would react to me finally showing up at home again.

Eldon Rafferty drove slow like he wasn't used to maneuvering on the road in a motor vehicle. And maybe he wasn't. The last I remembered he still drove a horse and wagon.

"Well. My wife is pleased you come. Your father's ailing, you know. It's good you come to see about him."

My stomach was tight, and I felt like my throat was all bound up with knots. But I made myself answer him smoothly. "Thank you so much for the ride."

"No problem. Ain't far."

We rode in silence. Nearly five miles to the farm. The house looked almost the same, but older, in need of some time and attention. One of the trees in the front yard had toppled over and still lay where it fell.

"Have a good evening now," Mr. Rafferty said. "Tell your pappy how-do."

"I will. Thank you."

I stood in the yard as he drove away, this whole thing not even seeming real. Maybe I'd wake in a moment's time and find Eliza cuddled beside me and the scent of Marigold's fresh biscuits already in the air.

Skeeter the dog limped out to meet me. He'd been young and spry not so awfully long ago, but now he looked gray and tired, the years catching up with him. He didn't bark, just stood and nuzzled my hand with his nose.

"Just like always, huh, Skeeter? Need a little attention?"

I petted the dog, leaned and gave him a hug. For some reason the simple act brought tears to my eyes. Would I be able to do this much for my father? Would he let me get even half so close?

I took a deep breath. I was here. It was real. And I would have to go inside. The breeze caught my skirt and gave it a swirl, and I kept hold of the shawl Marigold had given me, to make sure I didn't drop it out here in the unmowed grass.

I knocked just once and then opened the door, not wanting to make him get up if he were lying down. "Hello? Father?"

He didn't answer till I was fully in the room and had closed the door behind me.

"Well. Let me look at you."

He was propped at the head of a bed someone must have moved downstairs for him. That and a padded rocking chair dominated what had once been Mother's delicately furnished sitting room.

"Mr. Rafferty said to tell you hello." It seemed a safe way to answer him, at least for now.

"Um-hum. Did he ask a lot of questions?"

"None."

"Good. Don't need nobody knowin' our business."

I stepped a little closer. He looked a bit gray, but it was difficult to tell with the curtains closed. "Are you all right?"

"'Course I'm not. Or I'd be out in the orchard where I belong. Still daylight."

I moved to the chair near him. "Can you tell me about the problem?"

"Heart's bad," he grumbled with a frown. "Done told you that already in the letter."

Maybe it wouldn't get any better. At least he was talking to me and not yelling. I decided to be really brave. "God loves you, Father. Just like Mama used to say. And—and I do too."

He seemed to have a catch in his throat all of a sudden. When he found his voice, it was a good deal quieter. "Well, if you do, seems like you'd want to fix us some supper. I ain't et for hours. How 'bout you?"

"Not since St. Louis. What would you like?"

"Don't care. Anything you can find that's worth fixin'."

I thought about presenting Marigold's scones first thing, but maybe that would be better for a snack later, or breakfast tomorrow. I really wanted to cook something, if only to give my hands something busy to do for a few minutes in the kitchen away from him. I needed to think a little, breathe a little, in the next room before speaking to him again.

I certainly didn't find the same problem here as at the Kurchers'. Father had an abundance of groceries of all sorts as if he'd just gone to market and brought home plenty of everything he could find. Some of it still sat in boxes and bags, waiting to be unpacked.

The dishes were done, but besides that, it looked like nothing in the kitchen had been cleaned for a month. A dead bug lay on the floor beneath the table, and I saw the telltale sign of mice on a countertop.

I wished he'd told me what he'd like to eat. I saw a sausage in the icebox and decided on biscuits and gravy. I knew he liked that. At least he had years ago when I was a child.

I worked in silence, and he waited in silence. When it was finally ready, I wasn't sure whether he was able to come to the table, so I carried two plates right to him in the sitting room.

He took a good look at the food I'd handed him and shook his head. "Train's got you all mixed up, girl. It ain't breakfast time." He lifted the fork to his mouth. "Still, I ain't et nothing this good in a long time."

I smiled. I cleaned off my plate in peace. We didn't say much more that night. He didn't say he was glad I'd come, or ask about Eliza, even when I gave him the picture she'd drawn. I cleaned up the dishes and then started washing the countertops and table. When I looked in on him, he'd gone to sleep, so I swept and mopped the floor before taking a break again in the big rocker.

This time he woke and turned his eyes to me. "Doctor'll be here Monday."

"Does he come often?"

"Twice a week. Used to be more, but I made him quit. Orville comes in every day. He's my hired man. Been doing the harvest. He's the one brought in the groceries."

"Good. I'm glad you've got help."

"He ain't help. He's working for his own benefit. Wants to buy this place. If he can keep it from falling down too bad, so much the better for him when I'm gone."

I was stunned to hear him speak of such things so casually, and surprised to find the words so deeply cutting to me.

"What does the doctor say?"

"Girl, I already told you it's my heart!"

"I know, but—"

"Ask him Monday if you gotta have every detail. I don't wanna talk no more."

"All right." I sat quietly rocking for a moment, and then got up again to clean the grime off the stovetop. In a little while I heard him snore. It was dark already. Maybe he'd sleep through the night this time. Quietly, I carried my bag upstairs, finding the dust and cobwebs thick, but otherwise the place almost as I'd last seen it.

Father and Mother hadn't shared a room in years, and I'd recognized the bed downstairs as the one that used to be in the room Father had claimed, that should have belonged to my brother James. Mother's room would be on the right at the top of the stairs, and I turned to it first, perhaps trying to find some sparkle of her light in what had become such a dark and dismal place. Little had been touched there, though the bedcovers weren't straight and the dresser top was bare of some of the trinkets I was used to seeing. The room made me sad, I'm not sure why, except that Mother had been sad here so often, and I missed her.

I went to what had been my own room next door. It too was almost the same. I plopped my bag there on the foot of the bed, lit the lamp, and parted the curtains with a sigh. A twinkle of starlight met my gaze, and I thought of the times I'd stared out this window as a child, wishing my life could be different.

"Leah!"

The sudden call jolted me, it was so unexpected. Father hollering my name. What could be wrong? I ran down the stairs as fast as I could, nearly tripping at the bottom.

"Yes? Father, what's wrong?"

He looked pale in the dimness. "I—I thought maybe you'd left."

My heart was pounding, and I didn't know what to think of my large, frightening father suddenly seeming weak, even frightened, at the idea that he might have been left alone. "Oh no, Father. I'm staying the night. More than one night if it's all right with you. I'd just gone to take my bag upstairs."

"All right then." He settled his head onto the pillow again. "If that's the way you want it."

"Is it all right if I sleep upstairs?"

"'Course it's all right. You don't see no second bed down here, do you?"

He seemed to be trying to sound as cantankerous as ever, but I could discern the softening in his voice, in his heart. He was glad I was here, even if he'd never be able to say it. Marigold had been right about that. My presence was a comfort somehow, and I was glad.

The next day was strange, and I wished I were in church with Eliza. Father didn't want to talk to me. He only wanted to hear me working about the house and know that I was close by. He appreciated the food I made, and he ate it heartily, which I took to be a good sign. But he would not answer the simplest question about his ailment or much of anything else. I began to wonder why he'd asked me to come.

Finally that night when I brought him ham and potatoes, he asked if I would mind if he sold the farm to Orville.

"No, Father. Not if that's what you want. It's all right. And if he's been a good worker, I suppose it's his due."

"A good worker, I guess. But with him hoping it'll all be his, I still say it's to his own benefit."

"Has he been getting the crops to harvest for you?"

"Three years now," Father admitted. "Though I been able to do most things myself till this year. Still, he brings the harvest in, and he sells at a good price. Can't complain for the yield of the crop this year, that I can say, though some farmers in the area have struggled a little."

"Orville must know his job well, then. Is he one of the Williams boys? I seem to remember an Orville in that family."

"That's right. And he aims to marry up with that Markert girl. You remember her? They're wanting to raise 'em a family here, I guess."

I took a deep breath. It was with mixed feelings that I thought of my family home being sold. But it was no more than right. Inevitable. I could hardly tell him I'd rather keep it for myself. It was too much for Eliza and me to maintain, and he didn't want Eliza here anyway. He still hadn't spoken of her.

"What are you doing in Illinois, anyway?" he finally asked.

"Upkeep at a boardinghouse," I told him for lack of a better answer. "Cleaning and laundry and such."

"Well. I guess that's honest work."

Did he disapprove? I thought he might, but he hadn't come flat out and railed over it like I might have expected. He was completely calm. But still I wondered.

Only later did I consider that he might have been trying to figure out if I were established there, or if I might be willing to consider coming home.

That night he didn't snore as he'd done the previous night. For some reason it made me anxious, and I eased down the stairs gently several times just to check on him. His coarse breathing reassured me, and I would go back to bed, though I lay in the darkness, near tears from missing Eliza beside me. Finally I rose to the window, thinking of the silly song Marigold had taught her. The moon was bright outside my window, and it strangely made me smile.

On Monday, I was anxious for the doctor's arrival from the moment I got out of bed. But Father was testier than he had been and would not even tell me what time to expect him.

"Go find Orville!" he shouted. "Tell him I want him to scythe the grass in my front yard. I am not growin' a hay field!"

"Yes, sir," I answered, though I wasn't sure at all where to find Orville.

I walked out to the barn, taking the time to pet Skeeter again on the way. It looked a little wind-whipped and bare of some of the rusted old implements that used to sit gathering dust in the stalls.

But there was no hired man here. Only a barn cat, with a very mangled field mouse in its jaws. I didn't recognize the cat, but figured it was surely a descendent of Jewels, my favorite pet as a child.

I walked through the orchard, where most of the trees were already bare and showed the handiwork of the hired man better than anywhere else. They were neatly pruned and cared for, just as Father had implied. No reason not to expect that there'd been a decent crop. Finally I saw a tall skinny fellow in the distance, digging by hand in the potato field.

"Hello!" I called. "Are you Orville?"

He stopped. He stared a moment, and he started walking toward me, shovel in hand. "Late crop," he explained when he was close enough. "I like to stagger the plantings so there's harvest every week or so till frost."

"Orville Williams? I'm Leah Wiskirk Breckenridge."

"Oh yes. Glad to see you again. Heard you might be coming."

He looked terribly nervous.

"You've done a fine job with the orchard."

"Thank you."

"Father would like you to see to some mowing in the front yard. Does he normally ask you to do things outside of the orchard or fields?"

"Not every day, ma'am. Just every time he takes a notion."

I smiled a little. I could definitely picture that, and I hoped Father hadn't been too hard.

"I'll get right to it. Thanks for coming all the way out here to tell me."

"It's all right. It was nice to walk through the orchard again anyway."

He started walking back with me, still seeming awfully anxious. "You like the orchard real well then?" he asked.

"I always have. Something about fruit trees that makes me smile. Unless of course, Father's yelling at me to get out of them."

I don't know why I'd told him that. It wasn't the sort of thing you talk about with a near stranger. But this was not a normal circumstance, and I guess I didn't care about behaving according to convention.

"Think you might like to be moving back home, then?"

Here was that same idea again. "I haven't thought much about it," I answered honestly. "But you'd rather like to claim the farm for yourself, I understand. Right?"

He nearly dropped the shovel he'd carried. "Uh—yeah, if it don't bother you none, that is. It suits my purpose. I know I could make a decent go a' things here. I been doin' it. Or close as I could come to it in the circumstance. And it's less than three miles from the folks that's gonna be my in-laws. That's kinda important to Olivia right now."

"Olivia Markert?"

"Yeah. Maybe you know we're engaged."

"My father mentioned that."

"I'd pay a fair price. I understand good value."

"Of course. But it's really my father's decision."

He stopped and seemed to have to swallow hard to get the next words out. "Pardon me for saying, ma'am. But I ain't real sure he's gonna make the decision. I've asked him twice, and he says the place is his till he's dead and gone 'cause he's not gonna live nowhere else."

"That sounds like him."

"But the doctor says he could go any day."

My heart nearly skipped a beat at such words.

"Beggin' your pardon, ma'am. But I'm hurtin' to know what

I should do. I'm needin' to make a way awful bad for my future family, but I ain't even been paid in a month. I ain't meanin' to complain. I just need to know where I stand."

I'd had no idea that I'd have to cope with a circumstance like this. I assured him that I'd see to it he was paid fairly for his time. "Do you have a record of your hours? And your previous pay?"

"Yes, ma'am. I been jottin' it all down. And the previous wages oughta be in your father's books. I don't know where those are, but they'd have any verification you need, on my previous work."

"Thank you, sir. I'll see if I can find them."

"He may be strapped for cash right now, ma'am, and I could understand that, with paying the doctor and everything. I'd just appreciate a paper or something, testifying to what I'm owed."

"All right. I don't see a problem with that. But I will have to speak with my father."

He fumbled a bit with his hat. "He may not like that. He . . . uh . . . he seems to think I don't need paid no more if I aim to make this place mine. And I'd agree, I would, ma'am, if there was an agreement to that effect. But there ain't been none for certain, so I gots no guarantees."

I nodded. "I'll talk to him."

"I'm wishin' him well. I really am."

"Of course."

"And I ain't meanin' to complain."

"It's all right. I understand."

I'd seen my father browbeat workers before, till they didn't know from one day to the next what their wages were, or from one minute to the next if they still had a job. That this man had hung on for three years spoke well for him.

I wondered how it might wear on him that he'd been asked to stop digging a cash crop and cut my father's grass. Still I left him to the work and walked back to the house.

"How long has it been since you paid Orville?" I questioned when I reached father's bedside.

"Why?"

"Just wondering."

"I tol' you. He's working for hisself."

"Maybe. In a way, everybody does. But he's also working for you and you have to pay his wages in a timely manner. What do you normally pay for a day?"

"Get outta my house!" he suddenly roared at me. "You ain't givin' him my harvest money! You ain't givin' him a dime!"

I could hear a vehicle pulling up outside, and I rushed to look out the door, hoping to see the doctor. And it was him, complete with black bag, dangling listening scope, and the same kind of hat as the doctor who'd come to treat the Kurchers.

I hurried out to talk to him in the yard.

"Leah?" He seemed very pleased.

"Yes, sir. Can you tell me how he is?" I hoped the man would understand that I needed to talk to him a few minutes away from my father's earshot. He seemed to.

"I'm glad you've come. I wasn't sure you would."

"But what's the problem?"

"I believe he has an enlarged heart. A very irregular rhythm. But he's doing much better the last couple of weeks. Before that, I wasn't sure he'd last this long. He's strong. He may go on for some time. But the condition is serious. And not treatable. He's already had more than one episode that nearly cost his life. I've ordered him to rest because he may not survive another one."

"What sort of episode?"

"A sudden collapse. An attack of the weakened heart muscle. Both times that young hired man carried him into the house and ran to fetch me."

"Then he saved his life?"

"Couldn't say for sure, but he could've laid there a long time before someone happened along to find him."

I glanced toward the other side of the driveway, where Orville was already hard at work.

"How much did your father tell you?" the doctor asked.

"Bad heart. Not another word of detail."

The doctor shook his head. “He’s a stubborn old mule.”

“You’re very right.”

I walked back in with the doctor, though Father had just been yelling for me to leave.

“Is it Monday already?” he yelled at the man. “Or are you doubling up on me again to charge me more?”

“You can’t pay me enough to come out and listen to you,” the doctor answered just as gruffly. “Now be quiet so I can hear your heart.”

Father obeyed and the doctor listened. I waited, neither of them paying me any attention.

“About the same,” the doctor said at last. “It sounds like it’s gonna be steady at first, and then it sort of trips up in its path and can’t seem to find its step again. Can you feel any of the palpitations?”

“Durn your fool palpitations,” Father answered. “It don’t like seeing you comin’. Knows you’re gonna bilk me of my hard-earned harvest cash.”

“I haven’t seen any of your cash, and you know it.”

It was a troublous day, all in all. Not only because I’d found out the seriousness of my father’s condition but also because his financial state was so uncertain. Exactly how much did he owe? Were there others as well? I tried to ask if he had money on hand, when he’d paid the doctor, or what he’d previously paid Orville for a day’s work, but any time I brought up anything of the sort, he yelled and raged, like old times. I gave up, because I was afraid of the strain on his heart.

I’d just have to search for his books and find out for myself. Under the circumstances, surely it wasn’t wrong. He needed help tending to business. He couldn’t go on refusing to deal with his obligations like this.

That night, I had a dream again of wandering along the railroad tracks as a little girl. I woke sweating, unnerved, and with my heart racing. I could almost imagine the sound of a train whistle right outside, though I knew that to be impossible.

The night was far from done, but I couldn't coax myself back to sleep. So I rose from my bed and wandered to my mother's room, just like I used to do as a child sometimes, when she didn't come to my bedside first. I wanted comfort from my troubled thoughts. Somehow my mind still sought it in Mother's room, though I couldn't be sure why.

There was nothing there but the emptiness, and I sat on the bed, lifted one of Mother's pillows, and hugged it to my chest.

"Oh, how I wish you were here," I whispered into the silence. "And I wish I weren't. I want to go back to Eliza. I can't straighten things out for Father, or help him through this illness. He doesn't even want me to. I don't even know why he wanted me here."

I lay my head to the bed, looking around the room in the dimness. Several of the things that had been Mother's were gone. Sold, perhaps, I didn't know. But much that was hers remained. A brush and mirror. The jewelry box. The bulky shape of her big Bible on the shelf.

I had John's Bible, but for some reason I'd left it at Marigold's. Maybe it was a strange thought, but I suddenly wanted to hold that Bible in my hands, as though cradling something that had been so precious to my mother would help me to feel her near me again.

I rose and lit the lamp.

"Lord, help me," I prayed. I don't know why.

And then I reached the dusty book from its shelf. First I brushed it off with my hand, and tears came to my eyes. Father had kept this, but not downstairs where he could see it or use it. At least it was still here. Surely he wouldn't care if I claimed it for my own.

I lifted the dusty cover and parted the pages. It opened easily to a place near the beginning where Mother had stuck a thin sheet of paper. Notes on a sermon, perhaps? Or a message from a friend? I unfolded the brittle paper, written in Mother's handwriting, and my breath stopped in my throat as I read the words on top. *Dear Leah.*

A letter. To me. After all this time. It was like heaven opened up and talking. My hands started shaking and my eyes watered so that I could scarcely read. But read this I must.

Dear Leah,

I write this to you because I love you so very much and you need to understand the truth. Please don't blame your father. He didn't want me to tell you, maybe because he thinks it would make matters worse. I disagree because you have already suffered so much. Still he forbids it. And he is your father, to be respected even when he is not understood.

I had to stop and wipe my eyes with a bit of my sleeve. I didn't know yet what she meant, but it seemed that she was here now and knew this present situation. There was no date on this letter, so I had no way to know when she had written it.

You've been plagued too long by the train dreams. And I wanted to explain to you from the beginning.

My heart raced and my hands felt numb. Oh. Mother! Oh, Lord God, would I really get an answer?

Dearest Leah, I know you were too young to remember what happened on the day your brother died. And you must never, never blame yourself. You were just an innocent toddler, and I'd been ill with the jaundice. I should have watched you more carefully. But instead I went to rest and left you in your brother's charge.

He was a good boy, a courageous and gentle big brother who loved you more than my words could suffice to say. But he was a boy, with his eyes on toads and fishing worms, and you got away from him on your little toddling legs.

I was suddenly shaking so badly that I almost dropped the book. I could remember this. Vaguely. It seemed to come to me out of my dreams.

Whether the sand and rocks or the swaying flowers that flourished along the tracks, something drew your attention, and you must have been up the little slope and on the ties before he saw where you'd gone. I heard him call your name, and then I heard the train whistle. I ran, but I couldn't get there fast enough. Your father heard the train whistle too, but I don't know why he ran. He didn't hear the voices. Somehow he just knew. We thought you were both gone. You were on the tracks and he ran so quickly to grab you. And then the train . . . it was too horrible, Leah, to ever describe. We found you screaming in the ditch on the other side. James must have pushed you, with no time to jump himself. You'd crawled and found his severed leg. I pulled you away from it, and you screamed for hours.

I had to stop. I had to try to take a deep breath, several deep breaths to fight away the panic, the nausea that tried to resurface. My dreams. They were real. Why hadn't they told me when I was old enough to understand? Because Father didn't want to? I had to read on.

Your father searched till he found James' body, and we buried him in the Northridge cemetery. We moved less than a year later, because you couldn't bear the sound of the trains rumbling through our backyard and I couldn't stand the memory. But moving was not the remedy we'd thought it would be. The dreams plagued you, as though you could still hear the whistle of trains in the stillness of night.

Forgive us, Leah, for not explaining to you how your brother died.

Especially forgive your father. James was his joy, and he was broken, utterly shattered as a man and as a father when we lost him. Perhaps he blamed you in a way, because James had lost his life in sparing yours. But do not ever blame yourself. You were only two years old, and your brother did what he did for you willingly.

The words blurred on the page before me, and it was a long time before I could finish. So much this was, to finally understand. But there was more. Something else Mother had written at the close of her letter.

Try to be patient with your father. I know he's difficult. He wasn't always this way. He's a good man soured by a broken heart. Love him anyway, Leah, for my sake if you can. I know if you are reading this, it must mean that I am gone. But let me hold you in spirit, my darling daughter, and pray your tears away. Deep in his heart, I know your father loves you. And I will love you ever.
Mother

I folded the paper carefully and tucked it back into the same page. And then I hugged her Bible to my chest and wept until the night was far gone. I must have eventually slept, because in the morning Mother's Bible lay to one side and I found myself sprawled with my hands over my head, eyes and cheeks still wet.

36

Leah

Talking to Father was different after that. I kept picturing him wandering a train track, searching for my brother's broken body, and I could scarcely contain the tears, even right in front of him.

He must have resented me deeply for trying to act like the son he longed for. Maybe he'd even wished that James had not reached me in time, that it might have been me that was killed and not him.

Or maybe he just didn't want the reminder night after night after night. What torture that must have been to hear my screams.

I tried to hug my father that next day. I tried to tell him again that I loved him. He only pushed me away and told me to go and make him a sandwich.

Finally I decided I couldn't hide from this any longer. And why should he? Mother had wanted everything to be in the open. It should be. I couldn't bear it any other way.

When his sandwich was done, I sat in the rocker beside my father's bed. He said nothing, only lay there, staring at the ceiling as he so often did.

"Father?"

He took his time to answer. "What?"

"I need to talk to you."

He snorted. "Well, you're talking. Get on with it."

"I—I found a letter. In Mother's Bible—"

"What are you doing looking at that?" He seemed very shaken. Might he already know?

"I knew she wouldn't mind me reading her Bible. And I—I left mine in Andersonville."

He turned his head, but just for a moment. Just before he did, I thought I'd caught the glimpse of a tear.

"The letter was addressed to me. She told me about James's death. And . . . I wanted you to know that I'm so sorry."

He stunned me by throwing his cover off and clear to one side. "About what? About what, girl? She told you not to be blaming yourself! She said that plenty plain!"

I couldn't speak for a moment. He'd read it. He knew every word. And yet he'd left it there for me to find. When he so easily could have destroyed it.

"I'm sorry anyway, that it happened. For the pain it must have been for you and Mother, to lose a son—"

"I guess you understand that yourself now, don't you, girl?"

His words were almost cold, and yet edged with a pain that was clear in his face.

"Yes. Yes, Papa, I do."

Slowly his hand moved to mine. I could scarcely believe it, but he held my fingers cupped in his for a long time, and neither of us spoke. Tears flowed down my cheeks and I gave up all attempts to restrain them. Finally, he reached for his own hanky and gave it to me.

"Wipe your nose, girl. Before you drip."

I didn't answer, just obeyed him quietly and then handed the hanky back to him.

He was different after that. When I asked him again about

Orville's pay, he told me there was an envelope of cash under the foot of his bed if I wanted to give him some of it.

"It won't be enough. There's the doctor and the grocer in town to pay too. I been using their credit most the summer."

I found his book of records in a drawer in the kitchen, and based on that, I could get a pretty good idea of what should have been paid all this time. But his records simply stopped weeks ago. Like he'd just ceased doing anything. But maybe he couldn't. Maybe he was just expecting to die.

I told him I'd pay the doctor and the grocer but I'd like to speak with Orville about another arrangement. He'd done right. He'd done the best he could, as far as I could see, even when his pay had stopped. He'd saved my father's life in all likelihood, with no thanks for it.

"We could set a fair price for the farm," I told my father. "And deduct the amount you owe him. If he agrees, it'd be like he'd made payments already. And if he'll keep working, keep checking in on you and helping where you need help, you could keep paying him, or letting him make payments against the farm, whichever you'd rather. He really wants it. And I don't feel like denying him."

I knew Father wasn't happy. But he agreed. He sat up more. He walked around the house a little, even went to the porch once to yell out at Orville to trim along the fence better. I went to talk to Orville's future bride about coming to cook and clean for my father sometimes after I left. And I was glad to know they'd be marrying within the month and had a place to stay at her parents' farm until they could move into one of their own.

I started missing Eliza so much I could barely take another moment. And maybe I'd gotten things settled here enough that I could leave. Then when I was telling Father that I'd need to be going soon, he finally mentioned her name.

"Where'd you leave your little Eliza, anyway?"

"With some very dear friends."

"Don't you think it's high time you got yourself back to her?"

"Yes." I couldn't help a smile. "I absolutely do."

"I want you on that next train, girl. Can't be leaving my granddaughter with strangers after this, you hear me? Next time you bring her along."

"Yes, Father."

I would never have thought I'd see anything from my father that I could interpret as tenderness. But he'd shown me differently. And I was amazed by it. But of course he was right, and my own heart had been telling me the same thing. It was time to go back to Andersonville.

"I'll come back, Father. If you want me to."

"I may not live another day."

"I think you will. Maybe you could have been gone, back when the doctor says you were at your worst. But it's better now. I think the good Lord has brought you through a storm."

"You sound like your mother."

"Good. That's a compliment."

He touched my hand again, just for a moment, and I'll never forget it for as long as I live. But then he pulled away and snorted at me. "Make me another sandwich. And then go down the road, will you, and find yourself a ride to that train."

I did just what he said, with a smile on my face. And I felt a lightness I'd never known before. A burden gone away. Without thinking about it, I found myself praying a simple prayer. *Thank you, Jesus. For Father. For Mother. For James. And peace . . .*

37

Leah

Coming home to Andersonville seemed almost unreal. I called ahead to Mr. Abraham's house, so I knew they'd be waiting for me at the depot. But still it was joyous and new to see them from the train window.

I hadn't known if Josiah would be there, but he was, standing a little away from the others. I wondered if he'd told Marigold what had happened between us.

Eliza was bouncing up and down, nearly beside herself with excitement. And I could share that feeling, so immense was the happiness and the peace I was feeling inside. I dropped my bag as soon as my feet left the train steps, so I could fly and take her into my arms. Out of the corner of my eye, I could see Josiah going to retrieve the bag for me, and I thought of the last time Eliza and I had greeted each other so fondly after being apart.

He must never have had such a homecoming, coming from a difficult childhood and with no child of his own. No wonder Marigold had hugged him that day and assured him he was loved.

Eliza squeezed me, kissed my cheek three or four times, and

asked me how her grandpa was, all without ever managing to stand still. I lifted her and twirled her around, just to be doing.

"I love you," I told her. "I am so glad to be back. And don't worry. Your grandfather's doing better. Much better."

"Maybe next time I can go and see him?"

"Yes, dear. And he would like that."

"Really?" Her big eyes grew even wider.

"Yes. Really. I told you he was much better."

Marigold smiled. I gave her a hug with Eliza still clinging to my side. And then greeted Mr. Abraham with a shake of the hand. Josiah stayed back from us, my bag in his hand.

"Thank you," I told him. And he nodded his head, something deep and solemn in his eyes.

There was no splitting up and going to two separate houses when we got back. Marigold ushered everyone in to her kitchen table and fed us tea and scones. They told me another boarder had stopped in while I was gone, a traveling man who'd only needed to stay a few days. But Mr. Abraham had made Josiah move right back in with Marigold so he'd be here in the boardinghouse to spend his nights while the stranger was here.

"I'd rather such a thing not happen again," Mr. Abraham confessed. "I don't like the idea of a stranger roaming the house over here. I never have, but it's never been my place to say. Until now. So I've asked Josiah to stay and keep a watch on things until the spring, the Passover time, when I'd like to claim my bride."

My mouth flew open. "Marigold!"

They both smiled, and Eliza giggled with glee. I didn't even worry what Eliza and I would do then. Marigold and Eliza would say that the Lord would provide. And I believed it. With all my heart. He'd already worked a miracle with my father. Nothing was impossible to him.

I noticed Josiah watching me as we ate and laughed together around the table. But he remained quiet, letting the rest of us do almost all the talking. But later, after Mr. Abraham had gone home and I'd tucked Eliza into bed, I met him on the stairway, and we both stopped.

"I'm glad you're back," he said. "I'm glad things went well."

"Thank you."

"How was the return ride, on the train?"

"So very much better."

He looked like he was afraid again, almost like the way he'd seemed in the Kurchers' kitchen when I'd refused to be the one to drive. His hand fidgeted on the rail and he cleared his throat a couple of times. Finally, he just lowered himself to the step where he'd stood, sitting practically at my feet. "Can I talk to you?"

He looked like a little boy, tussled hair, uncertain eyes and all.

I sat on a step near him, so we were both perched halfway up in Marigold's front hall.

"I need to apologize," he began.

My heart thundered, and I immediately began to protest. "Oh no. You did nothing wrong. You helped me. Really. I was in such a state I don't think I could have managed on my own."

He smiled, a frightened little smile, and tears came to his eyes. "That's kind of what I thought."

"But then—why apologize?"

"Not for the train." He smiled a little wider. "I should have known better. I should have listened to Marigold, but more than that, what the Lord was trying to do here. It was wrong of me to be so rude to you, to try to make you promise something that would never have been right. The truth is, you helped me, maybe more than you know. And I didn't think I'd ever be able to help you. But I guess I did. In some small way."

"No. A big way. A very big way."

He looked beyond me, up into the rafters. "What I'm trying to say is, since I've already been proved wrong on that point, I was wondering . . . if you wouldn't find it too uncomfortable . . . I just want to know . . . if you'd have any objection to claiming me for a friend."

I could see the hope in his face, like a child's, the hunger to be accepted. "That would be wonderful," I told him. "If you'd also accept me as your friend."

He lowered his eyes and looked for a moment into mine. "I think I can do that."

He pulled himself to his feet and offered me his hand. With fluttering heart, I took it and he lifted me gently but then turned his eyes away again.

"I know your loss is still recent. I don't expect anything more of you, so don't be worryin'. Just friendship. That's enough."

"Thank you," I told him, feeling suddenly warm inside. "More than you know."

His eyes returned to mine for a fleeting instant with a twinkle of light, a depth of emotion rare and almost lovely. *I could respect a man like this,* I caught myself thinking. *Maybe even love a man like this one day.*

He took my hand, gave it a little shake. Then he walked on up the steps away from me.

"Josiah," I called before he could disappear.

"Yes?" He stopped on a stair and stood stiff.

"God bless you."

I could see his shoulders relax. He turned just a little. "God bless you too, Leah Breckenridge."

Then he went on to his room and left me on the stairs alone. I'd just been going down to fetch fresh towels, but it took me a moment now to remember that.

Another miracle. Another gift from heaven. I don't know why I thought of it like that. Josiah was nothing like my father. But I saw a miracle just the same. I saw grace and peace melt a barrier from a strong man's heart, and I felt like singing. Except that I was afraid I might wake Eliza, and maybe even Marigold.

But no. I'd probably not wake Marigold. She was probably still up. Praying. For the hurt to be healed, the poor to be fed, and everything to come aright in this world.

I skipped down the stairway and twirled once or twice in the hall. Wouldn't Eliza think I was funny if she saw me now? But she'd understand. That girl had no trouble comprehending joy. And not so long ago, I'd thought I'd never feel it again. Now I felt full to overflowing.

You are so good, God! Even when I doubted you, you never turned away. I love you. I thank you, for every wonder that you've wrought. Hope. Grace. And your precious gift of peace. Thank you, thank you, God!

Leisha Kelly is the author of many popular historical fiction books, including *Julia's Hope*, *Emma's Gift*, *Katie's Dream*, *Till Morning Is Nigh*, and the Country Road Chronicles. As L.A. Kelly, she is also the author of *Tahn*, *Return to Alastair*, and *The Scarlet Trefoil*. She and her husband have two children and live in a small Illinois town where she has served many years on her local library board. Leisha is also busy as a speaker in the surrounding area and a youth and children's minister at her home church.

For more information on Leisha and her books, go to www.leishakelly.com.

A Reluctant War Hero Returns Home . . . and Encounters a New Chance at Love

A HEARTWARMING STORY of tender love and fresh starts that will capture your heart.

Revell
a division of Baker Publishing Group
www.RevellBooks.com

Available Wherever Books Are Sold